AS THE CROW FLIES

FLIES

THE WESTPORT FIGHT

A Novel

By Curt Iles

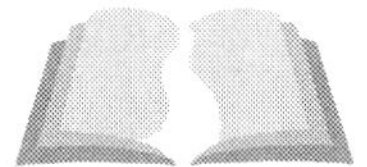

Creekbank Stories
Curt Iles
Every Journey has a Story.
www.creekbank.net

ISBN Trade Paperback 978-0-9705236-7-9
ISBN Larger Print 978-0-9705236-8-6
ISBN e-book 978-0-9826492-0-6
Library of Congress EPCN number pfh65973

Learn more at
www.creekbank.net
Creekbank Stories
PO Box 6060
Alexandria, LA 71307

Please address all corrections, criticisms, and questions to
creekbank.stories@gmail.com

Book formatting by Botherine Consultations.
Anthony Mugisha/ www.botherineconsult.com/ +256 703 694863
Map by Debra Tyler at DebraBirdArts.
Cover design by Lan Gao
www.langaodesign.com

Cover painting by Bill Iles "Camp Road."

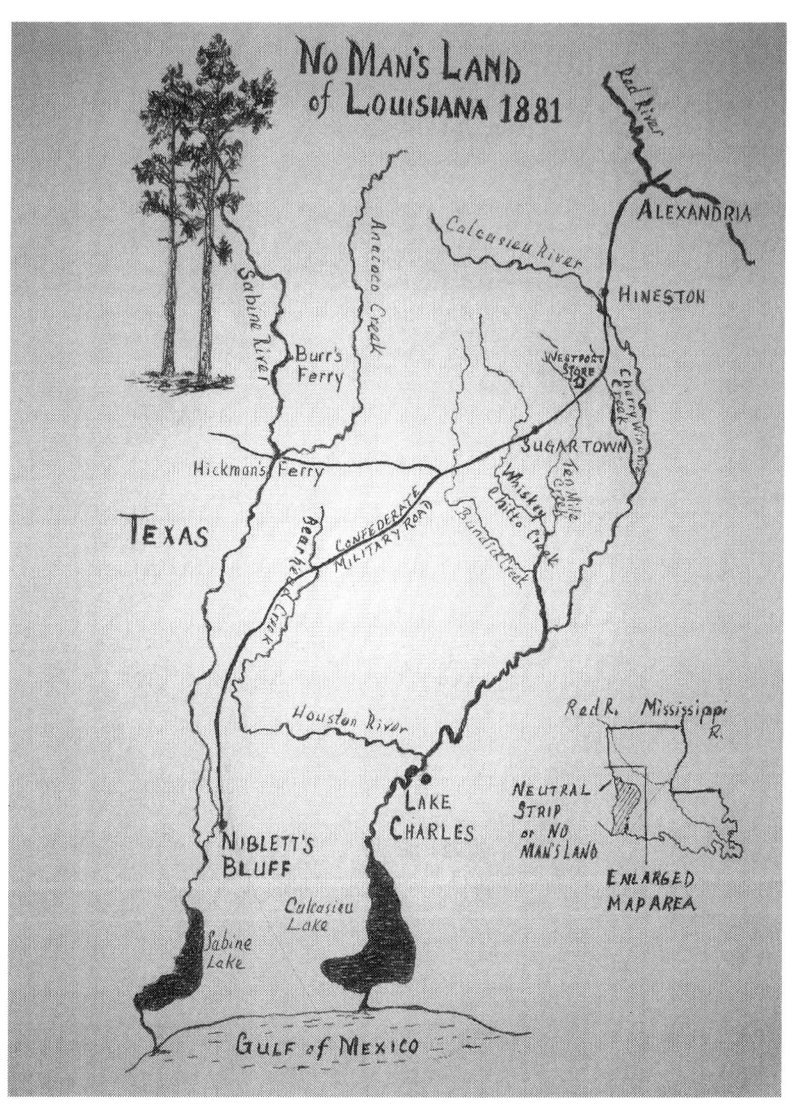

Map by Debra Tyler   DebraBird Graphics   Dry Creek, Louisiana

DEDICATION

To T-Bone Perkins, the most faithful friend a man could ever have, and to Greg Johnson, my model for Unk Dyal, who possesses the kindest heart I know.

Special Thanks

So many people chose to become involved in the publication *of As the Crow Flies*. An incomplete list is at the end of the book. There are several crows who flew high, straight, and fast. Without their help, this book would've never happened.

Thanks to Alycia Morales, Paul Conant, Allen Green, Debra Tyler, Linda Schekman, Anthony Mugisha, Wayne Mullins, Jade Ross, Clay Iles, and Robin Iles.

I appreciate my uncle, Bill Iles, for allowing the use of his painting "Camp Road" as part of the cover. Uncle Bill, thanks for a lifetime of encouragement.

As always, my rock in life is my sweet wife, DeDe. I could do nothing without her support, belief, and understanding.

Other books by Curt Iles

Deep Roots

A Good Place

The Wayfaring Stranger

The Mockingbird's Song

Hearts across the Water

Wind in the Pines

The Old House

Stories from the Creekbank

Trampled Grass

A Spent Bullet

Uncle Sam. A Horse's Tale

Christmas Jelly

Learn more at www.creekbank.net

Most are also available as e-books at Amazon Kindle.

BOOK ONE – DRIFTING

We have no power over external things, and the good that ought to
be is found only within ourselves.
– Epictetus

CHAPTER 1

AT THE RIVER

September 30, 1881

My name is Missouri Cotton, and I was born into a family of thieves. That's how Pap, Ma, and a fifteen-year-old girl like me found ourselves stuck in Louisiana's No Man's Land in September 1881. Although Missouri was my given name, most folks called me Mizz.

Pap, eyeing the two riders who'd been trailing us for the past mile, hustled our wagon onto the Calcasieu River ferry.

Pap tossed a wadded dollar bill at the ferryman. "How far is it to Texas?"

"As the crow flies, it's 'bout fifty miles." The ferryman pocketed the dollar and nodded behind us. "Your rush to git to Texas have anything to do with those men?"

"Ain't your worry," Pap said. "I'm paying you double to get us across now."

The man unmoored the barge and began poling us across the Calcasieu River. One of the riders, cradling a long gun, dismounted and walked down to the river. He was crudely dressed and yelled, "Fellow, you can run, but you can't hide."

The second rider was the one who caught my attention. He was a tall man dressed in a long black coat and wore a dark felt hat pulled down over his eyes. When he dismounted and stood by his horse, he was at least six-and-a-half feet tall and walked with a limp. Even from this distance, I sensed he was dangerous. The question was about what he was doing at the river. I whispered, "Javert."

Pap grabbed my arm. "What'd you say?"

"Nothing. Just a name from a book."

Ma grabbed Pap's arm. "You sure they won't follow us?"

The ferryman, who had a gravelly voice, answered her question.

"Ma'am, them men won't cross past here. They're probably a posse, but their badges don't mean a thing on the west side of the Calcasieu." He nodded. "It's their Dead Line. They won't cross over into the Outlaw Strip if they can he'p it."

"Dead Line?" Ma said.

"They're Outsiders, and know their life is in danger if they cross." He glanced westward across the river. "This river is a Dead Line. They don't go among them people unless they have to."

"Those people?"

"Ma'am, you're heading into Redbone territory. Best to steer clear of 'em and keep moving west."

"What's a Redbone?"

You're entering their kingdom and you'll soon find out for yerself." The ferryman wiped his hands on his faded bib overalls. "Where you coming from?"

"Alexandria," Pap said. "We left there due to a, uh, a little misunderstanding."

The man spat as he glanced behind him. "I can see that. By the way, what's your name?"

"Whoa now, feller. You taking a census or something?" Pap who'd been drinking earlier was already approaching his surly stage, so I eased beside him, hoping to diffuse any trouble.

The ferryman raised his hand. "No offense meant. Jes' my job to know who's crossing the river, in case we need to notify y'all's next of kin."

"We're the . . ." Pap hesitated. "We're the, uh, Cotton family." Pap wasn't quite yet used to our new alias. He'd selected it two days ago as we passed through the ripe, white-topped cotton fields west of Alexandria. "My name's Henry Cotton, but I'm known as Slick. He nodded. "This here's my wife, Beulah Mae, and our daughter, Missouri." As Pap tied the team to a rail on the ferry, he said, "Is there a difference between No Man's Land and what you called The Outlaw Strip?"

"One and the same. Sometimes it's also called the Neutral Strip or simply, The Strip. It's always been disputed territory."

He glanced at our rickety wagon with its mismatched ox and mule team. "Normally, it's a four-day trip, but it'll take pert-near a week with that buzzard-bait pair pulling you."

Pap stiffened. "The mule's name is Maggie and her partner's Aunt Em. They may not look like much, but they got us here and will git us to Texas."

"Well, you won't find much between here and the Sabine River border 'cept pine thickets and hog wallows. The part of Louisiana you're entering ain't got much civilization and even less law." The ferryman grinned at Pap. "I reckon you'll fit in pretty well there if they don't kill you first."

Pap wiped his brow. "We'll be safe across the river?"

The Ferryman nodded at the riders on the receding far riverbank. "You'll be safe from them." He glanced westward across the river. "The question is whether you'll be safe over there."

The black-dressed stranger pranced his horse back and forth on the sand bar. I had the sickening feeling we'd not seen the last of him.

The ferry was now in the river's swift current, struggling to reach the far shore. As soon as we bumped against the far sand bar, Pap hurried our team off the ferry and up the steep-cut bank. The animals strained to get traction and move the wagon out of the loose sand. Pap impatiently cracked his whip above the team. "Haw, come on, girls, let's git." The wagon hesitated, jerked, and then Mag and Aunt Emma pulled us toward level ground.

At the top of the bluff bank, Pap pointed at a red sign nailed to a cypress tree. "Mizz, what's it say?"

"This crossing's called Hineston Ferry, and the road we're now on is Sugartown Road." Below it, a hand-scrawled sign was nailed. "The lower sign says, 'Abandon hope all ye who enter here.'"

"Sounds like our kind of place," Pap said.

Hope. What a word. I had abandoned my hope a long time ago and had no illusions crossing this river would change anything.

Someone had scratched another sentence in a foreign language. "What's that?"

The ferryman shrugged. "Somebody told me it was the same quote in Eye-talian or French." He walked beside us to the road. "Good luck. Stay on the road and keep amovin'." I heard him whisper under his breath. "Riffraff. "

Ma didn't hear the insult, being too busy leaning out her side of the buckboard.

Pap didn't hear it either. He'd lost most of his hearing in the War. Anyway, he was concentrating on making tracks into this so-called No Man's Land. "Are they still there?"

"As far as I can see, they're gone," Ma said.

Whatever this mysterious new land might hold, it was sure different from the open cotton plantation country of the lower Mississippi River Valley. We passed out of the hardwood river bottom into an endless green curtain of towering pines whose canopy blocked out the sun, casting the entire forest into cool shade.

There was an eerie silence unbroken only by the sound of wind in the pine crowns and our creaking wagon rolling on the thick carpet of pine straw. I hunkered down in the wagon, now understanding why this was called No Man's Land. It seemed a fearful place where humans were unwelcome.

A flock of cawing crows circled our wagon. Ma, using her hand to shield her eyes from the sun, said, "That murder of crows are a sign." Several of them landed, cawing and hopping about on the red clay road.

"Ma, I thought they were called a flock," I said.

Her eyes widened, and she spoke slowly. "No siree, Bob. That's a murder of crows, and they're trying to warn us."

"Of what?"

"Nothin' but trouble and prob'ly death."

"Where?"

"Up ahead." She turned to Pap, icy fear in her voice. "Henry, please turn back."

"Too late." Pap's hackles were up. "Woman, I don't wanna hear none of that flapdoodle."

As much as I hated to admit it, it was too late. There was no going back in this lifetime of river crossings. One less chance of my ever putting down roots and having a place to belong.

CHAPTER 2

IN THE PINES

September 30, 1881

Our wagon jostled along the narrow, rutted road, the left rear wheel squealing badly. It was evident the back axle wasn't taking us much farther.

"I can smell the wheel burning," Ma said. "I told you to get some axle grease."

Pap clenched his fist. "Woman, shut your mouth."

"It would not have hurt to asked a passing wagon for a little grease."

"I don't wanna hear no more of your sass."

"I just—"

"Shut up, or I'll shut you up."

As Ma pouted and Pap fumed, we rode in relative silence for a mile or so. I began humming "In the Pines," wishing that music might soothe the savage beast—or in this case, beasts. I hoped Ma with her strong alto would join in.

"In the Pines,
In the Pines.
Where the sun never shines,
And you shiver
When the cold wind blows."

As we neared a small branch, the wagon jolted to a stop. The wheel had finally frozen. Pap crawled under the wagon and as soon as he was out of earshot, Ma said, "Your pap's hard to be around when he gets like this."

"Then why in the world do you put up with him," I asked.

"Because he's my husband … and uh, your Pap."

"You could probably do better."

"Maybe so. He ain't the kind of man I wanted, but he's the kind of man I got."

"I believe I'd cut his throat one night while he's sleeping off a drunk."

"Don't talk about your Pap like that."

"Or I'd cut my own throat."

"Hush, Girl. Besides, I lean on him when I'm crazy, and he leans on me when he's drunk."

"What about when you're both off-kilter?"

"We jes' lean on each other."

"Well, if that's what marriage is, I believe I'll pass." The old bitterness seeped up. "Anyway, marriage shouldn't be about him hitting you."

"Mizz, he only hits me when's he been drinking."

"That's no excuse." I felt a familiar outrage rising in my chest. "His conning is gonna get us all in jail, or worse."

"He's pretty good at staying ahead of the game. I've always said he was so slick he could slide uphill."

Just then, Pap began cussing and kicking. He crawled from under the wagon. He'd raised up and cut his head on the axle. Blood ran down his face, and he angrily threw a monkey wrench at the wagon.

Ma sighed. "Mizz, go see if you can find a clean towel." She sat Pap down and tended to his wound. She was from a long line of Indian healers. Ma's gifts had been carefully passed down through generations of woods women. She could draw fire from a burn, cure poison ivy or mouth thrush, but her specialty was staunching bleeding. I never tired of watching it. I'd watched Ma staunch bleeding on a hunting dog that'd been ripped open by a hog's tusk. Another time, near Meridian, Mississippi, I watched her heal a neighbor boy who'd cut his leg bad on a cross-cut saw.

Ma pulled out a little bag of herbs she always carried. She wadded some leaves, spit on them, and applied them to Pap's cut. She placed her hand on Pap's head and whispered, "And when I passed by thee, and saw thee polluted in thine own blood, I said unto thee …Live; yea, Live."

She kept repeating this as Pap wiggled and cussed, but

amazingly the bleeding stopped.

"Are those words from the *Bible*?" I asked.

"It's in the book of Ezekiel." She closed her herb bag. "Mizz, I need to pass all of this onto you."

I was curious but wasn't sure I wanted any of that. I'd seen those gifts cause as much trouble as Pap's stealing. She swore these gifts came from God. Some folks agreed with this assessment, while others suspiciously viewed her, and her touch, as instruments of the Devil.

"Missouri, git my bottle," Pap said.

I acted as if I didn't hear him.

"My bottle. It's in my boot under the wagon."

I slowly made my way there, then reluctantly handed the whiskey jug to him.

He took a long slug. "Best painkiller there is."

Ma, under her breath, said, "He who puts a thief in his mouth to steal his brains."

"What'd you say, Woman?"

I stepped in. "She asked if the wagon was fixed."

He wiped his mouth. "This is as far as we're going for now."

"We should've turned back," Ma said.

To escape their coming storm, I slipped off the wagon, grabbed a bucket, and headed to the creek for water. Tom-Claws, our wagon cat, hopped down and followed me, meowing.

"Yep, I'm hungry too."

Rain frogs, sensing a change in the weather, croaked in anticipation.

Across the creek, a distant crow cawed.

The cat rubbed against my leg.

"Did you hear that, Tom-Claws?"

The crow, now closer, cawed again. A neighboring bird cawed from near our wagon. I shivered, wondering if Ma had heard it, too.

As if in recognition of our predicament, dusk fell and a cold rain began.

CHAPTER 3

TWO WAGONS

Friday, September 30

That first rainy night in No Man's Land, we made camp beside our broken-down wagon. My folks set up an old army tent in a nearby clearing. I preferred a pallet in the bed of the wagon where it was just Tom-Claws, my books, and me. Using a short candle, I hoped to read a few chapters before it went out. The rain intensified, causing me to position my bed away from the leaks in the canopy. I patted the double-bit ax I kept beside my pallet. You never knew when any varmints, especially the two-legged kind, might show up in the night.

The candle flickered for about ten minutes, then went out. I placed the book in my bag and settled down, dozing off to the drumming of rain on the canvas.

I woke to the sound of Ma scraping a pot, moved my ax, and then pulled out my *Bible*. The sizzling of bacon and wonderful aroma of fresh coffee filled the wagon. In spite of being stranded in this God-forsaken wilderness, any day starting with bacon and hot coffee had the chance to be a good day.

I peeked from the canopy to see Ma hunkered over the campfire. She smiled. "Morning, Mizz. How about a cup of hot coffee?"

Slowly, I stretched and crawled out into the open air. I sat on a log beside Ma. "Don't you ever get tired of cooking on the ground?"

"It's about the only way I know. It's been pert near a year since

I last cooked in a kitchen. This is just the way it is."

Pap, with a bandage on his head, came out of the tent and said, "Lookee there." A Conestoga wagon approached from the west. Pap sat beside me on the log, placing his Long Tom shotgun between his knees. "Don't forgit—our name is Cotton."

A man and teen girl sat on the buckboard of the wagon, framed by four blonde, curly-headed girls peering from the canvas opening.

Pap tipped his hat at the waggoneer. "Mornin'. Where y'all headed?"

"Alexandria." The man glanced back. "Then as far from here as possible." He stopped the wagon, and the passel of girls piled out. From behind the canvas, a baby's raspy cough caught my attention.

One of the girls looked about my age, and I followed her to the back flap of the wagon. "That baby has a graveyard cough."

"No doctors out here. That's why we're headed back to Alex."

Alex was how the locals shortened Alexandria, the main town in central Louisiana. They pronounced it Aleck as in smart aleck.

I peered under the canvas at a sad-eyed woman holding a newborn. The woman wiped her face, then looked away.

"Ma'am, my ma's a healer." I said. "She might can help with your baby."

"I'm afeared he's beyond help."

A hand touched my shoulder, and Ma's calm voice said, "I can sure try."

The mother's voice was desperate. "We done buried two other boys in this God-forsaken place, and I'm scared of losing another." She glanced at the girls who'd crowded around. "I can keep girls alive but ain't much good with boys."

Ma tenderly took the coughing, swaddled baby. "He's burning up with fever. What's his name?"

"Ain't named him yet." The woman gazed away. "Waiting to see if he makes it."

Ma's jaw tightened. "I'll try to help, but you gotta promise me you'll name this baby. Don't nobody deserve to live or die without a name."

The mother was chagrined and nodded at Ma. "What's your name?"

"Beulah. Beulah Mae Cotton, and this is my daughter, Mizz." Ma winked at me. "We're the Cotton family. Mizz, now how do you spell it?"

"It's C-o-t-t-o-n." Because our family name changed from town to town, it was a chore keeping her up with both saying and spelling our names.

Ma stepped toward the woman. "How long y'all been in this here country?"

"Going on two years." The woman nodded out to the back of the wagon where her husband and Pap were deep in discussion. "My man wanted homestead land. There's lots of free land out here, jes' ain't much of a life."

The woman called out, "Addie, come over here."

One of the younger girls walked over. "Look at how her arm is swoll'." The mother pointed. "Bessie's gettin' over a snakebite. She's the third one of the children bitten by a snake around that house. The collapsed chimney and underneath of our house was infested with copperheads. She was digging in the firewood, and a rattlesnake pilot nipped her. It was the stick that broke the donkey's back. We left the next day. Nothin' but bad luck."

"We ain't done much better in our wanderin'," Ma said.

"Where are you all headed?"

"Texas."

The mother put her hand on Ma's shoulder. "Lady, you'll never get your family through this strip alive. Turn around."

Ma whispered "crows" before shaking herself. "Let's take a look at your baby."

The mother handed her the baby. "How you gonna heal him?"

"With the help of the good Lord and the fire over there."

"Fire?" The mother grabbed for her baby.

"Please trust me," Ma said. "I need you to trust me."

The woman crossed her arms and stepped back.

We climbed out of the wagon, and Ma led us to the smoldering campfire where she knelt, muttered a prayer, pulled some dried herbs and roots from one of her satchels, and tossed them into the smoking embers. The fire flared up, giving off a thick gray smoke.

Ma unbundled the baby and held him directly above the smoke as he choked and screamed. The sisters' curious looks deepened to concern. The baby's father hurried over. "Whatcha doing to my baby?"

The mother waved him back. "Leave her alone. She's healing him."

It looked to me like Ma was killing him. In a soft voice, she hummed into the howling baby's ear, still wafting smoke in his face. Finished, she handed the baby to his mother. "All right, Momma. I've done my part." Ma stepped squarely in front of the mother. "Now it's your turn. What are you going to name this fine boy?"

The mother gazed at her red-faced, sputtering baby. "Cotton. I like it. We'll name him Cotton after y'all. All my other kids are cotton-tops. His name will be Cotton Nash." She winked. "If it's all right, with two O's."

Ma smiled. "Cotton's a good name for a boy. He's gonna grow up to be a fine man."

The baby was still wailing, but the mother mustered up a smile. "Thank you kindly."

Ma patted her shoulder. "You get to a doctor when you reach civilization across the river. He's gonna be fine."

The woman climbed onto the wagon. "Where'd you get your gift?"

"From the Lord."

"God's blessed you."

Ma laughed bitterly. "Not sure if it's a blessing or a curse."

The woman reached into her pocket. "I don't have much, but I'd like to give you something."

Ma held up her hand. "Nope, I don't take nothin' for helping. Ain't how it works."

I stole a look at Pap and wasn't surprised at his scowl.

The Cotton-top Nash family loaded onto their wagon. The baby had the dry heaves but wasn't coughing as badly.

I eased beside Ma. "You really think he'll make it?"

She nodded. "Yep, I do."

The wagon moved slowly away as the entire Nash clan waved. One word came to mind. *Lost.* They were just as lost as us. Drifting along lost.

Just as their wagon topped the hill, the lady shouted back, "God bless you."

Pap spat. "God he'ps those who he'p themselves, and we just missed our chance." He grabbed Ma's arm. "Them people wanted to give you something, and you turned them down. And us with a broken wagon and empty pockets."

Ma jerked away. "I've never taken money for my gift."

Pap held out a weathered paper. "That fellow on the wagon gave me his homestead deed. Said they weren't ever coming back and wouldn't need it." He handed the paper to me to read. It was a land deed filled with a scrambled mess of legal terms and descriptions. The man's legal name was Graham Nash, and the homestead deed was for a hundred and sixty acres in Calcasieu Parish near a place called Sugartown. I handed Pap the deed, and he put it in his vest pocket. "We're going to Texas but can check this out if we pass near there."

"I don't want nothin' to do with that house," Ma said. "The Nash woman said it'd been nothing but bad luck. Two of her kids got bit by rattlesnake pilots at the house."

"Ain't reason enough for us not to take a look."

"I don't plan to stay nowhere there's a nest of copperheads," Ma said.

I stepped between Ma and Pap, hoping to head off a fight. "Ma, I thought the lady said they were rattlesnakes?"

"She said rattlesnake pilots, another name for copperheads. Folks in the mountains call them that. They're bad news by either name."

Pap called me over. "Missouri, the man mentioned a general store about three miles past here. I'm sending you for supplies."

"How will I pay?"

He pulled out several wadded bills and a fistful of coins. "Here's a little, but it'll be up to you to get the rest." He winked. "Use your charm."

I held one of the bills to the light. "Is it real or counterfeit?"

"Does it matter? We need wagon grease, some flour, sugar, coffee, a half-pound of eight-penny nails, and tobacco, both smoking and chewing."

I held out the money. "This isn't enough."

He shrugged. "Beg it, steal it, or whatever, but bring it back."

"Can I get a candle?"

"As long as you bring back the other things."

I scratched the items on a scrap of paper and then read them back to Pap. Walking away, I rubbed my cheek. The bruise was nearly gone from the last time I'd returned empty-handed. I was determined this mission would be successful. Before he could add any items to my shopping list, I hurried away toward the store.

CHAPTER 4

STRANGER IN A STRANGE LAND

Saturday, October 1

I'd walked nearly a mile before I came to a creek crossing. An older man sat on the far bank, holding a fishing pole. Something about him gave me the creeps—I glanced up and down the creek for a safer crossing.

He halloed. "Use that log ri't there for crossin'. Don't worry, it ain't but knee-deep where the log ends."

I liked his sing-songy voice and let my guard down. "How's fishing?"

"Caught a perch or two. Be careful crossin'. My can of night crawlers is on the log."

I hiked up my skirt, walked the log, and then stepped off into the creek, gritting my teeth. "That's cold."

The stranger laughed. "Cherry Winchie's cold this time of the year."

"What's a Cherry Winchie?"

"It's what you're wading in, Sister. It's Cherry Winchie Creek."

I warily studied him as he waded toward me. He was Indian-looking and kind of dried up like old men often are ... as if he'd blow away in a strong gust.

He stood at the water's edge, hand out, wearing a lopsided grin. "Wanna know how it got its name?"

"Sounds as if you're going to tell me, whether I want to know or not."

He waved off my comment. "My grandma said it got its name from a Cherokee woman who lived on the creek. You know, Cherry ... Chero-kee."

He pointed behind me. "That side of the creek is called the Cherry Winchie Country. When you touch this side, you'll be in what we call the Ten Mile Country."

"What's the difference?"

He chuckled. "I guess the creek. It serves as a border, but that don't mean nothin' much. Our folks are on both sides."

Before I could ask more, he reached for my arm, and I instinctively stepped back.

He laughed. "Oh, don't worry about me. They say I'm just a harmless idjitt."

"A what?"

"Idjitt. I'm the village idjitt. You know, touched in the head." He had a musical herky-jerky manner of speaking. "My cornbread ain't all done, but they say I ain't the only one." We waded out of the creek together, where I sat on a stump and put on my shoes. I didn't take my eyes off him. He had a crooked permanent smile and piercing, smoky-black eyes that seemed to take in everything around him, including me. He was definitely part Indian as evidenced by his dark skin, high cheekbones, and lack of facial hair.

I sensed him as trustworthy. Besides, he was so old, I could easily outrun him if he started any trouble.

He browsed the ragged clouds. "That north wind is raw. Hog-butchering weather today, ain't it?"

I stared at the raggedly clouds hurrying southward.

"Sir, if you don't mind my asking, are you what they call a . . . Redbone?"

He stood to his full height, which wasn't much. "Redbone born and Redbone bred, and when I'm dead I'll be Redbone dead."

I laughed. "Well, that's pretty clear."

He held up a hand. "We're also called Ten Milers. Some of our folks take offense at being called a Redbone. So, I'd use the term Ten Miler until you get to know folks." He looked up at the tall pines. "Our area is called Ten Mile. It's our home and where our people have been for a hundred years or more."

He placed his arm beside mine. "Child, you and I are about the same skin color."

"I've always been dark." I looked down. "I try to hide my darkness by wearing long sleeves."

"You part Indian?"

"I guess so. My momma's people are Melungeons from the Carolina Mountains."

"Never heard of 'em."

"Ma says our people were Portuguese who were shipwrecked on the Atlantic coast and moved inland to the mountains, where we mixed with Indians, wildcats, and who knows what else?" I leaned closer to him. "Ma says folks in Carolina claim our people are part colored."

"Well, here's some good advice for you from Ol' Unk. Don't mention that you got black blood in you. That won't make you any friends around here."

"Thanks. Can I trust you to keep it under your hat?"

"With my life." He moved closer. "Where'd you get those eyes? One's brown and the other's green, and they're kind of mixed up, like there's a little bit of everything in them—and you."

I blushed. "People always notice my eyes."

Unk squinted into my face. "You got cat eyes, honey." He cocked his head as he studied my eyes. "By the way, where you be headed right now?"

"To the ... uh, store . . . across this creek."

"Well, if I'm going to help you, I need to know your name."

"Who said I wanted you to help me?" Suddenly, my mind went blank. "I'm Mizz ... Whitehead." I shook my head. "I mean Missouri Cotton." I still got confused from our ongoing aliases. Before we were the Whitehead family in Alexandria, we'd been the Greens in New Orleans. Pap liked colors. Said they made good aliases.

"Well, Miss-Miss-Uh-White-Cotton, mind if I walk witcha?"

"Well, if you're going to be my bodyguard, I need to know your name?"

"I'm Nathan Dyal, but folks around here just call me Unk." He grinned. "It appears I know my name better than you do your'ns. You must be using a summer name."

"A summer name?"

"Yeah, a fake name. I think they call it an elias.

I stifled a laugh. "Which way is the store?"

"Sure. I can remember how to git to the store and my name, but I have trouble keeping up with other simple stuff, like what day of the week is it?"

I counted on my fingers. "I believe it's Saturday. The first day of October." I reached down to tie my other shoe. "How far to the store?"

"As the crow hops, it's three miles," he said.

"I thought the saying was 'as the crow flies'?"

He shrugged. "Don't matter. It's pert-near three miles either way. Uphill or downhill. When you git to the store, will you check the big calendar to see what day it is?"

"Why don't you check it yourself?"

"I can't read, and besides I stay away from that store. There's been lots of trouble in the store lately."

"What kind?"

"Outsiders wanting our land." He bent over to pick up a blue jay feather. "Everywhere a feather falls is where an angel walked." He handed it to me. "Your first Ten Mile gift from the land."

"Speaking of land," I pointed down the road. "What's past this store?"

"Not much until the village of Sugartown. It's 'bout a twenty-mile walk."

"As the crow hops? Uphill or downhill?" I asked.

Unk grinned. "Either."

I nodded south. "My pap has a land deed that mentioned Sugartown. Have you been there?"

"Nope. My kind ain't welcome there."

"Kind?"

"I'm a Redbone. We don't travel much past Ten Mile Creek if we can help it." He squinted at me. "You've got lots of questions. You seem pretty smart for a girl who don't know her own name."

"And you're pretty nosey for a fellow who's touched in the head."

He grinned. "Well, dog my cats, Miss-Mizz. I believe you and me are going to get along real well." He led me around the mud holes in the road. "You can call me Unk, Ol' Unk, or Mister Unk."

He squinted at me. "Miss-Mizz, you got a lotta sand being out here alone in No Man's Land."

"Sand?"

"Yep, sand—or grit. You've got it, Miss-Mizz."

"You don't have to call me Miss."

"That's no problem, Miss-Mizz."

I'd made a new friend named Unk, but doubted he'd ever get my name straight.

We climbed a rise, and the store sat in a clearing in the pines. There wasn't anything fancy about the store. It was constructed of rough pine with sawmill slats as batting. Part of the building was two-story. What really caught my attention was how it just set there in the middle of the wilderness. It was a pioneer store, and I was excited to see the stock. A sign was above the porch.

Hatch and Moore Store

General Merchandise.

Westport, La.

"How long has the store been here?"

"About two years."

I took note of a skinny pole with an American flag snapping in the wind. The sun was shining on it and it contrasted with the green surrounding us in every direction. "I haven't seen many United States flags out here."

"Yeah, they're scarce as hen's apples on our side of the Calcasieu. The flag's the Irishman's statement that we live in 'Merica. These woods always been contested by the nations. Long before I was born, the Spanish and French fought over it, fighting and flying their own flags. When I was a boy, the land across the Sabine was owned by Spain, and then by them Mexicans." Unk, who was on a historical roll, pointed to the flag. "Then Lousianer became part of the United States, and that 'Merican flag flew there. Then 'bout twenty year ago, we broke away from the United States and tried to make our own country, and of course, being a new country, had to have their own flag." He shook his head. "You probably heard how that turned out."

Unk pointed at the United States flag. "Sometimes we nearly forgit who we belong to. The Irishman flies it to remind us we're 'Mericans. That's also why he bought the biggest one he could find."

"Well, it'd be hard to miss," I said. "Did the Irishman fight in the War of Rebellion?"

"For the Secesh side."

"That what?"

"The Secesh. You know, the Secessionists. The South. Most everybody here supported that side."

Just then a man cradling a long gun walked past the flagpole, spit on the ground, and joined a rough-looking crew in front of the store.

CHAPTER 5

THIEVING

Saturday, October 1

We were probably a hundred yards from the store when Unk Dyal saw the man walk past the flagpole and join a group of men clustered in front of the store. Unk's reaction was intense and immediate. As if he'd nearly stepped on a snake, he darted into the cover of the woods, roughly dragging me with him.

I pulled loose from his death grip. "What was that about?"

His voice trembled as he pointed toward the men. "Outsiders. Timber men who want our land. That cat-kicker with the rifle is named Musk. Iffen you get in his way, there'll be trouble."

"Iffen?"

"Yes, ma'am, stay out of his shadow iffen you don't want to git shot or hurt."

"How so?"

"A feud's been brewing 'tween our people and those fellers. Somebody's gonna get kilt 'fore it's over. Musk can't keep his mouth shut, and I figure he'll be the first one to kill …or be kilt." He shook me, rather harshly. "This place is jes' a powder keg waitin' on a spark."

I jerked away. "I'm going in the store."

"Please don't." There was real fear in his voice, but I was already walking toward the store. Unk called after me, "Ask for the Irishman—He'll he'p you. And don't forgit to check the calendar."

I waved. The group of men stopped talking as I neared but made no effort to move. The tall one squarely faced me, blocking the steps. "And who might you be?"

"Just passing through."

"A girl as pretty as you shouldn't be out here alone."

I nodded toward the woods. "Who said I was alone?"

The big man didn't move, evidently being the kind of bully who liked pulling his weight on someone smaller, especially women. Just as I readied myself to plow right past him, a voice echoed from the doorway. "Musk, you don't have enough manners to let a lady through?"

The voice had a slight lisp and was the interesting blend of a boy becoming a man, but that voice also had an air of authority. I looked up to see a ruddy, sandy-haired teenager a little older than me. He had a thin, peach-fuzz beard. I hadn't been here long enough to accurately separate the sheep from the goats, but he definitely wasn't a Redbone.

He stepped into the crowd of men with a laugh. "You fellows let that girl in. She may have a wad of money burning a hole in her pocket, and Lord knows we need it."

If you only knew.

At the sound of his voice, a three-legged black and tan hound bounded out from under the gallery and limped to the boy's side. He reached down to pet it. "Now, Lucky, be nice to our guest."

The men shuffled aside, and as I stepped onto the porch I asked, "What happened to the dog?"

"Huge cane brake rattler got him," the teen said. "He barely survived and was lucky to only lose his leg. That's how he got his nickname."

I knelt and petted the happy-faced hound. "What was his name before 'Lucky'?"

"Boo. He's scared of noises."

The boy was covered in flour dust from head to toe. He doffed his cap, smiling shyly. "My name's, uh, Dan'l Moore. Around here, I'm simply known as Dan. And who might you be?"

"I'm Missouri Cotton. Our wagon's broken down, and my father sent me for some, uh, supplies." I handed him my shopping list.

He studied it. "Do you need one candle or a bundle?"

"Only one." I lowered my head. He and I both knew folks didn't buy one candle at a time unless they were dirt poor.

He held out the list. "Who wrote this list for you?"

"I did."

"You can read and write?"

"Fairly."

"It's a rare skill in these parts."

"Speaking of rare, what's with the big American flag out there?"

"It's his reminder that we're Americans here. All of that crap about tribes and border wars is over." Dan laughed. "My brother Will who is the local historian claims we're flying an illegal flag. It's only got thirty-seven stars." He nodded toward the flag. "Will claims our flag, to be official, should have thirty-eight stars since the Colorado Territory became a state."

"Does it matter?"

"Nothing to anyone but Will Moore, but he'd argue with a fence post about it."

"I was told to ask for the Irishman," I said.

"He's my da." Seeing my confusion, he added, "Da. That's Irish for father."

"Do you work for your father?"

"Kind of." He glanced behind him and lowered his voice. "The truth is that he works for me." He winked, then disappeared into the store.

He returned with a man who could've been his twin, only twenty years older and a little stockier. He had the same-colored hair and beard of his son. "This is my father, Joe Moore. Everyone just calls him the Irishman."

"Where are you from, gearrchaile?" the Irishman asked.

"Sir?"

"*Gearrchaile.* Girl-child." He grinned. "I try to polish up on my Gaelic from time to time."

"I'm just passing through," I said.

He took out his pipe. "Another stranger in a strange land."

"Sir, that I am."

The Irishman seemed to size me up, which I didn't like one bit. It was always best when we kept a low profile. Never taking his eyes off me, he handed my list back. "Our wagon grease is out back." He motioned inside. "Shop until I get back."

His brogue reminded me of the Irish Channel of New Orleans. As I backed away from him, I couldn't decide if the Irishman would be a friend or foe.

As I pushed through the wide double door, the store smelled of horse feed, liniment, coffee, and tobacco. The walls were covered with all kinds of tools, rolls of wire, and pots and pans. A locked cash box sat on the counter. I wandered the three aisles, running my hand along a well-stocked shelf filled with rolls of gingham, calico, and denim fabric. Maybe someday I'd be fortunate enough to have something that pretty to wear. I looked around for the items on my list, carefully watching both doors.

Dan Moore sneaked right up behind me. "Boo."

I dropped several items. "It's not nice to scare folks like that."

"Wow, why are you so jumpy?"

"I'm just new, that's all." I retrieved my items. "Where's your wall calendar?"

He walked me to it. The calendar had a picture of a train station and advertised The *Louisiana Democrat*, Alexandria's main newspaper. The calendar's current page was for October 1881 and the first day of the month was circled. "Is today the first of October?"

"It is." Dan Moore pointed at the calendar. "We circle the day each morning, but don't cross it off till closing time. Folks come in weekly to settle arguments about what day of the month it is."

"Do you have other family that works here?"

"My younger brother, but he's not here today. Also, my mother works when she's well enough."

"What's wrong?"

"She's got Consumption."

Consumption. TB. Tuberculosis. Whatever you called it, it was the kiss of death in this part of the South.

I walked over to him, eager to change the subject. "Do you run the grist mill?"

He brushed flour off his shoulder. "How'd you guess?"

I pointed to the line on his forehead where his cap had been. "Your flour line gave you away."

Dan smiled, but it didn't remove the touch of sadness in his face. "We're near the end of the corn-gristing season, so we'll convert the mill to cutting lumber during the winter months."

Behind us, the Irishman coughed. "Dan, I believe they're waiting for you at the mill." He handed the grease to me. "What size nails do you need?"

"A half-pound of eight-penny."

He disappeared again into the storage room, leaving me on my own.

When the Irishman returned, I plunked my money on the counter. "We need flour with the money that's left over."

He counted my money, then measured out the flour. "Anything else?"

"Oh, I forgot. I need a candle."

"Just one?"

I nodded.

He put two candles on the counter. "Consider that lagniappe."

"What?"

"A little something extra. *Lagniappe.* That's what the Cajuns call it."

As I picked up the candles, I cringed at the term *something extra.* "Sir, you can remove some of the flour to make my money come out right."

"Nah. We're even enough. Anything else you need?"

"No, sir. That's good." I stuffed the items into my tote sack.

"Great. If you're happy, we're happy."

"Yes, sir. I guess I am happy."

He walked me to the door, and the way he studied me made my stomach churn. He took off his hat. "You sure are a stranger in a strange land."

I hurried out of the store, and to my relief Musk and the other men were gone.

A young man leaned against a gallery post, using the rough edge like a backscratcher between his shoulders. "Hi-yah." He was one of the Redbones. A little older than me and about two shades darker and, like Unk, he had no facial hair but a thick head of curly hair. "Where you from?"

"Just passing through."

He tipped his hat. "Moon Perkins, at your service."

I laughed. "That's an interesting name."

"Look at my face. It's kinda round like the moon. Everyone's got a nickname here in Ten Mile. I've got a brother named Squirrel and another one who goes by Worm."

He stepped closer and said, "You're already known as Wagon Girl and you live in the Cherry Winchie country.

I felt my face redden, causing Moon Perkins to laugh. "Everyone gets a nickname in Ten Mile."

I hurried away with a wave and about a quarter mile down the trail, Lucky the store dog caught up with me, panting hard. "Well, I guess three legs makes loping a little harder."

He wagged his tail and flashed the ever-ready smile that made him a celebrity around the store. "Well, it looks like I've made at least one new friend today."

I reached the spot where Unk Dyal had been hiding. Sure that he lurked nearby, I cupped my hands. "Today's Saturday, October first, in the year of our Lord, 1881."

My words echoed off the pines. Lucky, sitting on his haunches, whined. When I resumed walking, the dog trotted back toward the store. "So, you're deserting me? This must be your dead line."

As me and my guilty conscience scurried along the road toward the Cherry Winchie Creek crossing, a horse's snort startled me. Caught in the open road, I dashed for the cover of the trees and crouched in some merkle bushes.

"Come on out." It was the Irishman. He dismounted and stood on the road with his arms crossed. Lucky, no longer wagging his tail, stood stock-still beside him.

I stepped out. "Sir, something wrong?"

"You forgot about something at the store." He walked to a roadside red oak stump, sat and pulled out a pipe, tapping it against the stump. "I'd sure like a good smoke. Mind if I borrow some of your tobacco?"

"Tobacco? I don't have any tobacco."

He pointed. "It's in your left dress pocket."

Slowly, I pulled out the pack of tobacco and tossed it to him.

He filled his pipe, tamped the tobacco, and lit it. Puffing contentedly, he blew a fine cloud of blue smoke. "It's not every day I meet a pipe-smoking girl."

"I don't smoke a pipe."

"Or one your age who dips snuff." He put his hand out.

I pulled a tin of Garrett's Sweet Snuff out of my bag and sheepishly handed it to him. "Are you going to have me arrested?"

"Maybe." He rubbed his chin, watching me squirm. He reminded me of Tom-Claws torturing an injured mouse. The Irishman never lost his smile or took his eyes off me. I was close enough to notice they were green. They were similar to his son Dan's eyes, except the Irishman's were what I'd call fierce. And as those fierce eyes battled with that kind smile, I wondered which facial trait really defined this man. The answer to that would probably reveal my fate.

"Does anyone else know?" I said.

"Nope. No one but Lucky and me."

I bit my lip. "Are you going to tell Dan?"

His eyes twinkled. "Dan who?"

"Your son."

"Well, he told you that I worked for him, so I guess I'll have to." He paused and glanced at Lucky. "No, I don't plan on telling anyone unless it happens again."

"It won't."

"I'm sure it won't." He grinned. "Why wouldn't you want Dan to know?"

I felt my face redden. "Oh, I don't know."

The Irishman stood quickly, holding up the tobacco. "I need to talk with your father about this."

Hot tears rose, and I ducked my head.

His tone softened. "That is, if you've got a father."

I studied the ground in front of my toes. "He's the one who sent me to steal."

"Your father sent you to steal?"

"A good beating awaits me if I return empty-handed."

The Irishman collapsed back onto the stump, puffing so rapidly that the embers flared in his pipe. When he finally looked up, his eyes were also afire. He tossed the tobacco and snuff at my feet. "You take this on home."

As I shuffled away, he said, "And I'll expect to see you Monday by eight for work."

I stopped. "Work?"

"At the store. We're shorthanded right now and could use the help." He winked. "Besides, you showed yourself to be pretty handy around the store."

I cringed, and he laughed. "You'll be working off your tobacco stash."

"Are you serious?"

He mounted his horse. "See you Monday at eight. Don't come tomorrow 'cause it's Sunday." He whistled. "Let's go, Lucky."

As he turned for the store, I said, "I'm sorry about your wife being so sick."

He reined in, deep hurt in his eyes. "So am I."

I watched until the Irishman, Joe Moore, disappeared over the hill, and I stood a long time looking in both directions down the trail. Two men were on my mind. the Irishman and my pap. Comparing them wasn't fair, but it was hard to avoid.

I picked up my contraband, stuffed it in my tote bag, and walked toward the wagon.

The strangeness of this day had dizzied me. The Irishman's words echoed in my mind. A stranger in a strange land.

I knew one thing for sure. It was time for this stranger's life to change. And that was good, because it seemingly couldn't get any worse.

Pap and Ma were sitting by the campfire when I returned from my foraging mission. I silently handed Pap the contraband.

"Well?" He grunted. "How'd it go?"

"No problem."

"Is the store pretty well-stocked?"

"Not as well as it was." I climbed into the wagon. "I'm pretty tired. I'm going on to bed."

"You're not hungry?" Ma said. "I made some fresh corn dodgers."

"No ma'am. I've kind of lost my appetite. `I believe I'll call it a day."

CHAPTER 6

THE WESTPORT STORE

Monday, Oct. 3, 1881

Two days later before dawn, I hurried onto the footpath that took me to Sugartown Road. It was a cold morning with a gusty wind that made the top of those tall pine trees sing. I'd never seen trees that majestic. The layer of pine straw on the ground reminded me of a thick carpet I'd once walked on in the lobby of a fancy New Orleans hotel.

I started humming that song again,
"In the pines,
In the pines,
Where the sun never shines . . ."

I stopped. Someone—or something—was following me. I stepped behind a tree and picked up a good pine knot. As I suspected, it was Unk Dyal. I threw the knot at him. "What are you doing trailing me?"

He grinned. "I'm squirrel huntin'."

"You don't have a gun."

"Don't need one."

"You're making enough noise to scare off a deaf squirrel."

He rubbed his bad leg. "My limp makes it hard sneakin' up. I have trouble getting that leg to do what I tell it."

"Why're you following me?"

"Looking out for jaybirds like you is part of my job."

"How'd you know I'd be out this mornin'?"

"A little bird told me that you might need protection."

"Why don't you tell that little bird I don't need protecting."

"Yep, you do." He pointed to a side road. "About a quarter

mile down there is a turpentine camp. Do you know the kind of men who live and work there?" He waited until I nodded. "Those are desperate men, and desperate men do desperate things. That's one of the reasons why I'm keeping an eye on you."

I increased my tempo. "Well, Mister Guardian Angel, I don't want to be late for work."

He shuffled along beside me and never hushed. He poked my bag. "Whatcha got in your bag?"

"Work clothes."

"Kinda heavy for clothes."

"I also have a book."

"You can read?"

"Fairly."

He shook his head. "I wish I could read. But I ain't got no book sense. Eliza says I'll be able to read when I get to Heaven."

"Who's Eliza?"

"My niece. She looks after poor Ol' Unk."

"Can Eliza read?"

"A little." He tapped the bag again. "What book do you have?"

"If you'll tell me about the Irishman, I'll show you my book when we reach the store."

"The Irishman, Joe Moore? He showed up here about thirty-year ago. Had this story about getting in some trouble in Ireland, stowing away from there, landing in New Orleans, and ending up here in the Pineywoods."

"Do you know him well?"

"Sure. I was his first friend in Ten Mile. Took care of him."

"Kind of like you're doing me?"

"Yep. I always try to help Outsiders."

"Am I an Outsider?"

"You are. You kinda look like us Ten Milers, but you and your family ain't from here. You're an Outsider, and Ten Mile Folk don't trust Outsiders."

"Do they trust the Irishman?"

"As much as they can trust any Outsider. Besides, he married into our people. His wife Eliza is my niece."

"So, the Irishman's wife is a Redbone?"

"Dyed in the wool."

"But Dan doesn't look Redbone."

"Nope, but that's what he is on the inside. His older brother

Mayo looks as dark as me, but Dan and younger brother Will look Irish." Unk stopped at the crest of the hill. "I'll stay with you until the store opens."

We sat down on the galleried porch.

"Okay, show me your book," Unk said.

"I only own two books. One's the *Bible*." I pulled out the other thick book I carried. "And then I own this one."

Unk hefted it. "It's a big 'un."

"Four hundred and seventy-three pages."

He opened it, thumbing through the water-smudged pages and my loose-leaf notes, inserted throughout the damaged copy. "What happened to it?"

"My father threw it out in the rain one night."

Unk glanced up. "Why?"

"That's a story for another time."

"What's the name of your big book?"

"It's known in French as *Les Miserables* and this is the fourth book of five volumes."

Unk gawked. "Wow. Are the other ones this big?"

"Yep. Together, the five books are over sixteen hundred pages."

"Do you have the other four?"

"No." I patted his shoulder. "And that's a story for another day, too."

As Unk handed the book back to me, his blue jay feather fell out of the book.

"I use your feather as my bookmark," I said.

"What's a bookmark?"

"It's how I mark where I've stopped reading."

"You've read all of this?"

"I've probably read this volume seven times."

He cocked his head. "What's the name of it again?"

I pointed to the spine. "The French name is *Les Miserables*, but I'm not even sure how to pronounce it. In English, it means 'The Miserable Ones.' The lady that gave it to me shortened the title to

Les Mizz to help me pronounce it. I say it 'Lay-Mizz.' "

Unk laughed. "Lay-Mizz. That sounds like your name." He watched as I stuffed the book back in my canvas bag. "What's it about?"

I studied the sun that was breaking through the pines. "It's about a saint, a woman, a little girl, and a convict trying to escape his past."

"Does he—the convict—make it?"

"I'm not sure."

"Why not?"

"I've never read book five." I held up the fourth volume. "This volume is called *St. Denis* and ends with the convict and a whole host of characters hanging in the balance. By the way, the convict's name is Valjean. Jean Valjean, but he goes by a host of other names in the book."

"So, he had some summer names, too?" Unk stood. "I guess that's a story for another day."

I laughed. "One day I'll find *Volume Five* and then we'll know."

He handed me the blue jay feather. "Where feathers fall, angels have walked."

With Unk gone, I turned to my notes for *Volume One*, page 323. It was my favorite passage in the entire book. Just as the Bishop was telling the convict Valjean, who still went by his prison parole number, 24601, 'I've bought your soul for God,' I jumped at the sound of rattling keys in the door behind me. I dropped my book and it tumbled down the steps into the dirt, with all of my notes and drawings scattering across the yard.

The Irishman stuck his head out the door. "Morning. Didn't mean to startle you."

I gathered my papers and dusted off my book.

"Let me see that book," The Irishman said. "That's a mighty big book for a girl your size."

He held up *Les Mizz*. "What's it about?"

"It's the story of a fallen man who tries to leave his past behind and start a new life."

"Does he succeed?"

"I don't have the final volume yet, so I don't know."

I'd noticed that the Irishman, when pensive, pulled out his pipe. He probed his pockets for tobacco, and finding none simply held the unlit pipe in his hand.

"So, the man is trying to leave his past?" He said. "There's a whole host of men—and even women—in No Man's Land trying to get *past* their past. Hope the man in your book does a better job than most of them here. It seems most folks out here drag their past with them."

He stood. "It sounds kind of like my own story."

"I'd like to hear your story sometimes," I said.

"Well, that's for another day." He handed the book to me. "I warn you. There won't be much sitting on the gallery and reading here at the store."

"What's a gallery?" I asked.

"It's what you're sitting on. The porch. Folks this far south call it the gallery."

I stood on the steps. "No, sir. My book won't be any problem. I just brought it for safekeeping."

"Safekeeping?"

"Yes, sir. We live in a wagon, and I'm always afraid something, or someone, might destroy my books."

The Irishman stopped. "By the way, you don't have any tobacco on you, do you?"

I fumbled in my pockets. "Doggone if I didn't leave it at home."

He laughed. "I bet you did." The Irishman unbolted the doors. "If you work hard today, it'll pay off your tobacco debt to Hatch and Moore."

Eager to change the subject, I said, "Did you know President Garfield died?"

"I knew he'd been shot, but thought he'd survived."

"Blood poisoning. He died a couple of weeks ago. Mister Chester A. Arthur's our president now."

He shrugged. "Out here on the frontier, it really doesn't make much difference who's president." He tossed me an apron and brush broom. "Now, get this gallery cleaned off." He stopped at the door. "If you see anything, uh, suspicious, let me know."

"Like what?"

"Anybody hanging around, drinking, looking for trouble."

I pointed to Unk, who was sitting in a grove of young pines. "Suspicious like him?"

The Irishman waved. "Don't worry about him."

"You trust him?"

"With my life." He stopped at the door. "And so can you."

I moved on to sweeping the gallery, then to the yard arranging the dirt in large patterns.

Dan Moore walked up eyeing my artwork in the dust. "That looks like a snake. Da doesn't like snakes."

"Well, who does, and who is Da?"

"My father. Da is Gaelic for daddy. He's deathly afraid of snakes. It's the Irish in him. You know, that Saint Patrick story about throwing all the snakes and Devil out of Ireland."

"Do you believe that?"

He shrugged. "Da says they don't have snakes there. He claims Saint Patrick flung them out, and they all landed here in Louisiana."

I laughed. "How many are in your Louisiana family."

"Well, there's me, and then there's my younger brother, Will. My older brother Mayo lives in Alexandria, and my older sister lives in Shreveport. Three siblings didn't survive childhood."

"Does Will work at the store?"

"Not right now. He's on house arrest."

"How so?"

"It's a good story. He was part of a baby kidnapping at last month's brush arbor meeting. Follow me to the grist mill and I'll tell you the story."

I laid my broom down. I've always been a sucker for a good story.

CHAPTER 7

BRUSH ARBOR

October 3

It was about a quarter mile to the grist mill. As Dan Moore walked briskly, I said, "A baby kidnapping?"

Dan sighed and I knew he'd repeated the story dozens of times. "Well, last month we had a Brush Arbor Revival over at Occupy Church. Folks came in their wagons, and the mothers with babies made sure they parked close to the arbor. When the infants dozed off after feeding, the mothers laid them down on Methodist pallets in the wagon beds."

"What's that?"

"Blankets and clothing so the babies would be comfortable. Well, my brother Will and two other scalawags sneaked around in the dark and switched four of the sleeping babies. The mothers didn't realize they had the wrong baby until late that night or early the next morning. It took a full day untangling everything and getting the babies back into their correct homes."

"That's bad."

"It was an ill-fated kidnapping, and the fur did fly. As you can imagine, Will ain't the most popular boy in any of Ten Mile, especially around Occupy Church."

"You weren't in on the baby-swapping?"

"No way. I like a good prank, but that's crossing the line. Those mommas were like grizzly bears robbed of their cubs. Da whipped Will real good and put him on probation for the month. He's got double chores and isn't allowed to go anywhere without Da or Momma."

"Will sounds like quite a rascal."

"He manages to stay in lots of trouble. Most of it's harmless, but it lands him in hot water pretty often.

"He sounds like a character in my favorite book."

"What's the book?"

"It's French and I call it *Les Mizz*, and the bad boy is named Gavroche."

"Gavroche? What kind of name is that?"

"French. Gavroche is a gamin. That's a street urchin in Paris. He has a big heart, loud mouth, and is always breaking streetlights and stealing, then sharing his booty with someone worse off than him."

"That sounds a little like my brother Will, except we don't have streetlights in Ten Mile."

"I'm a little confused," I said. "You've mentioned No Man's Land, Ten Mile, and Westport. What are they?"

Dan drew two parallel lines in the dirt. "That's the rivers that serve as borders of what we call No Man's Land." He pointed at one of the lines. "This river here is the Calcasieu, where you crossed into No Man's Land."

He drew a third line. "This is Ten Mile Creek. All the land between the Calcasieu and past the creek is called 'Ten Mile.' It's the Redbone kingdom. Westport is the name of the store. Da named it after the town he came from—Westport, County Mayo, Ireland."

Before I could ask more, Dan said, "You'd better get back to sweeping before we both get fired. Now, what was the name of that bad boy in your book?"

"Gavroche."

As I hurried back toward the store, I heard Dan Moore laugh aloud. "Gavroche."

I spent the rest of the morning cleaning around the outside using the brush broom to attack the spider webs on the walls and eaves. Twice that day, I stuck my head inside and offered to help, but the Irishman gestured me away. It should not have surprised me. I wouldn't want a five-fingered discount thief in my store either, even one that was working off her debt.

At lunch, I sat on the gallery with my corn dodgers and book. I was surprised when Dan Moore brought me a plate of beans and cornbread.

"Here's some vittles."

I held up a cold corn dodger, but I waved him off. "I'm fine."

"That johnnycake can't compare to beans and cornbread."

"What's that?" I said.

"Johnnycake?" Dan laughed. "It's what you're holding."

"We've always called it a corn dodger." I said. "Or hoe cake, and I've eaten my fair share."

"Well, regardless, it don't stack up against a hot meal." He handed me the plate.

I didn't even bother being ladylike. I ate without taking a breath. It was hot and delicious, and I was some kind of hungry. "Who made this?"

"My mother."

"She is some cook."

"Yes, she is. Momma's been really sick but can still cook up a storm on her good days." He handed me another piece of cornbread. "All Redbone women can."

Between a mouthful, I said, "I still haven't got a handle on what a Redbone is."

Dan lowered his voice. "Be careful using that term Redbone in open conversation. Some of them take deep offense at the word. They usually call themselves Ten Milers, so that's what I call them. If you say Redbone, they might come at night and burn your pine knot pile."

I glanced around. "Okay then, what's a Redbone?"

"My momma says that the real question is, 'What's not in a Redbone?' We're a gumbo mixture of all kinds of groups that have settled in this No Man's Land. My kin can't even agree what strain of Indian blood flows in us. Maybe Cherokee, Choctaw, or Attakapas."

"Your mother sounds like a real character."

"She's one of a kind and has a full dose of the Outlaw Strip in her blood."

"You sound proud of that."

"I am."

"You're proud of being called an outlaw?"

"I'm proud of our independent spirit. We're rebels—it's the defining mark of Ten Mile. You've probably noticed we're a little standoffish to Outsiders."

"What about your daddy, the Irishman. Is he an Outsider?"

"He's still an Outsider. He's as close as you can get to being adopted, but he's Irish and will always be viewed as an Outsider."

"What about you?"

"Look at me." He held up his freckled arms. "Do I look Redbone? Will and I got the Irish side's looks." He touched my shoulder. "But don't forget this—I'm a one hundred percent Ten Miler on the inside."

"Does your looks cause problems in Ten Mile?"

"Not to folks who've known me all my life, but folks do judge a book by its cover. I'm afeared most locals will always view me as an Outsider."

He placed his arm beside mine, and the contrast was startling. "You're dark enough to fit in as a Ten Miler," Dan said. "You're as dark as my momma. What are you?"

"It's a mystery." I shrugged. "My folks won't talk much about their past. All I know is that Ma who's dark like me claims to be Melungeon."

"What's that?"

"It's some kind of mixture of reclusive folks in the Carolina mountains." I shrugged. "Sometimes it's better not to know."

Dan laughed. "I know what you mean. What's your daddy?"

"He claims to be Scots-Irish, but Ma says he's Sorry-Arsed."

"I didn't know that was a nationality, but I've known plenty from that clan."

Just then a large calico cat scooted past me.

"That's Esther," Dan said. "She runs the rat department here at the Westport Store."

"She looks healthy from all appearances."

"I think she's great with child. Or in her case, kittens."

I nodded at the sign on the storefront. "This store is the Hatch and Moore Store, but you just called it the Westport Store."

"Westport is where Da is from. It's a seaport town in County Mayo, Ireland. He gave this place the name after we built the store."

"Your father is Moore, so who is Hatch?"

"Captain Hatch was with my daddy in the Civil War. They served with the quartermaster's corps at Vicksburg. The Captain lives in Alexandria and is a silent partner in the store."

"Why'd they open a store in the middle of the woods?"

"Because there's nowhere to buy supplies between Hineston and Sugartown. It's a full day's wagon ride to either town, so this was a logical place to set up shop. The only problem is that the store is considered an Outsider's venture. "There's tension between the white trespassers and the locals. It's a simmering feud over grazing rights, timber, and land. This talk of bushwhacks and burnouts has folks on edge."

"What's a bushwhack?"

"An ambush. A specialty of my people."

"You say 'your people'," I said. "Which side are you on?"

"Both and neither."

"What will you do if fighting breaks out?"

"Try to keep my head down."

I pointed at a stack of coffins in the corner of the store. "Much need for these?"

"There's always demand for coffins in Ten Mile country." Dan led me to a closet containing a stack of several child-sized coffins. "Sadly, we sell as many of those as the big ones. Life can be fast, straight, and short here in No Man's Land . . ."

The Irishman coughed. "Daniel, you and uh, Missouri, better get back to work."

"Tell your wife that the beans and cornbread were wonderful."

"Will do."

Customers trickled in and out during the afternoon. I busied myself keeping the gallery and yard swept, whistling while I worked.

The Irishman walked out on the porch. "A whistling woman and a crowing hen . . . both will come to a very bad end."

I leaned on my broom. "I'll try to remember to silence my whistler."

"Just picking. Whistle away. It's a free country."

Lucky limped up to the Irishman. He nudged the dog's ears. "Have you had a good day?" He turned to me. "Lucky's a fine dog, but has one big problem. He's afraid of loud noises. Anything loud, be it thunder, gunfire, or fire poppers, sets him into a panic."

The Irishman nodded at the setting sun behind the pines. "Missouri, you've done a good day's work. As far as I'm concerned, we're even. You've paid your debt. You better hurry on before this short day catches you out in the open."

"I'm still sorry about what happened."

"It's in the past. Wasn't your fault anyway. Let me give you a word of advice. Don't stumble over anything behind you." He held out an envelope. "This is for later."

"What is it?"

"Lagniappe."

"Thanks. I like that word." I took a deep breath. "I do have one favor to ask." I was surprised at how shaky my voice was.

He nodded. "Go ahead."

"I … I'd like to come to work tomorrow. You could pay me in food or supplies. I believe I'd be good help, and to be real honest, we need money something bad."

He took a step back and stifled a smile. "Girl, you've got some kind of moxie."

"What's that?"

"Grit. Sand. A stubbornness. Moxie. It's an Indian word.

"Sir, is that a good or bad thing?"

"It can be either or both, but you've definitely got it." He shook his head. "Imagine the moxie of stealing from my store, then asking for a job?" He rubbed his chin. "Well, I do like the way you worked, and I'm prone to believe you won't have any more sticky fingers."

I dropped my head. "You can trust me, sir."

He studied me closely, then laughed. "Well, we'll find out. See you tomorrow morning bright and early." He walked about five steps, then stopped. "And remember, don't stumble over anything—"

"Behind you."

He waved. "Forward. Always forward."

I stepped off the gallery and was startled to see Pap wobbling toward the store. I hurried to him, wanting to keep him as far from the Irishman as possible. He was roaring drunk, slurring his words. "Where you been?"

"Helping out." I handed him the envelope.

"What's this?"

"My pay for the day from the store. It's a dollar."

He grabbed my arm. "How'd you get a job at that store?"

"It's a long story, but the bottom line is I made some money for us." It sickened me to give my hard-earned pay to him, but it beat a black eye.

He held it up to the light. "It's counterfeit. In fact, it's one of the dollars I sent with you yesterday."

I thought about a verse in Proverbs, "Who so diggeth a pit shall fall therein, and he that rolleth a stone, it will return upon him."

The stone had rolled back on us, and I wasn't sure whether to laugh or cry. Did the Irishman do this, or was it coincidence? Pap staggered toward the store, waving my dollar. "I want to trade this for the real thing."

"Pap. It's closed. Let's go home." I eased him in the direction of our campsite.

As we walked in the last daylight, I glimpsed a figure slipping along behind us. I was pretty sure it was Unk Dyal.

CHAPTER 8

A BIRTHDAY PROMISE

Monday, October 10, 1881

After about a week at the store, I'd settled into a routine. I was always the first at the store before the Irishman arrived to unlock later. He'd join me on the steps. As always, I was reading one of my two books—the *Bible* or *Les Mizz*. On this morning, I had them both.

The Irishman nodded at my *Bible*. "It's in as bad a shape as the big book. What happened?"

"They both got tossed out in the rain one night."

He picked up the *Bible*. Its pages had been stuck together due to being waterlogged. The ink hadn't run, but pulling the pages apart had made some passages illegible. The Irishman scowled at the Bible. "How'd this happen?"

"My pap's bad to drink. One night he got upset at me over some little nothing and in a fit tossed my books out of the wagon. It was raining a log-floater and he said he'd thrash me if I retrieved them. You can see the result."

"Your own father did this?"

"Yes, sir. I guess he knew where to hit where it hurt. As soon as he passed out, I retrieved the books. Took a week to dry the pages, pull them apart, and work on my smudged handwritten notes."

I held up the *Bible*. "I call it my waterproof *Bible*. It weathered the storm pretty well. It's missing a few pages from Revelations where Pap tore out some pages to start a fire. That's why I carry both books in this canvas sack for protection."

"The more I hear about your father, the less I like him."

As I left the store that afternoon, the Irishman stood in the doorway, "Remember, don't stumble—"

"Over anything behind me."

"If you stumble, let it be something in front—"

I hesitated before finishing my part, "And don't forget to get up."

"And keep your powder dry as well as your books."

I waved as I walked toward the grist mill. I wanted to talk to Dan Moore. I found him coated in corn flour. He smiled. "I'm kind of kivered in flour, huh?"

"Kivered?" I asked.

"Kivered. It's how Ten Milers say 'covered.' " He nodded. "So you're headed home to downtown Cherry Winchie?"

"If you can call a wagon a home."

"Home's where the heart is." He walked with me toward the tree line. In a fake Irish accent, he said, "May the road rise up to meet ye. And the wind be at your back. And the rain fall softly on the fields." He pointed. "Your bodyguard's awaiting."

Just then, Unk stepped out of the shadows.

"Well, I see you're in good hands," Dan said. "It's back to the grind for me."

I approached Unk. "Don't you have anything better to do?"

"I kinda like being your bodyguard. Fine day, ain't it?"

"I don't feel like talking today."

"That's all right. I can talk for both of us."

A crow flew over. "Do you believe in crows, Miss-Mizz?"

I nodded.

"Do you believe they carry messages?"

I shook my head.

The crow circled over us again. "Ol' Unk believes that any day with a crow in it is full of promise."

I shook my head vigorously, hoping he'd take a hint and shut up.

Surprisingly, he did, and we walked about a quarter mile before I kicked a rock as hard as I could. "Today's my birthday."

"Well, Happy Birthday, Miss-Mizz. Did they know it's your birthday at the store?"

"I didn't tell them."

Unk studied on this for a while. "How old are you today?"

"Sixteen."

"Well, I guess your Ma will have a birthday supper waiting for you."

"I doubt she remembered."

Unk stopped. "You could've reminded her."

"But I didn't. Some things aren't worth the trouble. Having to remind Ma didn't seem fair."

"Fair to who?"

"Her or me. It's not fair that my own mother would forget the date of the day she brought me into this world."

Unk scratched his head. "Folks in the woods ain't too good at keeping up with dates. Remember, you had to help Unk on what day of the week it was."

"But this is my own mother."

Unk stepped in front of me. "Maybe she's waiting to surprise you."

"Doubt it. This morning Ma was up making coffee over the campfire before I left for work. I kept waiting for her to say, 'Happy Birthday.' She probably doesn't even know what month it is, much less the date."

I nodded down the path. "I guess we'll see. By the way, when is your birthday?"

"Unk's not rightly sure. I always celebrate it on January the first."

"Why?"

"It's easy to remember, and folks are celebrating anyway, so it makes it easy for me to imagine they're shooting fire poppers and guns in the air 'cause it's Unk's birthday."

"What year were you born?"

He rubbed his chin. "I'm not rightly sure. I believe it was 1812 or 13."

"So, you're nearly seventy years old."

"Somewhere in the vicinity. I use 1812 'cause it's the year Lousianer became a state."

"You've always lived here?"

"Yep, don't plan on being nowhere else. This is home for Ol' Unk." He kicked a dried pile of cow manure out of the roadway. "How about you, Miss-Mizz? Where'd you have your last birthday?"

"I'm not sure. I believe it was New Orleans."

"You're not sure?"

"Unk, I've probably never had a birthday in the same place twice."

"That's hard to believe."

"It's just what happens when you don't have roots. Drifting does that to a soul. Just pounds you down flat and gives you tunnel vision. Surviving becomes the focus. Getting by. Existence. Dates cease to matter."

He limped around a hole in the road. "You sound bitter."

"I am. I just don't have much to believe in."

He took my hand. "Well, Unk says 'Happy Happy Birthday' to you, Miss-Mizz."

As we neared our wagon, Unk stopped. "This is ri't far enough for me." He hesitated, then looked me in the eyes. "What do you believe in?"

"Honestly, there's a whole lot more I don't believe in than I do."

Unk shook his head. "That's sad."

His comment irritated as well as saddened me. "Well, Mister Professor, what do you believe in?"

He nodded at the late evening stars. "Look at those first stars bravely appearing in the twilight. For starters, Unk believes in them stars. He believes in them 'cause he can see 'em. Unk don't understand all about them, but he believes in 'em 'cause he sees them each night. Miss-Mizz, do you believe in things you can't see?"

"I don't even believe in some of the things I can see."

Unk laughed. "That's all right for now, but you hang around the Ten Mile country long enough, and you might see things differently."

"I doubt it."

He ignored my skepticism. "Unk can't see a pine taproot, but I believe it's down there under the trunk. We had a hurricane 'bout twenty year ago, and it laid the yellow pines down by the thousands. It exposed the ones that were top heavy. They didn't have a deep enough taproot. Just proves there's strength in some things we can't see."

"Are you preaching to me?"

"Unk ain't smart enough to preach to nobody." He shrugged. "I'm just observing."

I chunked a clod of dirt at him. In spite of it, I couldn't work up a good mad at him. He was such a sweet combination of being simple and kind. "Why don't you walk to our wagon and meet my folks?" she asked.

He tipped his hat. "Thank you kindly, but I believe I'll pass. Your daddy mixes two things I try to stay away from—whiskey and shotguns." As he turned to go, he said, "Are you gonna tell 'em it's your birthday?"

"I believe I am. I'd made up my mind. I'm going to do something I'd been waiting to do for a long time.

"Miss-Mizz, you be careful what you say. You can't take back words." He squeezed my hand. "And Happy Birthday. You can't say no one wished you that today." He turned and tripped over a root, falling face first in the road. "And don't fergit to not stumble on nuthin' behind you."

I didn't answer. I'd heard that saw enough. I had too much baggage behind me not to stumble over some of it.

Ma had prepared a good supper of sawmill gravy, biscuits, and some fatback. We'd been eating lots of trail salad, but an early frost had ended our supply, and it wasn't a day too soon for me.

Ma set the plates of food on the ground. Pap sat on a stump while Ma and I each had a packing box for a chair.

"Missouri, pass me another helping of that gravy."

I handed the plate to Pap. Him being sober, I decided this was as good a time as ever. "Pap. Ma. I have an announcement."

Ma looked up, while Pap shoveled half a biscuit into his mouth.

"I've made up my mind on something today. I'm not stealing anymore."

Pap set his plate down. "What was that?"

"I won't be stealing anymore for you."

"You will if I tell you to."

"No, sir. You can order me. You can beat me, but I've made up my mind. I won't do it again."

He wiped his mouth on his sleeve. "Yes, you will."

"No, I won't."

He drew back his fist. Ma stepped between us, but I pushed her out of the way, exposing my chin. "You can hit me every day, but I won't do it. Never again. I won't be stealing. Not today. Not tomorrow. Not ever."

Pap threw his plate on the ground and stomped off into the dark.

"Missouri, what's got into you?" Ma said.

I shrugged. "I just made up my mind. I'm through with it."

"But, why today?"

"It's my birthday, and I'm giving myself a present."

"Today's your birthday?"

I nodded.

"Baby, I'm so sorry I forgot."

I lied. "It's all right." Tears stung my eyes. "You've got a lot on your mind."

"You're not going to steal?" Ma said. "You got religion or something?"

"No. I just realized how tired I am of all this. I will answer to God one day, but it's more about answering to myself now. I want to be able to look in a mirror and see someone I'm proud of. I realized today that my past doesn't have to be my future."

Ma pulled me close. "You know your Pap won't let this go."

"I'm game. I've made up my mind."

"You're both stubborn."

"I'm through stumbling on anything behind me. I'm moving forward." I broke down in tears—the first real cry I'd had in forever.

Ma held me a long time, stroking my hair. "I'm so sorry, Baby. Really sorry. Sorry about forgittin' your birthday. Sorry about this hell of a life we live. You deserve better."

"Ma, I love you. I don't expect you to be perfect."

"Well, that's good, because I'm a long way from it." She sighed. "And your Pap. I just think…"

I held up my hand. "I don't want to talk about him."

"Mizz, you sure are stubborn. I wonder if the man's ever been born that'll tame your gypsy soul."

"I'm not a gypsy."

"Deep down in your soul you are, and nothing and nobody can change that."

She began clearing the dishes, and I walked toward the creek. Brave fireflies blinked on and off in the trees. This cool spell was a harbinger of the end of lots of things, not just my stealing days. I sat on a log under the starlit canopy and watched as the fireflies flickered for probably the last time until next summer. The pesky mosquitos wouldn't last much longer either. The crickets chirped noisily, near deafening, until Pap interrupted them with his clinking of glass and cussing. He was getting pig-faced drunk.

Backlit by the lantern, Ma's silhouette danced on the wagon canvas as she sang an old spiritual. "I ain't studying war no more.

Gonna lay down my sleepy head down by the riverside. Gonna lay down my burden down by the riverside. I ain't gonna study war no more, study war no more. Ain't gonna study war no more…"

I couldn't remember the last time I'd heard her sing. This was my sixteenth birthday … the one I'd never forget. I didn't get a cake, but the gift of a promise. A present I'd given myself.

It was only a start. But it was a start.

I shivered, wondering where I'd be for my seventeenth birthday. I had no idea, but I hoped we'd be out of this God-forsaken country and in Texas.

CHAPTER 9

REVENGE

October 18, 1881

About a week after my birthday fiasco, we were finishing supper when Pap leaned back in his straight chair, "Missouri, there's something I been meanin' to tell you." I didn't like his smile, reflected by the dying campfire.

"Since your birthday, I been thinking about how you want to be treated like an adult. There's something you need to know." He nodded at Ma. "How can I put it? You're our daughter …but you're not."

I glanced at Ma. She looked clueless.

"I don't like where this is going," I said.

"When you were born, things were in a mess and … and your older sister Helen was about your age. She got involved with some white trash boy who worked on a nearby plantation in Carroll County, Georgia."

Ma's plate rattled as she put it down. "Henry, why are you doing this to our girl?"

Pap never took his eye off me. "Missouri wants to be treated like an adult, so she needs to know adult stuff." He smirked. "Anyway, Helen ran off with that sorry boy that'd been hanging around. She was gone about ten days. Came back with a broken heart, black eye, and a few months later after we'd moved on, Helen was obviously pregnant." He flicked a mosquito from his arm. "Pregnant with you."

They say revenge is a dish best served cold. Maybe that's why Pap waited an entire week to spring his trap. I knew he'd retaliate against my birthday promise, but I never saw this coming.

Ma wept quietly.

I kicked at a pile of leaves. "You mean Helen, who I thought was my sister, was really my mother?"

He nodded.

I turned to Ma. "So, you're my grandparents, instead of my mother and father?"

"That's the sum of it, Baby," she said.

I turned on Pa. "Why in the world are you telling me this now?"

"He's trying to hurt you." In one quick motion, Ma flung her plate at him. "This here's his way of getting even. You provoked him by refusing to steal anymore, and I knew he'd find some way to get even." She glanced around for something else to throw. "I didn't think you'd stoop this low."

He shrugged. "You wanted to know, didn't you, Missouri?"

My mouth wouldn't work.

But Ma's did. "Henry, you get out of my sight." She picked up a butcher knife and pointed it at him. "Out. Now!"

"Woman, you are not brave enough to try. I'd take it and use it on you."

"And you'd be doing me a favor." She tossed the knife at his feet. "You're not brave enough, either." He kicked the knife and huffed into the nearby tent. He lit the lantern and rattled around, his movement casting eerie shadows on the canvas.

"I can't believe he did this while sober," I said. "That made it hurt even deeper, since it was premeditated."

The sound of glass clinking echoed from the tent, and Ma put her hand on my shoulder. "Within an hour, he'll still be mean—and drunk to boot."

She sat beside me. "Mizz, I've meant to tell you a thousand times. You deserved to know. I wanted to tell you as a child, but your Pap wouldn't hear of it."

"What else about my life is a lie?"

"Honey, don't be angry."

"I have a right to be. Everything about my life is one big damnable lie." I rubbed my temples. "I can't believe it. My dead sister was really my mother."

"She was both. She loved you as much as any mother that's ever-drawn breath."

"What am I supposed to do? Just smile and go on?"

"I'm so sorry."

"Well, this does explain some things about our crazy family. So, the story about me being conceived in Missouri is a crock?"

"Afraid so. Helen picked your name. She claimed the short time we were in Missouri was the happiest of her life." Ma's voice softened. "Your Pap blamed himself for everything—letting Helen get mixed up with that guy in Georgia. Then we made the fateful trip to New Orleans. By then, you were nearly two, and Helen had just turned twenty. I had a nightmare about going to New Orleans and begged your Pap not to go. He ignored it, and we walked into a yellow fever epidemic."

"So that's really how Helen died?"

"She's the only one of us that got the yellow fever. She was dead by the next day."

"Is she buried there?"

"In a pauper's cemetery. We didn't have no money, and they wanted to get rid of bodies quickly. That's the time when your Pap's drinking really started. He ain't never been the same man since New Orleans. If I even mention Helen's name, he gets up and leaves the room."

"Ma, what was the man's name?"

"Who?"

"The man that was my father."

"It won't do you no good."

"Probably not, but I still want to know."

"Why do you want so much to know about the man that made you? He prob'ly don't even know you exist, and if he did, he wouldn't care a rat's tail about you. "

I shook my head. "I got a Daddy that don't even know I exist. And I don't even know his name."

"His name was Wilson. Buford Wilson."

She grasped my hand. "I've been a pretty fair mother to you, ain't I?"

"Yes'um."

"After New Orleans, there weren't nothing to do but soldier on. The War weren't many years over and times were hard."

I was still stunned. "I barely remember Helen. So, my sister is really my momma?"

"That's so."

I wiped my eyes on my sleeve. "And Pap ain't my daddy, and you're not my mother?"

"Nope." Ma stroked my hair. "Baby, your sister was a wonderful child."

I shoved her hand away, turned on my heel, and hurried away. The entire world was wobbling on its axis, and due to the tangle of emotion in me, I might fall off at any moment.

CHAPTER 10

COMINGS AND GOINGS

October 27, 1881

About ten days after spilling the beans about my sister Helen, Pap disappeared. No note or explanation. He saddled Maggie and was gone. It was more than ironic that he left just before Halloween. It seemed to be one of his favorite holidays, as to how he loved scaring me with stories of graveyards and haints.

To tell the truth, I enjoyed our time without his tirades and antics, but Ma felt differently. There was a lonely sadness about her. Nearly nightly, she had a case of what she called the 'sobbing spasms.' I'd just hold her tight and sing every verse I knew of "In the Pines." I had now memorized forty-eight of the verses and had even made up a few original ones.

On one of those long nights, Ma was darning a pair of worn socks as I read by a fluttering candle. A wind gust blew out both my candle and the lantern. We sat in complete darkness, illuminated only by the occasional distant lightning. The dark seemed a good place to say what was on my mind. "Ma, sometimes I think we'd be better off without him."

"Maybe . . . "She took a deep breath. "Then, maybe not."

"You ever wonder how different your life might be without Pap?"

"No. That's a waste of time. Like I told you, he ain't the kind of man I wanted, but he's the kind I got."

"Would you be better off without him?"

"Are you asking about me, or us?"

"Both."

"You might be better off. Me? I'm not so sure. We need each other. Occasionally, he's good to me."

"I'm glad you're happy with him."

"I didn't say I was happy."

"Ma, where do you think he's gone this time?"

"He'd mentioned slipping back across the river and running a Lucky Lady at that Hineston ferry crossing. Figured they wouldn't follow him back into No Man's Land."

"Since the wagon's fixed, why haven't we moved on?"

"Your Pap don't do nothing until he's ready."

"You ever wonder if there's a time he won't come back?"

"It's never happened yet."

"How would you feel if he didn't?"

"I guess we'd get on . . . How about you?"

I wanted to say *relieved*, but held my tongue, ashamed of feeling that way. "I guess I'd have lots of unanswered questions."

I relit the lantern and she returned to her stitching.

I changed the subject. "Is the Lucky Lady his best con?"

"Consistently, yes. People just can't resist. Your father knows how to make it look so easy with those three cards. That's how he got his nickname of Slick. His hands are quick enough that he often doesn't even need to cheat. Just beats them with sleight of hand." Ma said it as proudly as a banker's wife bragging about her husband. "All cons play off greed and arrogance."

"Can he do the Lucky Lady without you?"

"Oh, yeah. He'll pick up somebody as a shill for a cut of the profit."

"Ma, you know it'll be another woman. Doesn't that bother you that it'll be another woman?"

She dropped the sock. "Like I said, he ain't the kind of man I wanted—"

I finished for her. "...but he's the kind you got."

"Afraid so."

"Ma, I got one more question, but it's a hard one to ask you."

"Go ahead."

"Can a person rise above their raising?"

I immediately regretted my question, knowing it had hurt her deeply.

"I'm sorry ... I didn't mean it the way it sounded."

She held up her hand. "That's okay. I think I understand your question—"

"I don't mean it toward Pap and you."

"I understand." She took my hand. "Do I believe a person can rise above their raising? Sure, I do. All I have to do is look at you."

She kissed me on the forehead. "And you write that down in those notes you keep and remember it."

I quickly blew out my reading candle and stretched out on the pallet I called a bed. In the pitch darkness, I listened to Ma crying softly. It was a good while before I heard the soft snoring that meant Ma was asleep. It was much longer before I drifted off.

The next day as I was tending shop at the store, a man walked in, put his hands on his hips, and disdainfully surveyed the store. He was so tall he ducked under the doorframe. I immediately recognized the bounty hunter I'd nicknamed "Javert" at the river. He was dressed in a long, black riding coat, and although I couldn't see a weapon, he seemed dangerous. His black felt hat sat pulled low over his eyes.

Javert still had his slight limp, and I remembered the river ferryman's assurance that this man and his partners wouldn't cross the river and the Dead Line. Yet, here he was. He looked up from under his hat and I could make out the bird-of-prey look of this man with his sharp nose and long face. He also had shifty, beady eyes and nervously licked his lips. His eyes and lips reminded me of a rattler I'd encountered the week before on my walk to work. We'd studied each other, and those cat-eyes and flicking tongue gave me the heebie-jeebies. I found a stout stick and dispatched the snake.

As I watched this man in the Westport Store, I wished I'd had that same stout stick. Instead, I tried to smile. "Can I help you, sir?"

"Maybe so. Maybe not." He picked up a can of baking soda, then set it down.

I glanced out the window and could see his horse tied to the post. "You're traveling alone through the No Man's Land. We don't see that often."

"Who said I was by myself?" He stepped toward me, and I was glad the counter separated us. "Actually, I'm here on business."

"What kind?"

"Probably nothing that concerns you." He smirked. "Or, maybe it might. How long have you been living here?"

"Long enough."

He pulled out a wanted poster with a pretty fair sketch of Pap. It listed several aliases and crimes he was wanted for. "You ever seen him?"

"What's the color of his hair?"

"Kind of bald with reddish hair, light-skinned with a red face."

I pointed to my face. "Everyone around here is as dark as the ace of spades. We don't take to outsiders. Especially redheaded ones with a long list of offenses. Never seen him before."

"Where's the proprietor of this store?"

"That would be the Irishman, Mister Joe Moore. He's over at the gristmill. Would you like to speak with him?"

"I would."

"Good. I'll go get him. May I tell him your name?"

"My name's not important. Go get the man."

I hurried to the mill, relieved to be out of this man's sight. He wouldn't tell me his name but I knew he would always be Javert to me. I called the Irishman outside the loud mill. "There's a stranger here who wants to see you."

"About what?"

"He's a bounty hunter."

He lifted his eyebrows. "And what brings you to that conclusion?"

"He's got a wanted poster with my pap's likeness. The sketch looks a lot like you too, so, you got a good alibi?" This drew a smirk from the Irishman.

"We saw this same fellow at the ferry crossing in Hineston," I said. "We were told his ilk didn't cross into No Man's Land."

"Normally, they don't, if they've got good sense." The Irishman took off his apron. "Well, let me go meet him."

I grabbed his arm. "You won't give up my pap, will you?"

"I don't have any reason to. What happens across the river is none of our business on this side."

The hunter was pacing back and forth on the gallery. The Irishman greeted him and slowly led him to the hitching post. The Irishman pointed south, then east. The bounty hunter mounted his horse, tipped his hat, and rode back toward Hineston and civilization. I hoped it was my last glimpse of the man I had come to call Javert.

The Irishman came into the store. "He described a man like your daddy and the likeness did bear a resemblance."

"To who?"

"To both of us." The Irishman grinned and pulled out his pipe. "Sounds like your father left a good trail of angry people in his wake."

"It's the story of our life."

"Where's your father now?"

"He disappeared about a week ago."

"Where to?"

"We don't know, but I figure he's up to no good back across the river."

"Well, I hope he and that fellow don't cross paths."

"You didn't tell Javert anything, did you?"

"Who is Javert?"

"It's my name for the bounty hunter. It comes from the name of a lawman in *Les Miserables.*"

The Irishman put his hand on my shoulder "The fellow wouldn't tell me his name. Missouri, don't worry. Folks here won't give your daddy up. It's our code of silence concerning Outsiders. Ten Milers can be the tightest lipped people in the world. And if that fellow hangs around and asks too many questions, he may get a bullet in the back. Besides, most of us here in No Man's Land have been chased at one time or another."

"I heard that's how you got here."

"Well, trouble's what got me on the road." He took out his trusty pipe and lit it. "Times were hard during the Potato Famine in Ireland. I was just a teen, and my family depended on me pretty heavy. About all we had were a few sheep. One day a pack of dogs attacked our flock, and as I chased them off, I beat the most aggressive dog to death with my shovel. It was my bad luck that it belonged to one of the local English Nobleman."

"What's a Nobleman?"

The Irishman scowled. "In Europe, it's a class of people born into nobility. You have land, privileges, and prestige that cannot be earned by the lower classes."

"That's down right un-American," I said.

He laughed. "Another reason I love it here. Anyway, the rich Nobleman quickly placed a price on my young Irish head, and I wisely made my leave of Westport Town before the High Sheriff found me. Stowed away on a ship that was bound for America." He held up his hands. "That's how I got here."

"Westport. So your store is named after your hometown?" I asked.

"Yep, and how this neck of the woods became known as Westport." He took a long puff. "By the way, your Pap sounds like a real tomcat. Just remember, what a fellow did 'fore he arrived in Westport isn't important, but *what* he does *here* makes all the difference. I hope your Pap remembers that. Folks here have a way of meting out their own justice."

I returned home from work shaken and got out my copy of *Les Miserables*. Since the weather had turned cooler and the mosquitoes lessened, I flopped down on a pallet outside the tent and read every dog-eared page about Javert, the lawman who doggedly pursued Jean Valjean.

I'd always had mixed emotions about Javert in *Les Mizz*. He was a solid officer who lived by the law of justice. His dogged pursuit of Valjean was built on a belief that a man cannot change. Valjean had broken parole and ditched his yellow parole card, so he must be brought to justice.

I hoped the fictional Javert was wrong, both in the book, and in general. I wondered what part he would play in *Volume Five*. Would he end as a villain or hero?

I set my book aside and studied the sky. The Louisiana humidity is lower in the fall, and the night sky could be stunning. Earlier that summer, I'd read in the *Louisiana Democrat* about what was called the Great Comet of 1881. The article stated that the comet was presently only visible in the northern latitudes, but predicted it'd be visible in our part of the South by year's end. During a spell of cool clear nights, I'd put a pallet out on the ground, build a good pine-knot fire, and watch for the comet.

On this November night, I first spotted the comet on the NW horizon close to the North Star. I called to Ma, who was in the wagon. "Come out here and see something."

She was dressed in her bedclothes but sat beside me on the pallet.

"Look at that. It's the comet."

She studied it a long time before saying, "It's an omen of bad things."

I'd expected something like this. "Why does every sign predict bad things?"

"Baby, I just call it as I see it."

"It's always death or something bad. We're due some good news."

"A similar comet appeared just afore the Civil War broke out in 1861." Ma lay back on the pallet. "Lots of folks are convinced it caused the War. They didn't know where it came from, and that fear of the unknown scared them."

"Kind of like us?"

"Exactly."

I poked the fire with a long stick. "Ma, tell me about the other children?"

She stared into the fire for a long time. "Besides you and Helen? Well, there was a boy named Rob that died of the croup in the Carolinas. Then, we had twin boys that died at birth. Buried in Tennessee on the edge of a long-forgotten town. Like that Nash woman, I didn't even bother to name them, since they weren't around long enough." Ma sighed. "Seems like I can't keep boys alive." She tweaked my nose. "But look at you, Mizz. You're healthy as a horse. Then there was the other boy."

"Who?" I said.

"The boy we picked up."

"What?" I'd never heard this before.

"He was a street kid that attached himself to us in West Tennessee. I'm not sure if we adopted him or he us."

"I don't remember him."

"You were too little, but my how he loved you."

"What was his name?"

"His given name was Jephthah, but we called him Jep."

"What happened to him?"

"That's the hardest part. We never were sure. It was us, your sister Helen, you, and the boy. We were staying in a river town, and then Jep just disappeared into thin air."

I saw the pain as she spoke his name. "You never saw him again?"

"No note left behind. He left his clothes. We don't know if he drowned, was kidnapped, or was kilt. Or maybe just left. We'll never know. That's the hardest part. Not knowing. We'd already lost the other boys. We'd wanted a boy so bad, especially your

Pap."

Ma sat up and took a sip from her cup of cold coffee. "I wonder if Jep's looking at this same comet tonight somewhere?" Tears streamed down her cheeks, and she flung the dregs of her cup into the fire.

"Ma, you believe he's still alive, don't you?"

"I just know in my mother's heart that he is."

I sat in silence watching the comet slowly sink to the tree line. There's nothing worse than no closure. In its own way, it's worse than death. An open sore that won't or can't heal.

She sat up. "I wonder if your pap is looking at this same comet?"

I held my tongue. *He's not my father. He's my grandfather, and he's not much use at neither.*

She lay there a long time. The silence was sacred, which I knew better than to break.

Once the comet set behind the horizon, I said, "You miss Pap, don't you?"

She stared off into the darkness. "More than I thought I would."

I wouldn't admit it, but I kind of missed him, too.

CHAPTER 11

MISS ELIZA

Friday, November 4, 1881

Pap was still gone, so Ma and I used his absence to make a move. One of my challenges was that each day I was forced to wade Cherry Winchie Creek to get to the store, and when it flooded, I couldn't cross at all.

During a dry spell, the Moore men came with their own team of oxen and moved our wagon across the creek at a good ford and parked the wagon in a spot where the swamp ended and the pines began again. I was now a mile closer to work and didn't have to worry about the creek.

Our new spot also had a good view of the night sky, but a full moon dimmed the comet on our first night across the creek. I didn't sleep well under the bright moonlight, so I dressed for work early and studied the comet on my walk to the store. I identified with this lonely traveler way out in the cold night sky.

I reached the store and pulled up one of the cowhide rockers that sat on the gallery. The first redbird's chirping quickly followed the last of the owls' hooting. Lucky, who'd followed me from the wagon, snuggled up beside my leg.

As dawn crept in, I pulled out *Les Miserables*, flipping to my notes where poor Fantine had fallen from grace. In spite of how it seems silly, I began telling the story to Lucky. Dogs are generally better listeners than people. Don't believe it? When's the last time you saw a human's ears prick up at a human voice?

I cleared my throat. "This young woman, Fantine has lost everything. She's been fired from her factory job and is sinking into a life of disrepute."

Lucky cocked his head as if wondering what disrepute meant.

"Fantine, now penniless, must find money to support her daughter. First, Fantine cuts and sells her long hair, then sells her front teeth. Finally, she has fallen so far that the only thing she has left to sell is her body."

I nodded at the dog. "I'll explain that some other time."

The book's hero, the former criminal Jean Valjean, is now the wealthy factory owner as well as mayor of the town. As you imagine, he goes by an alias. Lucky, that's something me and my family know all about. He's being doggedly pursued by a lawman named Javert."

I glanced at the smiling dog. "Excuse that word *doggedly*. Well, the ex-criminal, Valjean, who now is the rich mayor, takes pity on poor Fantine, but she spits in his face, blaming him for the loss of her job."

I looked up from my book notes at Lucky. "That's what you call biting the hand that feeds you."

Lucky made no comment on my remark, so I continued my narrative. "In spite of this, Valjean listens to the dying Fantine's story of her lost daughter, Cosette, and promises to find the child and rescue her from an evil family holding her as a child slave. From that point in the book, Valjean's one mission in life is finding and protecting the child Cosette."

I rubbed my eyes with my sleeve. Lucky whined at me.

"Don't worry, Lucky. It's just a story in a book. It's not even true."

But in my heart of hearts, I wondered if like Cosette, there was a hero out there who'd rescue me from this pitiful life I was living.

I petted my listener on the head. "Let me tell you a little secret. I'd come to parallel every character in the book with someone here in Westport.

"For me, sweet Fantine is my lost sister Helen. I'll tell you more about her some other time.

"Cosette is the character I most identify with—trying to find her way in the world and in love. I'm Cosette.

"As Cosette becomes a teen, she falls in love with a young man named Marius. For me, that's Dan'l Moore, but don't you tell a soul."

Lucky grinned as if making a solemn oath.

"And Jean Valjean is the Irishman. Valjean went to prison for stealing a loaf of bread to feed his family. From the Irishman's story, he killed a Nobleman's dog that was mauling his sheep. The Irishman would've paid for it with his life if he hadn't run."

I glanced at Lucky. "I think even you can justify that dog-killing." I lowered my voice. "But I also believe Valjean could be my father. I call him Pap. My pap's not a good man most of the time, but I hope he can change just like Valjean.

"And just like Valjean being pursued by the lawman Javert, there's a bounty hunter after Pap. I'm hoping this No Man's Land is beyond his reach."

Lucky hopped up and walked to the porch edge. I smelled pipe smoke and saw the shadow of a man at the porch corner.

"Who's there?" I said, but I knew who it was. "Mr. Irishman, how long have you been standing there?"

"Long enough to know you talk to dogs."

"What ... what did you hear?"

"Didn't hear a ... thing." He tromped up the steps and unlocked the chain and padlock on the front doors.

"You're right early." He motioned me in. "Let me get some kindling, and we'll have a good fire. Why don't you get the coffee pot ready?"

Soon a fire was blazing, and the incomparable smell of brewing coffee filled the store.

He handed me a hot mug.

"What did you really hear out there?" I asked.

"That you're a good storyteller."

"That's all?"

He nodded. "That's all."

I knew he was lying. He'd heard every word including my comparing him to Valjean.

The Irishman threw another log on the firedog. "You know, we didn't use wood for fires in Ireland."

"Why not?"

"It's simple. We didn't have many trees. I was told there were plenty in the past, but the bloody English cut them down when they took over our country. My father always said, 'The trees of Ireland are in the furniture of England.' " He pulled up three chairs and motioned me to sit.

"Well, what did y'all build fires with?" I said.

"Peat. It's decayed plant matter." He laughed at my shrug. "You dig it out of the ground in squares. After it's dried, it burns as good as wood."

"Never heard of it."

"Burns with a blue smoke and gives off an aroma that I haven't smelled in over thirty years."

"Do you ever wish to go back to Ireland?"

He stared into the fire. "Sometimes I think about it, but this is where my life is now. Probably all the folks I knew back home are dead or gone." He poured both of us a cup of coffee. "That's all behind me."

"And you don't wanna stumble over what's behind you."

"Mizz, you're a quick study." The Irishman stood as a gaunt lady wrapped in a quilt shuffled in the back door. The Irishman moved the third chair closer to the fire, and the woman took a seat. She studied me with a wry smile. "Child, scoot your chair over here. You must be the famous Missouri Cotton."

"And you've got to be Miss Eliza Moore."

She reached out her hand. In spite of her frailty, her grip was as strong as most men. It belied a strength that the disease was trying to hide. Next, I noticed her deep, dark eyes that immediately made me think of Unk. And her skin was dark like mine. But her defining mark was a strong jaw that sickness or age couldn't hide.

"Can I call you Miss Eliza?"

"I've been called far worse. You can call me Eliza if I can call you Child."

"You and Unk look a lot alike."

"He's my momma's younger brother."

"So, you're one of the Ten Milers, aren't you?"

"Yep. I can't hide what I am. Wouldn't want to anyway."

A cat ran out from under her feet. "Have you met Esther?"

"Briefly."

"Esther's our ratter. She keeps the store mouse-free. In return, we provide lodging and food." She motioned to the cat. "Come up here, Queen Esther." The cat leaped onto her lap.

The Irishman said, "I'm going to let you three cats keep the fire going. There's work to be done."

I turned to Miss Eliza. "So, Esther belongs to y'all?"

"Child, a cat don't belong to nobody. They're one of the last undomesticated animals on God's green earth." She scratched the cat's large head. "Ain't that so, Queen Esther?"

Miss Eliza studied me for a long time as I sat uncomfortably at attention. She squinted. "Hmm, I've never seen eyes quite like yours. Your left one's brown, and I guess I'd call the other hazel. But it's more than just the color. You've got cat eyes. Kinda like Esther's. The rest of you looks domesticated, but those eyes ain't been tamed." She winked. "At least not yet."

"Ma says the man's never been born that'll tame my gypsy soul."

"I guess we'll see. Who are your people?"

"My mother and me, we look like . . ." I groped for the right word. "We look like y'all."

"I can see that. Those eyes make me wonder about your roots. My son Dan told me that your mother's folks come from where North Carolina and Tennessee meet."

"I'm not sure I'd call it roots because I've never been there. Never known none of my people except Pap and Ma."

"No one?"

"No, ma'am. All I've got is a photo of my grandparents on my momma's side."

Miss Eliza laughed. "I had thirty-nine cousins on just my Daddy's side, and all lived within twenty miles." Seeing a housefly, she said, "Hand me that flyswatter."

After dispatching the fly, she laughed, "The best tools ever invented are flyswatters and 12-gauge shotguns."

I laughed. "That's a pair. Now, back to all of your cousins, did you know them all?"

"Yep. Some better than others. Five were double first cousins."

"What's that?"

"We shared grandparents. My mother's sister married my father's brother. That meant that Uncle Tom and Aunt Jess's kids were my double first cousins."

Miss Eliza stirred the fire before squinting at me long enough that I looked away. "Child, what is your real family name?"

"I think it's Musselwhite. But we've had so many aliases, I'm not rightly sure."

Miss Eliza rubbed her chin. "My folks talked about a wagon train that arrived here early in the century. Rumor had it, at the Mississippi they made a death pact never to reveal their origins. The folks in the wagon train all changed their names 'fore crossing the big river. Word was they came from the corner of North Caroliner." She whispered conspiratorially. "Some of them even swapped wives when they changed their names. My daddy always said they reshuffled their cards. He even claimed one of our neighbors went from a joker to a queen when they re-dealt the wives."

I liked her sense of humor.

"Speaking of cards, my daddy said some in that wagon train was as black as the ace of spades. They kept moving and ended up in East Texas. I jes' wonder, Child, if those wagon folks might be some of your own people."

Being uncomfortable with the subject, I said, "How'd this become a neutral territory?"

"So this lawless area is what drew your people here?"

"At least some of them."

"How about the Irishman? How'd he get here?"

"Whoa, that's a long story. In a nutshell, Joe Moore just dropped out of the sky. Told us he'd come from Ireland by way of New Orleans and came to No Man's Land, or as he called it, Rio Hondo, to stake a claim. He tried courting me and didn't get too far. You've probably noticed that our people are a little clannish and don't take kindly to Outsiders. That's what he was until the fire."

"The fire?"

"In 1850. We had a huge ice storm that winter. It left piles of limbs and debris in the forest. In February before the grass turned green, some timber men set a fire on a day with a strong north wind and low humidity. They were trying to burn out the locals to get a hold of their land. The fire spread quickly, and the north wind whipped it across the ground, as well as up in the crown of the trees. An old widow we called Aunt Mollie Weeks lived near the forks above West Bay Swamp where the fire was worst. Joe Moore, that crazy Irishman, rode his horse into the creek, up the far bank, and then full tilt through the fire. I was sure we'd seen the last of him. Thirty minutes later, he burst out of the smoke with Aunt Mollie in the saddle behind him. She was hanging on for dear life and yelling like an Indian. That's the day that Irishman became one of us."

She smiled. "That day was also the day I made up my mind to marry him come hell or high water." She winked. "And here we are thirty years later. I've been down sick for the past two years. I'm not much use to anybody, and Joe Moore ought to knock me in the head and bury me in a stump hole, but he's cheerfully taken care of me. When he promised to care for me in sickness or health, he meant it." She took my hand. "Child, I hope you find a man like that for yourself."

She had a coughing fit and put a rag over her mouth. It took a minute or so for her to regain her breath.

"What's wrong with you, Miss Eliza?"

She lowered her voice. "I've got Consumption, Tuberculosis. It's in my lungs and my stomach. I've spent so much time on the pot and in our outhouse that I learned to play the harmonica."

I wasn't sure she was serious until she pulled one from her dress pocket.

"Sometime when it's just you and me, I'll play 'The Eighth of January' for you." She pocketed the harmonica and folded the rag in her lap. "Now tell me, Child, where were you born?"

"In Georgia, I believe."

"Georgia. Then how'd you get the name Missouri?"

"My mother always told me I was conceived in Missouri."

"Whoa, Child." She laughed. "I guess it's better than being named Big Brass Bed."

I had to get in on the fun. "Well, that'd be better than being named Hayloft."

She snorted. "We'll stick with Missouri. How old are you?"

"Just turned sixteen in October. When's your birthday, Miss Eliza?"

"April 6. Whip-poor-will Day."

"What's that?"

"My people swear you can always hear a whippoorwill calling on the sixth of April. You'll have to celebrate my birthday with our family."

"If we're still here. Your birthday is over three months away. We'll probably be gone by then."

"You don't feel that you belong, do you?"

"No, but I dream about it."

"Missouri, you told me about your mother. What about your father?"

"Not much to tell."

"Joe Moore told me a little about him."

I hung my head. "I'm sorry."

"Child, you're not responsible for your folks." Miss Eliza rested her chin in her hand. "Is he really your father?"

Her question startled me. "Well, yes … and no. I had a sister named Helen who was seventeen years older than me. She died of yellow fever in New Orleans when I was about two. I faintly remember her. Anyway, when Helen died, the wheels began falling off our wagon. Pap went to drinking really bad, and Ma started going into her dark place."

"I can understand. I lost a child. It don't ever stop hurting."

"How old was she?" I asked.

"It was a he, and his name was Patrick. He died while Joe Moore was off in the War. Patrick was just two years old. Just got sick real quick and was gone." Tears filled her eyes. "Just gone. When we buried him, they put a part of me in that grave. I don't even have a photo to remember him by. I've about forgotten how he looked."

"I'm sorry."

"Thank you." She shifted in her chair. "Now, you were telling about your family."

"Last week, my daddy spilled the beans that my sister Helen wasn't my sister. She was really my mother."

Miss Eliza sat up. "So, let me catch up here. The woman you *thought* was your sister is *really* your mother?"

I nodded.

"So, you thought was your mother is really your grandmother?"

"Yes'um."

Miss Eliza shrugged. "So?"

I stood. "So? It's turned my world upside down, and I'm just angry about it. What else in my life is a lie?"

"Do you think your momma, or grandma, loves you any less?"

"No, but I can't get over fifteen years of withholding the truth."

"Why hadn't she told you?"

"Said she'd meant to."

"Why'd your daddy drop the cannonball now?"

"It was revenge."

"Huh?" She stared into my eyes. "Are you glad you know now?"

"I'm not sure. I wish I'd known my *real* mom."

"You do. Your grandma's been your mother. There's a whole lot worse things than that. You've also got a man you thought was your father, and he's really your grandfather. So?"

"Pap's not much of nothing."

"I can't be the judge of that, Child. But he's who you've got. Has he taken care of you?"

"Most of the time. Pap's okay when he's sober, which is about half the time." I placed my hand on hers. "Miss Eliza, you're a good listener."

"I'm just an old, sick woman who don't have nothing to do 'cept listen."

I stood. "I better get to work." I leaned down close to her. "Miss Eliza, do you know what it's like to lose hope? You know, being sick and all?"

She studied the fire. "Can't say I do. How 'bout you?"

I hung my head. I couldn't lie to this woman. "I don't have much hope."

"Well, I'll tell you what. I'm an old woman who's dyin'. I don't have much time left, but I do have hope. Maybe I can pass some of it on to you before I'm gone."

I sat back beside her. "I'd like it better than buttermilk. Better than anything in the world."

She gripped my hand. "I want to know the story about those five books of which you've only got one."

"I'm warning you, it might take a while."

"Honey, all I've got is time. You go tell Joe Moore I need you more than him for the moment. Anyway, there ain't no business coming in until the day warms."

I got the Irishman's permission to visit more with Miss Eliza. He rolled his eyes. "You'll figure out pretty quick that she runs the show around here."

I settled in a rocker by hers. "Miss Eliza, during my lifetime, my family has drifted all over the South. We've mostly stuck to the river cities where my pap could pull off schemes.

"Last year we arrived in New Orleans and spent the rest of that year there and into early 1881. About a month after arriving, I got a job cleaning house for a rich lady in the Garden District.

"The setting room had these huge double doors with one side

held open by a stack of five books. They were all entitled *Les Miserables* and each one was a separate volume by the same author, Victor Hugo.

I steepled my fingers. "Now, one day during my lunch break, I picked up the first volume, sub-titled 'Fantine,' and immediately was drawn into the story. I've always had a vivid imagination, and before I knew it, I was off in France following an ex-convict named Jean Valjean. I also met a kindly Bishop, a woman of the streets named Fantine, and her orphan daughter, Cosette."

"How long did you read?" Miss Eliza said.

"I have no idea, but suddenly the lady of the house confronted me. 'I hired you to *clean*, not *read* my books.'

"I dropped the book, knowing for sure I'd been sacked. But the book had fallen open to the page I was on. When she saw how far I'd read, she was amused. She picked up *Volume One* from the carpet. 'So you're a reader?'

'Yes, ma'am. It's how I'm getting my education.'

'No school?'

I ducked my head. 'Very little.'

'Would you like to borrow *Volume One*?' She asked. "I warn you. Hugo wrote the longest novel ever written. Few people finish it.'

The lady pronounced the French title, *Les Miserables*, which was gibberish to me, and then explained that it meant 'The Miserable Ones' in English. Because I had so much trouble with the French pronunciation, we agreed to call it *Les Mizz*."

Miss Eliza Moore laughed out loud. "Like your name. *Lay-Mizz*."

"Yes-um, I was speechless that she'd trust me with one of her books. I bought a canvas bag and carefully transported the first volume home. The next month was one of the best of my life. Pap was staying out of trouble, Ma and I were both bringing home cash, and I spent each night deep in *Les Mizz*. I spent a good deal of my pay on coal oil and candles. The book took the sting of living in a wagon in a mosquito-infested swampy area of New Orleans."

Miss Eliza took a fresh dip of snuff. "This is some kind of story."

"Yes'um. Over the next month, I faithfully worked my way through the first four volumes, carefully returning each one when finished. I also bought a spiral notebook and kept an outline of the story and the shifting cast of characters.

"The lady of the house prepared lunch for us each day for the sole purpose of discussing the story. My lunch breaks went longer and longer, but I worked hard to earn my pay and keep access to the books."

"I was nearing the end of *Volume Four: St. Denis*, when Pap ran afoul of the law big-time. That night we pulled up stakes and sneaked our wagon onto a barge going upriver to the Red River town of Alexandria."

Miss Eliza patted my knee. "What about the book you had?"

"I had Volume *Four*, titled *St. Denis*, and it didn't belong to me. At the same time, I was owed a week's pay that I couldn't collect. So, I didn't steal it. It was a trade. A week's work for that book.

"Miss Eliza, the problem was, I had the fourth of *five* volumes and the story was in limbo. I've nearly driven myself crazy wondering what happens in the last volume. I thought I'd find the books in Alexandria, but during our time there, in spite of searching high and low, I found no trace of any of the volumes.

"I read and re-read *Volume Four* of *Les Mizz* until I just about have it memorized. I have my notebook and have organized my outline and character list of the first three volumes. My notebook even contains about a thirty-page version of how I think the story ends in *Volume Five*."

She spat into the fire, causing it to sizzle. "You are some kind of serious."

"We left and arrived here, but I have very little hope of finding my book in No Man's Land. I'm hoping for better luck in Texas."

Miss Eliza laughed. "Mizz, you're in No Man's Land, but it could also be called no-books-land. You can't eat books, so most folks have little use for the written word, plus most of us don't read well or at all." She laughed. I don't think you'll find Texas much better."

She took my hand. "Look, you'd better git to work before that tightwad Irishman docks your pay."

CHAPTER 12

AN INVITATION

Wednesday, November 23, 1881

"My momma wants to see you today."

I leaned on my broom and studied Dan Moore. "What about?"

"She wouldn't say. Said it was a secret. Told me to walk you there."

It was my least favorite type of Louisiana winter day—foggy, humid, and balmy. Dan and I slapped at mosquitoes as we walked side by side on the Military Road. The recent rains and wagon traffic had left ruts and water-filled potholes. As we stepped around a mud hole, I slipped and Dan grabbed my hand.

I liked the fact that he didn't let go.

"Dan, my pap showed up last night. He'd been gone for most of the month."

"Where had he been?"

"Wouldn't say. The only clue was the roll of bills he pulled out. Ma said that it was thick enough to choke a dog."

"That's good for your family with Christmas and winter coming on."

"It might be, and it might not. Pap is good at losing it just as quick as he got it."

"How do you think he got it?"

"I don't know and was afraid to ask."

Dan hopped over a wagon rut. "Some things are best left unknown."

"Speaking of unknowns, I'm worried about your mother."

Dan's face darkened, and he looked away, but I continued. "The few times I've seen her at the store, her cough has worsened."

He walked about a hundred yards before he spoke. "She's been spitting up blood." This was followed by, "It'll usually start raining within a day of fog like this. Listen to those geese up in the fog."

The geese made several passes over us. Dan stopped. "They're lost up in that fog."

"I know how they feel," I said.

He blinked. "Is that how you feel?"

"Sometimes." I should've been more honest. "Dan, most of the time, I don't quite know how to talk to you about your mother. I can't just act like she's not bad sick."

His grip tightened. "I just can't talk about it."

"I'm sorry I brought it up."

He slapped at a mosquito. "No, Mizz. I want to talk with you about her. I just can't handle it right now."

"You let me know when you want to."

He let go of my hand. "I will."

The Moore homestead came into view through the fog. Dan stepped away from me. Was it because he didn't want his family to see us holding hands?

It was my first visit to the Moore cabin. It was a new-looking dogtrot cabin. Smoke circled from a mud-daubed chimney.

"How long have y'all lived here?"

"About a year. When Da opened the store two years ago, we were still living over in Vernon Parish. Once he had things running, he built the store and we all moved here."

Dan stepped up on the gallery and spread his arms. "And this here's where we live."

"It looks homey."

Dan glanced up in confusion.

"I said it looks homey, not homely. It's homey in a welcoming kind of way."

"Oh." Dan held the screen door as I stepped into the darkened front room. The curtains were drawn, and as my eyes adjusted, I could see Miss Eliza, graying hair unpinned, propped up in her bed. Her shoulders weren't covered, and I was shocked at the thinness of her arms. It appeared a brisk wind could break her bones. I'd seen this before in folks with the grip of Consumption. It was well named. The disease seemed to suck the life out of a person until they were just a shell of bones and taut skin.

She smiled weakly. "Child, come over here, so I can see you better."

As I walked toward her, I kicked the chamber pot, spilling urine all over the hardwood floor. "I'm so sorry, ma'am."

"It's not your fault. I shouldn't have left it there." She motioned. "Dan, get a rag and bucket of well water."

I glanced around the sickroom, trying not to wrinkle my nose as a sneeze built up. There are certain sensory items sick rooms have in common—the darkness, rumpled sheets, and a side table topped with an array of medicine bottles. Most of all, it was the smells of sickness—candle wax, liniment, and urine. But the real sense in the room was one of impending death. Like Dan's air that you could cut with a knife, the sense of doom hung in this room.

In spite of this, the room was spotless. "Miss Eliza, I love your house. Everything is so clean and neat."

"Well, it's a right challenge with everything else. I've got a colored woman named Bertha from the Turpentine Camp who cleans three days a week. That's what I want to talk to you about."

Dan returned with a bucket and mop. "Here we go."

Miss Eliza tried to rise out of the bed. "Thank you, son. Now you git on back to the store."

I took the bucket and began swabbing the floor.

"You don't have to do that. I can handle it later."

"I made the mess. I can clean it up."

"Well, we both made the mess. I started it, and you finished it."

I stopped and looked at her. She was laughing, and her eyes sparkled. This spunky wood woman had a little more fight left in her than I'd first thought.

She motioned me to a chair by the bed. "I been wanting to talk with you about helping me here at the house."

"Doing what?"

"I told you about my cleaning lady, Bertha. She and her man are leaving next week for Alabama. I'd like for you to take over."

"What about my job at the store?"

"I'll pay you better than that tightwad Irishman." Miss Eliza winked. "Seriously, I've already cleared it with him. In fact, you can still work there. You'll start here Monday.

My new work schedule had me at the store in the mornings and with Miss Eliza each afternoon. As I arrived on my third day, she said, "Dr. Hamilton, who lives in Hineston, is coming this afternoon."

"That's good."

"I guess so. I'm not sure any human can help me now."

She was probably correct, but I couldn't say it.

"Child, I can see you're worried. Don't be. This is gonna be all right."

"How do you know that?"

"I've lost a lot but still have my faith. This is just my bitter cup to drink. It's my thorn in the flesh. I'm at peace with it."

I had so many questions, but now wasn't the time.

"Did you bring your book?"

"As always."

"Why don't you read a little to me."

"I'd better get to cleaning."

She took my hand. "That can wait. I need your company more than your cleaning."

I opened *Les Miserables*. "Where do you want me to start?"

"Right wherever you're at."

"Well, just before Fantine dies, Jean Valjean, who's on the straight and narrow now, promises to find her orphaned daughter, Cosette, and give her a good life."

"So Valjean the criminal becomes a good man?"

"Yes'um. He even changes his name to Monsieur Madeline, opens a factory, and becomes the mayor of a provincial town.

"Here's the best part. Valjean finds where little Cosette is being mistreated by a mean innkeeper and his wife by the name of Thernadier. They treat Cosette like a slave and Valjean gladly pays a high price to free her. He adopts her and they escape to Paris to begin a new life.

"Somewhere along the way, Valjean buries the money he has amassed as mayor and factory owner."

Miss Eliza pointed a bony finger. "So people can change."

"At least in books." I shut my copy of *Les Mizz*. "I'm not sure in real life that a person can rise above their raising."

"Missouri, I'm sure of it. I've seen it with my own naked eye. These woods are full of folks who turned out a lot better than they should've. I married one of them."

I moved my feather bookmark. "Well, Jean Valjean, with little

Cosette with him, is still fleeing the Lawman Javert, who wants to put him back in prison."

"For stealing that loaf of bread?"

"No, he'd served his time for that and several escape attempts. But Valjean is required to carry a yellow card showing that he is an ex-convict. He refuses to wear it and disappears. The rest of the book has Javert chasing Valjean.

"Valjean, who continues to use various aliases, ends up in Paris, and he and Cosette find refuge in a convent."

"What's that?"

"A home for nuns where no men are allowed. Cosette is taken in by the nuns and Valjean is allowed to stay as the gardener. This allows them to hide from the Lawman Javert for a period of years."

Within a few minutes, she'd nodded off.

Doctor Hamilton arrived later that afternoon. He was the mystery man in this part of No Man's Land. He was young, dapper, refined, and had supposedly come from good money in Virginia. Folks couldn't figure out how or why a man like him would choose to make a go along the Calcasieu River and in No Man's Land. I wondered if he, like Valjean the Mayor, had a secret in his past that had driven him from Virginia to No Man's Land.

Doc, as he was called, also was a silent partner in the Westport Store along with Captain Hatch and the Irishman.

Doctor Hamilton nodded at me as he set his black bag on the nightstand. "Eliza, you're still losing weight."

I rose from my chair. "Do you want me to leave?"

She raised her hand. "No, Child. Stand over there. I need a second set of ears." She nodded. "Doctor Hamilton, this is my nursemaid, Missouri Cotton. Most people call her Mizz."

"That's an unusual name."

"There's a good story behind it," she said, "but it ain't for mixed company."

Dr. Hamilton examined her for about ten minutes.

"How's my lungs?"

"Lots of fluid in there." He folded his stethoscope. "How's

your appetite?"

"Poor."

"Still having diarrhea?"

"What? The girl here is working on her muscles carrying this chamber pot in and out."

He probed her stomach.

"That hurts. Something's in there, ain't it?"

"It could be. That's the thing about Consumption. We think of it as only on the lungs, but it can spread to different parts of the body." He sat in the chair and removed his glasses. "Eliza, would you be willing to go to Alexandria and see a colleague of mine?"

She pulled herself up in the bed. "I'm willing to do about anything to feel better. How long would I be gone?"

"A week to ten days. He'd probably want to see you, try out a medicine or two, and examine you again before sending you home."

"Could I wait and go after Christmas?"

Dr. Hamilton fumbled in his bag before looking up. "You don't need to wait."

"I see." She calmly smoothed her blanket.

He walked to the front door. "I need a good smoke. I'll go to the store and bring Joe back."

Miss Eliza turned to me. "Missouri, if I go to Alexandria, I want you to go with me." It was the first time she'd addressed me by my given name.

"Won't the Irishman want to go?"

"With Christmas season at the store, it'll be hard for him to be gone that long."

"What about one of your sons?"

"I may take one of the boys, but I need a woman to go with me. We'd be staying with my son Mayo and his family."

"What would I be doing?"

"Jes' being with me. Helping clean up after my messes and being a second set of ears."

"What about my job at the store?"

"I'll take care of that. You'd still be paid. You'd be my nurse. But if you go, you must promise me one thing. You won't let them keep me up there."

I shook my head. "Miss Eliza, you may outlive me."

"That's doubtful. Promise me, you'll bring me home one way or the other.”

I nodded.

“Missouri, I want you to say it.”

“I promise.”

She winked. “I was Ten Mile born and I'm Ten Mile bred, and when I'm gone, I'll be Ten Mile dead. And it's real important to me that I’m buried near my family, especially my baby.”

I wanted to know more about this lost baby, but now wasn't the time.

She glanced out the window. “This is where I’ve lived, and it’s where I plan on turning up my toes.”

I didn’t want to cry in front of her, so I hurried toward the door, then stopped. “Miss Eliza, you hardly know me and—”

“Missouri, I’m a good judge of character. I like what I see in you.” She ran her hand through her hair. “One more thing. Ask your mother to come by for a cup of coffee. I want to get her permission for you going.”

The Irishman didn’t speak as he hurried into the house, with the screen door slamming shut. Dr. Hamilton, a few steps behind, nodded as he walked by.

I went and sat in a rocker on the porch, not sure if I should leave or stay. The fog hadn't lifted, and I heard the geese still circling. I leaned by the door so I could hear the discussion about Miss Eliza's prognosis. The doc explained to both of the Moore’s how serious this was. The Irishman had a multitude of questions, for many of which Doctor Hamilton had no answer.

After about fifteen minutes, the Doctor joined me. He sat on the gallery swing and puffed on a pipe. After eyeing me carefully, he said, “I’ve heard there’s medicine in your family.”

How had he heard this? My voice was shaky. “My mother’s a natural healer.”

“Some might call her a witch doctor.”

I nodded. I’d learned a long time ago not to waste my breath defending my mother.

He unfolded a newspaper from his vest. “Do you believe your mother can heal?”

“On some things, I’m sure.”

“Why doesn’t she try to heal Eliza?”

“First of all, I don’t think she’s been asked. Secondly, Miss Eliza’s sickness is not her type.”

Doctor Hamilton sniffed and began reading his paper.

In the house, the Irishman said, "I'll drop everything and take you."

I had to lean closer to hear Miss Eliza. "No, you need to keep things going here. Let one of the boys drive the wagon. We'll stay with Mayo and do just fine."

"Doc, come help us on this," the Irishman called.

I sat petting Lucky, singing softly.

The Irishman stuck his head out the door. "Who you talking to?"

"The best dog in Westport."

The Irishman nodded. "Come in here. Eliza says you're willing to go with her to Alexandria?"

"Yes, sir." I followed him until we were at her bedside again.

He turned to his wife. "That's fine, Honey, but I'm going, too. I'll accompany y'all to Alex in our extra wagon. Once I'm satisfied with your care, I'll get supplies and return to Westport. One of the boys can drive the other wagon with you in it. I'll need Dan to stay here and look after the mill and store, so I'll probably send Will."

"Do you think Will's ready for Alex?" Miss Eliza said.

The Irishman rubbed his chin. "Might be a better question, is Alex ready for Will Moore?"

Even Doctor Hamilton laughed.

CHAPTER 13

PEACEMAKER

November 23

I was back at the store that afternoon, when Moon Perkins' brother, Squirrel, walked in. I always avoided him because he had trouble keeping his hands to himself.

Ten minutes later, a stranger suddenly stomped through the front door, and headed straight for Squirrel. He unsheathed a Bowie knife as long as my arm and made his way toward the unsuspecting skinny Redbone.

I shouted. "Heads up, Squirrel." This gave him time to put a shelf between him and the knife as the stranger circled Squirrel. "So, you're the fellow that's been plowing with my heifer."

Squirrel pulled his folding Barlow knife from his pocket, then wrapped his jacket around his free arm, and took a defensive stance. The stranger charged like a wild bull, knocking Squirrel over a counter, and scattering canned goods. Squirrel, belying his nickname, was back on his feet in an instant, slashing at his tormentor with his much smaller knife. Blood flew as they sliced one another on the arms, circling each other in the aisle.

Suddenly, a deafening shot rang out in the store. I turned to see Doctor Hamilton with pistol raised in his hand, straddling his open medical bag.

His warning shot had hit the ceiling, and pieces of splinters fell. The shot didn't seem to faze the combatants, so Doctor Hamilton fired a second shot into the floor between them. Dust flew up from the floorboards, and the fighters stopped in their tracks.

Squirrel, seeing Doctor Hamilton with the smoking gun in his hand, shook his head. "You're a dadgum doctor, and you're shooting at us?" He was catching his breath. "Didn't you take some kind of oath to heal folks ... not shoot 'em?"

Doc pointed at the opponents. "I'll wing both of you. Then I guess I'll come stitch y'all up ... or sign your death certificates."

The fighters, unsure if the doctor really meant business, stood breathless, still enraged, their knives at the ready.

Doctor Hamilton motioned his gun at Squirrel. "You fold your knife and leave out the back door."

Squirrel obeyed. "Fine with me. I don't want no trouble with this feller."

The stranger flashed his knife. "You should've thought about that afore you fooled around with my wife."

I now understood the plowing with my heifer reference. It was some obscure biblical reference, and in spite of the dire situation, I couldn't suppress a giggle.

Squirrel seemed content to leave the store with his intestines intact. As he eased past, he said, "Thanks, Doc. I was a little out-knifed."

"I'd recommend you heed his advice and plow with your own heifer. Sarah won't be happy when this gets to her."

The stranger was still poised, but Doc Hamilton stood in the doorway with his weapon pointed. "Fellow, I will shoot you."

The stranger re-sheathed his knife. "Sooner or later, I'll git him, and I'll probably come after you too."

Doc dropped his pistol back in his black bag. "When you cool off, you'll realize I saved your life today. You're not from here and don't know the ways of these folks. When you enter No Man's Land to fight a man, you'd best be ready to fight his kin, neighbors, and even enemies. You may've killed Squirrel, but you would never have seen your side of the Calcasieu again." He nodded out the window. "I'd advise you to get on that horse of yours and spur it straight for the river."

The stranger, mumbling and cussing as he went out the door, mounted his horse, and galloped out of sight.

Doctor Hamilton winked at me. "Just another day at the office in Ten Mile."

"Can I see that pistol?"

He reached in his bag and held it up by the handle.

It was the most beautiful thing I'd ever seen. "Can I hold it?"

He passed it to me by the barrel. "Careful, it's loaded for bear."

Using both hands, I held it up. It was shiny, cold, and possessed a power I could feel. "What is it?"

"It's a Colt .45 revolver. It's pretty new and hard to get hold of."

"I bet it's expensive."

"Worth every dollar."

I counted the cylinder holes. "Shoots six times without reloading?"

"Yep. I had four more rounds to go." He watched my fascination with the pistol. "It's nicknamed the Peacemaker over in Texas."

I gripped its wooden handle and felt the balance and craftsmanship. "Well, it brought the peace for Squirrel today," I grinned. "By the way, what's a doctor doing carrying a pistol like that?"

"You never know what kind of varmint you might come up on when making one's rounds."

"The Peacemaker, huh? What's one cost?"

"Way more than you'd make in the store in a year."

Carefully mimicking his style, I handed the pistol back to him barrel down and handle down. "I will own one of these."

"I'm sure you will, Girl. And I feel for the fool who may end up on the other end of it."

The Irishman, trailed by Will, rushed in. "What happened?"

"Two fellows were having a little argument." Doc winked at me. "And Mizz and I persuaded them to take it somewhere else."

The Irishman put his boot on the splintered floor board, then stared at Doc Hamilton. "Looks like someone's a poor shot."

"Just send me a bill." Doc glanced at the bullet hole in the ceiling. "And for that one too." He picked up his bag. "They just don't make lumber like they used to."

CHAPTER 14

PERMISSION

November 23

That evening, I carefully mentioned the proposed Alexandria trip to Ma. She wasn't thrilled about it, even though I fudged and said I'd only be gone for a week.

She twisted her apron. "I'm not sure Alexandria is a good place for any of our family to resurface."

"I'm willing to take a chance. Besides, it'll be good pay."

"Still, it's a chance I'd rather you not take. Why don't you take it up with your Pap tomorrow? If he says you can go, I won't fight it." She turned toward the tent where Pap was snoring. "Just make sure you catch him between the hangover and the next drinking episode."

"That doesn't leave much of an opening."

She laughed. "It don't, does it?"

The next morning, I studied Pap as he lay around most of the day like an old dog that'd been hunted out. He seemed relaxed, which I figured had a lot to do with the cash he was carrying.

At supper, I sat by him. "Pap, I need your permission on something."

He glanced up from the campfire.

"Miss Eliza Moore wants me to go with her to Alexandria next week."

"Why's she want you going there?"

"She's going to the doctor. Wants me to be her helper on the trip while she's there."

"How long would you be gone?"

I glanced at Ma. "Maybe, uh, a week."

Pap slammed his fist down. "No. Those folks in Alexandria might recognize you and connect the dots."

I'd made up my mind to go regardless but preferred permission over forgiveness. It's true that getting forgiveness is a sight easier than getting permission, but I preferred the latter, so I unleashed my plan. "Pap, there's several good reasons to go. First of all, I'll get paid extra. Secondly, the folks at the store told me satsumas sell like hotcakes right before Christmas. Supposedly, a steamboat brings a boatload of fruit upriver each Christmas season. I could buy as much fruit as I had money for and easily quadruple our profit here in Westport. Most folks here never see a piece of fruit."

"Our profit?"

I had Pap's attention, but not his permission, so I poured it on. "The Irishman said that he'd advance my pay. Along with what I've saved, I have money for about fifteen crates of satsumas. With good luck, I might clear over eighty dollars profit. If you send some of the grub stake you have, I could double your money."

I turned to Ma. "And it'd be honest profit."

"How do you know we could sell all of them?" Pap said.

"It's about the only Christmas gift most people get out here—a satsuma and maybe a stick of peppermint."

Pap, seeing those dollar signs, reluctantly gave his approval. "Well, I guess it's worth a try."

Ma, slower to come around, muttered, "What if you get off there and get sick?"

"It's not yellow fever or malaria season. Besides, you know how healthy I am."

Ma crossed her arms. "When would you leave?"

"Next Monday."

We sat around the campfire as the embers burned lower, wondering if any of us would sleep that night. Pap was already counting his money, while Ma was worrying about what disease or varmint would get me. Me? I was a strange blend of excitement and nervousness. Excited to be going on an adventure. Nervous, wondering if there'd really be any satsumas for sale in Alexandria, Louisiana, and speculating if anyone would connect me with the infamous Whitehead family that had bilked a handful of the town's finest citizens.

CHAPTER 15

THE BIG RACE

Saturday, December 10, 1881

Two days before we left for Alexandria, a horse race was held in Ten Mile. Country people—and I'm one of them—love events. Whether it's camp meeting, fistfight, duel, funeral, chimney daubing, foot race, log roll, or a barn dance, they'll come.

But what folks loved best was a horse race. Ma always said the same folks who were jumping pews the previous week at a revival meeting would be the first in line to put their money down on a horse race.

And this wasn't just any horse race in the Ten Mile country. It was a challenge race between the Redbones and Outsiders. Much more than winnings rested on this race. For the entire week at the store, the horse race was all anyone wanted to talk about.

My pap loved a horse race nearly as much as he liked liquor, and that's saying a lot. Knowing there'd be plenty of money and liquor at the race, he was up early and ready to go on race day. Ma had forbidden me to go, saying that it was all of the Devil. She reluctantly gave in and allowed me to go, so long as I promised to keep an eye on Pap. "Don't let him lose our money."

Pap scoffed. "It's not our money. I earned it honestly across the river."

"Henry, it's all we got." She turned to me. "I'm going to spend the morning with Miss Eliza Moore. She's had a bad week and her men are all at the race."

Pap, in a chipper mood, laughed as we hurried away toward the racetrack. It was a two-mile walk from Cherry Winchie Creek to the Bush Racetrack. On the way, Pap relived all of the cheating he'd seen at horse races. "One time in Alabama, a fellow bit off the end of a hot pepper and stuffed it up his horse's behind. My, my, didn't that baby run."

"You're making that up."

"Missouri, I'd swear on a stack of Bibles. I've also heard of rubbing salt on the horse's rear end. Another time, I believe it was in north Florida, a fellow tied a banty rooster to his horse's mane. That horse ran like crazy trying to get rid of it, and the other horses were too scared to pass it." Pap was on a roll. "An Irishman told me of burying a frog in the lane of the opposing horse, said it'd give them the evil eye every time." He stopped. "Have I told you about the evil eye?"

I rolled my eyes. "Only a hundred times."

For the next mile, I received a barrel full of history about the evil eye and how every culture believes in some aspect of this curse.

We arrived at the bush track to find a crowd of Ten Milers already milling about. Each group—the Redbones and the Outsiders—had collectively put up a purse of a hundred dollars, which was a king's ransom.

Pap pointed to the Redbone horse. "They call him Flying Bob."

The horse had beautiful pinto markings, and although small, looked strong and sure-footed. Ten Milers were real livestock people and took great pride in their sleek cattle, sheep, woods hogs, and horses. Especially their horses.

Moon Perkins's brother Robert, who was known as "Worm," would be the jockey on the Ten Mile horse. He was a regular customer at the store and was always flirting with me, trying to make me laugh at bad jokes. Seeing me, Worm tipped his cap. "Put your money on the right horse now, Sister."

There were only a few Outsiders present, and they stood off in a clump. One of them pointed in the distance and hollered, "Here he comes." A crowd of people and riders arrived, escorting the opposing horse.

Pap whistled. "That's a big son of a gun." He asked a passing Outsider, "Tell me about that horse."

The man swelled with pride. "He's named Palomino Gold and has reportedly never lost a race. Supposedly came from one of those plantations on the river."

"Who's riding him?"

"That's Buck Davis, a local jockey."

A small knot of Outsiders stood to the side by Palomino Gold. The horse was a fine specimen as the sun gleamed off his golden coat and white mane. Comparing the two horses, Palomino Gold looked like the obvious winner.

The two groups were segregated around their respective mounts. Most of the men were armed, which wasn't unusual. This was a frontier. There were a multitude of reasons to carry a firearm.

Most of the attendees had ridden their own horses to the race. There was a mix of fine-spirited mounts, Indian ponies, swaybacks, old grays, and what Pap described as "crowbaits" and "farm chunks." The track was a rudimentary straight stretch cut out of the pines. The stumps had been removed, and stakes with white flagging marked the perimeter of the course. Pap started from the finish line and carefully stepped off to where the race would start. He spun around and made long steps back to where I stood. "It's about three arpents."

"What?"

"Right at two hundred yards. It's far enough that the big Palomino should get up a good head of steam." He took a stick and jabbed the mud off the soles of his boots. "Track's a little muddy. That'll be to the advantage of the smaller horse."

Pap then proceeded over to the Ten Mile pony and measured it to the withers, then announced loudly, "Fourteen-point-two hands high."

A small crowd followed him to Palomino Gold. He measured twice before whistling. "Sixteen hands on the dot." He took out his bandana and wiped his face. "Hard to beat. Hard to beat." He then waded into the crowd. I secretly prayed folks had their wallets secured.

A local Redbone, Simon Morrow, who supplied the liquor from the Hatch and Moore store, stood by a long table. He and the Irishman worked together and had some kind of handshake agreement on splitting the profits. And profits plenty there would be on this festive day. Morrow had several kegs set up where a long line of thirsty men tanked up. It worried me to see Pap imbibing among a circle of laughing Ten Mile men.

Ruth Wray, a local girl I'd met at the store, walked over. "Missouri, don't touch none of that red liquor. It'll kill from a thousand yards." She laughed. "Who you got your money on?"

"Honey, I worked way too hard all week rolling barrels at the store to lose it here." I nodded at the smaller Ten Mile horse. "It looks like a pony up against that big horse."

Ruth took out a dollar bill. "The bigger they are, the harder they fall."

The betting was set up on a pine stump. A man known in the community as Cooter represented the Redbones. Gordon Musgrove stood beside Cooter, representing the Outsiders. Musk, as he was known to both sides, was proudly part Indian and had the olive complexion and high cheekbones to show for it. I wondered why he was affiliated with the Outsiders when he much more resembled the Redbones. Since my earlier run-in with him at the store, I always steered clear of him.

Men on both sides were placing their bets with Musk and Cooter. There was good-natured jabbering among the bettors, but I sensed an uneasy tension among the crowd.

I looked around for Pap. He was back at the big horse. If I hadn't known better, I'd believed he was whispering in its ear. I just hoped he didn't have a red pepper or banty rooster.

With a wad of bills in his hand, Pap made his way to the betting stump. I hurried beside him. "Pap, you promised Ma you wouldn't lose our money."

He jerked away. "It ain't our money." His face was flushed as he set a stack of bills on the stump. "This goes on the mustang pony."

I grabbed his elbow. "You said the Palomino…"

He jerked free of my arm. "I know what I'm doing. I got close enough to that big Palomino to see the eye color of the horseflies on its mane. It can't win."

"What were you doing over there?"

"Just making my final calculations." After putting his money down and getting his marker sheet, he made a beeline toward the kegs.

I walked away, shaking my head. I wanted to be as far away from Pap as possible when he lost his money.

I saw Will Moore in the crowd, and he waved. "Who're you for?"

"If I was a betting woman, I'd put my money on the big one."

"Good deal. That's what I've done. Ten dollars, in fact."

I whistled. "Whoa. That's a smart amount of money."

"I expect to double it today."

Musk, standing on a stump, announced that betting would cease in ten minutes. Clutches of men made last-minute inspections of the two steeds as if they'd spot something assuring their money was on the winner.

I moved out of the crowd and headed toward a grove of pines. An older colored man with cotton-white hair and a beard sat on a nearby log. I'd seen him around the store but never met him. He was an ex-slave that lived near the Turpentine Camp.

I sat on the opposite end of the log. "So, you're Uncle Rube?"

"That's what they call me." He had a harsh voice that made it sound as if he was crunching gravel. His speaking style contrasted with his kindly eyes and steady smile.

"Unk Dyal told me I should meet you."

"You're Missouri, ain't you? Unk told me about you."

I felt comfortable with him, so I cut to the chase. "If you don't mind me asking, how'd a man like you end up in the middle of Ten Mile?"

"It's a long story. Well, I was born down in lower Rapides Parish on one of the plantations near Cheneyville…"

He stopped when a big white man walked over with a shovel. He tossed it at Uncle Rube's feet. "Hey boy, go over there and fill in those holes. I don't want a horse breaking a leg in it."

Uncle Rube sidled over and wordlessly filled the holes then knocked the mud off the shovel before returning to his end of the log. "Missouri, you don't think it looks bad you sitting here with me?"

"I'm on my end of the log and you're on yours." I studied him. "Uncle Rube, does that bother you when that man called you that?"

"Called me what?"

"Boy."

He grinned. "I been called that so long I thought it was my name."

"You're old enough to be that fellow's daddy, and he calls you boy. Doesn't it bother you a little?"

"I guess if I dwelt on it. That fellow there is just the product of poor raising. His folks didn't teach him to show respect to elders. It don't matter if an older man or woman is black, white, or purple, they deserve respect. The *Bible* even speaks to that." He rubbed his chin. "It's somewhere in the 'Postle Paul's epis'les. 'Never speak harshly to an elder.'"

He chuckled. "There was a plantation I worked on afore the War. The lady of the house was some kind of hard on the women workers. Nothing was ever done quite right or quick enough. A house slave we called Aunt Mamie had worked in the kitchen for years. She was always humming and smiling. It seems as if the Master's wife couldn't pinch that smile off Aunt Mamie's face. I asked her one day, 'Auntie, how do you act so kindly to that old biddy?' "

"She smiled. 'I just let it roll off my back and go on. Then at some point when ain't nobody looking, I spit in whatever I'm cooking. It keeps the bitterness at bay, and I can carry on with a good spirit.' "

"Is that true?" I said.

Uncle Rube winked. "Do you think I'd lie about that? Now, don't tell a soul."

I studied Uncle Rube. "Do you spit in white people's soup?"

"No way, but I got my own ways to keep that bitterness away."

"How so?"

"Child, iffen I tell you, I might hafta kill you."

"You sound like Unk Dyal."

"He learned that saying from me."

"I bet you two make a pair."

Just then, Moon Perkins trotted toward me. I turned to Uncle Rube. "Excuse me."

Moon waved a five-dollar bill. "Wagon Girl, I'll place a bet with you that our horse will win."

"I don't have five dollars."

"Don't need it. If the big horse wins, you get five dollars. If our horse wins, you owe me a kiss."

I clicked my tongue.

"I'll even go as far as giving odds on our horse winning by a full length."

"You sound confident. Your brother's riding. Do you have some inside information?"

He lowered his voice. "Let's just say a little bird told me." He pressed the bill into my hand. "If my horse loses, you keep the five dollars. If my horse wins, you can still keep the money. I just want my kiss."

Against my better judgment, I stuffed the bill into my pocket.

A tall, well-dressed man stepped up on a stump and announced that the race would begin at the far end of the track.

As the jockeys walked their mounts to the starting line, I asked Moon, "Who's the announcer?"

"Solounge LaCaze. He's a Creole."

"What's that?"

"Shh, listen up."

LaCaze, in a strong voice, boomed, "First horse across the line wins. May the best horse win."

The crowd whooped and hollered. A man holding a white handkerchief stepped onto the track in front of the two horses. "That's LaCaze's younger brother, Louis. He's the starter."

The younger LaCaze dropped the hankie, and the horses were off.

The crowd was bunched all along the finish line. The recent rains made the track slick in places and the smaller, sure-footed pony took the early lead. Soon, the Outsider's horse began gaining ground. Both jockeys used their whips, and clods of mud flew in every direction. The big horse took, and then built, a steady lead. The whites waved their arms and cheered. As the horses reached the halfway marker, something strange happened. The big horse, safely in the lead, veered off course to the left. Jockey Davis furiously jerked on his reins and flailed with his crop, finally forcing his horse back onto the track.

The smaller Ten Mile horse remained straight and true and quickly made up ground. As they neared the fifty-yard marker, they were neck and neck. There wasn't a man or woman sitting as everyone craned to watch the horses down the homestretch.

The big horse was back in the lead, but nearing the finish line, it veered left again, sending spectators scampering out of its path. The Ten Mile pony ran straight and true and crossed the finish line a length ahead.

After throwing their hats in the air, the Ten Milers yapped and hugged each other. They surged toward the winning horse. Meanwhile, in various stages of disbelief, the Outsiders stood as if frozen.

The only Outsider rejoicing was Pap. "Doubled my money. Too much sugar for a dime. Too much." I walked away as if I didn't know him. He wasn't making any friends among the whites, while the Redbones gladly welcomed him into their victory parade. He joined the Redbones in pulling Jockey Perkins off his horse, hoisting him onto their shoulders.

By now, the Outsiders had gathered around their losing horse, Palomino Gold, as a low buzz of anger built. Buck Davis jumped down into a knot of men studying their horse. Then Davis rushed the winning crowd. "We was cheated." He pointed to the right rein, which was nearly sliced in two. Suddenly, it was clear why the horse had listed to the left. "Some sorry SOB sliced my rein." Davis pushed people aside, forcing his way toward the Redbone horse. He got in Worm Perkins's face. "You won 'cause someone cut my rein."

Har'm Morrow stepped forward. "Didn't nobody here cut your rein. You're just a sore loser."

The two groups shoved on each other, even as the winning bettors jockeyed in line for their money. Pap was third in line.

Several folks grabbed their children and fled. One woman pulled at her teenaged son as he hurried toward the melee. "Let's git. There's gonna be trouble."

Ruth Wray, grinning and holding up her winnings, grabbed me by the arm. "Bigger the tree, the louder it falls."

Will Moore walked by me. He had his hat pulled down nearly over his eyes.

I tried to console him. "Bad luck, Will. I'm sorry."

"Luck had nothin' to do with it. It was fixed."

Most folks were like me—too spell-bound by the tumult to move. The crowd surged in, trying to see the sliced rein for themselves. I was right by the big horse and could easily see the fresh leather. Evidently, just before the race, someone had cut it.

The only thing that prevented more violence was how quickly the Redbones cleared out. Jockey Perkins and his mount trotted off, and the other Ten Milers, after collecting their winnings, disappeared into the timber like spooked deer.

Only the losers stood in the clearing, cussing and examining the cut rein. Gordon Musgrove fingered his rifle. "Winged Pegasus couldn't have won this rigged race."

Pap whistled. "Let's go home, Missouri." He patted his bulging pocket with a big ol' southern grin.

Musgrove walked over to him and poked him hard in the chest. "Fellow, I don't like the way you look."

Pap shrugged. "I just had a hunch, that's all. A hunch. As the good book says, 'The horse is made ready for the day of battle, but victory rests with the Lord.' ”

Musk stepped closer. "If I find out you had anything to do with this, I'll kill you."

I stepped between them. "If you'll excuse us, we're going home." I got a hold of Pap's arm and jerked him away.

Musgrove stepped in front of me. "Girl, you ain't seen the last of me."

Walking fast, I turned Pap toward our campsite. I waited for a command to stop or the sound of a rifle cocking and was relieved to hear neither.

CHAPTER 16

MOON

December 10

Moon Perkins was waiting at the edge of the pines, and waved me over. "All right, Wagon Girl, I'm ready for my kiss."

I pointed a finger in his face. "You knew about the cut rein."

"I honestly knew nothin' about it."

I studied him. For some reason, I believed him.

"So, I'm ready," he said.

I nodded at Pap. "You'll get it, but not in front of the whole wide world."

"That's even better. Just tell me when and where."

"Right. Just don't expect too much."

"I'm expecting a good kiss, not no sisterly peck."

I held out his five-dollar bill. "I'm a girl who keeps my word."

He stuffed his hands in his pockets. "The money's yours. I just want my kiss."

I held out the bill. "There won't be a kiss unless you take your money back."

He reluctantly took the money. "I want my kiss more than that money, and I expect my money's worth."

"And you'll get it, but there's one more part of the deal."

"What?"

"You'll have to stop calling me Wagon Girl."

Moon grinned. "Fair enough."

I looked around for Pap and he was already a quarter mile ahead. I finally caught up with him at our campsite, where he was sitting in a chair, a cup of coffee balanced on his knee, whistling one of his tuneless songs. I took note that a full whiskey bottle was at his feet.

"Your mother's still gone to that dying woman's house."

"Her name's Eliza Moore, and I'd appreciate you not calling her 'that dying woman.' " Spreading my scarf, I sat down on my log. "You're right proud of yourself, aren't you?"

He patted his bulging pocket. "Got reason to be."

"Pap, I'm only going to ask this one time. Did you cut that rein?"

He grinned. "They ain't never sent a man to the pen for keeping his mouth shut."

"You did it."

"If I tell ye, I'd have to kill ye."

I just shook my head. An approaching cold front whipped the top of the pines, causing the long straw needles to fall in a curtain around us.

Pap turned his collar up. "Storm's coming."

"Probably in more ways than one."

He pulled out his growing wad of bills. "Your ma said it was enough to choke a dog. Now, it's enough to choke a horse."

I shifted on my log seat. "It might be enough to choke a man."

"Yep, what a way to go. Missouri, I'm beginning to really like this place. No law to get in the way of a fellow making an honest living."

"I like it too, but for different reasons."

Pap scanned the pines. "It seems more like home than the open cotton country."

"Do you think we could stay awhile?"

"I still want to see Texas." He stepped in front of me. "Would you turn me in if I'd cut that rein?"

"No, sir."

"I thought your new promise to go straight might make you a turncoat."

"I made that promise to myself, but I don't—I can't—control you."

"So, there is some honor among thieves?"

"More like honor among family."

"I am still your daddy, and you'll do what I say."

"Within reason, I will."

"We'll see."

I stood. "Speaking of turncoats, which side are you on in this local feud?"

"Just like in the Civil War, whichever side is winning."

"You were a turncoat."

"Nope, I was flexible."

"Pap, you'd better be careful among these people."

"Which ones? I ain't scared of them Outsiders. Got a little more respect for the Redbones." He kicked at an anthill. "So, you made a bet on a kiss with that Redbone boy?"

"He kind of pushed it on me, but I guess I did."

"You plan to keep your promise?"

"I will."

"Why didn't you keep his five dollars?"

"Kiss or not, I want him to know I can't be bought."

His face softened. "Missouri, I want you to know that in spite of everything, you are my daughter…"

I wasn't sure if it was his good luck, the first shot of whiskey, or his true feelings. I looked away. "No, I'm your granddaughter."

"But I love you like a daughter."

I'm not sure I'd ever heard him say that word, love, especially in relation to me. I wondered if it was the alcohol speaking. I glanced again, but the bottle at his feet was full. When he was drinking, the whistling stopped, and his tongue became sharp and mean.

He broke off a piece of pine bark. "Do you think you'll ever forgive me?"

"For what?"

"Telling you the truth about who you are, then running off and disappearing for two weeks."

"You asking if I can forgive you, or will I?"

"Both."

"I'm working on it. I will work on it."

"I guess that's all I can ask or expect."

CHAPTER 17

HINESTON

Monday, December 12, 1881

Right on time, we left Ten Mile for Alexandria. As the crow flies, it's twenty miles from Ten Mile to the river crossing at Hineston. In a road wagon during the winter muddy season, it seems like much more. That, coupled with Miss Eliza's condition, slowed our journey.

The Irishman drove the larger lead wagon with his horse, Vernon II, tied behind. His plan was to buy supplies and then return to the Westport Store once Miss Eliza was settled in Alexandria.

Will Moore followed in the second wagon, where under a canopy Miss Eliza lay on a pallet. I sat by her, holding her hand. Every time the wagon hit a hole, she gritted her teeth and moaned.

I squeezed her hand. "I'm sorry the ride is so rough."

"It can't be helped. Will's doing the best he can." She tried to sit up. "Will, don't forget to stop at Oakland Cemetery."

"Yes'um; it's about four more miles," Will said.

Eventually, in spite of the rough ride, Miss Eliza drifted off to sleep. When she relaxed her grip on my hand, I climbed onto the buckboard beside Will.

We rode in silence, the clip-clop of the team and creaking wagon the only sounds. It was the longest I'd ever seen Will Moore silent. "You're sure quiet."

"Got a lot on my mind." He clicked to the team.

"What's up?"

"I'm mainly worried about Momma."

"I hope the doctor in Alex can help your mother."

"Missouri, you know there ain't but one way that Consumption ends. My momma's dying, and I can't do a damn thing about it."

Will pulled on the reins. "We're nearly to Oakland."

"Why are we stopping there?"

"It's where most of Momma's family is buried." He leaned under the canopy. "Momma, we're about there." He stood and cupped his hands. "Da, Momma wants to stop here."

The Irishman pulled his wagon to the road edge and hurried back. "What's up?"

"Momma wants to visit the graveyard."

I watched the Irishman's face darken. He pulled out his pipe and was soon furiously puffing away under a grove of holly trees. It was hard to know if the puffs were anger or sorrow. From inside the wagon, Miss Eliza said, "Will, if you and Mizz'll help me down, I want to make this visit."

The Irishman joined us, and after setting his pipe on the wagon seat, he and Will helped her to the ground. With her son and husband supporting her, she slowly made her way to a grove of pines. I hung back until she motioned for me to follow.

The cemetery was small and barely visible from the road.

The Irishman stopped at the edge of the cemetery as Will led his mother to a cluster of graves. As was the custom of the time, each grave was covered with a small grave house and picket fence enclosure.

"Missouri, come support me." Miss Eliza didn't even turn around.

I took her right arm as she walked toward a wizened cedar tree at the center of the cemetery.

She glanced back. "Joe Moore ain't coming. He can't take the sight of where our baby is buried. He's still tormented about the baby dying while he was off at war."

We stopped at a small grave—obviously a child's headstone. It was a simple slab with Patrick Moore 1863–1864 inscribed upon it.

"Yep, baby Patrick just got sick real bad. And he was gone. Jes gone."

All I could do was grip her arm tighter.

"Most every family in Ten Mile has buried at least one child. Many have buried a lot more. Patrick's the only one we lost, but it hurts like I lost a dozen."

She pointed to an adjacent grave. "That's where my parents are buried, and on the other side of the baby is where I'll be. Will, you make sure of that."

Will looked away and wiped his eyes.

I glanced back at the Irishman, who leaned against a pine, smoking his pipe.

I scanned the edge of the cemetery. There weren't any flowers in bloom, but I saw that a holly tree was in the corner of the cemetery. I broke off some limbs and made a crude bouquet, taking it to Miss Eliza.

She tenderly placed it on the baby's grave. "It don't seem right for a mother to bury a child. It's supposed to be the other way around."

Will Moore had heard enough. He walked quickly back toward the wagon.

I looked up in surprise as the Irishman approached and took Miss Eliza in his arms.

I eased back to the wagon, not looking back. This was a sacred moment that I had no business being near.

After about ten minutes, the couple slowly walked back to the wagons and our journey resumed. Within minutes, Miss Eliza fell asleep and dozed for nearly an hour. When she awoke, I caressed her hand. "What was baby Patrick like?"

"Oh, he was a happy child. A happy child in an unhappy time, and he was gone so quick." She sighed. "You know, I don't even have a picture of him."

Miss Eliza pointed to another weathered stone. "That's for my younger brother Eli, but he ain't buried there. He died in the Civil War and is buried somewhere over in Mississippi. It hurts my soul to think that he wasn't laid to rest here in the Pineywoods." She picked up a rock and put it in her pocket. "Eli was one of the first to go from these woods in late 1862. My folks couldn't talk him out of enlisting."

"Did most of the men here go off to the Civil War?" I asked.

"Originally, no. They viewed it as a rich man's war and weren't interested in dying for some plantation owners and their slaves."

"What changed to make them go?"

"When the Yankees invaded Louisiana, the War became personal. They were on our home turf."

"What caused the Irishman to go off to the War?"

"Now that's a long story. The Irishman won't talk about it, but maybe my son Mayo can tell you the story when we get to

Alexandria."

She turned her head toward to canvas wall. "If he will."

Tuesday, December 13

We camped that night on the side of the Sugartown Road and got an early start the next morning so we could make Hineston before nightfall. Our wagon reached the edge of the Calcasieu Swamp in late afternoon, riding out of the pines for the stark grayness of the bottomland in winter.

At the ferry landing, I pointed out the sign at river's edge. "Look at that. It says, 'Abandon hope all that enter here.'"

The Irishman had sidled up beside us. "That's from Dante. He wrote about the seven circles of Hell in a book. That same sign was posted at the entrance to Hell. 'Abandon hope—'"

"How'd you know that?" I asked.

"Believe it or not, I had a good education in Ireland up until the time of the Famine." The Irishman looked away. "But that was another time and another place."

Someone had scratched a sentence in some foreign language. "What's that?"

"I believe it's a Latin translation of Dante's quotation."

I took out my journal and wrote down both the English and Latin.

"Why are you writing that down?"

"Abandon Hope." I shrugged. "Never know when you might need to know something. "Why'd someone put that sign up?"

"It's how most folks on the other side of the river view No Man's Land. As a hopeless place."

"How do you view it?"

The Irishman and Miss Eliza answered in unison. "Home."

The Irishman walked down to the ferry landing. I turned to Miss Eliza. "Can I ask you something?"

She nodded.

"When I first met you, you called me Child, but then you started calling me Missouri or Mizz. Why?"

"One's your given name and I like the shortened version too. They're both good names. Be proud of who you are. Ol' Solomon in Proverbs says, "A good name is to be desired above great riches.""

"I believe I'd like to have both."

"You've already got one. A good name. Your good name's not tied to your daddy or any alias. It's tied to you.""

Finishing her sermon, she took a fresh dip of snuff and then said, "Every tub sits on its own bottom. You ain't responsible for no one else's good name, 'cept yours.""

Hineston was the last outpost before travelers crossed the river into No Man's Land, built on a high riverbank where it was protected from the floodwaters of the river.

A family named Miller ran the only boarding house in Hineston. We checked into our rooms. I couldn't believe I had a small closet with a rope bed. I hadn't slept in a real bed since New Orleans. After a good supper, we sat around the front room fireplace with Mr. and Mrs. Miller.

Mr. Miller was real curious about the Irishman and the Big Store in Westport. Will leaned over to me. "He's a little nosey, ain't he?"

Miss Eliza, louder than she realized, said, "A little? He's a lot."

The man, absorbed in his questioning, paid us no mind, but his wife giggled along with us.

The Irishman tried to change the conversation. "When did y'all open this boarding house?"

"Before the War, we had a plantation near Cheneyville on Bayou Beouf. When General Banks and his crew retreated through central Louisiana, the Yankees burned our place, and our slaves ran off to follow the army. All that was left was a lone chimney. So, the wife and I lost our plantation acreage to taxes during the Occupation."

He saw the puzzled look on my face and spat. "The Occupation. That's what I call Reconstruction. The enemy occupied our land and told us how to live. At first, we tried to make a go of it in Alexandria, then about five years ago we moved here to Hineston and opened this boarding house."

The Irishman lit his pipe. "How are y'all doing now?"

"Just getting by. Reconstruction and them carpetbaggers and scalawags have made it impossible for an honest man to make a good living. The deck's stacked."

Without interruption, Mr. Miller went on about the unfairness of life in general and Louisiana in particular. We were his captive audience. Finally, the Irishman yawned. "Well, we've got an early day tomorrow if we're going to make Alexandria. I believe we'll turn in."

Will and I helped Miss Eliza up the stairs. Before I went to my small room, she said, "Sit right here. I wanna tell you something."

She took a dip of snuff. "That Mr. Miller, he'd rain on anybody's parade. There's nothing sadder than a bitter man, unless it's a bitter old man."

I smoothed her dress. "I know *bitter*. I live with my pap, the infamous Henry Cotton, and no one does bitter better. But I got a question for you. How'd y'all not become bitter?"

Her eyes filled with tears. "It ain't been easy. Like everyone, we've had our share of disappointments and tragedy. The Lord's helped me along. Besides, bitterness is like drinking poison and hoping it kills someone else."

Will was standing in the door. "It seems Mr. Miller has drank his bitterness down to the dregs."

"Yep, the War was hard on everyone, but those who had a lot suffered the most. Mr. and Mrs. Miller went from having folks waiting on them to being servants themselves. That's a tough adjustment for anyone to make, and few can do so."

I stood. "My ma always said that we were poor before the War, and the Reconstruction years just made us poorer."

"Us too. I guess in a way it's a blessing."

I started in Miss Eliza's wagon next morning as we got an early start for our full day's ride to Alexandria. The road from Hineston improved as we traveled along beside Bayou Rapides. We'd left the pines and were surrounded by fallow cotton fields stretching in every direction.

"Miss Eliza, when we came through here three months ago, the fields were white with cotton. Now, it's just drab red dirt."

She sat up. "I've never liked this open country. I miss the confines of the pines."

I laughed. "Confines of the pines. You're a regular poet. This open country just feels more breathable. By the way, how many times have you been to Alex?"

"Maybe a dozen. Don't go unless there's a reason."

"Different strokes for different folks."

"That's the way it is." Miss Eliza started humming "In the Pines."

"Little girl little girl,
Where did you stay last night?
In the pines, in the pines,
Where the sun doesn't shine
And you shiver when the cold wind blows."

"What's that song talking about?" I said.

"The pines represent darkness and death."

"I've heard there's about twenty variations of the song that talk about trains, black girls, death, decapitation, and everything else under the full moon."

We took turns singing it, humming it, and discussing the verses.

When we stopped for a break mid-morning, the Irishman walked over. "Mizz, come ride with me, so the wife'll rest."

After we'd ridden a mile, he said, "You've come a long way since that first day at the Westport Store."

"I really appreciate how y'all have made me feel so at home."

"My Eliza thinks you hung the moon." He clicked at the team. "And my boys Dan and Will have taken a shine to you."

I studied his face, trying to read anything into his statement. The silence was uncomfortable enough so that I said, "How'd you get like this?"

"Like what?"

"How'd you not become bitter?"

"Bitter like that Mr. Miller in Hineston?" He rubbed his scuffed boot on the footboard. "When I stowed away on the ship in Ireland, I was just as bitter as Mr. Miller. I had a well-tended hatred of everyone who'd ever wronged me. My stowaway ship was French, and once the crew discovered me, they treated me pretty rough.

"But there was one man aboard that treated me kindly. His name was Gill, and he was an Englishman. Now, I hated the English. Everything bad that had happened to Ireland could be traced back to the English. However, Gill the Englishman became my first and only friend on that ship. We had plenty of time to visit, and Gill had this natural skill of sharing wisdom without sounding preachy or stuffy."

The Irishman removed a weathered silver compass from his pocket. "When we made landfall at New Orleans, the Englishman Gill gave me this compass. I tried to turn it down, saying that it was too nice of a gift. Gill said that was the very reason he was giving it to me. It was nice, and he wanted me to have it. I'll never forget his parting words. 'A man starting a new life in a new country needs a good compass to guide him. Besides, you stubborn Irishmen all have a heaping dose of *mettle*, and when you hold this metal compass, remember where you came from.'

"I promised Gill I'd take good care of that compass and the wise words that went with it. Right there, I made a vow to become a better man, not a bitter one. I've got lots of faults, but when I promise someone something, I try to be a man of my word."

He let me hold the compass. "Sometimes when I've felt bitter, I pull out this compass and remember the fellow who gave this to me and my promise to him."

We stopped to rest the team and Will joined us as his father continued his story. "A few months after leaving New Orleans, I worked my way upriver and arrived here in No Man's Land. That's when I met my second teacher, Joseph Willis."

"Father Joseph Willis, as we called him, was born as the son of a North Carolina plantation owner and his mixed-race Indian slave. When his rich father died, his uncles cheated Joseph Willis out of his father's estate, so he pulled up roots, left the Carolinas, and ended up here. He started a string of Baptist churches up and down the Texas Road, including Occupy.

"Occupy's an odd name for a church," I said.

As the Irishman filled his pipe, Will took up the story. "Occupy comes from one of the parables of Jesus when he was talking about a master giving out money to his farm hands. Before the master leaves, he instructs the workers to 'Occupy till I come.' When Willis founded this church in 1832, most folks thought it wouldn't last. That's why he named it 'Occupy.'"

The Irishman puffed away. "When I arrived here in 1849, Joseph Willis befriended me and taught me my greatest lesson about leaving bitterness behind."

"How so?"

"I had to let it go. And the only way to get it out was to be filled with something else. Pastor Willis believed it needed to be with the help of Jesus. Over time, I got past that bitterness. I had folks to forgive on both sides of the Atlantic. I realized your past doesn't have to be your future."

"Say that again."

"Your past doesn't have to be your future."

"You really believe that?"

"Sure. The question is, do you?"

"I'm not sure." I handed the compass back to him.

"Mizz, it seems you don't believe you can break free from whatever is dogging your past. Life discourages us all, but we don't have to become or stay bitter. Our troubles will strengthen us or break us. It's just like any load—it's how we carry it that matters. It's like I say, 'Don't stumble over—'"

"Anything that's behind you." I nodded at smoke on the horizon. "Is that Alexandria?"

"It is." He studied me. "You look nervous."

"I am. We kind of left there in a hurry. There might be some bitter folks that remember me and my family."

"Did you do anything wrong?"

"Other than being my father's daughter, no. Not there. Pap made a lot of money swindling folks and didn't need my sticky fingers."

"Then don't worry. You don't have to answer for your father."

I wanted to believe that, but I just wasn't sure.

I shifted back to riding with Miss Eliza.

"You've got me hooked on your story. Tell me more," she said.

I held up my dog-eared copy of *Les Miserables, Volume Four*. "We're near the end of the fourth volume. When we finish it, we'll just start over or I can make up the ending."

She shifted on her pallet. "Mizz, I ain't got time left to wait on finding that last volume. You'll have to make it up for me. For now, let's finish book four."

I'd found that she enjoyed my narration much better than reading word for word. Using the book as my guide, I turned to page 393. "By the end of this volume, Cossette and Marius have fallen madly in love, against the wishes of the aging Jean Valjean."

"Now, let me keep this straight," Miss Eliza said. "Cosette is now beautiful and Marius is from a wealthy family who has chosen to live simply and poorly."

"Valjean, who is such a good man, isn't perfect. He develops a hatred for Marius and forbids her to see him. However, young love is strong and she slips off each evening to meet Marius secretly at a nearby park."

"Valjean doesn't know?"

"Nope. Now, Paris is full of political unrest and there is talk of fighting in the streets. Valjean, fearing for Cossette's future, makes plans for the two of them to leave for England.

"Of course, this will separate Marius and Cosette forever. This plunges Marius into deep despair and he throws himself in with a revolutionary group called ABC. In the year 1832 open revolt breaks out in Paris, and barricades are erected all over the city. In addition to serving as fortresses for the revolutionaries, it brings traffic and commerce in Paris to a stop. The government cannot allow this and marshals its army for attack on the barricades."

"It doesn't look good for Marius," Miss Eliza said.

"Well, Marius, who has given up hope of winning Cosette's hand, joins the throng at the barricade, having a death wish."

"He'd rather die than live without Cosette?"

"That's true love."

"What's the barricade like?" She asked.

"They've blocked the narrow street with wagons, carts, doors, and all manner of debris. The National Army is strong and well-armed. The city has not rallied to the ABC and its revolution like their leaders expected."

"Near the end of this volume, our friend Javert, still working for the government, infiltrates the revolt at the barricade, but is unmasked as a spy by the boy Gavroche."

I stopped. "That's the rascal that reminds you of Will."

"They're both jaybirds for sure."

"The leader of the revolt binds Javert and orders his execution."

"Well, I'm glad that bad man is gonna get his just desserts. I've never liked him," she said.

I held up the book. "As this volume ends, Valjean puts on a National Guard uniform and leaves the hideaway from which he and Cosette are scheduled to leave for England. He uses his uniform to slip through the Army lines and to the barricades. He is armed and on a mission. Is he going there to kill the spy Javert or kill Marius and be rid of this rival to Cosette's affection?"

Miss Eliza scoffed. "I don't believe either are true."

"But the writer Hugo shows that Valjean's hatred and distrust of Marius is that deep."

She shook her head. "I just can't believe this good man would do that."

"Remember, he is an ex-convict and has never been painted as perfect." I leaned in. "At the barricade, Valjean arrives, takes off his uniform and announces his intention to join the revolt.

"The night is tense as the steady footsteps of hundreds of Army infantrymen gather near the barricade. Every evidence is of a full-scale assault on the outnumbered revolutionists."

I slammed the book shut. "And that's where the story ends until we find *Volume Five*."

Miss Eliza laid back on her pallet, exhausted. "I've got to live long enough for you to find this book and tell me what happens. You know we Redbones love a good story more than anyone. I want you to spend every spare minute in Alex searching for that book."

"But I'm going to help you."

"You finding out how this story ends is the best way you can help Eliza Clark Moore. In the meantime, you must tell me your version of the last book."

"I will, but not today. You need to rest."

CHAPTER 18

A PEARL NECKLACE

Wednesday, December 14

My second view of Alexandria wasn't any more impressive than the first. The first visit had featured three inches of summer dust. On this winter visit, I sank ankle deep in red mud.

The Irishman climbed down from his wagon and used a board to make it to a makeshift sidewalk. "You can pick your poison. Louisiana dust or Louisiana mud."

We made our way through the busy streets to the home of the Moore's oldest son, Mayo. He owned a blacksmith shop on Seventh Street and lived in a house behind his business.

I'd heard so many stories about Mayo and was surprised when I met him. He was a perfect blend of his parents with his mother's Indian features and the green eyes and smile of his Irish father.

That smile faded when he helped his mother out of the wagon. "Mother, you've lost a lot more weight. I wished I'd known y'all were coming. The wife's gone to Shreveport to visit her folks."

"Son, this trip came up quick, and there's no way to get word quick out of Ten Mile."

"I'm glad you're here. I bet they're going to be able to make you feel better."

Miss Eliza's lips tightened.

I walked by Mayo toward his house. "I bet your mother was a beautiful younger woman," I said.

"She still is."

"I'm sorry if I offended you, I didn't mean she no longer is."

"No offense. She's been sick a long time, and those crows done landed at the corner of her eyes, but she's still the most beautiful woman I know." He winked. "Next to my wife, of course."

The next morning as we went to the doctor's office, ragged clouds pushed by a strong south wind flowed overhead. "My bones tell me there's a change in the weather." Miss Eliza cocked her ear. "Listen to those geese fighting that wind."

A long vee of snow and blue geese came into view.

Miss Eliza and I entered the small, crowded waiting room at Dr. Harvey's office on Murray Street and took our place on a long bench. The Irishman and Will were buying supplies for the store and would join us later.

A big-bosomed city lady was seated beside us. She scooted away and whispered in a prissy stage whisper. "I cannot believe they let their kind in here."

I glanced at Miss Eliza. She'd either not heard the catty remark or had chosen not to respond. I tried to stare a hole through the woman.

"Well, I don't have to sit by them." She took her purse and moved across the room.

I'd had enough. "Ma'am, are you talking about us?"

She smirked. "Yes. You and that old squaw."

My face flushed. "What you'd call her?"

"You heard me."

I pounced before I knew what I'd done. I meant to just get in Prissy's face, but I tripped and fell on top of her. "I'm going to scratch your eyes out. You don't talk about my momma like that." She shoved me off, and as I fell I grabbed a handful of necklace. I jumped off the floor, determined to finish my scratch-out-your-eyes threat, but someone pinned my arms behind me.

I twisted to find a wide-eyed Will Moore. "Whoa now, Nelly."

I glanced at Miss Eliza, who had the same gaze as her son. She put her hand over her mouth. "Oh, my soul."

Mrs. Prissy stood in front of me. "You broke my necklace."

The necklace was clinched in my fist. I tossed it to her. "You're lucky that's all I broke."

"You owe me for breaking it."

Miss Eliza stepped between us. "Lady, send the repair bill care of the Old Squaw at the Ten Mile Reservation."

Mrs. Prissy stormed to the door. "I'll be back with the sheriff."

Miss Eliza sat down. "It'd be a shame to have a boring day."

Will sat between us. "I bet she'll watch her mouth next time."

Miss Eliza giggled. "Missouri, you sure bounced off that big-busted woman."

"It was a sight, wasn't it?"

"You told her that I was your momma."

I placed my hand on hers. "You kinda are."

Miss Eliza glanced around the room where the other patients sat in silence, as if what we had was catching. "It's always a good day when the circus comes to town, ain't it?"

The Irishman walked in. "How are things here?"

Will made a fist. "You just missed Missouri kicking a city woman's butt."

"What for?"

"She called Momma a bad name."

"Then she had it coming."

"But the city woman went to get the sheriff."

The Irishman shook his head. "I can't leave you women alone without y'all getting into a mess."

A man who I assumed to be Dr. Harvey stood in the office doorway. "I heard there was a little trouble out here?" He glanced at his chart. "I'm ready for Mrs. Eliza Moore."

The Irishman told Will, "Son, go get Captain Hatch. If the Sheriff comes, he can help us."

Mrs. Eliza took my hand. "Missouri, you come with me and Joe Moore."

The doctor led us into a small room. "I'm Doctor Harvey." He shook Joe Moore's hand and then Miss Eliza's.

"That's quite a grip for a sick lady."

The doctor turned to me. "And who might you be?"

"I'm Missouri Cotton."

The doctor peered over his reading glasses. "I'll be sure to watch my mouth around you. According to my nurse, you got with that brassy woman out there."

He listened intently to Miss Eliza's chest and asked a multitude of questions. After about ten minutes, he took off his glasses. "Mrs. Moore, you're a sick woman, but you knew that before you came here. Consumption is a tough thing to fight."

"How long do I have?"

He cleared his throat. "It's not a matter of how long. It's just that your condition is very advanced."

"How long?"

"Maybe a year." The doctor fidgeted. "I'm sure you'd tried all of the quack medical cures out there."

"I've tried a few but none helped."

"I'd like to start you on a new medicine that's helped some on that cough. I'll consult with one of my colleagues here on any other approaches we could use. We'll also write up a summary for Dr. Hamilton." He stood. "I'd like for you to come back in four days, and let's see where you're at. Mr. Moore, I'd like you to come also." He eyed me up and down. "It's up to you if you want to bring your bodyguard."

We helped Miss Eliza up and walked her into the outer office, where a greeting committee waited. A deputy stood with his hands on his hips. Will stood beside a well-dressed man, whom I supposed was Captain Hatch. Mrs. Prissy, her necklace in hand, pointed at me. "She attacked me."

"I tripped and fell on you." I stepped closer to Miss Eliza. "Besides, you should not've talked bad about my momma."

The deputy looked at Miss Eliza. "Is this your mother?"

"Not by blood, but by heart," I said.

The sheriff looked puzzled. "By heart?"

"That's where we're connected. It's just as strong as blood."

Captain Hatch stepped into the fray. "Deputy Willie, we'll take care of paying for this woman's necklace." He nodded at us. "These ladies are business associates of mine. Mrs. Moore's husband and I own a store across the Calcasieu, and this young lady works for us. I can, uh, vouch for her character." He held out a twenty-dollar bill to Mrs. Prissy. "I believe that will take care of a new necklace."

Prissy snatched at it, but Hatch drew it back, holding out his other hand. "We're buying the necklace from you."

"No way. That money's to repair it."

"You know it's not worth twenty dollars. It's not even real. It's fake."

Miss Eliza whispered under her breath, "Fake like you."

"It's a family heirloom."

Hatch pocketed his bill, and the woman's tone changed. "Well, I do want to get this over with. I'll take twenty-five dollars and not a penny less.”

“Twenty-two fifty, and that’s my last offer.” Captain Hatch pulled out a receipt book. “Now, if you’ll sign this, releasing my associates from all responsibility.”

Prissy scribbled her name, took the money, dropped the necklace on the floor, and left in a huff.

Hatch picked up the necklace and handed it to me. “I believe this is yours.”

The deputy eyed me. “What’s your name?”

“Missouri Cotton.”

“Haven’t I seen you before?”

I remembered him well. He’d questioned Pap the day before we cleared out of Alexandria. “I don’t think so.”

“I’d swear I’ve seen you before.” He looked at his watch. “I’d best be going.” He nodded at me. “And I’d best not see you again, at least not in something like this.”

“Yes, sir.”

I clutched my new necklace as we walked down the muddy street. The Irishman led the way as Will and I walked on each side of Miss Eliza. In spite of the sobering report, she was in good spirits. “Hand me that necklace. Now that was better than any medicine.” She stopped and looked me in the eyes. “Missouri, how’d that deputy know you?”

I shrugged. “He’d questioned Pap about some trouble when we were here earlier in the year. I guess he recognized me.”

She rose to her full height. “I’ll just ask one time. Were you involved in anything here that I need to know about?”

“Other than being my pap’s daughter? That’s the only thing I’m guilty of here.”

“What did your Pap do?” Will said.

“Nearly got himself killed by conning some fellows. We had to clear out really quick, and that’s how we ended up in Ten Mile.”

That night at the Moore household on Seventh Street, Will and Miss Eliza recounted the day’s tale blow by blow for Mayo Moore. He made them act it out three more times.

They say laughter is the best medicine, and for at least one night it was true among the Moore clan. How I’d taken up for Miss Eliza had made me a hero.

But my laughter died when I thought of the deputy. I had a gut feeling I hadn’t seen the last of him.

CHAPTER 19

SEARCHING

Thursday, December 15

I was up early and out the door on a search-and-rescue mission. Pulling my collar up, I leaned in against the bitter north wind blowing down the streets of Alexandria. Cities always seemed colder on windy days.

My mission that day was to find two things. Satsumas and that fifth volume of *Les Miserables*.

I'd secured this trip promising Pap a boatload of satsumas and riches. I was off in search of the riverfront or a fruit stand. As I passed by a livery stable, a rangy middle-aged man called out. "What's a girl like you doing walking the streets?"

"I'm looking for satsumas."

The man stopped whittling a match and pointed with his knife. "Haven't I seen you before?"

"I don't think so. I've just arrived from across the river to shop for the store where I work."

"What store is that?" He said.

"The Hatch and Moore Store in Ten Mile."

He picked his teeth with his sharpened matchstick. "You sure you weren't here a few months ago?"

"Maybe, but I don't think so."

The man leaned inside the doorway. "Boss, come take a look out here."

A well-dressed man with a long white moustache stepped out. "What do you have, Buzzard?"

"Boss, you remember that scoundrel who ran the scam down on Front Street?"

Boss grimaced. "It'd be hard to forget him with the way he

lightened my wallet."

Buzzard nodded. "Wasn't this girl with him?"

Boss stared long and hard. "I don't think so."

"I'd swear she was with him." Buzzard leered at me. "I wouldn't forget a woman that looks like her."

"No, sir. I live over in No Man's Land. Way past Hineston."

Boss walked closer. "My name is Perry. Raymond Perry. How long you been in No Man's Land?"

"About two or three months."

"Were you here in Alex before that?"

I ducked my head. "For a little while."

Perry leaned in closer. "I remember you. I'd never forget your eyes. You were with him."

Buzzard threw down his toothpick. "I'm going to get the sheriff."

"Wait a minute, Buzzard," Mr. Perry said. "What are you going to tell the sheriff? That we got greedy and got snookered in a scheme we had no business in? That's the whole reason we've kept it quiet."

"But the sheriff sent out a posse looking for that fellow. This girl here might lead to him. I'd like to get hold of that rascal."

Perry nodded. "So would I, but I'm not ready to reveal how stupid we were. Besides, if this girl is his daughter, what are you gonna do? Hold her hostage?"

He turned to me. "Was that man your father?"

"Kind of."

"What do you mean kind of?"

"He's really my grandpa."

"Is he over in No Man's Land?"

"When I left, he was, sir."

"Well, you tell him if he pulls one of his schemes among those people, he'll end up swingin' from a rope." He kicked a dirt clod at me. "You tell him, you hear?"

"If I see him, I will."

Buzzard was still pacing angrily and murmuring under his breath. Boss turned to him, "Well, Buzzard, since you're so torn up over it, why don't you go over there into No Man's Land and fetch him? "

"Cross the Dead Line? I ain't that torn up." His voice sounded hurt. "But, Boss, you sound like you're defending him. You lost more money than I did."

"That fellow just took advantage of our greed. It's water under the bridge." He turned to me. "Your father was an artist. Give him my compliments, and tell him if we ever cross paths again, I'll kill him."

"Sir, if I may, I'll move on."

Mr. Perry nodded.

I turned. "Where can I find satsumas and a library?"

He laughed. "I'm afraid to ask what satsumas have to do with books. I hope it's not another con."

"No sir. Word is a boatload of fruit is arriving this week from New Orleans. I'm buying them for our store."

"There is a boat that shows up about now, but I haven't seen it this year. Books? We don't have a library, but go to Elliott Street and find John's General Store and ask for Mrs. Willie. She's Alexandria's book expert." Boss returned into the store, chuckling. "Satsumas and libraries."

Buzzard roughly grabbed my arm and pulled me right up to his face. He smelled like stale beer and tobacco. "You ain't seen the last of me." As he released his grip, he pushed me away. "It'll be different next time."

CHAPTER 20

BOOTS AND BOOKS

December 15

Trying to put Buzzard and his death breath out of my mind, I continued hunting for *Les Miserables: Volume Five*.

I continued looking behind to make sure Buzzard wasn't following me. I found John's General Store at the end of Elliott Street. I met Mrs. Willie and told her about my mission to find *Les Miserables*. She removed her glasses. "Honey, I don't think we have those books, but you're welcome to look in our storage room."

An entire wall of the dark room was stacked with musty books. I happily began digging around through the titles. I found a rat-eaten copy of *Aesop's Fables* and set it aside. Every time I moved a book, silverfish scurried about. On a table were a few copies of the *Louisiana Democrat*. As I skimmed through them, I found an article about the ongoing trial of Charles Guiteau, the alleged assassin of President Garfield. As usual, the paper took a dim view of anything done by the Republican administration in Washington.

I was startled away from my reading by Mrs. Willie shaking my arm. "Honey, did you find what you're looking for?"

"No ma'am." I held up *Aesop's Fables*. "But I'd like to buy this one."

"Look at the shape it's in. Take it. It's yours." She put her glasses back on. "There's a Yankee lady who lives on Foisy Street. Word is that she has a fine library of books. Her husband is a cotton trader down on the levee not two blocks from here. He'll be easy to find. He's got a peg leg."

"What's his name?"

"Something like Platt or Pratt."

After thanking her, I was on my way. As usual, the Alexandria waterfront was crowded, and I wound my way around looking for a man with a peg leg. A roustabout was leaning on his loading wagon. "I'm looking for a Mister Platt. He's only got one leg."

He wiped his face. "There's two of 'em over there."

"Two what?"

"Two men with one leg."

"One leg between them?"

The roustabout grinned. "No, they've got two between them. Each one only has one leg. They're sitting at the checkerboard by the bank."

The two older checker players were arguing, so I edged forward. One wore a faded-blue greatcoat, and that and his accent confirmed that he was the Yankee. He smiled at his opponent. "Crown me."

His opponent sported a faded Rebel cavalry cap that had once been gray. Both men had long beards. And sure enough, each had a peg leg.

As I approached them, Rebel eyed me. "You wanna play the winner?"

"I'm not very good at checkers."

"Well, neither are we." He nodded at his partner. "Be careful coming over here, Sis. Bluecoat's people burnt this town once and he might do it again. He'll steal your spoons and silverware, too."

Bluecoat moved a black checker and never looked up. "Rumor's always been that the Jayhawkers burnt the town as a smoke screen to plunder their own people. It weren't the Yankees."

Reb winked at me. "That's Damn Yankees."

Curiosity has always got me in trouble. I walked up to the checkerboard. "How'd y'all lose those legs?"

Reb looked up. "How'd you get so nosey at such a young age?"

"Just curious. What's your name, mister?"

Reb put out his hand. "Abram B. Terry."

I shook his hand. "It's nice meeting you, Mister Abraham."

Bluecoat snickered. "His name's Abram, not Abraham. Ask him why."

Reb spat. "Abraham Lincoln's the one that started this whole shooting match. I changed my name when I got home from the War. I now go by Abram."

I studied their peg legs. "It looks like one of you lost a left leg and the other his right." Bluecoat grinned. "You're right observant."

"Are you Mister Pratt?"

"No, but I am Mister Plott. How can I help you?"

"I'm looking for a book."

Bluecoat looked up. "Now that's a request I don't hear every day."

"It's by Victor Hugo and it's called *Les Miserables*. Do you think—"

"Never heard of it. I mainly only read the newspaper for cotton prices, but my wife has spent her inheritance and my cotton profit on books. She might have it." He moved a checker. "Let me finish beating Reb, I'll take you to our house."

Reb looked up from the checkerboard. "Don't be seen with him. He's a carpetbagger and it'll hurt your reputation." It was difficult to know when they were joking or serious. I pulled up a stool and watched them finish their game. Reb's earlier statement that neither were good at checkers was a front. They each moved with the careful deliberation of long-time players as they jawed back and forth between moves.

I moved my stool closer. "Seriously, how'd you lose your legs?"

Bluecoat shook his head. "Lost mine at Vicksburg, Mississippi."

Reb tapped his leg. "Lost mine the same day up at Gettysburg. Pickett's Charge. Friday, July 3, 1863. Yankees captured me, cut my leg off, and buried it in a stump hole before they shipped what was left of me north to a prison camp. That's where I cooled my heels—or rather, heel—till the War ended." I laughed and Reb gave me a stern look. "Now, it ain't funny." But he couldn't hide a grin underneath his long beard.

I turned to Bluecoat. "What about you?"

"A Rebel sniper got it on the last day at Vicksburg. I was the final casualty. Lost it to the hip." He nodded at Reb. "His is only to the knee."

"What's a Yankee like you doing here in Louisiana?" I said.

"I came down here to make a fortune in cotton after the War, and I am still waiting to make it."

"So you really are a carpetbagger?"

He nodded at his checkers partner. "Nope. Carpetbaggers made quick money and then cleared out before Reconstruction ended."

Reb smirked. "It wasn't Reconstruction. It was an occupation by your people."

Bluecoat shrugged. "Well, I've stayed and still haven't made any money."

A young man walked up and put his hand on Reb's shoulder. "Pop, don't you and this Yankee have anything better to do than tell lies to this girl?" He turned to me. "My name's Terry." He pointed to the Rebel. "I'm his son. I don't know your name, but I've heard of you."

"How's that?"

"That you're feisty and don't take gruff off smart-tongued city women."

"I see my fame has preceded me."

"I'm not sure it's fame. I'd call it notoriety."

"Is Terry your first name or last?"

"Both."

"Both?"

"My full name is Terry Terry." He pointed at Reb. "Blame him."

I stepped away from the checker match. "Okay, Terry Terry, tell me more about your father and that Yankee."

"Just call me Terry."

"First or last?"

"Either." I liked his easy-going smile.

"That's my father, Abram Terry in the Rebel cap. He and I run a sawmill on the edge of town. He's a native of Alexandria and came straight home when the War ended, and they let him out of that prisoner-of-war camp. He just came home with one less leg than he left with."

He nodded at the other player. "The Yankee's real name is Hiram Plott, but he's only known as Bluecoat. He came down here a few years ago as a cotton speculator. That keg and checkerboard is his office. He sits right there checking the river traffic, talking with the planters coming in and out of this bank.

"My pop, Reb, and Bluecoat weren't friends until last Christmas. It all started when my momma surprised Pop with a new pair of boots from Hardtner's Boot Store on Murray Street. It was a sacrificial gift from my mother who'd saved egg money all year to buy the boots. When he opened the box, and held up the boots, he cried like a baby."

Terry pointed at his father's peg leg. "Of course, the right boot wasn't much use for him. So Christmas afternoon, Pop had me hitch the wagon, and we came into town. Yank, even on Christmas Day, was sitting at his whiskey barrel office, checkerboard in place. My pop opened his tote sack and took out the brand-new right boot, tossing it against the barrel, scattering the checkers—"

"It was the right size and right boot. 9-E. Perfect fit." Terry smiled. "My pop nodded at his own new matching left boot. 'Christmas gift … for both of us.' Blue coat stood unsteadily and couldn't speak for a good fifteen seconds, then he simply said, 'Thank you' as tears rolled down his cheeks."

Terry nodded at the two veterans. "Up to this moment, he and my father had coolly viewed the other as the enemy. But after the boot incident and a subsequent game of checkers over a pot of hot coffee, a comradeship was born." Terry nodded at them. "They've been playing every week since."

I turned to Terry. "That's a great story. So, they're friends and have peace?"

He laughed. "It's more complex than that. I'd call it a truce."

"Have they ever addressed each other by their given names?"

"Nope. Just 'Bluecoat' and 'Reb.' "

Terry walked to the checkerboard. "Are y'all about through?"

Bluecoat moved once more. "You're trapped. My win."

"I let you win so it wouldn't embarrass you in front of this girl."

Bluecoat stood with the help of a thick staff. "Same time next week, and you'll buy the coffee." He bowed. "We're ready to go, your Royal Highness, and look for that book."

Reb got in a final broadside. "As slow as he hobbles, you'll probably not make Foisy Street by dark-thirty."

As I walked, I asked, "Mr. Plott, how will he get Reb home?"

"Why don't you just call me Bluecoat? Mr. Plott was my father, not me."

"All right, Mr. Bluecoat, how will Reb get home?"

"Terry will get their wagon from the sawmill and take him home."

He nodded down the street. "Here comes my daughter from the tailor's shop."

A tall blonde approached and Bluecoat said, "This is Amanda, my youngest daughter. I didn't catch your name?"

"It's Missouri Cotton."

"Missouri Cotton is looking for a book," Bluecoat said.

Amanda's eyes lit up. "What book?"

"It's called *Les Miserables* by Victor Hugo."

"I've heard of it, but never seen it around Alex. My mother's the local book expert. We'll ask her." Amanda stepped away from her father. "I saw you visiting with Terry."

From her expression, I immediately knew there was something strong between them. "Now, I ain't trying to steal your man."

"Did I say he was my man?"

"No, but your face showed it." I nodded at her father. "Does Bluecoat, I mean your father, know about y'all?"

"Neither of our families know. When they find out, it'll probably rekindle the Civil War and test the friendship between our two fathers."

"Will they give their permission?"

"I don't know. We're probably going to run off and get married. It's a lot easier to get forgiveness than to get permission."

"Why are you telling me about you and Terry?"

"I guess you seem trustworthy." She slowed so her father could catch up with us.

"Your boyfriend's really named Terry Terry?"

"Crazy, ain't it? Walk home with me."

We reached their house and I realized Bluecoat's talking about not making any money was only a joke. Their home was palatial, and suddenly I felt extremely small. These people were out of my league.

Evidently, Amanda sensed this. "Oh, come off it. You're as welcome here as can be. Let's go ask Mother about that book."

I'd never been in a house this nice. Amanda directed me to a plush couch that I sank into. I sat there nervously for about ten minutes, seemingly sinking deeper and deeper into the couch. I hoped I could get up when needed. "Come in here, Missouri." I struggled to my feet and met Amanda in the largest room of books I'd ever seen. Her mother, who Amanda strongly favored said in a strong New England accent. "We've got lots of books, but I'm afraid I've never procured a copy of any of Hugo's works so far.

The word *procured* percolated in my mind. "Thank you kindly, Mrs. Plott."

"I'll ask around among my few friends here."

It saddened me the way she said *few friends*. Being a Northerner in Alexandria could not have been an easy life. I wondered how she'd take the news of her daughter in love with a Southern boy.

While I was out gallivanting around, things had been busy at Mayo's home. Since our arrival in Alexandria, the Irishman and Will had bought supplies for the store. The plan was for the Irishman to leave the next morning for Westport. But when I reached the Moore home, the Irishman was tarping his loaded wagon. He'd decided to leave mid-afternoon and camp beside the Bayou Rapides Road. This would allow him to reach Westport the next day by nightfall. He was busy instructing Will and me about how to do things over the next week. "Oh, and one more thing. See if you can find some peppermints. They sell great at Christmastime."

Miss Eliza was having a bad day and was in the bed. She and the Irishman talked a long time as Will and I waited on the porch. When the Irishman came out, he said, "All right, I'm leaving you two with two jobs. Take care of your mother." He peered at me. "And try to stay out of jail."

Will nodded to the wagon. "You got your rifle loaded?"

Joe Moore nodded. "Yep. When your momma sees the doctor again and feels like traveling, come on home. Just don't get caught out on the road at night." He climbed on his wagon, waved, and began the trek to No Man's Land. The plan was for us to follow in about a week.

I spent most of the afternoon at Miss Eliza's bedside as she slept. I read until I ran out of candle light, then I made a pallet on the floor and spent the night beside her.

CHAPTER 21

SATSUMAS

Friday, December 16

Ophelia, Mayo's wife, returned the next afternoon. She'd received a telegraph about the Moores' arrival and returned to Alexandria by train. She was super nice to the Moore family, but seemed to have a standoffish attitude toward me. I sensed that she viewed me as second rate and brown trash.

So I went about my rat-killing in Alexandria. I had no desire to be underfoot or trouble. I resumed my satsuma search. Mayo insisted that Will accompany me. I hadn't told anyone about my encounter with Buzzard, so I was glad to have him along. He and I headed for the levee. I was sweating that satsuma boat. We wandered the levee looking for arrivals, carefully avoiding the Livery Stable and Buzzard. I had a plan B and C, but neither would make the profit my satsumas would.

People often use the statement, "When my ship comes in," and that was my hope for this day. We were there on the levee that afternoon when a steamer called the *Hannibal* arrived from New Orleans.

Longshoremen were already unloading the cargo. We hurried up the gangplank. I found a man with his arms crossed. He looked important, so I asked, "Sir, do you happen to have any satsumas?"

"According to the manifest, there are seventy cases."

"How would I go about buying some?"

He pointed to a man wearing a derby hat. "Swisher over there can tell you."

I hurried over. "Sir, could I buy some crates of your satsumas?"

Derby Hat kept walking. "They're spoken for. John's Grocery is buying them."

"All of them?"

He glanced up from his papers with a hint of irritation. "All but twenty crates. They're going upriver to Natchitoches."

"How much are they paying?"

He shook his head at Will and me. "What are you street urchins doing on my boat?"

"We're doing business for the Hatch and Moore General Store in Westport, Louisiana."

"Never heard of it."

"How much will they pay per crate in Natchitoches?"

He ran his finger down the manifest. "Looks like fifteen dollars per case. I'll get $300 for the lot.

"I'll give you $12 per for the twenty cases. That's $240."

"They're promised in Natchitoches."

"Trouble is, you'll never make Natchitoches. The river's dropped here at the rapids. Your draft is too deep, and this is as far upriver as you're going. Spoiled satsumas won't sell well back in New Orleans."

"You don't have the money."

"I pulled out Pap and my wad of money, licked my fingers, and began peeling off twenty-dollar bills. Nothing speaks quite like cold, hard cash. "Here you are, sir."

I pointed at Will. "And we'll even haul them off ourselves."

"You are quite the little business woman. It's a deal." He folded the bills and stuffed them into his pocket. "Besides, as determined as you are, I'm afraid you'd rob me at gunpoint if I didn't sell them to you."

I pointed. "Set my crates over there in the shade. My partner here will be back with a wagon."

Will, also being a businessman, couldn't resist. "Sir, you don't have any peppermints for sale, do you?"

Derby hat picked up a stick. "Both of you urchins. Off my boat."

We hurried back ashore. Will pulled on my sleeve. "Missouri, what's an urchin?"

"It's a word used by Dickens for beggar children."

"Who's Dickens?"

"He's an English writer who wrote books about poor people in London."

"Let's name our business Street Urchins and Sons."

"Let's not get ahead of ourselves. You go get the wagon, and I'll guard our contraband."

I sat on a crate and watched the fascinating scene along the levee. There's nothing quite like a port city. Alexandria wasn't New Orleans or Mobile, but the riverside had the same intensity that those ports had.

I saw my friend Buzzard walking the levee. I pulled my scarf over my face and faded into the shade of a building. His big knife was in a scabbard on his belt. He kept putting his hand in his right boot. I imagined he had a derringer in there. He was bad news, and as he walked past I was glad he hadn't spotted me.

Will arrived with the wagon and we loaded up our crates. In celebration of completing our mission, we each sucked on a fresh Louisiana satsuma on the way back to the Mayo Moore house. When Will reached for another one, I slapped his hand away. "We'll have to be careful, or we'll eat up our profit afore we reach Westport."

CHAPTER 22

HEADED HOME

Saturday, December 17

The next morning, I had breakfast with Mayo Moore as Miss Eliza sat across the table nursing her second cup of coffee.

As Mayo took a big bite of pancake, he said, "Momma, are you ready to go to the doctor?"

"Might as well get it over with." Mayo, Ophelia, Will, and I helped Miss Eliza onto the wagon.

Sadly, Miss Eliza's second visit wasn't any more helpful than the first. The medicine hadn't helped her, and every breath was labored. Doctor Harvey was obviously distressed. "I am so sorry you're not better. I want to try one more medicine."

Miss Eliza took his hand. "It's not your fault. It's jes' the way it is."

He tore off a script. "Would you try this medicine? How long do you plan to be in town?"

Mayo spoke up. "She'll be here another week."

"All right. I'd like to see you at the end of the week."

We were a sad lot as we loaded her onto the wagon. The air was thick with tension, and I said, "If I can be excused, I'm gonna walk to the levee for some fresh air. I'll see y'all back at Mayo's house."

I made my way along the levee then turned away from the river. My goal was Foisy Street to see Amanda Plott.

As I rounded an isolated corner, Buzzard stepped out. "I told you that I'd see you again." I turned to run, but he grabbed me by the arm. "I'm getting what I'm owed out of you." He pressed the hilt of his knife into my ribs. "I'll use the other end if needed." As he dragged me down a dead-end alley, he tore the bandana from his neck and stuffed it in my mouth. I struggled mightily, but he was much stronger and meaner. He shoved me to the ground, pinning my hands back. I closed my eyes and turned my head. I'd rather have died than be assaulted by him.

Suddenly, there was a loud whack and Buzzard collapsed onto my body. I rolled him off to see Will Moore holding an ax handle. I jerked the bandana out of my mouth and shakily stood, dusting off my dress. "Thanks."

We both stood over Buzzard. He lay still, blood pouring from a wound on the back of his head. Additionally, blood trickled from his ear.

"Is he dead?" I said.

Will dropped the ax handle. "I don't know, but let's git."

I scooped up my book, and we ran several blocks before Will stopped. "Let's slow down. We're creating too much suspicion running."

Out of breath, I put my hands on my knees. "What do we do now?"

"Absolutely nothing," Will said. "He got what he deserved whether he's dead or alive." He took my hand. "We've gotta keep this between us."

"You saved my life. Mum's the word."

He brushed the dirt off my shoulder. "Missouri, it's good you have a secret admirer. If I hadn't been following you, you'd be in a fix."

"Thanks. He got what he deserves."

"Where were you going?" Will said.

I held up my book. "Going to trade this one in." The cover was torn and mud-coated from my tangle with Buzzard. "I'm afraid it's ruined, but I must return it."

Will looked behind us. "Well, you can't be seen in that area right now. If either of us are connected to Buzzard, we'll be reading your book in a jail cell."

Will and I hurried on to Mayo's house, every step taking us away from Buzzard's body in the alley.

Miss Eliza was laying on a couch when we rushed in. She sat up. "You two look flushed. What's going on?"

Will, always quick on the draw, said, "Momma, it's just love, and it's hard to hide."

"Well, you're not hiding it too well. You two had better wash up and look presentable."

That night, I slept on a pallet at the foot of Miss Eliza's bed. It was a rough night as she coughed and moaned. Her breathing was labored and at several points seemed to cease. All throughout the night I rose to make sure she was alive.

Close to daybreak, she began fighting and crying, evidently in the middle of a nightmare. I crawled on the bed beside her. "It's all right. You're right here and safe in Mayo's house."

She got a death grip on my arm. "I had a bad dream. I dreamt they'd cut down all the pines on our side of the river."

"Who?"

"Outsiders. They came with all kinds of machines and contraptions. When they finished there weren't nothin' left but stumps and sawdust."

I patted her hand. "It was just a dream."

"But it seemed so real." She lay her head back. "I jes' wonder if you'll see that in your lifetime."

"I can't imagine that ever happening."

"I hear-tell it's happened in other places." She closed her eyes. "I won't live to see it, and I hope you don't either."

She drifted off to sleep as I lay beside her. Hours later, she woke me and I sat up to daylight streaming through the window.

"Missouri, I've made up my mind. We're going home."

I propped up on an elbow. "But the doctor wants to see you—"

"I don't care. I'm going home to the Pines. That's where I belong, not here."

I shrugged. "Well, you'll have to get that past Mayo and Will."

"You leave that to me. You'd best be packing your things. We're headed to Ten Mile."

Needless to say, there was a battle royale between Miss Eliza and her sons. Ophelia and I stayed in the kitchen but heard every word.

Finally, Miss Eliza stomped her foot. "I'm going home. Will, if you won't load me in the wagon, I'll start on foot."

"Momma, you can't—"

"I not only can, but I'm going, and if I'm your momma, you'll help me."

"But why this sudden decision?"

"I had a dream last night. It's clear to me that if I stay here, I'll die. I want to die in the Pineywoods. It's where I was born and where I plan to turn up my toes." She turned to Mayo and Ophelia. "My decision has nothing to do with y'all. Ophelia, you've done everything to take care of me. It's just that this ain't where I belong."

Mayo lowered his head. "I can tell your mind's made up. I won't stop you, but I sure wish Daddy was here to talk sense to you."

"That's another reason I want to go home. That's where he is, and I want to be with him." She pulled out her snuff can. "Besides, these doctors here can't help me. Only the Lord can, and I figure He's as powerful across the river as He is in Alexandria."

No one was happier to leave Alexandria than Miss Eliza, unless it was Will Moore and me. I was used to being on the run because of my father, but this time it was trouble of my own making.

The wagon was loaded. Miss Eliza lay on her bed in the wagon, and we began the trip back to Ten Mile.

I sat by Will, and when we were sure his mother was asleep, I let out a deep breath. "I hope we're out of the fire."

Will took up the slack in the reins. "I'll be glad when we get back across the river. Now that we're fugitives from the law, I understand the lure of the Outlaw Strip."

"We're not fugitives. It was self-defense."

That afternoon, Miss Eliza was perkier. She motioned to me. "Child, what do you think happens in the next book of *Les Mizz*?"

"Be careful getting me started."

Will sat on the buckboard. "Momma, she won't hush about that book."

Miss Eliza had a coughing fit then wheezed. "Child, we've got miles of riding left in this wagon. It'll make the journey go faster."

I drew a breath. "Well, I'll start with the spy Javert. I've never thought of him as a bad man, just one who can't be flexible when it comes to the law. That's why he can't let Valjean and his yellow card go free.

"Anyway, at the barricades, he vows to fight with the revolt if freed. Being a man of his word, he fights bravely and during the heat of the battle, he bravely saves Valjean's life before he is killed himself. He dies with his chips all cashed in and as a happy man."

Miss Eliza closed her eyes. "I like that."

"Valjean, who arrived to kill Marius, changes his mind and tricks young Marius to go on a mission with him to steal a nearby cannon. When they reach a safe spot. Valjean knocks Marius out, and carries him to the safe house where Cosette awaits. Marius is tied to a chair to prevent him from returning to the battle when he awakes.

Miss Eliza nodded approvingly. "I knew he wouldn't kill that boy. Valjean had it in him to save him."

I held up my hand. "The small number of revolters at the barricade is wiped out by the attacking army. All of Marius's friends die.

Marius awakes to find himself alive and with Cossette. He doesn't remember anything about the battle or Valjean's trickery. He believes that he was concussed by a cannon blast, then saved by Valjean, whom he now recognizes as Cossette's father.

"Valjean completes his plans for their trip to America. Before leaving he and Marius go to the countryside and dig up Valjean's buried treasure."

Miss Eliza leaned on her elbow. "Did they find it all?"

"Every coin. After the lavish wedding of Marius and Cossette, the three of them (Valjean) immigrate to New Orleans where they learn to fit into the city's unique French culture and they all live happily ever after. Their kinfolks live there until this day."

I scooted over by Miss Eliza and lowered my voice. "In fact, the

New Orleans lady whose house I cleaned is their grandchild. She's named Fantine in memory of her great-grandmother."

Miss Eliza scoffed. "Get out of here. That's not true."

I shrugged. "Remember, it's just fiction, and I can make it up any way I want."

"So, they lived happily ever after?" `Miss Eliza said.

"That's the way *my* story ends."

She gripped my arm. "Mizz, you've got to find that last book before I die." Her eyes darkened. "What about that bad man who tried to kidnap Cosette?

"Thernadier and his wife? In *my book*, they end up in prison for attempted murder while trying to rob a priest."

Miss Eliza nodded. "Yep, the past will catch up. A fellow's chickens will eventually come home to roost."

My stomach tightened. I looked up and Will arched his eyebrows. I could still visualize Buzzard lying in a pool of blood. That episode was one chicken I hoped didn't cross the Calcasieu.

Miss Eliza repeated as if to herself. "So they lived happily ever after."

"That's the way my story ends." I took her hand. "Now, how would *you* end the story?"

"I doubt if I could improve on your version, but I'd have them live happily ever after too." Tears filled her eyes. "Well, stories, especially love stories, don't always end like we think they will."

Exhausted, she lay back on her pallet, and in a few minutes, was sleeping soundly.

Will held the reins in his hand. "You're pretty good at putting her out. I don't think you realize how much she loves you."

"Well, I love her too."

Will, never taking his eyes off the road ahead, said, "Do you think what happened to Buzzard will ever catch up with us?"

"I sure hope not." I blew out a breath. "Crossing back across that river made me feel a lot further from it." Bone-weary, I lay down in the wagon bed beside Miss Eliza, and, in spite of the rough road, was soon asleep.

Mine was also a contented sleep. I dreamt, and they were good dreams. Satsumas sold. Christmas money in hand. Presents for Pap and Ma. A new dress for me. Settling down in Ten Mile. Marrying and raising a passel of happy kids in the Pineywoods.

I awoke at the Calcasieu ferry. This crossing didn't have the same foreboding as our crossing six weeks ago had. I felt as if I was returning home. I was still searching for who I was and where I belonged. Those two interlocking circles defined my life, but for the first time, I felt as if I was moving toward answers to those two questions.

CHAPTER 23

OCCUPY

Sunday, December 18

Two days after our return from Alexandria, Ruth Wray was in the store and invited me to Christmas services at Occupy Church. Since she was munching on one of my satsumas and had a dozen more in a sack, I was in no position to say no.

So on the Sunday before Christmas, I nervously tried to pick out the best dress I had, which still wasn't much, worked on my hair, and tried to look presentable. I was so nervous I could hardly button up my dress. My family seldom attended church, and it was usually when Pap wanted something. He knew it was a good place to gain sympathy and a freewill offering. Ma, although deeply religious, never felt at home in any meetinghouse. She felt as if everyone looked down on her.

When Ruth Wray showed up, I draped my blanket over my shoulders as a shawl, and we briskly headed out into the cold morning. I was shivering. "What kind of church is this?"

"A forty-gallon Baptist Church."

"What?"

"Forty-gallon Baptists. Deep-water Baptists. We believe in dunking people under when we baptize them."

I blew out a frosty breath. "I hope no one's getting baptized today."

"Not today. Occupy's a half-time church and only meets every other Sunday. Today's the last time we'll meet before the new year."

A few steps later, she looked me in the eye. "Did you know they call you Wagon Girl?"

I looked away. "I don't care for that name."

"People don't mean nothin' by it." She stepped around a cow

pie in the road. "And they call your daddy the Wagon Man. While you've been gone to Alexandria, a lot's gone on about that horse race. There's still a good bit of jawing between our people and the Outsiders over if the race was fair.

"Tensions are pretty high," Ruth said. "I've got a white boyfriend, Frank Taylor, who's with a surveying crew. Last time he paid a visit to our house, my father told him he wasn't welcome around our place and should stay on his side of the river."

Ruth Wray stopped in the road and stood directly in front of me. "Missouri, there's going to be real trouble. The day is approaching when my people are going to drive the Outsiders out."

"What about Frank, your boyfriend?"

Ruth twirled a small twig in her hand. "I've asked him to lay low. He's a target."

"A target for what?"

"The way things always get settled in this part of the world— ambushes, burnouts, and sniping—they all send the same message to move on."

"What about me and my family?"

"You and your folks would be wise to watch your backs and be ready to leave."

I let go of her hand. "What about the Irishman and his family?"

"I'd advise the same for them."

We resumed our walk and soon neared the gate of the meetinghouse just as the bell pealed. I waited for it to stop. "Ruth, what about Irishman's store?"

"He'll have a tough decision to make." She refused to answer any more of my questions as we entered the churchyard, hushing me. "We'll talk about it later."

A good-natured crowd was gathered in the churchyard. The men were smoking around a fire, and the women were busy rounding up the children.

There was nothing special about Occupy Church. It was built of board and batting, and a thin coat of whitewash gave it a little respectability. There wasn't a steeple, instead a homemade cross was nailed to the front peak. A hand-lettered sign hung above the porch. Occupy Baptist Church Established 1832.

"You know how Occupy got its name?" Ruth said.

"Will Moore told me. Y'all and this church ain't going anywhere."

Ruth's eyes hardened in a way I'd never seen. "Those timber men and Outsiders think they'll drive us out of here and lay claim to our land. They've done it before in other places, and groups like ours got pushed westward or onto some sorry piece of land, thus allowing civilization to creep in.

Ruth nodded at the Occupy sign. "Our name says a lot about how we feel about this land. We ain't goin' nowhere. We've occupied this area and don't plan to be pushed out by nobody."

"So you think there'll be a fight, no matter what?"

"Sooner or later, I'm afeared."

Ruth broke her twig and tossed it aside. "That's another trait of our people. When trouble arrives from the outside, Redbones will always band together to fight off the approaching enemy. That's what's happening now with the Outsiders."

I hesitated at the church steps. "I'm an Outsider. Are you sure I'm welcome inside?"

"Missouri, don't worry none about that. You're with me. And besides, this is the house of the Lord, and it's Christmas."

As we entered, I whispered, "Will the Moore family be here?"

Ruth pointed to an open pew. "Probably not. Since the trouble heated up, they've stayed away."

As we sat, I heard someone behind me whisper, "Wagon Girl."

I scoured the crowded church for any familiar face, but didn't find one until I spotted Unk Dyal. He grinned and waved.

"This is called Sunday School. They're teaching *Bible* stories to the children, but it's also a time for teaching folks to read. That's how it got its name.

I wasn't much interested in organized religion, but if this was a place where I could get book learning and books to read, I was for it.

A woman led the children in songs, which is how they did most of their learning. I picked up a dog-eared hymnal and was soon absorbed in studying the songs.

Ruth elbowed me. "Stand up. The song service has started."

I felt like that proverbial fish out of the pond, not knowing when to stand, sit, sing, or bow, but after several songs, I began to relax. It was hard to feel unwelcome in the midst of this kind of singing. I've always loved harmony, and these Ten Milers had perfected it. Due to the deficit in hymnals and many being illiterate, what they sang just came from the heart. They let it loose and let it fly.

Most of the songs weren't familiar, but there was one I really connected with. It was titled, "Come Thou Fount of Every Blessing," and I read the verses long after the singing had stopped. One line really got my attention.

"Jesus sought me as a stranger
Wandering from the fold of God.
He to rescue me from danger,
Interposed his precious blood."

I put my finger on one line and whispered to Ruth, "What's interposed?"

"I'm not positive, but I believe it means to come between."

"Prone to wander, Lord I feel it.
Prone to leave the God I love.
Here's my heart, Lord,
Take and seal it.
Seal it for thy courts above."

When the song service ended, I marked the page for that song and quietly stuffed the hymnal into my book bag. I knew they wouldn't need it for at least two weeks, which would allow plenty of time to study it and write down the words.

Just as I bagged my contraband, Dan Moore walked into the church. A murmur followed him down the aisle. He stepped around two girls and sat right by me.

Even though Dan was born in Ten Mile, he looked different from everyone else in the building, including me. His siblings looked like Redbones, but Dan would've fit in back in County Mayo. He smiled at me and nodded at Ruth Wray. If he was nervous, he didn't show it. Unk, who was his great uncle, turned in his pew and waved.

In the midst of Dan's arrival, the preacher had stepped to the pulpit. He was a local and looked, as well as talked, in the Ten Mile. He turned in his *Bible* and read what he called "The Parable of the Lost Coin."

Unk leaned back. "I'll warn ye, he's long-jawed."

Ruth giggled. "Hope you brought your lunch."

The preacher held up a gold coin.

Unk Dyal sneezed, and someone behind us said, "God bless you."

"This-here woman lost a coin. She had a bunch of them but

lost one. It bothered her fiercely, so she searched high and low, then low and high. Got out her brush broom and swept the floor clean. Did the same thing on the gallery and probably in the front yard. Moved everything."

The preacher pulled out a handkerchief and wiped his brow. He was a natural storyteller with the rhythm and timing of effective speakers. "She had one of her boys crawl under the house with a lantern and see if that coin had fallen through the cracks. Looked in every nook and cranny. And lo and behold, she found it."

He held up his shiny coin again. "The *Bible* doesn't tell us where or how she found it. Just that she did. And she went to rejoicing. Called the neighbors in. They had a party. She'd found her lost coin."

Every time he mentioned the coin, Unk jumped as if someone was poking him with a stick. I couldn't take my eyes off him as he twisted and turned as if in torment. Dan was tickled, so I leaned over. "What's wrong with Unk?"

"I'll tell you more after church."

I had plenty of time to watch, because the sermon went on and on. I reckon due to how the visiting preacher wouldn't be back for two weeks, he wanted to make sure the congregation got their money's worth.

A voice behind me said, "Whoa, I've always believed in feeding the cows good, but you don't have to give them all of the hay in the barn."

A child said, "I'm hungry" only to be shushed by an adult.

Unk was no longer tormented by the coin references. He was sound asleep and snoring softly. He'd slid down in the rough pew with the back of his head resting against the top of it.

The preacher was unaware, or cared little, for the restlessness in the pews. He walked all over the church wiping his face with a bandana, wandering in and out of the Scriptures.

Finally, he shut his *Bible* and his voice lowered. "Folks, Jesus is still hunting for lost coins. And lost sheep. And lost sons."

A wag behind me said, "He's nearly finished. He's bringing the horse into the barn."

Ruth put her hand over her mouth. "And not a moment too soon."

The preacher stepped from behind the pulpit down onto the floor. "Now, let me be perfectly frank with you. Most folks view us

Ten Milers as lost. Lost coins. Lost sheep. We've always been underdogs. On the edge of society, but Jesus don't look at us like that."

This brought a scattering of Amens.

It was also the moment that Unk began snoring louder with his mouth open.

Dan whispered, "If it went to raining, Unk would drown." Ruth snorted, trying to resist laughing. I wasn't doing much better. Several of the adults turned and gave us a graveyard look, and that only tickled us more.

The preacher had had enough. "It's fitting to have a little more respect for the Lord's house and His Word. I got a few more bites of this apple and would 'ppreciate a little respect 'til I finish."

It embarrassed me. I lowered my head and tried to think about sad things, like when Spencer my childhood dog died.

Thankfully, the service drew to a close. There was a time of what they called an invitation, and when it ended an older man stood and finally brought the service to an end.

After sitting for hours, I hurried to the line at the outhouse. By the time I came out, most of the crowd was gone. Ruth was waiting for me with an older woman. "Missouri, this is Aunt Bertha. She wanted a word with you."

Aunt Bertha nodded. "Are you born again?"

I glanced at Ruth, then shrugged. "I sure hope not."

I immediately knew I'd given the wrong answer. "I'm sorry. I just haven't been in church much."

"Well then, are you a Christian?" Aunt Bertha said.

"Sure I am. Ain't every American? But I don't think I've been born-again or whatever it is."

She laughed. "Baby, there ain't no other kind of Christian. You're either born again or ye ain't." Then she hugged me so close I smelt the talcum powder under her dress. "I hope that next time I see you, you can say you're born again."

"Well, I hope so too, ma'am."

CHAPTER 24

BURIED TREASURE

Sunday, December 18

The three of us—Ruth Wray, Dan Moore, and I—walked away from Occupy, talking about the upcoming Christmas holiday. "By the way," Ruth said, "There's going to be a Christmas Eve-Eve dance this Friday night at the H'arm Morrow Homestead. Why don't you two join me?"

Dan took his hat off. "I believe I'll pass. Any mixture of firewater, firearms, and Redbones isn't a safe place for someone like me."

"But you're one of us—born, bred, and raised here," Ruth said. "Missouri, what about you? Can you come?"

I stopped walking. "Well, I don't know about showing up at a man's house named *Harm*."

"His real name is Hiram, but it got shortened as a boy, so he's known as H'arm," Ruth said. "I'll be by the store on Friday about four o'clock. It's Christmas Eve-Eve."

"Christmas Eve-Eve?"

"Yep, Friday is the day before Christmas Eve. It's Christmas Eve-Eve."

Dan laughed. "Unk calls it Christmas Adam-Eve."

"Well, either way, it's two days before Christmas." Ruth stopped as we reached the Steep Gully fork. "Well, I'm going this way. I guess it's safe to leave you two alone."

"Oh, we'll be all right," I said as Dan turned red.

Ruth grinned. "It's kinda frowned on in our culture for two young people to be alone together."

I put my hands on my hips. "Well, I really don't give a wit for what folks think."

We girls stared at Dan, who said, "Well …uh … I guess neither do I. Besides, we're walking home from church in broad daylight."

Ruth goosed Dan. "Okay, then you're in charge of getting Missouri home safely. Can you handle it?"

"I reckon I can."

As soon as we were got out of earshot, I asked Dan, "Is that the real reason you don't want to go to the dance?"

"There's two good reasons— Eliza Moore and the feud. If my momma found out I went, she'd thrash me and never let me forget it. Secondly, the feud has got folks on edge. A dance like that is just the place for trouble to break out."

"Do you think I shouldn't go?"

"Missouri, I can't tell you what to do, but if you go, I'd step real lightly, and not let Ruth out of your sight."

I touched his elbow. "Now, what's the deal about Unk and the lost coin?"

"It's a well-known story that began about thirty years ago when a man traveling through these parts was robbed and murdered. He was carrying two bags of gold coins."

I held up my hand. "How do you know about all of this?"

"That's where Unk comes in. He was watching from the edge of the woods and saw the killer—a ne'er-do-well named Amos Long—do the dirty deed. Unk followed Long and watched him bury the contraband. Later that night, Unk dug up the bounty and re-buried the coins in a red-dirt ant colony."

"How many coins were there?"

"That's still debated. Unk doesn't count real good, so the amount varied from telling to telling."

"He buried the coins in an anthill?"

"Right in the middle of a town-ant colony where the dirt always looks as if it's been freshly dug."

"What about this Amos Long?"

When he returned to where he'd buried his coins, he couldn't find 'em. He spent the rest of his years in Ten Mile digging up that whole area."

"So the robber was robbed? Did he ever discover it was Unk?"

"Nope. No one ever suspected him.

"And here's the best part," Dan said. "About this time, folks started finding single gold coins left on their gallery or outdoor washstands. If a family was going through hard times or crops had failed, they'd discover a coin. This went on even through the hard Civil War years." Dan drew a breath. "Anyhoo, about the end of the War is when Unk got the idea to move the buried treasure. The town ants had abandoned their colony, so he moved the coins to a nearby spot. Something spooked him about that spot, so he moved them again a week later. And that's when it all went south. Unk couldn't find the coins. My brother Mayo whom you met in Alexandria went with him on many nighttime digging forays. Unk claimed he'd marked the spot with a pine-knot stob driven in the ground and an X carved on two nearby trees. They never had any luck finding the markers or the money."

"Do you think someone else dug up the coins?"

"Nope. I think in hiding the coins, Unk Dyal hid them from himself."

"Have you looked for them?"

"Sure. Everyone in my family has. Unk thinks that originally there were about seventy-five coins, and he either gave away or spent about twenty of them."

I blew out a breath. "That means there're over fifty gold coins buried somewhere out there. That's a king's ransom."

Dan laughed. "And that's the reason Unk kept fidgeting when the preacher mentioned that lost coin. It reminded him there's those lost gold coins moldering somewhere in the Ten Mile soil."

"Is Unk still looking for them?"

"Missouri, that's the best part of the story. Uncle Mayo told me they were digging one night the year after the War ended. Suddenly, Unk threw down his spade and sat on a stump and said, 'I'm through hunting them.' And he was. Mayo said Unk has never mentioned them again, other than to say he was glad to be rid of them."

"I'd like to see where he thinks he buried his coins."

"You'd be wasting your time. Everybody in Ten Mile has dug there at one time or the other." Dan laughed. "Looks like a herd of pigs been rooting." Our wagon came into view, and Dan stopped. "I think this is as far as I'd better go."

"You're welcome to come speak to my folks."

"I think I'll pass today."

We both knew Pap was the reason for Dan's refusal. For a brief moment, I thought he might kiss me, but he turned away. "I'll see you at the store tomorrow."

"Thanks for bringing me home."

I hoped my disappointment showed. I walked a ways before turning to look back. Dan Moore was still in his tracks, hands in his pockets. I would have given a handful of Unk's coins to know what was on his mind.

CHAPTER 25

A PRELUDE: SURVEYORS

Monday, December 19

On the wettest and coldest day so far in December 1881, four rugged rough men came into the store, shaking the rain and cold off them and hurrying toward the fireplace.

They were government surveyors. The oldest member of the crew carried a transit in a large wooden box and a tripod, placing his load in the corner. Two younger men placed their stack poles and metal measuring tapes by the other equipment.

The men at the bar, a mixture of Redbones and Outsiders, eyed the interlopers. The older surveyor tipped his hat. He had a Scottish brogue and a smile to match. "You fellows mind if we join you for some strong drink?"

Whiskey Morrow put down his drink. "According to what you're here for."

The surveyor nodded at his equipment. "Just putting in land lines for the government."

"That's my land you crossed yesterday."

"I'm sure it is. Our survey ain't taking nothing from nobody. Just marking it out in grids."

"That's always the first step in the gov'ment taking land," Morrow said.

"You can take that up in the Rapides Courthouse. We're just doing our job."

"I don't go to the Rapides Courthouse. Every Redbone I've known who's been to the courthouse left from there for the parish jail."

A younger Redbone staggered to the corner, grabbed one of the stack poles, and broke it over his knee. "Y'all ain't welcome here."

He then reached for the wooden transit box, but another surveyor grabbed it away. The older surveyor pulled his pistol. "You'd best leave that box alone. That transit telescope costs me nearly a year's salary, and I won't have you messing with it."

Several men around the bar had quietly drawn their weapons in a true Mexican standoff. The Irishman who'd been quietly tending bar stepped out between the two groups. "There won't be any shooting in my establishment. This store sits not far from the 31st Parallel, and it's registered in Alexandria under my name. I got papers to prove it."

He nodded at the Redbone who'd broken the stack pole. "Roscoe, instead of breaking government property, you ought to go to the Courthouse and make sure your land deed is in order."

Whiskey Morrow stood. "Irishman, you're not from here. My blood's been living on this land for four generations. We don't need a piece of paper or some pencil pusher in Alexandria to make it official."

"Well then, Whiskey, you'd best get with the modern way of things. If you don't have papers, you're considered a squatter. Some timber company or speculator will be coming in to take your land.

"Over my dead body."

"Probably so." The Irishman turned to the surveyors and to the men at the bar. "Drinks on the house." He nodded at Roscoe. "And you'll buy the second round for breaking that pole." Roscoe looked as if he was ready to shoot the Irishman, but cursing he holstered his pistol and put a small handful of coins on the counter.

Ruth Wray had told me her new boyfriend was a surveyor, so I asked, "Are any of you Ruth Wray's sweetheart?"

One of the younger men grinned. "I'm trying to be." He held out his hand. "I'm Frank Taylor. How do you know Ruth?"

"I'm new here, and she's been nice to me. Tell her I said hello."

"I will. I'll see her Friday night at a Christmas dance near here."

I remembered Dan's uneasiness about the dance. "Are you sure you'll be welcome?"

Frank Taylor grinned. "I plan to find out." He hurried to the other surveyors who after finishing their drinks were busy spending the rest of their paychecks in the Hatch and Moore Store.

Most of the locals had filtered out of the store to safer locales. I sidled beside the Irishman. "One of these days you're gonna get shot stepping into crossfires like that," I said.

He shrugged. "This is my establishment, and I'll run it the way I please. Half of the success of dealing with these people is making them think you're not afraid."

"You weren't scared?"

The Irishman's hand shook as he picked up his drink. "I'm pretty sure I wet my britches when they pulled those guns."

CHAPTER 26

THE WINTER SOLSTICE

Wednesday, December 21, 1881

Winter in Louisiana is a strange animal. There'll be periods of rain and humid cold that cut through layers of clothes. Then, after the cold, there might be mild days and nights for the next week.

Today, four days before Christmas, was the latter. After the recent cold spell, it turned warm and muggy with a lingering fog, and I stepped right beside a sluggish chicken snake on my way to the store. As the fog lifted, northward moving clouds obscured the sun which only shyly peeked out.

It was a busy day at the Westport Store. For most of the morning, folks wandered in and out, stocking up for Christmas. My two crates of satsumas, as well as the peppermints I'd bought, were popular at the store. Jingling coins and dollar bills filled my pocket.

The Irishman was in good form. The store's inventory was being whittled down, and that meant money in his pockets. He was in a reflective mood.

"Follow me out on the porch. I want to show you something. It's the Winter Solstice, shortest day of the year. It's a big deal in my home country." He pointed to a ridge to the southwest. "See how there's a gap with no trees on the horizon. That's called a solstice gap. Today the sun will set at its most southern point. That's where the gap begins. Starting tomorrow, the sun will gradually move higher in the sky until"—he pointed to the other end of the gap— "the summer solstice arrives in June. Then the sun will be at its extreme the other way."

"Who cut that gap in the trees?"

"I did. Near my home in Ireland, five huge rocks formed a line going down to the Atlantic. Each rock had an etched notch. On the Winter Solstice, you could stand behind the first rock and the notches would line up with the position of the setting sun. My da always took us to the rocks on December 21 to watch the sun set behind the mountains across the bay. I often wondered how someone had been observant enough to notch the rocks for the solstice."

"Do you miss Ireland?"

"There's things about it I miss, but this is my home." He pointed to the gap in the trees. "We don't have rocks here, so I made my own solstice gap."

"Why was the Winter Solstice a key day in the Irish year?"

"In our culture, which relied on growing food to survive, the solstice assured us that the days would slowly lengthen. Winter would lessen. We planned the days to plant from the solstice.

"Many times the days between December and April were when food became scarce in northern latitudes like Ireland. Sometimes people would starve. The solstice was a measuring stick as to how long before we could plant and begin storing up for another year."

I looked up to see an impatient customer. "I want to buy a dozen of those satsumas."

The Irishman waved and went out the door.

That afternoon things slowed down, and I was counting my personal stash when Uncle Rube wandered in. After laying his fiddle case on the counter, he returned with a bag of coffee beans and chewing tobacco. "How have you been, Miss Missouri?"

"I'm fine. How's your music playing?"

"Christmas is a good time for parties and no party is complete without good fiddlin'."

"Would you like a satsuma?"

"I believe I will." He carefully peeled it, slowly munching on each wedge.

"Uncle Rube, Can I ask you a question?"

"Shoot?"

"Did you have love—and family—at one time?"

He sat on an upturned nail keg. "Sure. I was born about the year of 1820. So, I'm right-near sixty years old. Didn't know nothing about my daddy. My mom never said." He held out his arm. "You can look at me and tell my father was prob'ly part white. Being mixed sure has caused me lots of trouble. I don't belong to no one.

"Anyway, Momma, me, and three siblings lived on that plantation. I guess things were all right. I didn't know they could be better but had seen worse. Belonging to someone else ain't no good. I'd always had this burning desire to be free."

"How'd you get free?"

"It took a war." He slowly filled and tamped his pipe before walking to the fireplace and using an ember to light it. "When I was about ten, the master sold my two brothers down the river to a plantation near New Orleans."

He puffed a long time before speaking. "It was a bitter day when they loaded those boys up on a steamer. I don't believe my momma ever got over that day." He shook his head. "I was twenty when they were taken away. When the War came to Lousianer twenty years later, everything changed. When the Yankees came through the Red River country, lots of slaves left their plantations and followed the Union army as they retreated toward New Orleans.

"I was a married man by this time. Me and the wife, Bernadine, had five children. Somehow in the confusion, we got separated. I spent several years searching for them up and down the river. Finally, I just gave up and moved on."

"Did you marry again?"

"No, ma'am. The War had ended, and I was now a free man. 'Cept I didn't have no family to share my freedom with. Had to learn how to be free." He cocked his head to the side. "But it was still a sweet thing being free. I was living near Colfax and saw some bad things happen, and that's when I decided to get out of cotton country. So I made a decision to be a wanderin' colored man in the Pineywoods, and this is where I've been for the last eight years or so.

"For a while I worked in a turpentine camp, but I found out I could make more money playing music, so I moved in and out of both the White folk and Redbone worlds. I play music for their dances, get-togethers, and weddings."

"Where do you live?"

"In a log house out on Steep Gully near the Turpentine Camp. I don't bother nobody, and nobody bothers me."

He picked up his tobacco and coffee. "I better be going. What do I owe you for the satsuma?"

"It's your Christmas present."

"I thank you kindly." I walked to the gallery edge with him. He took a deep breath and nodded at the ragged clouds. "I believes I smell rain."

A crow landed in the far corner of the yard scratching around the entrance of the grist mill. "Uncle Rube, do you believe in crows as an omen?"

"Sure I do. They can be good or bad omens. Omens can warn us." He scratched his gray beard. "And other times they guide us. Point ya to where you're going." He eyed me. "Why are you asking me this?"

I nodded at the lone crow watching us. "Look at that crow. How many does it take to make a murder?"

He wiped his hands on an old towel in his back pocket. "Just one. Kinda like Cain and Abel. It only takes one."

"One crow?"

"Nope, one man."

We stood there listening to the harsh caw-caw-cawing of the crow. As he stepped off the gallery, the first raindrops splattered on the old man's back. Uncle Rube untied his mule and rode in the direction of Sugartown. The crow took flight, circled the store a few times, and disappeared over the horizon.

The Irishman walked by and I said, "Do you believe in crows?"

"Those silly superstitions? No." He took a puff on his pipe. "In Ireland, a raven, a larger cousin of crows, got in a church house, and the people went crazy. They felt it was a message from the devil. They couldn't get it out, so they finally tore off part of the roof. Some parishioners never went back." He spat. "I've never believed in that foolishness over there, and still don't here." He glanced at me. "Do you?"

"I'm trying not to."

I left the store a little early and found a stump at the edge of the woods. I was under a stand of pines and only a few drops of rain made their way to my back. I hoped to catch a glimpse of the sunset on the Winter Solstice.

I popped a peppermint in my mouth and sat facing west. As if on cue, the clouds parted enough to view the sun as it slowly set exactly along the southern edge of the tree gap.

"My word, it just proves there is a God."

Lucky thumped his tail on the pine straw. I patted his head. "It's the shortest day of the year, so that means it's also the longest night of the year. Let's get home before the rain sets in."

CHAPTER 27

THE DANCE

Eve of Christmas Eve
Friday, December 23, 1881

The locals streamed in and out of the store on Friday with only one thing on their minds being tonight's dance. The host of the dance, Mr. H'arm Moore, had always been cordial with me at the store. I always gave him a peppermint when he came into the store, so he called me "Sweet." I felt pretty comfortable going to his house if Ruth was with me.

Mr. H'arm was also a first cousin of Simon Morrow. Simon was known by his nickname of "Whiskey," because he was the liquor agent for the Westport Store. He'd be busy at tonight's dance.

Right on time at 4:00, Ruth showed up in a pretty lacy dress at the store. I was ashamed of what I was wearing, but Ruth Wray wouldn't hear of me backing out. I'd already told my folks I'd be spending the night with Ruth, carefully omitting the part about the dance.

After the rain of the previous two days, the weather had broken off cold, so we hurried in the evening chill. It was right at dusk, and the planet Venus and a fingernail slice of the waxing moon stood above the trees.

As Ruth and I neared the lights of Mister H'arm's home, music and happy voices echoed off the pines. The gallery was already packed with young folks, and through lamp-lit windows, I could see couples dancing in the front yard.

In the side yard, a group of men circled a large pine-knot pile, passing a bottle and laughing loudly. As we passed them, my stomach tightened. "Ruth, are you sure I'm welcome?"

"Missouri, you're my guest. There's nothing to worry about. Besides, you look like one of us."

"What if your man, Frank Taylor, shows up?"

"He promised to stay away."

I shrugged. "I just know that I heard him say he might come."

Ruth laughed as we walked up on the large gallery. "He ain't that crazy."

The bare living room was wall to wall with dancing couples swaying on the rough cabin floor. Near the hearth of a large fireplace, Uncle Rube played his fiddle, tapping out time with his boot. He nodded at me as I walked by. Next to Uncle Rube was the most popular place in the house. The keg where bartender Whiskey Morrow busily exchanging red liquor for money.

I found a rickety cowhide chair beside where two large bull-dogged-faced women sat, surveying the dance floor.

Moon Perkins walked over. "Didn't expect to see you here."

I nodded at Ruth who was already on the dance floor. "Ruth invited me."

"I haven't seen you since the horse race."

I shifted on the cowhide chair. "The Outsiders are still saying your brother won the race by cheating. They claim your people cut the rein on their horse."

Moon took a swig from his bottle. "I was told your daddy did it. Anyway, where have you been?"

"I've been in Alex with the Irishman's wife. She's dying of Consumption."

"She's a good woman, and that's a bad way to die."

I whispered, "Who are the two bulldog women on the other side of me?"

"They're the chaperones for the dance, making sure nothing gets out of hand."

"It looks as if they're a little late."

"Don't underestimate them. In our culture, the women usually have the final say."

Moon sat his bottle down. "Will you dance with me?"

I glanced at the bulldogs. "Will they approve?"

He walked to the ladies and squatted in front of them. One of them eyed me, smiled slightly, and nodded.

Moon walked over and put his hand out as I stood shakily. "I'll warn you. I'm not too good at this."

Honestly, Moon Perkins wasn't much better than me, but we managed. When the song soon ended, he held on to my arm.

"How about one more?"

I leaned a little closer. "Sure."

Over his shoulder, I watched as Ruth danced with her third partner. So far there was no sign of Ruth's surveyor boyfriend, Frank Taylor.

On the third verse of this song, Moon stopped and stepped on my toe. I followed his glance to the front door.

Frank Taylor stood in the doorway.

"What's he doing here?" Moon said.

Even though Uncle Rube was still playing, most of the dancing couples had stopped and all eyes were on the intruder. Ruth Wray was the last person to spot him. When she did, she hurried from her partner and confronted Frank. "What are you doing here?"

As the crowd surged around Ruth and Taylor, Uncle Rube caught my attention and waved me over. "Somebody's got to get that fool out of here."

"What?"

Back in the huddle, Moon Perkins shoved himself between Frank Taylor and Ruth Wray. "Fellow, this ain't where you belong. I'd recommend you walk back out that door you just came in."

Taylor, whose false bravado was alcohol-fueled, said, "This is a free country. I got as much right to be here as anyone."

"These aren't your people. Leave." Perkins jabbed a finger in his chest and then pointed. "There's the door."

Suddenly H'arm Morrow stepped between them. "This is my house and my dance. If you guys want to tussle, take it outside."

Taylor looked around at the thirty or so folks surrounding him. He knew he'd walked into a hornet's nest, but he couldn't lose face. "I'll do what I …"

A smaller man shook Taylor by the shirt. "I'm thinkin' you'd better git on your hoss and ride, stranger."

Ruth Wray pulled on the man's arm. "Daddy, let him go."

In the midst of all this scuffling, I grabbed Frank Taylor by the arm, jerking him free from Ruth's daddy. Loudly, I said, "Frank Taylor, I told you not to come see me here."

The crowd turned toward me. Ruth's mouth dropped.

"Frank, the best thing you can do is walk me home. Right now."

Moon Perkins stood quietly. "You're leaving with him?"

I leaned toward Ruth. "Only to keep him from gettin' kilt." I roughly grabbed Taylor's elbow and led him away, whispering, "Don't say a word."

I turned to Moon. "I really enjoyed dancing with you."

He tried to bar my way. "Mizz, you've got to decide who you are."

"Maybe so, but not tonight." I hugged Frank Taylor closely. "Tonight I'm choosing him." I glanced back at Ruth, trying to sneak a wink. "I'm sorry to steal your man, but you had to find out sooner or later."

Her mouth moved but nothing came out.

I shoved a reluctant Frank Taylor toward the door, brushing past Moon as he tried to block our way.

The group of men around the campfire now had formed a narrow gauntlet at the gallery steps. I whispered to Taylor. "Don't say a word."

One of the men made an off-color remark that I wouldn't repeat in mixed company. Another said, "This is going to be a rawhide fight. Nothing but a rawhide fight will do."

I felt Taylor stiffen, so I got a new grip. "You've got to decide. Would you rather be a dead lion or a live dog?"

Once we cleared the yard, I shoved Frank Taylor as hard as I could. "You are a fool. You had no business being there. You promised Ruth you'd stay away."

"I just couldn't stand the thought of her dancing with all of these young bucks."

"Well, you were stupid." I picked up a stick in the road. By chance it was a thorn thistle. It cut my hand, but I figured it was just the weapon I needed.

"What's that for?"

I popped him across the hand, drawing blood. "You never know when you might encounter a varmint in these woods."

"Why'd you drag me outta there like that?" He waved his hand in the air. "After what you told Ruth, I'll never get this straight with her."

"I did it for her." I squared up to look him in the eyes. "You put her life in danger tonight. She would've taken a bullet or knife for you."

I steamed in silence for the next mile, until we came to the first crossroads. I pointed him toward where the surveyor camp was. "You go on home and get sober."

As I took the opposite fork, Frank said, "Where are you going?"

"Home."

"It ain't safe, you being alone."

"The farther I'm away from you, the safer I feel."

I hustled along in the dark, stumbling over several roots before reaching our wagon and quickly getting under the covers on my pallet. I didn't even take time to change clothes. I lay thinking for a long time.

In the nearby tent, Pap whistled his infamous dead-drunk snore. I heard Ma flouncing, so I eased out of the wagon into her tent.

She sleepily turned over. "I thought you were staying with that friend of yours."

"I was, but things got out of hand."

"You didn't walk back here by yourself, did you?"

"No ma'am. I had a good chaperone." I lay beside her. "Ma, I'm in the middle of a mess. Do you know what a rawhide fight is?"

"Never heard of it."

"It's what folks around here call a fight to the death. There's going to be a rawhide fight here with the Outsiders."

Ma pulled me close. "Tomorrow's Christmas Eve. There won't be trouble then. It's the birthday of the Prince of Peace, so I bet the peace will hold." She brushed the hair out of my eyes. "Why don't you sleep in here with us tonight? It's gonna be all right. Tomorrow's a brand new day."

That made sense. I drifted off to sleep, tired but hopeful.

BOOK TWO – FIGHTING

The horse is made ready for the day of battle, but victory rests with the Lord.
– Proverbs 21:31

CHAPTER 28

THE DAY OF BATTLE

Christmas Eve
Saturday, December 24, 1881

I woke early the next morning, still ill at ease about the events from the dance. After feeding Tom-Claws some clabbered milk, I hurried to work. I wasn't confident that Frank Taylor had enough sense and sobriety to inform the Irishman about the threats from the dance.

The Irishman was sitting on the store porch. He removed his pipe. "G'mornin' and Merry Christmas."

"And the same to you, sir." I sat by him. "I heard some talk at last night's dance."

"About what?"

"Trouble about ambushing folks coming to the store today."

The Irishman relit his pipe. "I had a late visitor, Uncle Rube, who made it very clear. He made the rounds all night warning folks of a planned ambush at Chinnapin Gulch. The Ten Milers planned to surprise folks on their way here to Christmas shop. 'Ol Rube saved a bunch of lives."

"What do we do now?"

"Just go about our business and stay calm. After you organize the fabrics, I want you out on the gallery watching for trouble approaching."

I spent most of the morning working in the corner of the store where the pretty things for women were. A few customers trickled in, but the warnings had evidently scared away lots of folks.

The shoppers who did come in were in a friendly mood. Christmas Eve was a special day, whether one had much money or not. There might not be a lot of presents, but most everyone would get a piece of fruit, peppermints, extra food, and time together. The Irishman had made sure we were well-stocked with lard, flour, salt, and whiskey. Especially lots of whiskey. Additionally, the Irishman had also stocked up on firearms and ammunition during his recent Alexandria shopping.

Buck Davis, who'd been the losing jockey in the horse race, liked hanging around the store. He was kind of oily and always had a big chaw of tobacco. He hung around on the front porch, which at this moment I was sweeping clean.

A wagon pulled up to the hitching post, and I recognized Gordon Musgrove. Tying his team to the rail, Musk bounded up the steps as if he owned the place. He was tall and rangy with a full head of hair that was beginning to turn whitish gray. He never wore a hat, which was tied to his vanity about his thick dark hair.

Buck Davis leaned on a post. "Mornin' Musk."

At this exact moment is when Moon Perkins, with a new coiled bullwhip in his hand walked out of the store.

Musgrove, who evidently knew Moon Perkins was behind him, loudly said, "Buck, you got cheated on that horse race. If it'd been me, I would've gotten that money or whipped Worm Perkins."

Moon, holding his bullwhip, stepped up. "Well, maybe you want to try and whip his brother." He unfurled the whip and seemed poised to strike Musk. But in one quick motion, Moon dropped the whip and charged Musk, and the two men collided like angry bulls. It was a typical No Man's Land fight—not a lot of talking or arguing—just two men content to let their fists do the talking.

A mixed crowd of Ten Milers and Outsiders gathered in a semicircle and watched the fight from the porch, yard, and doorway, each side egging their man on.

Musk, being a timber man, was extremely strong and fought aggressively. Moon Perkins, who actually outweighed Musgrove, fought with a craftier strategy. Both circled each other trying to keep their backs to the building so no one could trip them or jump in.

As they charged each other, the sound of fist on bone and muscle resounded. Soon each man was breathing heavily.

Moon used his heft to score punches to his opponent's face. After one hard lick, Musk fell against the store wall but sprang back with a kick of his heavy boot. It caught Perkins flush on the jaw, staggering him. When Perkins stepped toward the gallery edge, I initially thought he was going to run, but he swung around the gallery post and used his momentum to bull-rush Musk. Moon clasped the timber man around the waist and using his head as a battering ram drove his opponent hard into the plank floor.

There was a loud thud and it was clear Musk had had the wind knocked out of him. Moon used this to his advantage, straddling Musk and pummeling him in the face. It was pretty clear at least from Musk's side that this fight was over. Moon had an animal-like ferocity as he struck him over and over.

I glanced around at the onlookers waiting for someone to stop Moon Perkins from beating Gordon Musgrove to death.

The Ten Milers, urging their man on, had no desire to stop the fight. The Outsiders stood frozen. The only movement was a younger man drawing his pistol. This fight appeared on the edge of bigger trouble.

It was then that John Watson, the most feared man in this part of the woods, stepped in. He'd evidently ridden up after the fight started.

Watching him gave me the hen flesh. He had a dangerous quality about him. He had reputedly killed several men and was a crack shot with the .45-caliber long rifle he always carried. Watson handed that rifle to a man and took two steps before landing a well-placed kick that knocked Moon Perkins clear of his victim. Perkins skidded across the gallery and turned to see what—or who—had stopped his triumph.

Watson with hands on his hips stood at the porch's edge.

Moon reached in his pocket but before he could do anything, Watson grabbed him by the shirt, and slung him out into the yard. Moon landed about ten feet away, between the gallery and hitching rack.

John Watson pointed. "You stay there until I tell you to move."

Amazingly, Moon obeyed.

The Irishman, who had watched all of this from the doorway, brushed past me and knelt beside the semi-conscious Gordon Musgrove. "Looks like that bad fall knocked the wind out of Gordon." He nodded at one of the men. "Ride over to Doc Hamilton's house and fetch him."

Just then, Doc Hamilton rode up.

Joe Moore called out, "Doc, it's good to see you. We need your help."

Musk, slowly getting his breath back, tried to speak but could only gasp. Doc leaned over him and told him to relax.

I glanced around the yard and saw the backs of the Ten Milers as they rode or ran into the woods. Behind me, someone said, "They'll be back."

After examining Musk, Doctor Hamilton stood. "He's taken a bad beating but should survive. Most of all, he's had the breath knocked out of him. A few minutes should make that better."

The Irishman nodded, and Dr. Hamilton and John Watson followed him into the store. They gathered in a far corner of the store in deep discussion. This situation was evidently much more serious than I realized.

I stood on the porch watching Gordon Musgrove trying to clear the cobwebs in his mind. Out in the yard Moon sat sullenly with arms across his knees. A few of his clan watched from the shelter of the trees.

The crowd on the gallery were all Outsiders and began moving toward Moon as they made threatening remarks. Moon Perkins sat quietly, evidently less afraid of the crowd than he was of John Watson.

The three cool-headed men—Watson, Dr. Hamilton, and the Irishman—walked out to the porch. The Irishman motioned. "Moon, get up and come inside."

Moon didn't move, instead glancing at Watson who nodded. Perkins got to his feet and followed them into the store.

Dr. Hamilton put a hand on Moon's shoulder. "You go upstairs and keep quiet and away from the windows. We'll see that you're safe and get you out."

Once again Moon looked to Watson for confirmation. The man nodded. "Do what he says." As Moon stood, the circle of Outsiders around him broke up. Still upset at the beating Moon had given their man Musk, they returned to the bar to drown their disappointment.

As he went upstairs, Moon reached in his boot. He glanced back and our eyes connected.

I suddenly remember a saying Ma often used when things lined up a certain way and fate took over. I walked to the Irishman. "The stars are in their courses."

"Huh?"

"The stars are in their courses. Events have started that none of us can control."

He put his hand on his hips. "This thing is long ways from over. You keep busy out here, and if anyone approaches, come tell me." It was quiet—maybe too quiet—and from time to time I sensed movement in the pines.

Suddenly, someone whispered from around the corner of the building. "Missouri. Missouri White-Cotton." It was Unk. This was the closest I'd ever seen him to the store. "You need to get out of here now. Trouble's coming." He stepped onto the gallery and grabbed my sleeve. "Git out of here now."

I jerked away. "I can't. I've got a job to do."

"Everyone in and around this building is in danger. Please leave." His voice trembled. "Please leave. Now."

"I'm not leaving." I grabbed my broom, turned my back, and went to sweeping. When I turned, Unk was limping away into the pines. I'd never seen him move so fast.

About thirty minutes later, a lone man rode out of the pines. I didn't recognize this older man, and as he neared I noticed the rifle held across his chest.

I tapped on the window to Dan. "Tell your daddy we've got company."

The Irishman stepped out onto the porch.

I slipped beside Dan. "Who's the rider?"

"It's Old Tom Perkins." He nodded upstairs. "Moon's father. He's come to get his son that we're holding hostage."

"Hostage?"

"That's the way the Ten Milers will see it. Doctor Hamilton's trying to protect him from that mob at the bar, but that's not how Old Mr. Tom will see it."

"Why do y'all call him 'Old Mr. Tom?'"

"It's a term of respect," Dan said. "He's the head of the Perkins clan. It's similar to how we call old-timers 'uncle or aunt.'"

Old Mr. Tom dismounted slowly and tied his horse. He didn't seem to be in any hurry, but his face was taut. Still cradling his rifle, he walked onto the porch. "I'm here to get my boy."

The Irishman motioned him inside. As they brushed by, I followed them into the store. The crowd drinking around the bar fell silent when they saw Old Mr. Tom with his rifle. Dr. Hamilton greeted the older Redbone politely. "Mr. Tom, let's talk over here."

Old Mr. Tom Perkins, Dr. Hamilton, and the Irishman eased to a vacant corner of the store. I heard snatches of the conversation as Dr. Hamilton calmly said, "We've got Moon upstairs for his own protection. As soon as we can, we'll slip your son out the back door," he nodded at the bar, "without that crowd knowing it."

Dr. Hamilton poured a glass of wine from a nearby keg and offered it to Old Mr. Tom. "Where do you want your son to meet you?"

Old Mr. Tom Perkins spoke through gritted teeth. "This ain't no time for drinking. You people done pushed my boys around too much. Nothing's going to settle this but a rawhide fight." He turned and strode across the plank floor for the door. The crowd at the bar crowded the doorway as Old Mister Tom climbed on his horse, drove his spurs into the mount's flanks, and wheeled away. A crowd of Ten Milers awaited him near the stand of pines. Perkins rode among them gesturing wildly toward the store. When he finished, the men melted back into the woods.

Dan stepped up beside me. "They'll be back."

"Why don't you just let Moon go?" I said.

"It's too dangerous now. We lost our chance at a peaceable outcome at the start. Should've got him out of here as soon as the fight ended."

"Where's Gordon Musgrove?"

"He's lying in the back of his wagon. I'm going to take him home directly." He took my arm. "Missouri, it's time for you to leave."

I touched his shoulder. "I'm not going anywhere … without you."

"Missouri, this is gonna get out of hand. Get out while you can."

I crossed my arms.

He shoved me. "Mizz, people are going to die here today."

"Then that's more reason to stay with you."

He grabbed me around the shoulders and manhandled me toward the steps.

I stiffened. "I'll just sit in the yard. I ain't going nowhere without you."

Dan released me. "I can't make you go, but I can beg you."

"I'm not going."

"I believe you're the most stubborn girl I've ever met."
"That's probably true."

CHAPTER 29

STUCK

Christmas Eve

When Dan huffed back inside the store, I went back to my sweeping, keeping a weather eye for trouble. The next half hour passed quietly as arriving customers, unaware of the trouble, hailed each other with holiday greetings and good wishes. They hurried out of the cold and into the store's warmth.

I went in to warm myself beside the fire. It was easy to sense the trouble spot at the bar. About six Outsiders, all friends of Gordon Musgrove, were getting holiday drunk; their anger over Musk's beating intensified by the alcohol. They talked loudly about what should be done to Moon Perkins.

I moved to the counter, where Hamp Dykes, one of our regular customers, had stacked a two-foot-high pile of items.

"Some Christmas shopping, Mr. Hamp?"

"Yep, I've got some timber money in my pocket. The wife and kids are gonna have a Christmas to remember."

I pointed to my dwindling supply of satsumas. "I bet your family would enjoy some fruit."

"I'm sure they would. Add a dozen to my order."

I totaled his purchase. "Merry Christmas, Mr. Hamp, to you and your family."

"Same to your'ns."

I walked with him to the doorway as he peeled a satsuma and tossed a slice in his mouth. "That's sweet."

We both froze at the sight of three armed Ten-Milers approaching the store in a hurry. Old Mr. Tom Perkins was in the middle. Simon Morrow was to the left, and a third man, rifle at the ready, was on the right. The way they all carried their rifles revealed malicious intent.

The fact that the men were carrying long rifles wasn't unusual. This was gun country, and few men went anywhere unarmed. What concerned me was how they carried their guns at the ready, as well as the briskness of their approach. They stepped up on the front stoop, where the Irishman met them at the doorway in a friendly but alert way.

Just then, a French man, by the name of LaCaze, left the store with a bag of feed over his shoulder. Simon Morrow leveled his shotgun at LaCaze's chest. The Irishman leapt between the two men, moving the shotgun aside. "Whiskey, don't do it."

The Ten Miler, his face a mask of hatred, leveled his gun at the Irishman's face. "Out of my way."

The Irishman grabbed the gun barrel, forcing it down. "Simon, don't do this. Not here. Not today."

LaCaze heavily dropped his bag of feed and retreated back into the store. The Irishman, never taking his eyes off Simon Morrow, walked slowly backward, hands in the air, before joining LaCaze inside the store. The store's double doors slammed with a thud, and I heard metallic grating as the bolt slid shut and they were barricaded in ... and I was stuck outside. Talk about No Man's Land—that's where I was. Or rather, it was No-Woman's-Land at the moment.

The three Ten Milers—Perkins, Morrow, and the mystery man—stepped off the porch. Mystery man raised his shotgun and blasted the front door, scattering splinters all over the porch. It left a washtub-sized pattern of buckshot on the wood frame.

The siege had begun as a steady rain of potshots rang out from the woods, thudding into the thick pine walls. Lucky whimpered beside me, and I petted him. "It's going to be all right. Hopefully they're not shooting dogs or girls."

Suddenly, a rifle fired from the store window not a foot from my left ear. The concussion was deafening. A piece of pine bark exploded from a tree about fifty yards away. I knew a .45 caliber rifle when I heard it. The shot had come from Watson. His aim was true, and the attacker behind the pine ran for safer ground—or in this case, a bigger tree.

This unleashed a return of clattering fire from the woods.

Staying on the gallery wasn't an option. I had two bleak choices. run away into the woods and hopefully free passage to our family's campsite or get inside the store. I surveyed for anything I could use as a white flag.

I was an outside Outsider. Ironically, the other outsiders were inside the store. My knees went weak just thinking about the tempting target I'd be as I ran the gauntlet between the store and the woods.

On all fours, I crawled to the front door. "Open that door. Let me in."

A voice grunted. "Who's out there?"

"It's me, Missouri. I work here."

"Too dangerous."

I begged to no avail then scooted back to my shaded spot in the corner and hunkered back down. Lucky edged closer, paws over his head.

A squad of men using the pines for cover edged toward the store from two sides. I was in an exposed spot and staying there was no longer an option.

I knew from the store inventory there was plenty of ammunition to withstand an attack. The store was a fortress that wouldn't be easily overrun. However, the Ten Milers had the advantage of free movement plus the cover of the woods.

My motive for getting inside the store, come hell or high water, was Dan Moore. I thought about calling for him but didn't. If he came out to rescue me, he'd be an easy target. I wasn't quite sure which side the Moore family was on in this scramble, but anyone moving about was fair game.

A few minutes later, I heard Dan's voice. "Missouri, are you out there?"

I steeled myself not to answer.

I heard groaning near the porch. Gordon Musgrove, still punch drunk from his thrashing, had slipped out of his wagon and was crouched behind the water trough. He motioned me toward him, but I shook my head. "Musk, you've got to get inside. If they find you out here, you're dead."

He seemed too addled to move.

I was just as scared but knew staying on the gallery was a dead end. I slipped along the side of the store, careful to stay away from the windows, which were both giving and drawing the most fire. Eyeing the woods, I felt that I could run this gauntlet away from the store and back to our wagon.

An advancing number of Ten Milers approached the store.

Suddenly, Old Tom Perkins appeared from around the corner and raised his gun at me.

I raised my hands and stood. "Mr. Tom, it's me. Missouri Cotton. I work in the store."

He lowered his gun. "Girlie-Girl, you gotta decide if you're gonna run with the rabbits or hunt with the hounds. Which side are you on?" He then motioned for me to move.

I took a deep breath and ran. Feet don't fail me now. On my first step, I tripped over Lucky. The hound whimpered before lunging back under the porch. Regaining my balance, I crouched and ran, trying to make myself as small a target as possible.

But I didn't run for the woods. Instead, I raced around the store, headed for the back door. A voice called from the trees, "Don't shoot. It's just a girl."

Rounding the side of the building, I bumped into a man squatting beside some barrels. It was the jockey, Buck Davis. He grabbed for me. "Stay here. It's safer."

I never slowed, instead sprinting for the back door. Just as I arrived, a pistol shot sounded from inside, followed by the deeper report of a rifle. I bounded onto the back gallery and jerked on the door. "Let me in." Of course it was locked tighter than Dick's hatband. I pounded. "It's Missouri. Missouri Cotton. Let me in!"

I put my ear to the door and heard shouting followed by two more shots. Suddenly the door flung open as a bullet whistled past my ear. Moon Perkins tumbled out knocking me down and causing me to hit my head hard on the gallery edge. Woozily, I looked up at Moon who was bleeding from his left arm and held a small derringer in his right. "Moon, what's going…"

His face and the slate sky spun and then things went black.

CHAPTER 30

THE SIEGE

Christmas Eve

I woke with a pounding head and rattling gunfire echoing around me. I looked up at the ceiling, realizing I was in the store. Someone had wedged me between two towering heaps of flour sacks. Whoa, I was inside with the Outsiders.

As my head cleared, I tried to remember how I'd got there. Slowly, my footrace and collision with Moon flashed through my brain. I tried to remember why I had run to the store instead of following Old Mr. Tom's command to flee for the safety of the woods.

I sat up and surveyed the store. Dan and Will Moore sat behind the counter beside their father who watched out the window. As I studied them, I realized the Moore family was the reason I'd chosen to get inside the store instead of fleeing to the woods. These people had become my family in my Ten Mile sojourn. Being with them inside the Hatch and Moore Store might not be the safest place to be, but it was where I knew I belonged.

Just past the Moore's, Doctor Hamilton, dapper as always, peered out the edge of another window. John Watson stood on the other side of the same window, bracing his big rifle against the window frame.

The Frenchman LaCaze sat by a window on the other end of the store. Sam Nolan, a local farmer who'd also been caught inside the store, sat on an overturned washtub, smoking a cigarette.

A timber man named Sanders with a bloody bandage on his leg and pistol in hand, crouched and moved from window to window on the back side of the store.

Frank Taylor the surveyor held a shotgun in one hand and a whiskey bottle in the other. He was getting royally drunk, and his shaky hands made me wonder how much help he'd be. I feared he was a greater threat to accidently shoot one of us than an attacker.

So there were ten of us, counting yours truly, inside the store. All of them except me, Dan, and Will sported full beards and had the look of men who'd spent most of their lives outdoors and knew how to handle a weapon. All of them, with the possible exception of the surveyor, were Civil War veterans.

I wondered how many attackers were outside. From the sound of the gunfire, it was a whole lot more than ten.

Frank Taylor, between slugs on his bottle, first noticed me. He slurred loudly, "Hey, Sleeping Beauty's awake." Taylor nodded at the Irishman. "You sure we can trust her?"

I cut him off. "I saved your sorry hide last night, and you're questioning my loyalty? I'm in here because I want to be." I glanced around the room. "All of the rest of you got caught inside. I chose to be here. Before this is over, you'll be glad I'm here."

The Irishman walked over. "Well, Missouri, you put yourself right in the middle of a mess."

I smoothed my skirt and brushed the hair out of my eyes. "It seems so, don't it?"

"You should've left while you could, but now that you're here and if you're up to it, you can help out by keeping us watered."

I knelt shakily. "I'll help where needed."

"Just stay low and away from the windows."

I crawled over to where Dan and Will sat.

"I told you to leave," Dan said angrily.

"Well, I didn't."

Will crawled closer. "Did you see Moon Perkins?"

"He knocked me down when he bolted out. He was bleeding. What happened?"

"Daddy planned to let him go, but some of the other fellows wanted to hold him as a bargaining chip. Evidently he had a derringer and shot his way out." Will pointed at Sam Nolan, who had a blood-soaked bandana on his leg. "He grazed Sam."

"I saw him reaching in his boot as he went up the stairs," I said.

A bullet whizzed through the window passing just above our heads. We all ducked and Will scooted closer to me.

John Watson from his side of the window said to Doctor Hamilton, "They're fighting like Marion men. Many of the grandfathers of the Redbone men shooting at us served with Francis Marion in the Carolinas during the American Revolution."

"Who's Marion?" I asked Dan.

"Francis Marion was called the Swamp Fox. He and his ragtag army fought off the British with a small army using guerilla-style attacks. Joseph Willis and several of the early Redbone men who came with him were proud of being Marion Men. They'll snipe at us all day, then try to overrun or smoke us out tonight."

I rubbed my arm wondering if my dark skin and being a girl would make a difference if they overran the store.

I was among a quorum of white Outsiders who were the rabbits in this battle. That's how I felt. Like a hunted rabbit.

The hounds, the Redbones, had us surrounded.

A steady volley of fire came from the pines, answered by single shots from the windows of the store. Sam Nolan motioned to Will Moore. "Bring me another shot of that whiskey."

Will rolled a bottle toward the thirsty fighter. Will winked at me. "Dan and I are kind of the official bartenders."

I caught a sound that made me feel sick. Caught between the shooters on both sides were the horses hitched to the rack. They were whinnying in fright and struggling to break loose. All of the shooting had spooked the five of them. Two were tied to Musk's wagon, and three more saddled mounts were next to them. One of them, blood streaming down its flank, had caught some shotgun pellets and was in great pain and panicked, which affected the other horses, too. It angered me that these innocent animals were caught in the middle of a feud started by two stupid groups of humans.

I scooted over to a side wall, which seemed safer than being out in the open part of the store. I heard voices outside, and it chilled me to the marrow as I listened. A man in a shrill voice was begging for his life. "Please don't shoot me. I ain't got no dog in this fight. I'm not even armed. Just came here to get Christmas supplies." It was Hamp Dykes, the last customer I'd served before the shooting broke out.

The sharp crack of a rifle was followed by silence. I put my ear against the wall and heard only low moaning. Footsteps approached, followed by the horrible repetitive sound of a blunt object cracking bone. Someone was beating him.

The moaning stopped, and I thought about those crows. I crawled toward Dan. "Somebody just killed Hamp Dykes."

"How do you know?"

"I recognized his voice. He was my last customer before the fighting broke out."

Dan shook his head. "Missouri, you should've listened to me. This is no place for you."

"I did what I had to do."

"You shoulda listened." He took a swig of whiskey, then wiped his mouth. "There's two things I don't like, and both of them are women who won't listen."

"I listen when I should. There was no way I was leaving you in here alone."

"I'm not alone."

"That's not what I meant. I chose to be here by your side."

I squeezed beside him. "Do you think we'll get out of this?"

"It's gonna be tough sledding."

I sighed. "Let's at least call a truce between us."

Before he could answer, a shotgun blast resounded from the other side of the store. Dan and I crawled to the nearest window and saw a body lying in a widening circle of blood in the dust. It was Old Mr. Tom Perkins. He'd caught a full load of buckshot as he came around the side of the store.

By the window, Frank Taylor took a long slug of whiskey, then reloaded his shotgun.

"He's dead," I whispered.

Dan shook his head. "You live by the sword. You die by the sword."

Because Mr. Tom's death happened in front of the store, all the Ten Milers saw it. This changed the skirmish to a loud bombardment.

"It's now truly a rawhide fight—a fight to the death," Dan said.

Moon, from a vantage point near an outbuilding, had evidently witnessed his father's death, and this resulted in him making fearless charges toward the store, dodging from tree to tree. It looked as if he was on a suicide mission.

I crawled to my earlier peephole to have a better view. I could see Gordon Musgrove still hiding behind the water trough, and this shielded him from the firing from both sides.

Moon had evidently spied Musgrove on an earlier charge and

now saw the opportunity to finish the fight that had started on the store porch. He raced to Musgrove and fired several pistol shots into him. Looking up, he then shot into the window and fled.

Musk's body convulsed with each shot, then Moon ran back to his outbuilding corner. Three men had died in the span of five minutes. I wondered how many more were destined for the same fate on this Christmas Eve.

The Irishman scampered to my spot. "What was that?"

"Young Perkins just kilt Musgrove. I saw it through this hole."

Peering through the hole, the Irishman said, "I can't see much."

Watson, from his window vantage point, said, "Musk is dead."

From my knothole, I studied Musk's body carefully. At first, I thought it was only my imagination, but it appeared Musk's chest moved. I also saw a tiny wisp of frosted breath in the cold air. "He's still alive."

The Irishman leaned over taking my place at the knothole. "He's not moving."

"I saw his breath, and where there's breath there's life."

Dr. Hamilton took his turn at the knothole, then glanced skeptically at me. "Appears dead to me."

"I swear I saw his frosty breath."

A nearby bullet splintered wood near us forcing us to move away.

"That was close," the Doctor said as he, the Irishman, and Watson huddled together.

"The girl swore she saw him move and detected breath," Doctor Hamilton said.

"We've got to help him," the Irishman said. "He's bleeding to death."

"I'm not positive he's even alive," Dr. Hamilton said. "Besides, if we send a man out there, they'll cut him down, and then we've got more of a problem."

I raised my hand. "I'll go."

CHAPTER 31

THE RESCUE

Christmas Eve

I stood there feeling foolish. My hand still in the air. The Irishman glared at me. "Mizz, be quiet, and stay out of the way."

When I refused to move, he tossed his head toward the window. "Missouri Cotton, go over there and keep an eye out the corner of that window."

As I reluctantly crawled away and sat between Dan and Will, I realized the Irishman had never called me by my full name.

For the next few minutes, there was obvious disagreement among the three leaders over whether, and how, to rescue Musgrove. Finally, the Irishman stepped away from the group. "Dan, you and Will come over here."

A chill rushed over me as the Irishman said, "I need one of you to go out there and see if Musk is alive."

Dan stepped forward. "I'll do it."

The Irishman handed him a white rag. "Unbolt that front door."

Dan stepped to a shelf and pocketed a small mirror.

I barred the doorway. "They'll shoot him."

"We can't just leave Musk out there," the Irishman said.

"But Dan's your son."

"He volunteered."

"No, he didn't."

Dan shoved me out of the way. "I volunteered." He slipped sideways through the slightly ajar door.

I watched through my knothole as he knelt in the dust by the prone timber man shaking his shoulders. He then took out a small mirror and held it near Musgrove's mouth. Just as a shot splintered the Hatch and Moore sign that hung on the gallery edge, he turned toward the door, nodded at his father, and bounded back inside the store. "Da, he's alive. He fogged the mirror."

"Are you sure?"

"He groaned when I shook him."

Dr. Hamilton, Watson, and the Irishman reconvened in the corner of the store. Dan took Will by the arm, and they walked over to the men. "Da, Will and I will bring him in."

I grabbed Dan's arm. "I can't let you go out there again."

He was embarrassed, but I didn't care. "They'll shoot you. You heard that shot."

"That was just a warning shot aimed for the sign."

"But the next one might be aimed for you or Will."

"Missouri, move out of the way." Dan took a deep breath. "I've got to do this. I'm gonna do this. Will, are you with me?"

"Every step of the way, Brother."

Everyone watched as the two brothers eased out the door. What they didn't see was me grab a knife off the counter, tuck it in my waistband, and slip out the cracked door as they bounded off the porch.

Dan and Will, crouching low, ran to where Musk lay. Dan grabbed Musk by the shoulders while Will struggled with the big man's legs. They hadn't noticed me until I grabbed Musk's other leg. Dan cussed me all the way up the steps as the three of us dragged Musk to the door. When we reached the doorway, I let go, pulled my knife, and ran back into the yard.

The panicked horses had continued their whinnying and snorting all morning. Slipping behind the hitching posts, I cut the reins of the saddled trio and whacked them on the withers. Then I quickly dropped the trace chains on the wagon pair, hollering and whooping as they loped away.

A shot echoed nearby, and I wasn't sure if it was incoming or outgoing. Crouching, I zigzagged my way toward the store entrance. "Hold that door open!"

When Lucky heard my voice, he charged out from under the store and bounded into the store between my feet. This tripped me, and as I fell, the knife, which was in my right hand, sliced my leg as pretty as you please. I was bleeding like the proverbial stuck pig, and all of the men thought I'd been shot. They dragged me over by Musk. The Irishman and his boys knelt around me.

"Where are you hit?"

"I'm not hit. I'm cut." I held up the knife.

"Girl, you truly are a pistol," Doctor Hamilton said.

Dan stood, his hands shaking. "I need a shot of whiskey."

Will, gasping for breath said, "I need a clean pair of pants." Even in our dire situation, everyone had a good laugh.

Everyone laughed except Dan, who shook me by the arm. "You are crazy! You coulda been killed!"

"But I wasn't."

The Irishman stood over me. "Moxie. It's what you are. It's who you are. It's probably gonna get you killed, but you've got a full dose of moxie."

The rough board floor was blood-streaked from where they'd dragged Musk inside, and the blood from my cut was mingling with his.

Doctor Hamilton worked over him. "We don't have much time to waste." During this, the Ten Milers peppered the store with shot and slugs as if to remind us we were still in the middle of a siege.

Doctor Hamilton, who was clearly now in control, said, "The rest of you need to watch at the windows in case they rush us." He pointed at me. "You help me with Musk." He glanced at my wound, then threw me an old shirt. "Wrap this around your leg. You'll need stitches, but first we've got to try to save Musk."

They'd laid him by the stack of flour sacks. His face was gray, and blood pooled on a wound in his upper leg.

"He's bleeding out." Doctor Hamilton motioned to me. "Get over here and help me."

Now, I'm no Florence Nightingale, but I was willing to help any way possible. I usually fainted flat at the sight of blood, but something took a hold of me and I felt no fear or dizziness. The good doctor dressed Musgrove's numerous wounds as I tore a tattered sheet into strips. The worst wound was in his right thigh which continued to ooze blood.

Doctor Hamilton worked feverishly. "It must've clipped an artery. Find me a belt or rope."

Will, standing behind me, pulled off his belt. Just as he did, he fainted and fell against the flour sack, slowing sliding to the floor.

Doctor Hamilton laid the belt beside Musk. "Mizz, "If he keeps bleeding, we'll use this tourniquet. He'll lose his leg, but we'll save his life. For now, you keep pressure on his leg." He placed my hands over the wound and showed me how to use my body weight as a pressure point. "Keep a tight grip and don't let up for nothing. "I'll go take a look at the surveyor."

During the hullabaloo of Musk's rescue, Frank Taylor had caught a shrapnel splinter right below his eye. He was bleeding badly, and being really drunk, was screaming that he was dying.

Musgrove was the one who appeared dead, but I kept pressure on his leg. When I got a new grip and pressed on the leg wound, he groaned and an eyelid flickered. In spite of my efforts, he was still bleeding. The deep red blood spurted between my fingers with each beat of his heart. We were losing him. I looked at the belt but couldn't move. If I took my hand off his leg, I felt sure he'd bleed out before I could position the belt. Besides, I had no idea where to put it or how tight to apply it as a tourniquet.

Suddenly I knew what I must do. Something I'd vowed to never do. I glanced around to make sure no one was watching, then I removed my hands off his leg. The spurt of the blood nearly made me faint, but I couldn't stop now.

I didn't completely remember the biblical verse Ma used to staunch bleeding. It came from Ezekiel, and I'd tried to memorize it. In this desperate moment, I tried my best to recite it. "And when I passed by thee, and saw thee polluted in thine own blood, I said unto thee …Live; yea, Live." I wasn't much on praying. "Lord, I probably ain't saying the words right, but heal this fellow as only you can. Amen."

Musk was still bleeding. As I reached for the belt, "Jesus, if you can, and I believe you can, stop this bleeding. Save Musk's life." I put the belt around his thigh, but before I could notch it, the blood flow ebbed.

I was sure he'd bled out and was dead. I took his pulse in his neck and found the faintest of heartbeat. Suddenly he sighed deeply and didn't take another breath. I was sure he'd died. But he slowly began taking shallow breaths. The bleeding had stopped, so I covered him with a horse blanket to his waist.

In a few minutes some color returned to Musk's cheeks and his breathing picked up. I was shaking and was the most tired I'd ever been. I plopped down between Musk and Will and closed my eyes.

Suddenly, Musk grabbed my arm. I tried to jerk away, but he had me in a death grip.

"Can you hear me?" I said.

His eyes tried to focus on my face. I knelt beside him, peering over the flour sacks to make sure no one was within earshot. I glanced at Will. He was still out.

I leaned down in Musk's ear. "Mr. Gordon Musgrove, I don't know you from Adam's housecat, and you're not a real good man, but I'm convinced even the worst of men can change. I'm not sure what happened with your leg, but somehow or another God stopped you from bleeding to death."

In my fertile imagination, I saw the bishop handing the candlesticks and silver to Jean Valjean. Son, I've bought your soul for God.

I peered into his glassy eyes. "Listen here, you're going to live and be a different man. You're going to be a man of God."

Musk tried to mouth words, then released his grip.

Someone coughed to my right, and I glanced up to see Dan, arms folded.

"What's wrong with my brother?"

"Little too much blood for him." My eyes narrowed. "What'd you see?"

"I couldn't tell or hear, but it looked like a serious conversation."

"You should've told me you were standing there."

"Look, I just walked up." He frowned. "His leg's quit bleeding. What happened?"

"I'm not so sure I know."

He nodded at Musk. "I thought for sure our buddy would be dead by now." He took a knee beside me. "You did something to him. What was it?"

"I prayed for him, that's all."

"And you think that's why the bleeding stopped?"

I shrugged. "I figure God stopped the bleeding."

"Sure, but I suspect he used you to do it."

I stared at my bloodstained hands. "All that matters is that Musk is gonna live."

Dan scooted close enough that I smelled the whiskey on his breath. "Word around Ten Mile is that your momma is a faith healer and can stop bleeding and even cure burns."

"It's true she's got gifts." I grabbed him hard by the shirtsleeve. "But you remember this Dan Moore, I ain't my momma." I started crying. "Promise me you won't say anything about this to anyone."

"If that's what you want, I won't." He shook his head. "Missouri, I don't quite know what to make of you." He stood hurriedly, picked up a rifle, and resumed his watch near a window. Periodically, he glanced my way where I sat huddled by Musk and Will. Gunfire continued to pepper the store. Suddenly, all I wanted was to bolt from this store, run home to Pap and Ma, and sleep for the next three days. I closed my eyes and leaned against a flour sack.

Doctor Hamilton nudged me awake with his boot. Looking at me with the belt in my hand and Musk covered with the horse blanket, he angrily said, "I thought I told you to keep pressure on his leg." He knelt by Musk. "Is he dead?"

I shook my head. "The bleeding stopped."

Pulling the blanket back, he inspected the wound, and then eyed me. "What happened?"

"I'm not sure. I just know he stopped bleeding."

Dan stood behind Doc. He held his finger to his lips and winked.

Doctor Hamilton opened his bag. "Well, let's get your leg stitched up."

During the tumult of the past hour, I'd nearly forgotten about my wound. He removed the blood-caked bandage, and my long slice began bleeding again. "It's going to hurt."

I looked away. Up to now, I'd handled the blood fine, but seeing my own dizzied me. I winced as he stitched from my knee toward the ankle. Trying to ignore the pain, I said, "Some kind of Christmas, huh?"

Doctor Hamilton sighed. "Kind of ironic that this is happening on Christmas Eve. Nearly on the birthday of the Prince of Peace."

"I wonder if Christmases will ever seem the same after today."

He grimaced. "We need to survive this Christmas before we worry about future ones."

"What happens next?"

"Hopefully we get out of here alive. If we do, we'll need to clear out of this country. It won't be safe for any of us."

I pointed at the Irishman. "What about him?"

He shrugged. "You'll have to ask him. He was brave enough to start this store past the Dead Line. I'm one of his partners, but it'll be his decision whether to stay or throw in his chips."

He tied the last stitch. "Fourteen stitches. That was pretty brave, or stupid, of you going out there."

"I did what I had to do."

He smiled. "Pistol, I guess you did."

CHAPTER 32

THE LONGEST DAY

Christmas Eve, 4:00 p.m.

Although the solstice was only three days past and the daylight hours were short this Christmas Eve, it seemed as if the sun would never set. It reminded me of the Biblical story where Joshua was fighting some pagan tribe, and God made the sun stand still.

Of course, darkness wouldn't improve our situation at the Westport Store. The Ten Milers had freedom of movement and knew how to operate at night. A full-throated charge would probably overrun the store just like at the Texas Alamo.

Tom Perkins and Hamp Dykes lay dead in the yard. Gordon Musgrove lay five feet from me clinging to life. There were probably more dead or wounded in the trees. I put my head in my hands. How were Pap and Ma? Where was Unk? Was Miss Eliza safe?

The Irishman, sensing my fear, sat on the floor by me. He pulled out the weathered compass. "Why don't you hold this for a while? You showed a while ago you've got the mettle."

"Mr. Joe, I don't quite understand that word, *mettle*."

"What did you call me?" He shifted on the rough planks.

"Mr. Joe?"

"You've always called me the Irishman. I've never heard you call me by my name."

"Is that all right?"

He smiled. "I'd right prefer it. It sounds a lot more …" he glanced away. "It just sounds more personal." He quickly stood. "And *mettle*. It's just like the other word I use for you, *moxie*. It means you're tough and have grit."

I held out the compass. "This is yours."

"Why don't you keep it until this is over. I always rub it in my pocket when I get a little nervous; it might help you in the same way."

Without another word, Mr. Joe Moore went back to his lookout spot near the west window.

At this point in the fight, the attacks had concentrated on the front side of the store. John Watson, who had coolly assumed command of our outpost, had placed shooters at the two rear windows. The shots became sporadic. Were our besiegers running low on ammunition or saving it for a nighttime assault? Inside, we had plenty of ammo and food but were store-bound.

Watson's calm nature seemed to galvanize the rest of us. He took a position with his .45 rifle, and using the window frame to brace his gun, he began sniping at those hiding behind trees. Each shot brought flying bark or a yelp of pain.

From the trees came a series of yelping, whooping, and the shrillest noise I'd ever heard. It was a combination of the Ten Miler men and their women. The women were yipping with what Mr. Joe called "keening."

The men were yelling what I knew to be some kind of battle cry. The men inside the store gazed at each other. John Watson grinned. "Been a long time since I heard the Rebel Yell."

Doctor Hamilton stepped to the window. "It always sounds a lot different in battle than on a fox hunt."

"They're fixing to charge us." Watson directed each man to a specific shooting point. "Remember to aim low and make every shot count. There's a lot more of them than us, but we've just got to stem the tide and break their momentum."

With that, the yelling intensified and I watched a staggered line of Ten Milers charging the store. Watson turned to the men at the back windows. "Keep a watch for a flank attack." Just then a shot threw splinters all over the frame he was aiming from, forcing him to move to a new firing position.

The Ten Milers had the numerical advantage and the momentum, but it's difficult to make a full-throated assault while stopping to shoot. Additionally, dusk had shaded the store windows making it difficult to see Watson and the others. Because the charge was from the west, the attackers were silhouetted against the horizon. John Watson went to work. His steady aim seemed to slow the attack in its tracks.

One of the Ten Milers, who was braver than the rest, had advanced ahead of the others using the trees, posts, and wagons for cover. It appeared his plan was to flank us, and then fire at close range through one of the windows. However, his aggression outweighed his caution. He stopped and was caught in a crossfire of rifle and shotgun blasts. As the attacker crumpled to the ground, his gun went off, tearing a large hole in the ground. The man never moved.

Mr. Joe went to the window. "My God, it's Whiskey." Simon "Whiskey" Morrow had been Moore's friend and business partner in supplying the thirsty Baptists in the area with strong liquor. He had also been the one who pointed the gun in both LaCaze's, and then Moore's face, at the outset of the fight.

Now he lay dead at the corner of the Hatch and Moore store.

The store defenders glanced around. At least three of them had fired, but it was unclear who had killed Whiskey Morrow.

John Watson stepped to the center of the store. "Men, it don't matter which of us fired the fatal shot. He put himself in a position where we had no choice." He leaned his rifle against the counter. "But our story will be that I did. I live across the river and it'll be best if I'm blamed for it.

Out in the trees, the attackers had watched their bravest man and leader shot down. There was much yelling and the shrill sound of the women keening as the attack broke down. As they retreated back into the woods, a silent sadness permeated the store. All of us were glad to be alive, but each of us knew Simon and considered him a friend.

Mr. Joe said, "It's a lot different killing someone you know rather than a stranger. That's the sad part of a feud. There's a familiarity that makes it personal."

Will handed all of the men a big shot of whiskey. He handed the last glass to John Watson. "Where'd you learn to shoot like that?"

"Shooting Yankees."

"That's some kind of shooting."

"Just like anything else. You do it enough, you get better."

"It was a stupid war. A rich man's war and a poor man's fight. When I found out late in the War about the substitute rule, I packed my things and went home."

"What was that?"

"If a man had twenty or more slaves, he could send a substitute soldier in the place of himself or his sons. That did it for me."

"You deserted."

"No, I just went home."

Two pieces of buckshot shattered the wall not a foot from Watson's head.

He didn't flinch, but I hunkered down, and said, "You didn't seem scared at being hit?"

"Girl, I believe in fate. A bullet won't get you unless it's got your name on it. They ain't made the bullet yet with my name on it."

I shifted against the flour sack. *Famous last words.*

He added, "Besides, most of them were shooting shotguns and old rifles not as accurate or effective from the trees. That's why I was determined to keep them at a safe distance."

It seemed as if Simon Morrow's death and darkness took the fight out of both groups. Sporadic firing continued, but began to peter out as darkness fell.

Esther the cat, seemingly unfazed by the noise and shooting, purred against my leg.

Mr. Joe, his bag against a molasses barrel, sat forlornly. Trying to make conversation, I asked, "You were in the siege at Vicksburg?"

"Yep. Seldom saw who we were shooting at. Thought we'd starve to death. Toward the end, we ate rats." He glanced at Esther. "We were in competition with the stray cats."

"What's rat taste like?"

He winked. "Kind of a cross between possum and squirrel. Word was that some of the men ate cats and dogs." He nudged his cat. "Esther, if this siege goes on long enough, we might have you for Christmas dinner."

I made a face like I was gagging, not letting on that in tough times our family had dined on all of the above. I changed the subject. "Mr. Joe, what did you do at Vicksburg?"

"Oh, I was in the Quartermaster Corps. Supplies and food. By the end of the siege, we didn't have nothing to give out. We just lived in dug-out caves trying to avoid the mortars and snipers."

"When General Pemberton surrendered, I was relieved. No Yankee prison camp could've been worse than the siege. But ol'

Unconditional Surrender Grant fooled everyone. He didn't ship us north as prisoners. He paroled us."

"What's that?"

"We had to sign a paper swearing not to take up arms against the United States of America. By doing so, we received a paper parole granting us safe passage across the Mississippi River and back home. Lots of the men took the parole and went home, but I reenlisted and was back in the thick of it."

"It didn't bother you that you lied?"

"I didn't feel that it was a lie. I'd used my father's name when I signed. I should've taken my parole and gone home. I was wounded near the end of the War." He sighed. "After being gone for a year and a half, I was just thankful to make it home. Times weren't easy, and they never will be, but this is my home."

"After today, will you be able to stay?"

"Will I . . . or can I?"

"Both."

Tears filled his eyes as he glanced around the store rafters. "We've put everything we have into this store. I don't see how I can just walk away. I promised myself that I'd stay here until I turn up my toes."

"But if you stay, you might be turning up your toes a little earlier than needed."

"You've got a good point."

After a long, uncomfortable silence, I said, "Were most of these men in the War?"

"Yes."

"What about the Redbones?"

"Most of them were smart enough to stay out. They viewed it as a White Man's War and didn't see much sense in fighting for rich people to keep their slaves. So most of them sat it out. But not all; they're a fighting people. You heard those Rebel Yells. It wasn't their first time." He sighed. "That whole war was a lost cause."

I glanced around the darkened store. "Is this store a lost cause?"

"We'll see."

In the distance, horses clattered away, followed by a searing silence.

The siege was over. At least for now.

CHAPTER 33

DARKNESS

Christmas Eve, 6:00 p.m.

With darkness and the apparent withdrawal of the attackers, a new terror gripped us. The Redbones had a well-earned reputation as guerilla fighters and were adept at using the cover of darkness for bushwhacking. We blew out the lanterns, not wanting to pose a silhouette for any assassin lurking near the porch.

Watson, Doc, and the Irishman talked over our situation. "They'll be back tomorrow," Doctor Hamilton said. "We've got to get Musk out of here."

Watson peered out the window. "I suspect there's several of them just waiting for us to come outside."

"I'm most concerned about my wife," the Irishman said. "I can't stand the thought of her being at the house alone, wondering what's become of us."

"Da, do you think they'd hurt her?" Will said.

"Probably not. Her being a Redbone will protect her, but it's a known fact that her husband and two boys were in the store with the Outsiders. My biggest concern is that they'd hold her hostage to smoke us out."

Watson placed his rifle on the windowsill. "Speaking of smoking out, I wouldn't be surprised if they don't set fire to the store and outbuildings. That's why we need to stay alert and shoot at anything that moves outside."

I sat against my flour sacks and closed my eyes as the men continued. Dan came over and sat by me. "Well, we're stuck here for now."

"Looks that way."

"I've been thinking about your book, '*The Miserables.*' Tell me about that part where they build the barricades."

"The radicals, now including Marius, Cosette's lover, build barricades in the center of Paris. They use carts, wagons, anything to block the Army's advance. The one manned by Marius and his friends are on a narrow street. It is a long night as they listen to the tramp of infantrymen approaching and the rolling of cannon wheels over the cobblestones."

"What happens next."

"That's how *Volume Four* ends. I don't know what happens next."

"Kind of like where we're at right now."

I glanced around the store where I'd spent so many hours in the last three months. "I guess this is our barricade."

Finally, John Watson stood. "I've got cabin fever from being cooped up in here. I'm going out to see for myself." Doctor Hamilton followed him out the front door.

We sat in silence and waited for shooting or voices, but there were none until we heard Watson. "If there's anybody out here, speak your peace. We'd like to bring your dead to you." He repeated this several times, and the only response was a barred owl in the distance.

The rest of us headed for the door. I helped Frank Taylor to his feet, not sure if I'd ever seen a fellow drunker than he was—not even Pap. We left Musk propped up against the flour sacks and made our way toward a lantern light at the side of the store, where Doc Hamilton stood over Hamp Dykes' body.

It wasn't a pretty sight, and I immediately wished I hadn't seen it. He gripped the bag of satsumas I'd sold him. "I was the last person to talk to him."

Doc moved the lantern away. "He just had bad timing."

Four of the men loaded Hamp Dykes onto Musk's wagon.

I tripped over an object in the dark. It was Moon's bullwhip. I picked it up, twisted its coarse length in my hands, and handed it to the Irishman. "Moon dropped this when the fight started."

"Go put it behind the counter. I'll keep it for when, or if, I see him again."

We all slowly ventured out to where Simon Morrow and Old Mr. Tom lay. If an ambush awaited us, it would be here.

It was ironic that the two men lay within three steps of each other. As Doctor Hamilton held his lantern over their faces, it broke my heart to see these two men torn to shreds by buckshot. I didn't view them as the enemy. They were simply men who'd been pushed into a corner and, right or wrong, felt that the only way out was a rawhide fight. That's exactly what this battle had been for them. A fight to the death.

No one said a word as we stood in a semicircle around the men. I felt a deep sadness that this day, and their deaths, had forever changed this area we called Ten Mile.

As we returned to the store, I glanced at the waxing crescent moon low in the west, knowing it would set by midnight. Raggedy clouds passed over as Watson said, "I feel a change in the weather. I smell rain."

It seemed fitting that this Christmas Eve would end with a change in the weather. It didn't seem like a good omen.

The men sat on the gallery and discussed how reinforcements were needed to break the siege. There was a severe split in opinion of whether to send for help to Hineston or Sugartown.

Watson said, "Hineston 's closer, but I'm not sure they'd send help across the Dead Line. Sugartown's our best bet."

Sam Nolan spat. "Who will we send?"

Despite the darkness surrounding the circle of men, I could easily see each of them avoiding eye contact. Dan stood beside me, and I stomped his boot and whispered, "Don't even think about it."

Mister Joe turned to Dan. "Son, I need you to go fetch Uncle Rube. Stay in the dark and go to the Turpentine Camp. Get Rube and bring him here." He turned to the others. "Uncle Rube can get through safely to Sugartown."

I didn't like Dan leaving one bit but held my tongue. The next hour was long, and after what seemed like forever, we heard someone singing a slightly off-key version of "Silent Night."

The Irishman held up his hand. "Don't worry, it's Uncle Rube." Like a ghost, the old fiddler appeared astride his mule with Dan leading them.

Dr. Hamilton walked directly to Uncle Rube. "We need someone to ride to Sugartown and bring help. Are you willing to go?"

"I'll do my part to help. You'se already know that."

"We do, and that's why I sent for you." He handed Uncle Rube a folded note. "You go straight to the Sugartown post office and ask for a deputy named Cole. Wake him if he's asleep, and give him this note. No one but him should see it."

The Irishman turned to Will. "Son, go saddle up the roan for Uncle Rube. He's got a long night ahead of him." He turned to Uncle Rube. "You think you can make it through?"

"I've got my fiddle. If I'm stopped, I'll just say I'm headed to a Christmas dance."

"When they realize later that you went for help, things may get hot for you."

"I've got friends in Sugartown and will probably hang around for a few days, if you can spare your horse."

"If you send us help, you can keep it."

With no further word, Uncle Rube rode off into darkness down the Sugartown Road, singing the second verse of "Silent Night" in time with the clank of the lantern.

"Da, I'm sure glad he plays fiddle better than he sings," Dan said.

"Oh, he sings well. This is his mock-drunk singing. It'll let them know he's coming.

Dan sidled up beside his father. "You think he'll make it through?"

"He will." He glanced at the moon just above the treetops. "With luck, relief will arrive by later afternoon."

"What then?"

"Who knows? Our priority is keeping this thing from getting worse."

The rain began in earnest and brought another kind of chill with it. When Mr. Joe headed to build a fire inside the store, Watson put out a hand to stop him. "Many a person's been bushwhacked sitting beside a fire. It makes a tempting and easy target."

So we sat miserably inside the dark store. I huddled over near Gordon Musgrove, who was still unconscious but breathing better.

I finally dozed off to sleep and awoke to the men talking in the dark. "Someone's coming." I sat up and could hear the clattering sound of a horse approaching from the direction of the attack. Whoever it was didn't seem in a hurry nor care about making noise.

"It may be Uncle Rube, and he couldn't get through."

Watson, bracing his rifle against a gallery column, took aim.

As the horse clopped along, the rider whistled off tune. I didn't recognize the song but sure knew the whistler. I scooted to Watson. "Don't shoot. It's not one of them."

"Who is it, then?"

I tapped Watson. "It's my pap."

He didn't move his rifle. He said to him, "Are you alone?"

"Yep."

"Light a match. I wanna see your face."

A struck match illuminated the rough visage of my father. I expected to see drunk Pap. That's about the only way a man would ride into the aftermath of The Westport Fight in the dark.

As he alit from the horse, he shook, but it wasn't due to alcohol. Right now, he was a sober Pap. In fact, he was the soberest man in the vicinity of the store. He walked over to me and surprisingly hugged me. "Missouri, are you all right?"

"I'm fine. How'd you get here?"

"When I heard about the trouble, I feared you were in the middle of it." He struck a match and held it near my face. "You sure you ain't been hurt?"

"No, I'm fine."

Mr. Joe came forward. "How'd you get through?"

"A flag of truce." He held up a white shirt. "It usually worked well in the War. And besides, after the horse race, they consider me one of their Confederates."

"You were in the War?" Mister Joe said. "Whose side were you on?"

Pap blew out the match. "Fellow, I fought for whichever side was winning and had hot food and a dry place to sleep."

He belligerently poked Mr. Joe in the chest. "I hold you personally responsible for putting my daughter in danger."

Doctor Hamilton stepped between them. "Now, Mister ..."

"The name's Cotton. Henry Cotton." He turned on the doctor. "And whoever you are, I blame you, too."

"I'm Doctor James Hamilton."

"I don't know you from Adam's ox, but I still blame you." Pap nodded back into the woods. "Those fellows you're fighting let me through to get my daughter. They also said they wanted a ceasefire to remove their dead."

"That's fair enough," Doc said. "We've already moved them to the edge of the woods along the Sugartown Road."

Pap took me by the arm. "Missouri, I'm taking you home."

Doc stood beside our horse. "Why don't you stay till daylight. It'll be safer then."

"The quicker I can get Missouri away from the likes of y'all, the better. Besides, I didn't come through their lines alone. There's an odd-looking man with a limp waiting out there to lead us back."

Mr. Joe smiled. "Unk Dyal."

Pap shrugged. "They seem to all trust him. He said he'd take us back to our wagon."

Pap took me by the hand, but I broke loose and ran back to Mr. Joe, handing him his compass. "I believe this belongs to you."

"Did it help you?"

I grinned. "Sure did."

Pap helped me onto the horse, and as we headed toward the woods, he cupped his hands. "Ceasefire. Ceasefire on both sides. Attend to your wounded."

I'd never been sure about Pap's repeated stories about the Civil War, but he sounded like a man who knew the language of soldiering. "Pap, what did you really do in the War?"

"Everything and nothing."

"You sound like an officer."

"I was for a little while."

"You were an officer?"

"I impersonated one for a few days in late '64. It worked really well until I ran into a little trouble over selling cotton bales commandeered by the Union. Those Yankees stripped my rank, but it didn't matter. I was just borrowing the uniform."

We passed by where the bodies were laid out. If I hadn't known better, I'd swore they were sleeping, not dead.

Unk stepped out of the shadows. I reached down for his hand. "Thanks for helping."

He tipped his hat and put his finger to his lips, and then led us down the road toward a campfire located at the skirmish line from where the Redbones had staged their attack. A knot of six men stood around the fire. As we approached, they retreated into the trees.

Pap led the horse around them, but I pulled back on the reins and dismounted, walking over to the men. I didn't recognize any of them. "Your dead are lying beside the trail about fifty yards back. Unk and I will take you there."

Pap tried to grab my arm, but I pulled away. "Let it be. I need to do this."

When we reached the spot where Old Tom and Simon lay, several of them wailed. I'd never heard anything like it. Where I was from, men didn't cry. But Redbone men were strong, and they were never afraid to show any emotion, including tears.

I recognized Moon as he knelt over his father, sobbing. I leaned down, touched him on his bandaged arm, and softly kissed him on the cheek. "Moon, I'm so sorry."

He roughly pushed me away. At the same time, I remembered Moon had killed an innocent man, Hamp Dykes, in cold blood at the beginning of the fight. Everything about this day was complicated. There were no simple explanations or lines in the sand between the right and the wrong.

I wondered if over time Moon would blame himself for what happened.

Pap had followed us through the darkness and clutched my arm. "You've seen enough. Let's git home."

I stopped for one last glance at the grieving men. Here I was among the very men who'd been shooting at me all day, and all I felt was sympathy. I thought of that Scripture, "They sowed the wind and reaped the whirlwind." It was true on both sides. No one had won today. Men had died over nothing but pride and stubbornness.

Unk walked up. "I'm staying here. Y'all will be safe."

Pap led me on the horse deeper into the woods. It was a long time before the crying faded. This Christmas Eve in Westport was anything but festive. The few home places we passed shed no light. No lanterns or fires burned. Folks went to bed in the dark not wanting to be a silhouette target for a sniper or a bushwhacker.

As we crossed Cherry Winchie Creek, I said, "Pap, that was a mighty brave thing you did."

"I had to make sure you were all right." He hesitated. "Baby, I know I don't seem worth much as a father, or grandfather, but me and your Ma were worried sick about you. I would've walked through burning hell to get to you."

"That's kind of what it was like. Burning hell." I shivered as a chilly wind blew. "Thanks for coming."

A flock of geese honked in the far-off north. We reached our campsite just as the first few drops of rain splattered on the canvas of our tent.

Pap held up his hand. "Weather's changing. I smell ice in the air."

"Everything is changing," I said. I wasn't sure how long I lay awake, reliving a day I knew I'd never be able to forget.

I woke to gunfire in the night. Terror-filled, I grasped darkness, unsure of where I was. "Ma. Pap. Help me. They're shooting at me."

Ma put a hand on me. "Mizz, it ain't gunfire. It's an ice storm. Those are pine limbs popping due to the weight of the ice."

A shot rang out followed by a limb crashing to the ground. I shuddered as I tried to find sleep again.

CHAPTER 34

THE SADDEST CHRISTMAS

Christmas Day, 1881

As Christmas Day dawned dreary, cold, and miserable, Ma brought me a hot cup of coffee. A tent's not a good place to live in winter. They'd built a small pine-knot fire in the tent, and it smoked up our living space while giving off precious heat.

Ma redressed my knife wound and rubbed some herbs and cream over the stitches. "That was a bad cut."

As I drank my coffee, Ma pestered Pap, "We need to put up a lean-to or some permanent shelter. We've been in this Ten Mile country about as long as we stayed anywhere."

Pap looked up from the half-empty bottle he was steadily draining. "Our days are numbered here. We'll be pulling up stakes 'fore the week's over." I hated to hear it, but knew it was the truth. This was no longer a safe place for Outsiders, and in spite of our skin color and new friendships, we were counted with the whites.

Christmas is supposed to be the happiest day, but on this day, even the pines hung their heads in sorrow. Everything looked so different with the rain frozen on every tree, limb, and building. Icicles, something we seldom saw this far South, hung from everything. As the morning passed, the sun came out, and soon the icicles began dripping. It was as if all of Ten Mile was weeping over yesterday's events.

There would be no joy in Ten Mile that day. Everyone had lost someone or something. I'd lost a little innocence or naivety.

Ma finished her third cup of coffee, and as was her habit, slung the dregs into the fire where they sizzled. "I knew those crows were a sign."

"Ma, do you really think those crows were a premonition of

what happened at Westport yesterday?"

"Seems to me they were. Baby, birds are often sent to warn or guide us. It's not only true of crows, but hoot owls, mockingbirds, and such."

Pap overheard her crow talk and was ready for an argument. "Those birds didn't have nothin' to do with it. Quit filling the girl's head with that hogwash." It was never a good sign when they started off the day arguing. It meant storm clouds were on the horizon, and lightning would strike later that day.

"Henry, I want to go back east. Back to civilization."

"We ain't going nowhere until I say so, and when we do, it'll be to Texas."

"You act like getting to Texas will make everything great. It won't be no different, 'cause we'll all be the same."

Pa kicked an empty bushel basket, sending it against the canvas roof where it ripped a hole. He'd reluctantly used some of his horse race winnings to get the tent and wagon roadworthy. Now there was a tear in the tent roof. Without a word, he stepped out into the cold.

"And worst of all Henry, you'll be the same." Ma screamed. "A sorry drunken excuse for a man."

I was glad Pap didn't hear that, or he chose not to respond. Ma's flushed face fell to one of sorrow as she pulled me close. She stroked my hair. "I was worried about you."

"I was worried about me, too. I thought I was a goner a time or two. It was mighty brave of Pap coming for me."

"He was worried 'bout you." She paused her stroking and looked in my eyes. "He does care about you."

I turned away. "He sure has some strange ways of showing it." I stopped as Pap crashed about near the wagon. "I like the sober Pap a lot better than the drunk one."

"Me, too." She craned her ear. "But I'm afeared the drunk one will be with us today."

"Ma, I'm so tired of drifting."

"It's our lot." She stared into the fire. "At least for now."

"But it doesn't have to be mine."

"You're right." She took my hand in hers. "You're a fine-looking young lady. Your life can be a right bit better than what you have now."

"I want some roots."

"Then make sure you hitch your wagon to the right star. I pray for a better life for you."

I pulled my hand from hers. "Ma, I want yours to be better."

She folded her hands. "I'm afreered it's too late for me."

I sat up straight. "I saved a man's life inside the store yesterday."

She glanced up. "How so?"

"A fellow named Musk was bleeding to death from a gunshot wound. I took what I'd learned from you, and the bleeding stopped."

She lowered her voice. "Did anyone see you do it?"

"I think the oldest Moore boy came up and saw the end of it."

"Baby, be careful. Folks often don't know how to take that gift."

"Yes, ma'am, I saw it in Dan Moore's eyes. He wasn't sure what had happened but looked at me like I was some kind of freak."

"It goes with the territory."

"Then I don't want it."

"It's not a choice you make. It's a calling. It's a gift that you've been given, and you can't refuse a gift like that."

"I'm not sure it's a gift or a curse."

"Like I said before, it can be both."

I stood. "Ma, Unk Dyal is coming here later. He's taking me to the house of one of the men who was killed."

"Why would you want to do that?"

"The dead man's name was Dykes. He was the first one killed, and he'd bought some gifts for his children. When they moved his body, I picked up the bags of gifts, and I want to deliver them. Will you go with us?"

"How far is it?"

"About a thirty-minute walk down Cherry Winchie."

"I don't know about being out in this weather."

I glanced out past the tent flap. "The sky's clearing. Come with me. The walk'll do us both good."

"I'll go with you." Ma stood and worked at tidying the tent. She turned to me. "This family we're going to see. Are they White?"

"Yes'um."

"Will we be welcome?"

"I hope so. I'm waiting until Unk Dyal arrives. He promised to walk me toward the Dykes' place."

"Then I guess I'll go with you."

Unk showed up about mid-afternoon. "I've got news on two fronts. Firstly, six armed riders arrived an hour ago from Sugartown. They're guarding the store until things cool down."

I smiled. "So, Uncle Rube's mission bore fruit. What's the other news?"

Unk lowered his voice. "Solounge LaCaze made a visit to Har'm Morrow's place."

"Who is LaCaze?"

"He's a Creole rancher and the most respected man in these woods. His younger brother, Louis, was trapped in the store with y'all."

"Anyhow, Mr. Solounge LaCaze saddled up and rode to Har'm Morrow's house."

"Unk, how do you know this?"

"Well, I slipped along kinda quietly and saw it all." He nodded outside. "Let's get going, and I'll tell you the rest about LaCaze's visit."

Unk, Ma, and I began our slippery journey toward the home of Hamp Dykes. Their homestead was on the edge of the Ten Mile country. The ice was melting, but small trees remained bent in bizarre shapes. The ground under the big pines was littered with broken limbs. I shouldered the bundle of things Hamp Dykes had bought as we made our way.

"Unk, the younger LaCaze is the one the Irishman saved when he stepped between him and Old Mr. Tom Perkins's shotgun."

Unk put up his hand. "This is my story to tell. Anyway, early this morning the elder LaCaze rode by himself to the Morrow place. I don't know if the men were home or not, but only the women came out on the porch.

"LaCaze sat on his horse, rifle astride, and proceeded to tell them that if another white was harmed, they'd answer to him. I was close enough to hear Sister Morrow answer, 'We want peace, too,

Mr. Solounge.' ”

"Then he said, 'And peace is what we'll have.' With that, he turned his horse and rode slowly away."

"Were the men there?"

"I believe they were in the house but don't know for sure. The bottom line is that the message got delivered real clearly."

"Do you think the truce will hold?"

"I think it'll hold long enough for folks like y'all to clear out."

"Clear out?"

"Yep. Leave. Every Outsider here would be smart to get out quick. It probably won't be another open assault, just a matter of knocking off a person or family one at a time. Bushwhacking on the road. Burning folks out. It's best for y'all to get the jump on 'em."

As we neared the Dykes's cabin, I stopped at the sight of a group of White men gathered on the gallery edge, smoking and talking. They stopped when they saw us. Some children playing with a wagon hoop in the yard, stopped, watching our approach.

Unk stopped. "This is as far as Unk goes. I wouldn't be welcome in their yard. I hope y'all will."

Ma and I walked along the picket fence to the gate. One of the men cradled a double-barreled shotgun and broke away from the group to meet us at the gate. "What are you people doing here?"

I set my bundle on the fence. "I've got something for the Widow Dykes."

Mr. Shotgun barred the gate. "We don't need the likes of you 'round here."

Ma tugged on my sleeve. "Let's git."

I held up my hand. "Sir, we're not from here."

"Then who are you?"

I opened the gate. "I work at the Westport Store and sold Mr. Dykes some items just before he was killed. I thought it only proper to bring them here to his family."

A voice called from the porch. "Worm, these women are fine." It was Dan Moore. "The younger woman was with us during the fight."

A group of children gathered around me. One pulled on my sleeve. "Some bad men killed my Pa."

"I'm sorry, honey. I was there."

A pretty woman stepped from the porch. "You were at the

store?" She was much younger than Hamp Dykes, but I knew by her manner, she must be his wife.

"I work there. I sold him these things." I handed the sack toward her. "They belong to you."

She stepped through the crowd of men and took the sack. She didn't open it. Instead, she carefully studied Ma and me.

I stepped closer. "My name's Missouri. Missouri Cotton. This here's my ma, Beulah. We live up Cherry Winchie in a wagon."

"Oh, so you're the wagon girl who works at the store." She motioned us to the porch. "I'm Deborah Dykes. You ladies come in out of the cold."

Mrs. Dykes led us into the sitting room. Dan took off his hat as we entered the house. The first thing I saw and felt was the roaring fire in the fireplace. The heat of the room made me lightheaded. I hadn't eaten or drunk much in the last two days and was pretty dehydrated.

Hamp Dykes, fitted out in a white shirt and overalls, was laid out in a wooden coffin balanced on two sawhorses. Deborah Dykes led Ma and me to the coffin, which I recognized as the type sold at the store.

Ma put her arm around the widow. "He looks just like he's asleep."

Deborah Dykes winced. "He looks at peace, don't he?"

It was evident someone had worked hard at preparing his body. He looked a lot different than when we'd moved him last night.

The widow turned to me. "You talked to him afore he was kilt?"

"I helped him pick out the items for your children's Christmas. Look in the bundle."

She opened the bag and lovingly held each item. The four children crowded around and eagerly took their gifts. I'd forgotten that Dykes had bought some of my satsumas. They rolled out of the bag onto the floor and scattered across the room.

A wrapped package was in the bottom of the sack. Deborah Dykes tore it open and pulled out a calico dress I'd helped her husband select. She held it closely. "Where in the world did he get the money to buy all of this?"

"He told me he'd sold a bunch of timber near West Bay and kept it as a surprise for your Christmas."

She began weeping, and Ma embraced her. "I'm so sorry."

Through tears, Deborah said, "I rue the day we crossed the Calcasieu and entered this God-forsaken land. They warned us we were crossing the Dead Line." She nodded at the coffin. "And that's what it was for Hamp. That."

Ma stroked her hair. "What will you do now?"

"Clear out of here as quick as we can. I've got family up the Red River near Boyce. They'll take us in."

Ma kept petting on her, and I briefly worried she was going to pull out one of her spells or chants. But she was practicing a different kind of healing. comforting a young woman whose life had fallen apart. She was just loving on her, and that's what that poor woman needed right then.

I'd come here with trepidation. not sure of our welcome or the wisdom of bringing these gifts. However, right now I believed coming here was one of the best things I'd done in a long time.

Deborah lifted her head from Ma's shoulder. Tears streaked down her face, and she wiped at them with her tattered sleeve. "Tell me what he said in the store…"

"He was right excited about these gifts and how they'd be a surprise. It was evident he was mighty fond of you and the kids. He named each one as he picked out their gifts. Wanted each one of you to have a satsuma."

A commotion rose on the porch, and Deborah excused herself and stepped outside. I peeked outside and saw one of the men collaring Unk. He shoved Unk towards the widow. "We caught this one sulking around out by the road. I don't know what he was up to, but it weren't no good. Tried to run but Skunk Miller here chased him down."

It was Unk, and they manhandled him. I stepped out onto the porch. "That's my bodyguard, Unk Dyal."

"But he's one of them."

Dan, who was evidently welcome among this group of Outsiders, said, "He is, but he's my great uncle. Unk's a peacemaker. If he'd been there yesterday at the store, Mr. Hamp Dykes would probably be alive right now."

The fellow who had Unk by the collar said, "But he ain't right. I can look at him and see that."

Dan put his arm around Unk. "Maybe not, but he's got the purest heart there's ever been."

I turned to Widow Dykes. "Unk, this is … this is Mrs. Dykes."

She nodded in his direction. "You can call me Deborah."

I took Unk by the arm. "Her husband was one of the ones killed yesterday."

Unk stepped forward, released my arm hold, and hugged the woman. "I'm right sorry for what happened. I been praying for you."

Deborah Dykes led us back into the front room. Unk, hat in hand, stood a long time in front of the coffin.

"Did you know my husband?"

"I don't think so," Unk said. "How long have y'all been here?"

"Less than a year."

Most of the men from the gallery had crowded into the room. Everyone's eyes were on Unk and the Widow Dykes. In his simple way, he asked about her children, her farm, and the plans she and her husband had had. He knew just what to do and say. Just as important, he seemed to know what not to say. He was simply Unk Dyal.

I don't know if it was the heat of the room or what I'd been through, but I suddenly felt as if I might faint. "Please get me a chair to sit down in."

Deborah helped me over. "Honey, you feel hot to the touch."

"I think I just need a glass of water." The children gathered around me, and I was embarrassed being the center of attention, but this family was determined to lavish love on me. I was the last link between them and the man in that coffin.

Ma fanned me with a bonnet, and I whispered, "Don't do none of your magic on me. I'm fine."

Unk looked out the window. "Your bodyguard says we better git going if we're going to beat dark."

As we eased to the door, the children crowded around. "Merry Christmas."

Deborah Dykes nodded. "It's all right."

I hugged them. "Merry Christmas, children. Merry Christmas." I hurried away, no longer faint. Instead, I felt as if my heart was going to burst.

Our party of three walked silently down the creekside trail. Finally, Ma said, "Missouri, I've never been so proud of you." She turned to Unk. "And I'm a pretty good judge of character. You've got some healing ways, too."

"It's all from God."

We neared our wagon, where Pap sat under the lantern. Unk stopped. "I'd best be getting on." He took my hand. "I'll come by tomorrow morning. We're burying Old Mr. Tom Perkins at Occupy. Do you want to go?"

"Should I?"

"It's important that you be there."

Ma watched Unk fade into the pines. "I believe that little fellow is as strange as they come."

I nodded. "Strange, but good."

CHAPTER 35

GRAVEYARD DEAD

December 26, 1881

The day after Christmas had clear skies with a raw, blustery, cold wind. Although the ice had melted, it could still be felt in the air.

Unk met us early that morning, tipping his cap to Ma. "Ready to go? They're carrying Mr. Tom's body from his home place to Occupy."

The sun was low on the horizon. Unlike other places we'd lived farther north where ice or snow might stay on the ground for days or even weeks, here, it usually melted as quickly as it fell.

I nodded at several spindly pines bent over from the ice. "Unk, will those trees straighten up?"

"Hard to say. Some will. Others will always bear testimony to the ice storm by their shapes. Kind of like people, and how they react to trouble and trial."

Ma shook her head. "This place gives me the creeps."

Unk stopped and looked at Ma. "You don't care for Ten Mile?"

"Saw nothing but trouble when we entered this country." Ma pointed at me, "She likes it here."

I kicked a pinecone into the ditch. "I did until two days ago."

"I guess'um we're kind of like these trees," Unk said. "We'll take the storms and then do our best to straighten back up."

When we came within sight of the Perkins place, Ma hesitated. "Mizz, do you really think it's best—?"

"Ma, you're a Melungeon woman. They consider you part of their clan."

"Are you sure about being here?"

"I believe so." I took a deep breath. "I can't explain it, but I need to be here. I have to do this. I witnessed the last violent hour of Mr. Tom Perkins's life, and I consider his son, Moon, a friend."

"He wasn't too happy to see you on Christmas Eve night," Unk reminded me.

"He was standing over his dead daddy's body. I didn't expect a greeting.

Unk limped toward the Perkins homestead. "Y'all wait here at the fence corner."

Every Ten Miler for miles around was gathered at the Perkins homestead. A dozen rifles were lined up along the fence rail, and the gallery was crowded with wailing women. My knees felt weak.

Unk returned, hands in his pockets. "There's nothin' sadder than a Redbone funeral and nothin' more dangerous when we're riled."

"Are they sad or riled?" Ma said.

"Both."

Just then, a group of men carried Old Mr. Tom Perkins' coffin out of the house, and the wailing went up a shrill octave. The crowd surged around and behind the coffin. As the pallbearers loaded the coffin into a wagon, I saw Moon. In spite of his bandaged arm, he was helping heft his Daddy's coffin.

The slow procession to Occupy Graveyard began. As the wagon passed us, I quietly waved at Moon, and he nodded curtly. Several of the men stopped and stared. None tipped his hat.

Maybe this wasn't such a good idea. It was ironic that some of these folks were shooting at me two days ago. One fellow walked over and spat at my feet. "We know you were there. This rawhide fight ain't over." The crowd around him eyed us with a mixture of disdain and scorn, but the main emotion was raw sorrow. Deep, unspeakable sorrow.

What this sorrow would turn to in the coming days was uncertain, but today it was unvarnished grief at burying a family member and neighbor. These folks were grieving just as deeply as the Outsiders had yesterday at Hamp Dykes's wake. "Family is family," I said to Ma. "And blood is blood."

"I still think we ought to leave," Ma said.

I fell in line with the other mourners, and she and Unk joined me.

At the graveyard, a group of about forty more Ten Milers awaited the wagon's arrival. Several in the crowd had bandages that I surmised were the result of John Watson's eagle eye.

Unk pointed out another fresh grave to Ma. "That's where they buried the other Ten Miler, Simon Morrow, yesterday."

The pallbearers unloaded Mr. Tom's coffin. It wasn't like the stockpile ones at the Westport Store. It seemed appropriate that this Pineywoods man was being buried in a homemade longleaf pine box. Unk whispered, "Moon and his brother made the coffin themselves last night."

They sat the coffin down on some long two-by-fours over the grave. Two men pried the lid from the coffin, and then a long, snaking line of friends and neighbors passed by and paid their last respects.

Unk joined the procession, but Ma and I stayed respectfully back.

Finally, the Perkins family crowded around the open coffin. One by one and in small clumps, they said their goodbyes. It broke my heart as his wife, children, and young grandchildren wept over his body. I'm not sure I'd ever seen a grown man cry like Moon. It seemed as if he was going to crawl into the coffin. He wept so hard that most of his words were gibberish, but I clearly heard him repeating, "Daddy, I'm so sorry. This was all my fault."

Several men finally pulled Moon away, and they nailed the coffin shut. The hammer blows echoing off the surrounding pines only intensified the women's wailing. It just tore my heart open, and I wanted to run, but my legs wouldn't work.

Several Ten Milers, using ropes, slowly lowered Old Mr. Tom Perkins into his grave. Men and boys took turns shoveling dirt until the grave was filled. Moon picked up a handful of red clay and threw it on top of the heap. As the crowd dispersed, Moon walked over to me. Pointing his clay-smeared fist, he said, "Missouri, you tell your friends that this ain't over. I swear on my father's grave. This ain't the end of it."

I wanted to say something. Anything. To run to Moon and comfort him, but Ma held my arm. "Not now, Baby. This ain't the right time."

On the long walk back to our wagon, Ma, Unk, and I were all silent, deep in our own wells. Unk broke the silence. "It's ironic that they buried both of them near Joseph Willis's grave. These killings wouldna happened if Father Joseph Willis was still alive."

Ma, not familiar with the legend of Joseph Willis, said, "Who's that?"

"He founded Occupy Church. If Father Willis were still alive, this feud wouldn't be going on. He'd shame everybody into getting along."

"Did you know him?"

"Like the back of my hand." Unk picked up a twig and twirled it. "My favorite feud story happened when I was a boy. My Uncle Buck and another Redbone family were having an ongoing feud over an allegedly stolen pig. During the time of the feud, both men came to church armed, glaring at each other from across their pews. Father Willis stopped his sermon, took both men out to the churchyard, and dressed them down." Unk laughed. "The entire congregation watched from the windows and doorways. Uncle Buck and the other man went to crying and hugging, buried the hatchet, and returned to the altar, confessing their sins and trying to out forgive the other. It started a revival in Ten Mile."

"Wow. Did it last?" I said.

"Those two families have never had no trouble since. They feared Father Willis would come out of the grave if they backed off their promise to git along. That was the end of it, and I'm sure as shootin' that if Father Willis was alive today, Tom, Simon, and those others would still be alive." He threw down his twig. "The sad thing 'bout it is there weren't any winners in the Christmas Eve Fight. Nary a one."

"Whose side are you on?" Ma asked.

"Nobody's. There's right and wrong, good and bad men on both sides. Ain't neither side perfect. There's only been one perfect man, and they crucifried him."

I winked at Ma at Unk's use of the word *crucifried*.

Unk shook his head. "It'd take a good dose of Jesus to stop this fight."

"We're all losers," I said. "I've seen enough sadness to last a while."

Why do your people love fighting?" I asked Unk.

"We're just hot-headed. Guess it's in our blood. The smallest slight or insult can touch off trouble, dragging in families and clans to one side or the other. They'll scuffle back and forth until some outside threat comes along, then band together and fight side by side. That's the whole crux of this Outsider fight over the land and timber.

"Our people want things to be left alone. They don't want nobody messing with their pine thickets, bottomlands, and open-range livestock. The whites—the Outsiders—believe that everything is better when it gets changed. They call it civilization. Roads, sawmills, villages, railroads, and towns with laws and such. This feud—and it ain't over—is about two cultures clashing. Two cultures that can't, or won't, change or give in."

He stopped at the side trail going to the Turpentine Camp. "Unk's going home, unless I can he'p you."

Ma said, "We'll be fine."

As we passed the store, I pointed at the porch. "Ma, it could've all been avoided."

"How so?"

"When they took Moon Perkins inside the store, it set in motion the fight that followed," I said. "His daddy and their people could only see it one way. Moon was being held as a hostage."

"Why didn't they let him go?"

"They were trying to protect him from the mob of Outsiders that'd watched him pummel Gordon Musgrove," I said. "I heard Doctor Hamilton tell Moon, 'We're keeping you for your own protection.'"

"Ma, I thought about a saying you've used. 'The stars are in their courses.' The trouble and killing was going to happen regardless.

"That was the fatal mistake that led to the fight. Not letting him go right then. He was safe under the protection of Doctor Hamilton and the Irishman. But that's not how Moon's daddy, Old Mr. Tom Perkins, saw it. He saw his son as a hostage, and when he left with his son still held upstairs in the store, the die was cast.

"Old Tom said that there'd be a rawhide fight and there was no turning back. I'll always wonder what Old Mr. Tom told the crowd at the edge of the woods. Whether it was the truth, a lie, or exaggeration no longer mattered. The tinder was dry and any flash would've started it. The struggle for who really owns this area had to be fought."

"Eventually, the Outsiders always win," Ma said. "That's why my people in the Carolinas just kept getting pushed west. We finally ended up in some hidden mountain valleys where they just let us be."

I shook my head. "In this case, I'm not sure the Outsiders won. It looks like they're the ones who'll be moving on."

"Maybe so, but eventually civilization, and all it involves, will sweep over this area. They'll build railroads, cut the timber, hand out land deeds, tax the people to death, and start villages that become towns. A hundred years from today, this region won't look any different than how Georgia and Alabama look now." She waved her arm as if passing a benediction. "Yep, this place they call Ten Mile will be no different from areas back east that once were wild and free."

"What about us?"

"This ain't a place that's safe to stay. We'll move on."

"Where to?"

"I want to go back east to the cotton country, open sky, and cities. Your pap insists it's westward to Texas." She sighed. "So, it'll be Texas when we move on."

Texas. Moving on. I guess I should've known it was coming. It was foolish to get my hopes up. There were no roots for me here. And even worse, going would dash my best chance at love.

CHAPTER 36

UNDER THE MILKY WAY

December 28, 1881

Mr. Joe Moore reopened the Hatch and Moore store three days after Christmas, and I returned to work the day after that.

Customers were scarce, still unsure if it was safe. A pall had settled over the entire area, and no one wanted to be seen near the store.

The six Sugartown men guarded the store each night in shifts of three. Several of them weren't much older than me and entertained me with stories of life in Sugartown, which sounded much different than either Ten Mile or even Alexandria. Billy Reed, a boy about my age, mentioned a secondary school in Sugartown called the Baldwin Academy. "Students and boarders come from all over western Louisiana and even parts of Texas."

"Do you go to the Baldwin School?"

"Heck no. My family runs about a thousand head of sheep in the woods as well as several hundred head of rake-straw cattle.

"What breed is a rake straw?"

"Not a breed; it's 'cause they can survive the winter months by raking the longleaf pine straw back with their horns and muzzles to find grass protected from the frost." He smiled. "I spend lots of time in the woods tending the sheep, shooting wolves, and scaring off varmints, particularly the two-legged variety. I have plenty of time on my hands, so I read a lot."

"How'd you learn to read?"

"I went to school through the seventh grade at our one-room schoolhouse near our homestead." He winked. "It's known as the 'Who'd a Thought It' School.'"

"There's got to be a good story there," I said.

"Sure is. My Daddy donated some land near our home for a community school. The school got its name when they were finishing the frame and an old-timer rode by, stopped his horse, and asked, 'What are you boys building?'

"A school."

"The old fellow scanned the endless horizon of pine. 'A school? Who'd a thought it.' " Billy laughed. "And that name stuck."

"What do you read?"

"Anything I can get my hands on. Mostly those new dime store novels."

"I hope Sugartown is where we stop next," I said.

"Next?"

"Pap says we're pulling up stakes and moving out of here before more trouble breaks out."

"Probably a good idea. The six of us are riding back to Sugartown tomorrow after guarding the store tonight."

"Do you think they'll leave the store alone?"

"I'm not sure. We hear lots of coming and going during the night on the edge of the woods, but it might just be clumsy, big-footed raccoons for all I know. It's hard to figure out these people here. The store does them lots of good, but they evidently view it as an intrusion. I've got a running bet with my cousin Jim—he's also one of the guards—that they'll burn it down within a week."

That same day, Mr. Joe's business partner, Captain Hatch, arrived from Alexandria. Later that afternoon, Doctor Hamilton came in. The three co-owners spent all day discussing their options for the store. I listened in on all I could, but no clear consensus was formulated. The store, grist mill, and blacksmith shop had been financially lucrative, having no competition for business within a thirty-mile radius. But the fight had put future profitability up in the air.

I asked Dan about it. "What's going to happen?"

"The Sugartown men leave tomorrow. It'll be up to us to guard the store at night."

"Us?"

"Da, Will, and myself. The plan is to rotate and take turns."

"But you can't keep that up forever?"

"I guess we'll just play it by ear from there."

Mr. Joe and Will stayed that first night after the Sugartown men left. They came to work sleepy the next day, but reported that things were quiet.

Business picked up some as the week wore on, and I finally felt safe walking back and forth to the store. Unk always waited at Cherry Winchie to escort me from there.

Plus, I'd picked up another chaperone. Since the fight, Lucky followed me everywhere I went. All day he stayed near the store and spent his nights curled under the wagon. I'm not sure if he was protecting me, or if I was protecting him, but if you saw one of us, the other was near.

The next night, December 29, was Dan's turn to be the night watchman.

All afternoon, Mr. Joe and Dan argued about him staying by himself. Dan said he could do it, while Mr. Joe insisted he would stay too. They finally compromised. Mr. Joe would stay until midnight. If things were quiet, he'd leave Dan alone to finish the night shift.

I wiped the counters and swept the aisles, trying not to miss a word. As they planned, I made my own plan. I left work early that afternoon and fixed a traveling bag. As Ma, Pap, and I ate supper, I said, "Miss Eliza wants me to stay with her tonight." I wolfed down my stew. "I'll be back tomorrow after work."

Ma questioned me about my safety, and I insisted I'd be fine. "Unk's waiting at the creek crossing to escort me. Plus, I've got Lucky."

But staying with Miss Eliza wasn't the truth. I was on my own, and that's exactly what I wanted. I even had a name for my plan, the Boaz plan. In the biblical Book of Ruth, young Naomi slips into the grist mill and sleeps on the threshing floor by Boaz's feet. He wakes up to discover this sweet young thing alone with him. The Good Book doesn't go into what happened from there.

My Boaz Plan and I arrived at the store about dusk-dark. Will and Mr. Joe had built a big fire in front of the porch. They took turns on patrol, being careful to not get too close to the fire and make an easy silhouette for any shooter.

I found a lee in the pines and made a soft bed of pine needles where no one could see me. I had my books and a new candle—all I needed for a good night. Lucky nuzzled up against me. The moon, just past first quarter, bathed the pines in light. I could nearly read without my candle if I sat in the opening, but being hidden was my priority.

Everything was quiet around the store. I could faintly hear Dan and his father talking. I wondered how they must feel leaving a thriving business into which they'd poured everything.

Finally, Mr. Joe shouldered his firearm and left for home with a parting shout to Dan. "Fire your weapon if you need help."

After about a half hour, I made my move. I whistled like a quail.

Dan stopped in his tracks and raised his rifle. "Who's out there?"

I whistled again. Dan melted into the shadows in the lee of the store. "Speak now. Who's out there?"

"It's Bob White." I repeated my quail whistle.

"Mizz, is that you?"

I eased out of the pines and approached the store, Lucky trotting by my side.

"Girl, what in the world are you doing out here?"

"I've come to help you watch."

Dan looked around, uneasiness in his eyes. "Who knows you're here?"

"No one."

"Mizz, this don't appear right."

"Who said anything about appearing right?" I clucked at Lucky. "Besides, we aren't really alone."

"I'm kind of at a loss for words," he stammered. "I do want to do right."

"Dan, I want to do right, but I'm just not sure right now. We don't have much time."

"What do you mean?"

"Y'all are going back to Alexandria, aren't you?"

He motioned me over to a homemade bench by the water trough. "That's one of our options. We'd prefer to stay here with the store, mill, and smith shop, but we can't guard this place every night. We've decided to stay here and make a go of it and see what happens." He shifted on the bench. "What about y'all?"

"Pap's on his high horse on going to Texas." I reached for his hand. "It looks like we're going separate ways."

"I wish it weren't true."

"It doesn't have to be this way."

"How so?"

"We could leave together."

"What? You and me? Mizz, we ain't ready for that."

"But, Dan, if we leave here with one of us going west and the other east, we'll never see each other again. And I'm not ready for that to happen."

He rubbed his head. "You could stay here with us."

"I don't think your folks would approve."

"Well, Momma did make me promise to marry outside Ten Mile. And you're outside Ten Mile."

"But I'm still white trash to your folks."

"That's not how they view you. They love you."

"They view me as a good worker, but that's all. Good enough to work, not good enough to marry."

I waited for Dan to refute that, but his silence spoke volumes. I stood to leave.

"Mizz, don't leave."

He pointed to the quilt laid out on the ground. "Let's stretch out and watch the night sky. I've seen five falling stars already."

On this clear, cold night, the Milky Way was stunning as it stretched across the sky like a string of a million pearls. It seemed so close that you could reach up and grab a handful of stars.

A fine, red star blazed across the southern horizon. He pointed out the Big Dipper and the North Star. "Look at that square in the north."

"What is it?"

"The Square of Pegasus," Dan said. "That's the Flying Horse."

"I'm not sure I see the horse."

"It takes a little imagination." Dan moved the rifle from between us and scooted closer. "They claim in big cities you can't see the night sky like this."

"It's true. In New Orleans and Mobile you could see the bright stars, but nothing like what we're seeing."

"It's sad some folks never get to see this."

We lay in silence for several minutes waiting for another falling star.

Lucky growled, causing Dan to reach for his gun. And I reached for him. The next thing I knew, we were locked in an embrace, and I'd never been kissed like that. It was as if all the emotions we'd held in came out in this starlit night.

I loved this man named Dan Moore and wanted to be with him from now on. I wanted him so bad it hurt. And hurt it did.

We knew it probably couldn't last, but tonight that didn't matter. We lay there and let the pine-knot fire die out, oblivious to the cold or any Ten Mile arsonist who may have slipped up. The thing burning was our love, and on that night nothing else mattered.

It was our night, and no matter what happened the next day or next week, no one could take that away from me. I always said that night could be blamed on the Milky Way.

As I went to sleep in his arms, I said, "I love you, Dan'l Moore."

Instead of answering in kind, he said, "Why'd you call me *Dan'l?*"

I stared up into the Milky Way "That's what I'll call you for the rest of my life, *Dan'l Moore.*"

CHAPTER 37

THE BURNOUT

December 30, 1881

Sometimes we make decisions, and at other times decisions are made for us. That's the best way I know to describe the last week of 1881.

The Moore family had decided it seemed the storm was passing, and they might be able to keep their store open. Most of the other Outsiders were leaving or had already pulled out. When a wife fears her husband is facing death by a shot in the back, that wife usually gets her way. And most of those women felt that strongly about getting their man and children out of No Man's Land. Each day a family or two left with most coming by the store to say farewell.

Most retraced their steps back east toward civilization, leaving the Strip at Babb's Bridge or Hineston. Several moved deeper into the Strip but out of the Ten Mile Country. Their destination was Sugartown or the Sabine River and Texas beyond that. Pap and Ma and I planned to join that group.

At the store, the men who were leaving talked boisterously about how they should stay and help drive out the Redbones. They patted Mr. Joe on the back and congratulated him on having the courage to stay. But I saw relief in their eyes as they left the store and pointed their wagons away from Ten Mile.

The common gossip was whether a bullet or burnout would come first to Mr. Joe Moore. I hoped neither but feared the bushwhack way worse. Stores and houses can be rebuilt, but a double-barreled shot of buckshot from the darkness doesn't always leave room for repair.

Mr. Joe called us all together. "We're not going to guard the store at night. We can't stay up every night and still run a store, mill, and smith shop during the day."

Dan winked at me, and I blushed.

Will yawned. "I'll be glad to get back to a full night's sleep in a bed."

"Da, it's been a week since the fight," Dan said. "Don't you think if they were going to bother the store, they'd have done it by now?"

"I hope so. I guess we'll just have to wait and see. Another thing is that we've got to see more business returning. Right now, folks are voting with their feet."

That evening after closing, Mr. Joe and the boys backed two wagons to the store porch. They proceeded to load the most valuable inventory into them—guns, larger bore ammo, stoves, the best pots and pans, several clocks, and most of the red liquor and kegs. Mr. Joe caught me eyeing the liquor supply. "Well, it is our best seller and makes the most profit."

"And it'll kill you from ten thousand yards," I said.

He laughed. "It'll wing you from twenty."

Unk and I loaded the other wagon with the best ladies' wares—material, dresses, shawls, and sunhats.

As the boys tarped our load, the Irishman stood with his hands on his hips. "Not expecting trouble, but you can't be too careful." The Moore's and their wagons slipped off into the dark as Unk and I made our way toward my family's campsite.

I slept fitfully that night, fully expecting to wake up to see the glow of flames above the horizon, but I arrived at the store the next day to find everything in place. Mr. Joe Moore had a look of relief I hadn't seen since the fight. We all began to believe we might weather this storm.

Even though Pap was still talking about moving, he'd gotten used to my giving him part of my earnings from the store. I don't know if you'd call it a bribe or blackmail, but I hoped it would keep us here.

Most of our business that day was from the Ten Milers. They came in the stores in twos and threes, did their shopping quietly, paid, and left. Several men gathered around the spot near where Old Tom and Mr. Morrow had been shot. They talked a long time, and watching them gave me the willies.

We repeated the wagon loading that night after closing. Only this time, we only loaded one of the wagons. There was still lots of good inventory in the store, but most of it was too bulky to move daily. We also didn't want to give the impression we were selling out.

As we walked home, I asked Unk, "Do you think we'll make it?"

He grinned. "We?"

"Yeah, we. I feel a part of this store and family."

"Well, Miss-Mizz, we'll just see."

I wasn't sure what time of the night it was when Pap shook me awake. "Come take a look."

The red glow of fire was in the direction of the store. He put his arm around me. "I'm afeared it's the store."

Ma had joined us and simply shook her head. "This is a wicked place."

"Pap, will you walk with me there?"

"Let's get some warm clothes on and go take a look."

"I'm going, too," Ma said.

As we neared the store, flames licked the sky. The Hatch and Moore Store was engulfed. Lucky ran barking back and forth, and I panicked wondering where Esther was. They usually locked her in the store at night. The huge inferno was beyond us stopping it. Anything inside the store right now, including a cat, wasn't coming out.

A small group of men tried to keep the adjoining blacksmith shop from catching fire. Dan and Will ran back and forth from the water trough, sloshing buckets of water on the near wall of the smith shop.

The closest person to the fire was the Irishman. He had an ax and was attempting to cut down his flagpole and save his American flag. It was already singed along the edges. From inside the store, ammunition exploded causing most of the onlookers to scurry behind trees, but Mr. Joe flailed away at the pole. When he'd cut enough, he leaned against the pole and it and the flag fell with a thud. A fellow ran out of the crowd and threw dirt on the smoldering flag.

A knot of Redbones stood near where the flagpole fell. They weren't doing anything to help, simply observing the inferno. I was pretty sure whoever started this fire stood there among them. Just as I steeled myself to give me a good cussing, the frame of the store collapsed, scattering embers high into the sky as well as into the pine straw. Men with pine limbs beat out these mini-fires. The embers rained down on the blacksmith shop and its cypress shingle roof was soon engulfed.

I took another glance at the Redbone arsonists who'd not moved a foot to help. I abandoned any plan to say anything. Maybe another time.

Mr. Joe Moore stood with his arm around Miss Eliza as their life's savings and dreams literally went up in smoke.

I walked up beside them. "I'm so sorry."

He shrugged. "Well, there ain't nothing to do but roll up both sleeves and go to work." He kissed the top of his wife's head. "But it won't be here."

The flames reflected off Miss Eliza's tear-streaked face, which held a deep look of regret and lost dreams.

I looked away from her. "Where will you go?"

He made a fist. "Not sure. Probably back toward Hineston or Lecompte. I've taught school in the past. I could do it again." His strong Irish jaw, set with determination, was silhouetted against the flames.

I heard meowing from a nearby tree and ran over to find Esther in a small oak. Her tail was singed, but other than that she seemed fine. "Now, how'd you get out of there?" She crawled down the tree and into my arms and then rubbed her head alongside mine.

"Well, this is a new song. You must've gotten some arrogance burnt out of you. You've still got eight more lives to go."

We stayed until the fire died down. Dan and Will sat on a nearby log, crying. I went by and kissed each of them on top of the head, and then gave them some space.

With the first signs of daybreak, Pap, Ma, and I began the walk home. Ma stopped suddenly. "What if they burned us out while we were gone?" We hurried along, hoping against hope not to see flames from our campsite. Everything was just as we'd left it. Ma silently got a fire going to boil some coffee water.

I sat beside her, drawing in the dirt with a stick.

Pap stood over us. "Beulah and Missouri, the die is cast. We're leaving. They'll burn us out sooner or later if we stay. Like those people at the store, we'll just have to cut our losses and move on."

"Where will be go?" Ma asked.

"Sugartown. I want to see that homestead. It's on our way to Texas. I've still got the homestead deed from that Nash family.

Sugartown. It sounded like an interesting place, but all I could think of was that two ships were passing in the night. Dan and his family were going east. My family, with whatever name we'd be calling ourselves now, was continuing west.

CHAPTER 38

WILDFIRE

December 31, 1881
New Year's Eve

I returned to the store site that afternoon and found Dan still rummaging through the ashes.

"Luckily, we'd moved the guns and ammo out of the store, as well as most of the liquor," Dan said. "Everything else burnt up when the store burned down."

I burst out laughing. "Say that again?"

"What? It ain't funny."

"Say it again!"

"Everything inside burned up when the store burnt down."

"So some things burnt up and some burnt down?"

He finally caught on. "Guess it did, but it ain't funny."

"I agree, but the way you said it was."

He sat on a pile of rubble. "Burnt up and burnt down. It is funny, but our situation's not. We lost lots of stock."

"I know, and I'm sorry."

"I wished we'd gotten more stuff out of the blacksmith shop and mill." He held up a twisted set of tongs. "Some of the tools survived, but the fire messed most of them up."

"When are you leaving?" I said.

"In the next couple of days."

"Alexandria?"

"At least for the time being. What about y'all?"

"Westward. We plan to stop at Sugartown, then Texas."

Dan motioned me to sit by him. "Have you thought any more about going with us instead?"

"Dan'l, I just can't see it working. I wish I could, but I can't."

"We could make it work."

I shook my head. "I just don't think I can leave my poor ol' Momma alone at a time like this."

"Mizz, there comes a time when a person has to make a decision."

I glared at him. "You're right. Why don't you come west with us? We'll make a new start together there."

Dan's mouth moved, but no words came out. Finally, he said, "Mizz, you know that wouldn't work. I couldn't get along with your daddy for two days."

I fought the anger building up in me. It wasn't just Dan Moore, but at the moment it was all directed at him. "There comes a time to make a decision, and it looks like you're not willing to take that risk. At least not with a family like us."

I kicked a burnt washtub in the ashes, and my foot stuck in its encrusted side. Knocking it loose, I left in a huff. As I walked, I waited for Dan Moore to try to stop me, but he never did.

I was pretty bummed out when I arrived back at our wagon. Pap and Ma hadn't done one thing in the way of breaking camp and loading our stuff to move on. I walked to where they sat. "I thought we were leaving?"

"We are, but there's no reason to get in a hurry."

I scoffed. "There's enough burning and shooting around here to convince me we should've left already."

Pap sat on his stump. "We'll go when I say it's time to go."

I went to my tent and spent most of the day reading and sleeping. The blackness, which I called the Dreads, seemed to be settling over me.

Later that afternoon, I heard horses approach, so I stepped out of the tent. Moon Perkins and another fellow rode up to our campsite. Pap stepped back into the wagon for his gun.

Moon jumped off his horse. "Missouri, tell your Daddy he can put down his gun. He don't need it today."

Ma offered them a cup of coffee, but they refused. Moon nodded at the man with him. "This here's my cousin Cooter." Moon stepped closer to me. "Missouri, I'll cut right to the chase. Our people are determined to drive out the Outsiders once and for all. It ain't gonna be a pretty sight. I'd recommend that you and your family get out before the same thing happens to y'all."

"The same thing?"

"Yep, the same thing. Clear out. There's a wildfire burning here now, and it'll burn anything in its way including folks like yours."

"Why?"

"This place ain't big enough for your people and ours. And we don't have no intention of leavin'. Folks like y'all should."

"How soon?"

"Today if possible. Tomorrow at the latest. You'll need to get past the Dead Line."

Pap scratched his head. "It'll take a few days to pack up."

"Sir, you stay at your own risk and the risk of your family."

"I ain't much on anyone telling me what to do."

"I ain't telling you. I'm warning you. Warning you about the wildfire for your own good." He nodded at his cousin. "Cooter and me'd be in lots of trouble if our people knew we were even here."

"Then why are you warning us?" Pap said.

Moon glanced at me. "'Cause of her." His face was a strange mixture of anger, sorrow, and kindness.

Pap lowered his shotgun and went back in the tent.

Moon turned and walked his horse away, and I followed. Cooter fell back about twenty paces.

"Do the others know?" I asked.

"Who?"

"The whites."

"The burnout at the store was their message. I hope they heed it."

"But, the Moore family is part of your community," I said.

"Yep, but they were part of the fight and were on the wrong side. It's too late to bell the cat. One way or the other, they've got to go." Moon turned to walk away, but he had something to add. "By the way, the grist mill burned last night. Also, we've torched several pine-knot piles at area homes. That should send some strong messages." He stood ready to mount his horse, then stopped. "Missouri, I got one last question for you. Which man shot my daddy?"

I'd replayed that scene in my head a thousand times. "I'm not sure."

"I need to know."

"I understand, but—"

"If you don't tell me, I'm gonna kill each one of the men who were in the store. I'll do it one at a time from the oldest down to even the two young Moore ones."

"I can't tell you."

"Can't or won't?"

"Both."

He mounted his horse and as he wheeled to leave, I grabbed his rein. "I have one thing for you." I pulled him toward me and kissed him full on the mouth. I won't call it passionate on my part, but I didn't hold back, and it wasn't a quick kiss either. I thought he was going to fall off.

He pulled away and straightened up in the saddle.

"Moon, I owed you that one, and I'm a girl that keeps her promise."

He smiled slightly. "Well, I sure got my money's worth on that one. The only problem with a kiss like that is that it makes you want more."

"Just call it wildfire."

He tipped his hat. "It was that." He looked away. "Missouri Cotton, in another time, another place, we could've had something special."

He spurred his horse. "Let's get out of here, Cooter." I watched him disappear up the Sugartown Road. His words echoed off the pines.

Another time. Another place.

Wildfire.

CHAPTER 39

REFUGE

New Year's Eve

When I returned to our campsite, Pap was stirring the fire. He had his bottle at his side, and it was two fingers emptier than when I'd walked away with Moon. He sure hadn't poured it on the fire. That whiskey was in him, and that was never a good sign.

Ma stood over him. "Henry, we need to get out of here today."

"I ain't going nowhere until I git ready."

"You heard that man's warning. Mizz and I are leaving."

"You won't get a mile without me."

"We'll walk all the way back to Hineston if we have to."

"We'll leave when I get ready, and when we do, we're headed to Texas, not Hineston."

I slipped out of sight to stay clear of the developing storm. Anyway, I was working on a plan and needed a good walk to think. The Turpentine Camp about a mile away as the crow flies was my destination. In spite of its fierce reputation, it seemed our best hope at the moment. I'd never entered the Turpentine Camp alone. I'd always been there with either Unk or Pap. As I approached, the men all stopped their work and watched me approach.

Uncle Rube stepped out of a lean-to. "Miss-Mizz, what brings you here?"

"We need your help."

"Come sit over here." He motioned to the other men. "This is Miss-Mizz Cotton. She's the one that saved Gordon Musgrove during the fight."

Several of the men nodded but showed no other emotion.

"When did you get back from Sugartown, Uncle Rube?"

"Three nights ago. No one even suspicioned I was mixed up in the fight or the help arriving. Now tell me, what do you need?"

"We need a place of refuge. The Ten Milers have told us to get past the Dead Line by tomorrow. My pap is too stubborn, and presently too drunk, to load up and go."

Uncle Rube took a stick and drew in the dirt. "Well, what can we do?"

"Let us bring our wagon here until Pap gets the gumption and motivation to leave."

A turpentine worker named Solomon was filing his saw. "Rube, we don't need to get mixed up in this border feud. We have a hard enough time as it is."

"Well, we cain't just leave these people out on their own. War has been declared on them."

Solomon pointed his file. "And if we bring them here, war might be declared on us."

Uncle Rube stood. "I guess that's something we'll have to find out."

"You can't just make this decision on your own when it affects everyone in this camp," Solomon said.

"I don't think the locals view us as trespassers. I doubt if they'll even know we've taken in these refugees." He put his hat on and motioned to me. "Let's go git your wagon and stuff before it gets dark."

Just as I expected, Pap was passed out cold in the wagon when we reached our camp. It didn't take Ma, Uncle Rube, and me long to pack our tent and meager belongings and load them in the wagon. Uncle Rube helped hook up Maggie and Aunt Em, and we began toward the rough trail that led to the Turpentine Camp. Pap slept the entire bumpy ride, with a crooked smile on his face.

We rattled into the Turpentine Camp, and thirty or so men stood watching our arrival.

"Are you sure about us staying here?" Ma asked.

"It's the best plan for now."

"You trust these people?"

"Don't have much choice, do we?"

Several of the men led by Uncle Rube helped us set up camp. Later, a worker named Buck brought over a pan of cornbread and gravy. Ma stood. "I thank you kindly."

As I hungrily ate, I said, "Ma, when Pap comes to, he won't like us being here. You know how he is about black folk. He won't even eat something cooked by a colored person."

Ma took a big bite. "It's ironic that some folks won't touch food cooked by a colored person but will eat an egg for breakfast that came out of a chicken's butt."

She sniffed. "He didn't have good upbringing. If he was awake, I bet he'd eat this cornbread. It is something kind of good."

I went to bed full and fully amazed. Our welcome at the Turpentine Camp reinforced the amazing fact that the people you least expect help from are often the most generous.

It seemed that colored folks and white trash were the ones who could be depended on in a tight squeeze. I began recalling the characters in *Les Miserables* who, like us, were outcasts or riffraff, but would be the first persons to give someone the shirt off their backs.

I re-read my notes about the passage where the rascally street urchin Gavroche, one of my favorite characters in the book, takes in two poor orphan boys. He doesn't realize that they are his younger brothers, who like him, have been cast into the streets at the mercy of the world, just as he was a decade earlier.

In spite of having nothing, Gavroche scrounges the streets of Paris for food, feeds the boys, and takes them to his warm home inside the hollow statue of a huge elephant along the river.

I happily drifted off to sleep to the unique smells of a turpentine camp and the warmth of a hollow elephant statue.

CHAPTER 40

FAREWELLS

January 1, 1882

New Year's Day is as good as any for clearing out and moving on, and the foggy morning seemed fitting.

I've always loved the first day of the year, but felt bittersweet feelings about this one. In spite of everything that had happened, I was sad to leave the Ten Mile country. I couldn't imagine a prettier place, and in spite of the trouble and violence, I'd made some great friendships. And, for the first time in my life, I'd fallen in love. I would miss Westport.

At the same time, I was intrigued by what I'd heard about Sugartown. In crow-flying miles it was about twenty miles, and we'd easily reach it in two days. From Sugartown it was another forty-plus miles to the Texas border.

As we cinched down the last items in our wagon, I mentally went over the list of folks I'd probably never see again. A few I was glad to get shuck of, but most I would miss. It was amazing that in spite of the Fight, I'd made an equal number of friends on each side of the trouble.

Pap spent most of the first day of 1882 passed out drunk. I slipped away for a final visit to the Moore home. It broke my heart passing by the ashes of the store and outbuildings. At their home Dan was loading their belongings on a wagon.

"I'm so sorry."

He shrugged. "So am I, but it is what it is."

"Would you help us move our wagon to the creek crossing? Pap's passed out for the day."

"Sure, but you don't think he'll wake up and shoot me?"

"He's in no danger to anyone today. I came to say goodbye to your folks."

"My mother's in the house. Dan and Will are in the woods. Both are taking this move hard."

"Well, I'd like to see your mother before we leave."

Her sickbed was the only furnishing not taken out of the house. She motioned for me to sit beside her on the bed. "Mizz, I'm glad you came. She grasped my hand with her amazing strong grip. "I guess I'll never know the ending of your 'Miserables' story. I hope it's a happy one.

Tears filled her eyes. "And Missouri Cotton, I hope your story ends happy too."

I stood quickly. "Dan's walking with me part of the way back to our wagon. I'd better go before darkness catches us. I hate to leave without saying goodbye to Mr. Joe and Will."

"Joe Moore hates goodbyes worse than anyone, and I believe you'll see Will Moore again. I cannot imagine that jaybird not flying by Sugartown or wherever you are."

Miss Eliza pulled me close. "But I have a better idea. Child, come with us."

I backed away. "Are you serious?"

"If you are."

I wanted to say yes, but couldn't. Leaving Ma and Pap was something I hoped to do, but not today.

"No, ma'am. I can't. At least not now."

As fast as I could, I walked away.

Dan met me at the gate. "You're crying. It didn't go well?"

"It was just difficult."

We walked slowly toward the Turpentine Camp.

"We might walk together again," Dan said. "But it won't be in Ten Mile.

"Mizz, do you believe what we had was real?"

"Was real?" I wanted to slap him.

"That's not what I meant. I'm talking about our night under the Milky Way. Dan'l, even if I never see you again, I'll cherish that night until the day I die as an old woman. It was real. It's still real."

"Mizz, just because something's real doesn't mean it can last."

I bit my lip, holding back tears. "So, what's next?"

He shrugged. "We're pulling out for Alexandria this week. We'll regroup and go from there."

"Pap's bound and determined to reach Texas," I said.

He rolled up a coil of rope. "So this probably means goodbye?"

I waited. And waited.

Dan slowly coiled the rope.

"I guess we may not see you again," I said.

"Probably not." He put the rope over his shoulder.

I took his hand. "Dan'l, when we get settled, I'll write you at your brother Mayo's address. Then you can write me back at wherever we are."

"I will." He scanned the evening sky. "It's getting late. Neither of us need to be out at bushwhacking time."

He pulled me to him and we kissed long and hard, before I shoved him away. "Now git while you can. Stay alive so I can see you again."

He was thirty yards away when he turned. "I love you, Missouri Cotton."

He'd never said that before. I was so surprised that he was out of earshot before I could return his words.

Once again. Another place. Another time.

BOOK THREE – HEALING

Grace upon this road less traveled.
Grace beneath the pines, the pines.
Grace beneath the pines.
– Glen Hansard
"Grace Beneath the Pines"

CHAPTER 41

IF THE CREEK DON'T RISE

January 1, 1882

We moved our wagon down to a high and dry place near Occupy Church on the east bank of Ten Mile Creek. It was our last obstacle in leaving the Redbone Kingdom. The creek had been out of its banks since the Christmas Day ice storm and the subsequent rainy days. The creek had spread out over a half mile of the swamp. Until it receded back within its banks, the small ferry couldn't run.

We'd be ready to move when the creek dropped.

Pap, waking from his drunken stupor, was badly hung-over and miffed that we'd moved camp without his permission. Ma had had enough. "Henry, I don't need your permission or your forgiveness. While you were sleeping it off, Missouri and I took the liberty to save our lives. And yours."

I was standing by the wagon as a horse rider approached in the fog. I started to warn Pap but stopped when I realized it was Unk Dyal. I'd never seen him astride a horse.

As he neared, I studied Unk's horse. It was a big, strong, mottled mare with a blonde mane. Unk reined up beside me. "Mornin'."

"Unk, where'd you get that?"

He winked. "I stole it."

I helped him off the horse, and he nearly tumbled to the

ground. "Unk, I believe you're a little old and shaky to be riding a horse that high. How'd you get on her?"

"I led her to a high stump. It was quite the rodeo."

He handed the reins to me. "She's yours."

I shook my head. "What?"

"I got her for you."

"I can't take a horse from you."

"You've got to. It's impolite to refuse a gift among our people, and you shouldn't never look a gift horse in the eye."

I laughed. "I believe it's the mouth."

"Well, whatever. She's yours."

"Unk, you need a horse more than I do."

"Nah, I'd fall off and break a rib or arm or bust my head. Besides, I'm most comfortable using nature's carriage."

"What?"

He pointed down. "I'd rather foot it." He tapped the weathered brown saddle. "A fellow can miss a whole lot that far off the ground."

"You were the first friend I made here and by far the best. I shudder to think what would've become of me if you hadn't taken me under your wing." I touched the horse's mane. "This is an expensive horse."

"It's the best I could find. You deserve the very best, Miss-Mizz."

"Where you'd get that kind of money?"

He leaned close and whispered, "If I told you, I'd hafta kill you."

"Why does that not surprise me?" I hugged him. "I thought you'd lost your treasure?"

"I still got some squirreled away."

"I don't know what to say."

"Well, thank you's plenty good."

I stroked its mane. "What's its name?"

"No-Name."

"What?"

"It's a horse with no name. It's your horse, so you've got to name it."

"I can see she's a fine mare even if she ain't got no name."

"She doesn't have a name but does have a mane. You've got to name her."

I thought about Dan and my night under the Milky Way. "I think I'll call her Pegasus."

"That's an odd name."

"Pegasus is a mythological horse with wings. There's a constellation named for him."

"What's mythological?"

"Made up. Not true."

"Well, you don't need my persimmon to name her whatever."

"Unk, it's permission, not persimmon."

He winked. "Whatever. She's yours."

Pap and Ma were in the wagon, and he impatiently clicked to the team. "Let's go, girls."

Unk made a stirrup with his hands and helped me climb on my horse. He leaned up. "Your papers on this horse are in the saddlebag." He nodded at the wagon which was a quarter mile down the road. "Don't let your poppa get in a bind and try to sell off your horse. It's yours."

I looked down at him. "When will I see you again?"

"Never, unless you come back here."

Tears flowed down my cheeks. "I'm not sure that'll happen."

"Then, this is goodbye." He pulled out a bandana and wiped his forehead, then his eyes.

"Unk, you could leave with the Moore family. Your niece Eliza and her boys would gladly look after you."

"Leave Ten Mile? No way." He looked around the vast expanse of pines. "This is my country. It's where I was born, and it's where I'll turn up my toes."

"I'll send you a letter."

"I can't read."

"Somebody'll read it to you."

"We don't have no post office."

"I'll post it to Hineston and somebody can bring it to you."

"Miss-Mizz, next time I see you, I'll be able to read and write."

"You think so?"

"I know so." He grinned. "I'll write a sign pointing you to where I'm at. Right near them purly gates."

"Where?"

He laughed. "You know Unk don't talk real clear."

"Some of the wisest words I've ever heard have come from your mouth." I leaned down and kissed him on top of his head. "I won't forget you, Nathan Dyal."

"Nor you, Miss-Mizz Missouri White-Cotton-Whatever."

Tears blurred the road as I turned Pegasus and rode back toward Ten Mile as Unk walked beside me.

"I'd better get back to the creek." I dug my boots into Peg's flanks, and she took off like lightning. It felt as if she truly could fly.

Where the road turned, I looked back. Unk Dyal stood in the road, his right hand still high in the air.

It was as if he was frozen solid. Frozen in place.

Once again, I thought. Another time. Another place.

I waved, then spurred Pegasus and didn't look back.

When I rode up to wagon, Pap and Ma were sitting by the wagon

Pap stood, spilling his coffee. "Where'd you git that horse?"

"It's mine."

Ma put her hand over her mouth. "I believe it's the prettiest horse I ever seen."

"Who gave it to you?" Pap said.

"Unk Dyal."

Pap stepped to the horse and rubbed its mane. "What'd you do to git it?"

I didn't like Pap's tone. "I simply was his friend. Unk said it was my farewell gift."

Ma walked to the horse. "I do believe that little fellow is one of the strangest people I've ever met. He might even be part angel."

Pap, ever cynical, snorted. "Well, you'll have to feed it yourself." Under his breath he said, "Nobody gives a gift like that with no strings attached."

I wanted to slap him, but instead smiled. "I was his friend. It was really that simple."

About mid-afternoon, I had another visitor. Doctor James Hamilton rode up on a black stallion. He tipped his hat. "Missouri, I just wanted to see you off and give you a little gift."

"That's right kind of you."

He held up a small, tied tote sack. "It's just a little going away present."

He handed it to me, and I was surprised by the heft of the sack. I started to untie it, but he said, "Wait till I'm gone."

"Why?"

"I'm afraid you'll refuse to keep it if I'm still here."

With that, he doffed his hat, turned, and galloped away.

I ran after him. "Thank you, sir. Thank you."

He waved without looking back.

I quickly excused myself to the edge of the woods. I nervously untied the sack and reached in and pulled out a Colt .45. I knew it was the one he'd broken up the store knife fight with due to two notches on the handle. I lifted it and spun the cylinder. Taking aim down its barrel, I couldn't believe it was mine.

The tote sack also had about twenty loose cartridges and an envelope. I opened it and two silver coins fell out as I unfolded a note.

"Missouri,
The bravest girl I've ever met deserves the best gun one can own. Peacemaker is yours. Use it carefully, but use it as needed.

At Your Service,
Doctor James Hamilton"

I now had a horse named Pegasus and a pistol named Peacemaker. I glanced down at Lucky. "Folks been real nice to us lately, haven't they?

Lucky grinned and thumped his tail.

Several of the turpentine workers had decided to leave too. Their destination was Sugartown, and they camped with us. I don't know if it was strength in numbers or simply misery loves company, but it was good to not be alone.

One of the turpentine workers explained how the Sugartown Road was more commonly called the Confederate Road after the road crossed Ten Mile Creek and then its cousin, Six Mile. Since the War, it'd fallen into disrepair and was a challenge for any wagon.

He explained that at Sugartown the road split with both forks eventually leading to the Sabine River and Texas.

That was all Pap needed to hear. He felt as if getting there would solve all our problems. He talked so much about Texas that Ma began mockingly called it the Promised Land. Every time he mentioned Texas, she'd sing mockingly.

"I am bound for the promised land.
I am bound for the promised land.
Oh, who will come and go with me,
I am bound for the promised land."

I imagined we'd keep going until we reached the Pacific Ocean or fell off the edge of the earth. I didn't even know what was past Texas, but I reckoned we'd find out sooner or later.

Ma repeated the first verse of her new theme song,
"On Jordan's stormy banks
I stand and cast a wistful eye.
To Canaan's fair and happy land
Where my possessions lie."

I wasn't sure what that promised land would be like, but I knew I'd be riding a fine horse and well-armed when we arrived.

CHAPTER 42

QUEEN OF THE FRONTIER

January 3, 1882

On our third day of being stranded at Ten Mile Creek, the ferry operator announced that he'd resume service that afternoon. He had one catch. "Well, Ten Mile is still about twice as wide as normal, so I'm adding an extra dollar for passage."

Pap stepped forward to argue with him, but Ma beat him to the punch. "We'll be glad to pay a dollar more to get free of this country."

That afternoon we boarded the wobbly ferry and began our scary ride across Ten Mile. The creek was still spread across the woods, and the ferry had to dodge around floating logs and debris in the swift current. Every time we bumped into a tree, I expected the ferry to tip and dump the lot of us into the creek.

We finally reached safe ground and needed the help of the Turpentiners to push our wagon out of the silt and onto level ground.

Our destination was Sugartown, the only town between Ten Mile and Texas. Folks at the Westport Store called Sugartown "The Queen of the Frontier," and I surmised it was partly in jest. There wasn't anything I'd seen in the Pineywoods that looked like royalty.

As we ascended back into the pines, they took on a monotonous feeling. During our time in Ten Mile, I'd grown to love the canopy of longleafs, but now they seemed sinister and cast a pallor that I wished to escape. I believe it was the fear of the unknown. As far as the eye could see were tall longleaf pines. I petted Pegasus. "I hope you like pine trees." She snorted and the layer of pine straw in the road muffled her steps.

"Since you're a lady, how about if I shorten your name down and just call you 'Peg.'"

She didn't reply, so I assumed it was okay.

Later that day, we passed through a crossroads called Slabtown. It was well-named and there wasn't anything queenly about it. Folks kind of shunned us when they found out we'd come from Westport. One old-timer said we were about nine miles north of Sugartown and insisted the road was better on the next leg of our journey.

We spent the night past the Six Mile Creek ford. As our campfire burned out, Ma was laying by me. "A penny for your thoughts."

"I wonder what Sugartown and the next stage of our life will be like. I hope it'll be dull compared to our Ten Mile sojourn.

"It'd be hard to top that." She stroked my hair. "What was in that bag the doctor gave you?"

I wasn't ready to reveal about my pistol. "It was some medicine I might need later."

"Powerful medicine?"

"Yes, ma'am."

Ma sighed. "Well, here we are. Things seldom work out like we think they will. I've always heard that if you want to make God laugh, tell him your plans."

I turned over. "Well, I bet God's having a big ol' belly laugh right now at us."

"Just remember, He's in control."

"I hope He's in better control here than He was in Ten Mile."

"Child, don't talk like that. Lightning might strike us both."

"Good night, Ma."

Something else happened during our move from Ten Mile to Sugartown that troubled me greatly. My satsuma money disappeared. I kept it tied securely in a cloth bag and stashed away in one of drawers on the side of our wagon. I'd carefully covered it in old rags and only checked on it at night.

But the night before we reached Sugartown, my bag was missing. I searched everywhere to no avail. I wondered if I'd placed it on the ground the night before, but my biggest suspicion was Pap. Ma always said he could find a rusty penny in a pile of rocks.

So I reached Sugartown late the next afternoon much poorer than I'd left Ten Mile.

We made an immediate impression. That happens when you're in a dilapidated wagon pulled by a mismatched team of an ox and a mule with a three-legged hound trotting beside them.

I dropped Peg about twenty lengths behind the wagon. People came out on the porches of homes and businesses and silently watched our wagon pass.

One of three men playing cards at the Masonic Lodge stood and said towards Pap and Ma on the wagon, "You folks keep on moving."

We weren't getting a good start in Sugartown, but it didn't surprise me. Pap stopped the wagon at a general store. I tied Peg at the small post office and climbed off to have a look around. I'm ashamed to say I didn't want to be associated with my folks, at least not on my entrance into this new place.

To call Sugartown a city, or even a town, would've been an exaggeration, but it definitely qualified as civilization. There were three stores, two hotels, the afore-mentioned Lodge, a new-looking Baptist Church, and a boarding school. It was a two-story building painted white with several outbuildings attached. I couldn't wait until I had a chance to case the joint.

I caught up with my folks. Pap, hands in his suspenders, stood in the middle of the muddy main road. "They call it the Queen of the Frontier, and I guess that's what it is. But there don't look like there's much competition around for the title." He shrugged. "Say what you want about Sugartown, it is on the frontier. We didn't see nothin' but pine and swamps in the last six or seven miles."

It was clear Pap was no more impressed with Sugartown than Sugartown was with him.

By the second day of our arrival in Sugartown, I was the new kid in town. That's not saying much with everyone else's kin.

At the Sugartown Post Office, I saw one of the men who'd

come to guard the Westport Store in the days after the fight. He quickly spread the word that I'd been part of the Westport Fight. Soon the story about my part in the trouble was told and re-told. Each telling added a little more drama. Suddenly, I was the "queen of the frontier." I may have been white trash, but I was unusual white trash with a good story.

News that I'd been inside the store made me a local celebrity. Everywhere I went, folks wanted to ask about the fight. I didn't relish talking about it but couldn't avoid it. At least I got a new nickname. I was no longer called the Wagon Girl. I was now the Westport Girl.

In my first week there, I attained notoriety. I've always been confused by that word. It means being known for something. And that something can be for good or bad.

I was as lost as a goose in a hailstorm. I didn't know a person in Sugartown, although everyone seemed to know about me.

On our first Saturday evening there, I hung around one of the stores and a girl came up to me. She was about my age and had the blondest hair I'd ever seen. It was tied back in a long ponytail that reached to her waist.

"My name is Sabine, but everyone calls me Sonnet." She had a nice smile.

"I'm Missouri Cotton."

She laughed. "Our folks evidently knew how to pick out unusual names."

"Sabine, huh? What's your full name?"

"Sabine Sonnet Ireland."

"How'd you get that name?"

"Sonnet comes from my mother's love of Shakespeare. My daddy's from Texas and Momma's from here, so they compromised on the river that separates the two states for my first name."

"It's a good thing they didn't pick Calcasieu."

"Whoa. That'd be hard to say or spell. I've seen it spelt about six different ways."

"Calcasieu Sonnet Ireland," I said. "That's a mouthful." I smiled.

"Or Whiskey Chitto Sonnet Ireland. Or Calcasieu-Sabine Sonnet Ireland."

"That makes me dizzy," I said. "What do you want me to call

you?"

"Sonnet, by all means."

"You mentioned a Whiskey Chitto. What is that?"

"It's the next creek south of Sugartown. I have two uncles with a running argument on whether it's a creek or river. They also disagree on the name. One calls it Ouiska Chitto, and the other says it's Whiskey Chitto."

Sonnet was full of all kinds of stories, and I was grateful to have my first friend in Sugartown.

She twirled her ponytail. "Were you really in the Westport Fight?"

"I was there, but it was completely by accident and definitely not by choice. I didn't do much in the fight itself. I mainly crawled around on my hands and knees fetching ammunition or whiskey."

"I heard you got cut in the fight."

I hiked my skirt up to show part of my stitched leg. "It was self-inflicted." I nodded at Lucky who lay beside me. "I fell over my dog and cut myself."

"Word around the store is that you helped drag a wounded man to safety."

"I did, but there were three of us."

"Were you scared?"

"I messed in my step-ins."

"Really?"

"Not really, but I was that scared."

She took me by the hand. "Let me show you around town." Sonnet led us on a walking and talking tour of central Sugartown, supplying facts on every building and business. "That is the new Baptist Church, and next to it is the Masonic Lodge. They just moved the lodge building from Shiloh."

"Where's Shiloh?"

"It's another church south of the Whiskey Chitto."

I looked around at the hustle and bustle of Sugartown. They even had wooden sidewalks. The town gave the feeling that it was going somewhere.

Sonnet told how her father worked as a surveyor with one of the timber companies that was buying up local land. "My daddy says that these new arrivals are pumping cash into the economy, and there's no limit to how Sugartown can grow. There's talk of the railroad coming through here. If that happens, it will solidify

Sugartown as the hub of this part of Imperial Calcasieu Parish."

"I thought this was Vernon Parish?"

"No, we're part of the Imperial Calcasieu Parish. It takes up a big swath of southwestern Louisiana. The parish seat is in Lake Charles. Daddy says that when the railroad connects Lake Charles and Alexandria, they'll lay the tracks right through Sugartown. That will allow the timber to be harvested and shipped to the markets."

"They'd cut the pines?"

"Yep. That's progress." Sonnet laughed. "But they could never cut them all. The yellow longleaf pines stretch in every direction for at least fifty miles."

She stopped in front of the two-story school. "Do you know about the Academy?"

"I've heard about it."

"It is formally known as Professor W.H. Baldwin's Sugartown Academy for Males and Females."

"That's an ambitious name for a podunk town."

"Most of the time, we just call it the Baldwin School. Professor Doctor Baldwin, as he prefers to be called, arrived in Sugartown about four years before, displayed his diploma from the prestigious Columbia University in New York, and opened this school."

"Why'd he pick this backwater?" I asked.

"That's always been the mystery," Sonnet said. "But with his pedigree, Prof. Baldwin had instant success. His school appealed to those back-East mothers yearning for civilized and educated children."

"Do you attend?"

"Of course. Anyone who can afford to does." Sonnet walked to the schoolhouse door. "A new three-month term begins next week, and there are close to one hundred students registered. They come from all over this corner of Louisiana, as well as several from east Texas.

"Prof. Baldwin is a good teacher, but he's best as a great promoter and recruiter. And by far the thing he best promotes is himself ... as well as his school."

"Do they have a library?"

"Shelves of books."

I still couldn't believe it. "A library in this podunk little town?"

"The Baldwin School is no ordinary school."

"How do I get into the school?"

"There's an application process and fee, plus you have to take an entrance exam."

I had a new goal. I just had to get into this school. Of course, I had no idea how long we'd be here, but I started praying that this nearby homestead Pap wanted to see might be a place where we could put down roots. And if we put down roots, I'd find a way to get into the Baldwin Academy.

CHAPTER 43

A ROOF OVER OUR HEADS

January 1882

Pap had parked our wagon three miles south of Sugartown, determined to hide the fact that we lived in a wagon and Civil War tent. But in small communities, news travels fast, especially news about new people. I noticed several of the young people who'd welcomed me as the Westport Fight Girl kind of pulled back when they learned of my gypsy-like existence. It cut to the quick but didn't surprise me too much. Sooner or later, you always discover who your real friends are.

This morning Pap held up the land deed the Nash family had given us. "You don't look a gift horse in the mouth. I'm going to take a look. It might be fit for us to live in, or we might can sell it."

"Henry, why are you looking at a house place when your plans are to move on?"

He shrugged. "You never know what we might find. Come go with me for a look."

"I believe I'll pass."

"Mizz, how about you?"

"Sure, let me saddle my horse."

Pap and I rode into Sugartown and made our first stop at the Post Office. Several old men sat on the porch, evidently waiting for the mail. Pap whispered, "They look like desperadoes waiting on a train."

I tied Peg to a post. "It'd have to be a slow train for them to rob it."

Pap, pulling himself to his height and speaking in a real proper voice, said, "I've got a land deed here. Could any of you tell me about it?"

The men passed the deed around, briefly arguing about where it was. One of the men, more well-dressed than the others, held up the deed. "How'd you get this?"

"A fellow named Nash gave it to me near Hineston."

"I can see he signed it over to you, but why?"

"He owed me some money, and that made it right." I was always amazed at how quickly Pap could make up a plausible lie.

"Well, you don't want it."

Pap stepped forward. "It's my place now, and I'll be the judge of that."

The gentleman folded the deed. "Everybody that's lived there has had something bad happen to them. The Nash family was only the latest recipient of its bad luck."

"I don't believe in bad luck."

"Suit yourself." He sketched off a crude map of how to find the land. "It's south of here before the river crossing at the Whiskey Chitto. You'll come to a fork in the road and stay to the right. The house is on the north side of the road, and it's got a red door and broken-down chimney. Be careful. I was told there's a nest of copperheads under the floorboards."

This bleak report didn't deter Pap. He snatched his deed. "Appreciate your encouragement." As we saddled up, he said, "They ain't scaring me off it."

We rode south along the Confederate Road for two miles or so, following the landmarks until we reached the house. It was a typical dogtrot house and had definitely seen better days. The chimney had collapsed, and cypress shingles were missing in several spots. It sat in a pretty spot with young live oaks and several fruit trees. It was evident the Nash family had tried to make a go of it here. We stepped up onto the gallery; the creaking boards prompted us to walk carefully.

I kept thinking about those copperheads until Pap said, "Too cold for snakes to be moving now."

The windows and red door were covered in planks. Pap pried the door open and we walked into the front room. It had a rough plank floor and was connected to the chimney. The opposite room across the dogtrot was dirt-floored and had ample evidence that livestock had sheltered there.

I shivered. "I believe a rabbit just ran over my grave."

"Don't start any of your momma's crap about spirits and crows and spells."

"I just don't like the look of this place." I nodded at a patch of green palmetto plants. "This ground is too low. Those palmettos prove it. I bet it floods if the creek gets too high."

"What did they call that creek?"

I laughed. "Whiskey Chitto. I'm shocked you couldn't remember its name."

Even Pap laughed. "It sounds like where I oughta be." He stuck a hand through the gap in the logs. "The logs need chinking, and the roof needs work. Well, what do you really think?"

I was amazed at Pap asking my opinion. "Well, it's not exactly a mansion, but it beats the heck out of a wagon and tent. What about Ma?"

"She'll do as I say."

"It wouldn't hurt to let her see it and be part of the decision."

"She had her chance to come and passed on it."

I bit my tongue and went outside. The word mercurial was invented for Pap's personality. He could be kind and sensible, and then within a minute be as mean as one of those copperheads I knew were hibernating under that rotten floor. But I knew one thing for sure. He'd made up his mind, at least for the time being, that this would be where we stayed. It'd be the closest thing to a house we'd had since Alexandria. We'd have a real roof over our heads.

Pap made me promise not to mention to Ma about the horror stories about the previous occupants.

Ma wasn't crazy about the house when she saw it. As Ma shook her head, Pap said, "You've been saying you didn't have a pot to pee in or a window to throw it out." He nodded at the house as if it were an answer to her wish. "Now, here's your chance."

"It'll be a lot of work."

"We can do it. We can do it together."

I wanted to hug Pap and kiss him on top of his bald head. So we began moving in that afternoon. I took over the room on the right, shoveling out the dried manure. When I finished, I made a pallet on a rack of boards to sleep on. Pap took our army tent and stretched it across a wooden frame nailed to some sweet gums. This became home for Peg, Aunt Em, and Maggie.

Pa called our new home Poverty Knob. I nicknamed it Copperhead Acres. Ma just called it "that damn place."

It was sweet home at last.

CHAPTER 44

OPPORTUNITY KNOCKS

January 1882

On our third day in Sugartown, I decided to check out the Academy. School was out; the buildings seemed empty. My main goal was getting into the library. I had just about worn out 'Fantine' and 'Cosette.' It'd be a miracle to find the remaining book of *Les Miserable*s, but this library was my best bet.

The school building was unlocked, so I made my way through the hallway. I was sneaking around when I walked right into a stern-looking lady.

She looked me up and down. "And who might you be?"

"I'm Missouri Cotton. I was wishing to look at your library."

"My name is Lynne Collins, and I'm second in charge of the school under our headmaster and founder, Professor W. H. Baldwin." She pointed behind me. "The library is in there. It's not large, but it's the best around."

"May I take a look?"

I didn't like the way she was studying me. "Well, I guess so, but on future visits, you should announce your presence."

"Yes'um."

She walked me to a small room filled with the scent of musty, dusty paper and books. I inhaled deeply this smell that I always associated with books. I browsed up and down the wall of books. It wasn't a huge library but was stocked with the kinds of books I loved. There looked to be about a hundred or so of them, but to me it was as good as the famous Library at Alexandria. Alexandria, Egypt.

Miss Collins stood, arms crossed, watching me closely, as I tenderly touched the covers and pulled several volumes for a closer look. "You like reading?"

"Like the air I breathe."

"Where are you attending school?"

"I'm not."

"Where did you attend previously?"

"I, uh, I haven't had much schooling. We're always on the move."

"How'd you learn to read?"

"On my own."

She gave a hint of a smile and pushed a sheet of paper toward me. "Write your name and information down here. I'll tell Professor Baldwin about you."

"Is there any work around here in exchange for permission to read in your library?"

"How long will you be here?"

"At your school?"

"No, in town."

"I'm never sure as to what my pap will decide. We've moved into a house south of town, so I hope we'll be here a while." I stopped at the door. "May I come back tomorrow?"

"All right." She dismissed me with a curt nod. "That is all."

I backed out of the room.

The next day, I showed up at the library. I've known girls who get excited about going shopping or to a dance. That's the same way I've always felt about libraries. No one was on the premises of the Baldwin Academy, so I made myself at home. I examined the books, which were sorted by genre and category. Sadly, *Les Miserables* was not among the shelved books, so I settled instead for a newer book by Mark Twain entitled, *The Prince and the Pauper*.

At some point, Miss Collins entered and had a difficult time bringing me out of my book coma. "Young lady—Miss Cotton?"

I stared up at her. "I'm sorry."

"You were off in another world."

I held up Twain's book. "I was with the pauper in England."

"It's brand new. Professor Baldwin purchased a copy on a recent excursion to New Orleans. It's a good story about changing places."

I handed the book to her "It sounds pretty unlikely, but that's what I love about fiction…. Miss Collins, can I ask you a personal question?"

She glanced over her glasses. "Well … I guess so."

"It comes from Twain's book and the prince and the poor boy changing places. Do you think somebody can rise above their raising?"

She stepped around the desk, never taking her eyes off me. "I certainly hope so. Pray tell why you ask?"

"It's a question I ask lots of folks."

She picked up *The Prince and the Pauper*. "Well, Miss Missouri Cotton, do you believe someone can rise above their raising?"

"I sure hope so … but I'm not so sure." I rubbed my hand over the rough desktop. "Miss Collins, I love your library, but I was looking for a specific title. Have you heard of *Les Miserables* by Victor Hugo?"

"Professor Baldwin has a full set of the five Volumes of the novel in his office. He's a great fan of French Literature. Have you read it?"

"I've read the first four but can't find the final fifth volume."

"The professor is gone on business to Shreveport and he has the only key to his office. When he returns, I'm sure he'll be delighted to share the book with you."

I noticed a catch in her voice when she said, "he has the only key…." There seemed to be something mysterious about this Professor Baldwin.

"Miss Collins," I said. "Have you read all five Volumes?"

"Certainly."

"Did you like the story?"

She laughed. "It had too many twists and turns for me. Why do you like *Les Miserables* so much?"

"That's easy—that outcasts can get a new start and find love and roots."

"That's pretty deep for a girl your age." Miss Collins regained her stern schoolmarm's demeanor. "Well, if you borrow his copies, be sure not to write in the Professor's books."

"No ma'am, I'll take care of them like they were my own

children.”

I stopped at the door. “Do you mind telling me how the story ends?”

Miss Collins put her hands on her hips. “Now, do you really want me to give the story away?”

I smiled and waved. “Forget that I ever asked.”

She blocked my way and handed me Twain’s book. “This should keep you busy until the Professor gets back.”

I ran out the door, holding tightly to Mr. Twain. In a few days, I’d be holding Victor Hugo and *Volume Five, Jean Valjean,* of *Les Miserables.*

Before I left the library later that afternoon, Mrs. Collins asked me to return to the school the following day with my parents.

I chose not to tell them when I got home. Pap had a real hang-up about educated folks. Ma had always wanted me to have a formal education, but our lifestyle wasn't conducive to schooling.

I decided to make the school visit on my own late that afternoon. It had rained all night, but I showed up at the school in my best dress, embarrassed by my muddy shoes. I didn’t ride Peg to school because there was no place to tie her in the shade, and the livery stable charged ten cents a day.

Miss Collins put her hand over her mouth. “Kind of muddy out where you live?”

“Ma’am, it's muddy everywhere here.” I tried to stomp some of the mud off my boots. “I’m sorry my folks were prevented from coming with me. Maybe another day.”

She eyed me. “Professor Baldwin has returned and wishes to meet you. Evidently, he's heard about you. It seems you have quite the reputation.”

I wasn't sure how to respond. “I've always dreamed of being in school, but do you even have any openings?”

“It depends.”

“On what?”

“If a person—a girl—has school money.”

My heart sank.

Miss Collins led me to a large office in the opposite direction of the library. She motioned to a chair, and I sat.

"How much is school?"

"A semester is twenty-five dollars."

I was floored. "Twenty-five dollars?" I whistled. "That's a lot." I sadly thought about my satsuma money and vowed to go through all of Pap's belongings one more time tonight.

Just then, a distinguished-looking man walked in. Miss Collins stood. "This is Professor Doctor W.H. Baldwin, owner and headmaster of the Academy."

He wore pince-nez glasses perched low on his nose, and he peered over them, which gave the impression he was looking down on me. I squirmed in my seat.

"This young lady is inquiring about school," Miss Collins said.

He studied my muddy boots. "And who might you be?"

"I'm Missouri Cotton. My family has just moved here."

"From where?"

"We were last in Westport."

His eyes narrowed. "Westport?"

"Yes, sir."

He pointed a long finger. "Are you the famous girl who was inside the store during the fight?"

"Yes, sir."

"You are quite the young lady according to the stories going around." He wiped his forehead. "And you want to attend my school?"

"Yes, sir, but the money is well beyond what we have."

"What does your father do for a living?"

Boy, this was a tough one. "Uh, a little bit of everything." *And a lot of nothing.*

He leaned in closer, studying my face. I knew what was coming. "I'm not sure I've ever seen eyes quite like yours. They're not only different colors, but their pigment and pupils are quite unusual."

"I've heard that all of my life."

Miss Collins told the Professor about my dilemma with *Volume Five* of *Les Miserables*.

He asked me more about the story, and satisfied that I was serious, unlocked a nearby cabinet, and pulled out *Volume Five.*

As he unlocked the cabinet, I glanced at Miss Collins, but this time her face showed no reaction. I did notice that the entire office had cabinets and drawers, all closed and probably locked.

He handed the large book to me. "It's a tome, isn't it?"

I wasn't quite sure what a tome was, but quickly said, "It is that."

"Now, you'll leave the book in the library but can come by to read it anytime the building is unlocked."

I ran my hand over *Volume Five*, feeling the imprint of *Les Miserables Book Five, Jean Valjean*. I couldn't believe it.

Professor Baldwin stood. "I'd like to come by your home and meet your folks. Where do you live?"

I was careful. "Sir, our home is on this side of Whiskey Chitto. I don't want to trouble you coming out. Could I bring Ma here?"

Professor Baldwin stood and crisply said, "It won't be a bit of trouble coming out. Meet me here tomorrow at two o'clock. We'll ride out in my carriage and meet your folks."

I hurried to the library and began reading. I was only into about twenty pages and had learned about how Valjean removed his National Guard uniform and joined the revolutionists at the barricade when Miss Collins rapped on the door. "I'm locking up for the day."

I expected tomorrow to be a big day in more ways than one.

Now the question became how to broach the school subject with my parents, especially Pap. Catching him at the right moment was the key. And there weren't a lot of those good moments. I finally screwed up my courage. "Pap, do you know about the Baldwin Male and Female Academy in Sugartown?"

"School's for boys."

"No, it's a male and female academy. They're preparing young women to teach."

He was eating a bowl of stew and making a royal mess of it. He held his spoon aloft. "And…?"

"And the Professor is considering admitting me to the school."

"I don't know how long we'll be here."

"Please let me try it."

"You don't need no more education. I don't—"

"Pap, I'd also be working there. It could mean more money for our family." I hoped this familiar tactic would soften him up.

"We don't have no school money."

"I'm not asking for any. That's why the professor is coming out to meet y'all."

"I don't want you around those rich kids."

"From what I've seen of the student body, they're just country kids from all over the Pineywoods."

Ma spoke up. "It'd be a dream come true for Mizz."

"I don't care to hear one more word about it."

Ma and I backed out of the room. She whispered, "That went pretty well."

"Are you crazy? He shot it down."

"Not really. We created an opening. I'll take it from here. We'll be ready when your Professor Whoever comes tomorrow."

I hardly slept that night.

Ma and I planned for Pap to be gone. My chances were much better with him out of the picture.

Ma was as nervous as I was. We tried to spruce up the house and ourselves. All I can say is we made things better than they were.

Right at two o'clock, Professor Baldwin walked to his carriage outside the Academy. The driver jumped down and helped him up, and then I climbed up beside him.

On the ride out he said, "So you are a fellow lover of *Les Miserables.* He pronounced the title completely different from the way I did. I had lots of work to do on my *Francais.*

"It's my favorite book."

He took off his glasses. "Why do you think Hugo wrote it?"

"I'm no expert, but I believe he wrote it to show the humanity of mankind at its best as well as worst."

"Who is your favorite character?" he asked.

"I'd have to say Fantine. She gives up everything to save her daughter Cosette.

"Who is yours, Professor?"

"I've always loved the street urchin Gavroche with his spunk and pluck, but my favorite has to be Valjean."

"Prisoner 24601," I said.

He laughed. "24601. You really do know the book."

I felt as nervous as prisoner 24601 when we neared our home place.

He peered out of the carriage. "So, this is where you live?"

"For now. I apologize. I know it's humble."

"It is, but that's okay. All of us have to start somewhere." I guess my nervousness showed, because he added, "Honey, you can relax. I'm not trying to keep you out of our school. We're hunting ways to get you in."

Ma met us at the gate. Her hands shook as she invited Professor Baldwin into our house. She ducked her head. "Now, we don't have no school money."

Professor glanced around the interior of our front room. "I see. I'm not here to talk about money. I've heard about your daughter's bravery in that fight. I'd like to help her."

Ma sat up. "Who told you about Missouri and the fight?"

"Sam Nolan. He was one of the men caught inside. After the fight, he and his family moved here. Two of his children attend our Academy." Professor Baldwin laughed. "Sam Nolan has made quite the reputation reliving the fight. I wouldn't be surprised if he went on the road telling it with a medicine show or traveling preacher."

I relaxed. "I'm sure he's embellished it each time."

"I would expect nothing less. But in each telling, he's consistent about your part. Is it true you really went out and helped drag the wounded man inside?"

"The Moore brothers did most of the dragging. I just helped."

"Pretty brave."

"I figured they wouldn't shoot a woman."

"Not on purpose at least. Anyway, if you're willing to do some cleaning work at the school, I'd like to offer you a scholarship."

"I can attend your school?"

"Yes."

"Count me in. Will I stay there?"

"Not now. We're full up." He stood to leave. "We'll wait and see about boarding."

Ma and I walked him to the carriage. Professor Baldwin turned to me. "Missouri, you'll be new and different from most of our students."

I knew he was referring to my dark skin and rough ways.

"But if you work hard, you'll do well."

Just before Professor climbed into his carriage, my worst nightmare came true. Pap came staggering up and grabbed at the horse's reins. "What's going on here?" He squinted at the carriage. "What are you selling?"

Professor's voice was calm but firm. "A good education for your daughter."

Pap got right up in the professor's face. "What's a fellow from the great Columbia University doing out here in Sugartown, Louisiana? There's something's fishy about all of this."

Professor stepped back. "Sir, the only thing fishy about this is your breath." He'd evidently gotten a snoot full of Pap's infamous whiskey breath. Ma always said it could stop a charging grizzly in its tracks. "And in answer to your question, I'm here to provide a fundamental education to children like your daughter."

"I still think something's fishy."

Professor Baldwin climbed into the carriage. "Good day, sir." He motioned to the driver, who clicked to the horse. Pap took offense at being brushed off. "Hey, I'm not through with you. Come back here."

The carriage never slowed and Professor Baldwin never looked back. If I'd had my Colt .45, I'd have shot Pap. I would not've killed him, just winged him really good.

As the carriage receded up the road toward Sugartown following Pap's antics, I saw my chances for schooling disappearing also.

CHAPTER 45

24601

January 1882

I showed up at the school the next morning, not expecting admittance after Pap's actions. A stern Miss Collins was waiting at the door. "Professor Baldwin wishes to see you in his office." I entered expecting the worst. He sat behind his big desk that was piled high with papers and stacks of textbooks. He sat in a rolling chair that squeaked at his every move. "Sit down, Miss Cotton."

"Sir, I am so sorry for my father's words and actions."

He pulled out a cigar, lit it, and took a long drag. "You're not responsible for your father. You'll be judged here at the Academy by who you are and how you perform."

"I appreciate your mercy."

He sat his cigar in a tray. "So, your father likes to drink?"

"I'm afraid so."

"Does he have a job?"

"Not if he can help it."

He leaned across the desk. "To be honest, I fight a battle with the bottle myself, so I won't judge him on that." His face hardened. "However, being rude is inexcusable."

"I agree, sir, but may I ask a question?"

He nodded.

"Professor, do you think a person can change?"

He took a pull on his cigar. "I'd certainly hope so." He tipped the ashes in the tray. "Are you wondering if your father can change?"

"No sir. I'm wondering about myself."

He frowned. "Why would a girl your age need to change?"

"I been brought up rough around the edges. Lots of folks would call my family white trash or squatters. It shows itself from time to time. I'm afeared it'll show up here at the Academy."

The chair creaked as he leaned forward. "The correct grammar is 'I have been brought up' … and *afeared* is not a correct word. It's *afraid*."

I ducked my head. "That's why I need to be in your school."

"Well, we'll help you sand off some of those rough edges."

"I'm game."

He smiled. "Game for what?"

"To be the woman I was meant to be."

"And what woman do you think you're meant to be?"

"Kinder. Stronger. Smoother."

"Those are good goals." His rolling chair squeaked as he shifted his weight. "Now, back to your question. Can a person change? I'll answer your question with my own." He let the silence fill the room. "Jean Valjean. Did he change?"

"Sure. 24601. He leaves his old prison number behind. That's my favorite part of *Les Miserables*. A bad bitter man becomes a kind good man who lives a life of grace. I believe that was part of Hugo's reason for writing it. That's why we see his number— 24601—show up again and again. It's a reminder of who he was, not of who he's becoming."

"How did you feel when Valjean was given the job of killing the spy Javert?"

I'd only read this section recently and was still stunned by how it played out. "I was excited and sickened when I realized Valjean was finally going to get his revenge on Javert."

"Those are two divergent emotions." He watched me. I believe he was testing to see if I'd really read and understood the story.

"At first I felt excitement that Jean Valjean was finally going to get revenge on Javert. Javert had hounded an innocent Valjean for decades. It was time for what Hugo would probably call poetic justice. When he dropped the pistol and pulled out his sharp knife, I thought it was an appropriate way for the spy to die."

"Sickened?"

"Jean Valjean was no long Jean Valjean. He was LeBlanc. An old man who had changed in every way. It would spoil the whole story when he slit Javert's throat."

"So you liked the passage?"

"It was brilliant. Cutting the bonds loose of the man who'd spent a lifetime trying to put you back in chains."

"Well said." Professor Baldwin nodded. "What about the policeman, Javert?"

"No sir, I don't think he can, or is willing, to change. That's what leads him to jump into the Seine and end his life."

"Was Javert a bad man?"

"No sir, but he was a man so tied to the law that he seemed unable, or unwilling, to show mercy or flexibility."

"You've used that word mercy twice. How do you define it?"

"Not getting the punishment you deserve."

"Well said. You also said Valjean became a man of grace. What is that?"

"Grace is getting what you don't deserve. It's a gift."

He snubbed out his cigar. "Well, Miss Missouri Cotton, which of those two are you asking me for?"

I stared him straight in his eyes. "Professor, I'm asking for mercy for my pap's actions and begging for grace as an opportunity to attend your school."

He pulled out his pocket watch. "Then, it's time for your big changes to begin. Your first class starts in fifteen minutes."

"What will my schedule be?"

"We're starting you lightly. World Geography, European Literature, and Latin I."

"Latin?"

"It's an integral part of a good academy education."

"I have enough trouble with plain ol' English."

"If you'll study, you'll do fine," Professor Baldwin said.

"The semester's only two weeks old, and I'm already way behind."

He waved me off and stood from his creaky chair. "Let's get started, 24601."

He led me into a classroom with about fifteen students. I was amazed at how young many of them were, and they were all dressed much nicer than I was. One of the boys giggled at my muddy boots, and I heard a girl whisper, "It's the Westport Fight Girl."

Luckily I was seated next to Sonnet Ireland. She put a finger to her lips and smiled.

I was immediately way in over my head in World Geography which was taught by Miss Collins.

They were studying Africa, especially the European colonial powers and their grip on the continent. I listened and took laborious notes, keeping my head down to avoid any questions.

Geography ended and we stayed in the same classroom for our next subject, European Literature.

"I need to pee real bad," I said to Sonnet.

"You'll have to wait until after Literature." Sonnet leaned over. "Don't be nervous."

"I'm scared speechless."

"Just watch me," Sonnet said. "If you're put on the spot, I'll help you."

Professor Baldwin taught Literature. He introduced me and thankfully never asked me any questions. I immediately fell in love with Prof's obvious devotion to classical literature and books. He spoke so fast and passionately, that it was difficult to take notes. I furiously scribbled names, books, and dates. Sonnet leaned over and whispered. "Don't drop your pencil. If you do, you'll miss two pages of notes and fail the next test for sure."

The students around us giggled, causing Professor Baldwin to frown disapprovingly. "Miss Ireland, do you wish to address the class?"

"No, sir, I was just spelling *Chaucer* for Miss Cotton."

As I learned next, Professor Baldwin felt free to chase any and all rabbits. It was his school, and he was master of the classroom, but he had the rare ability to always bring the discussion back to the subject at hand. He rambled about Julius Caesar, who had no visible connection to this guy named Chaucer. "Now, let me mention about Shakespeare and his portrayal of Caesar. Even though Latin is after lunch, I'll ask for a translation of what were purportedly Caesar's last words before his assassination."

A boy tentatively raised his hand. "Et tu, Brute?"

"Was that a question or a statement?"

"Well, sir, it must've been a question, because it's translated, 'You too, Brutus?' "

"Correct."

Sonnet leaned over. "Marcus Weldon knows the answer to everything."

Professor pulled down a map of Europe and summarized the

conquests of the Romans under Caesar's generalship. "It was all of that success that eventually threatened his rivals in Rome and brought about his death." He used his pointer to jab a spot near Italy and France, then called on Sonnet, "Miss Ireland, can you tell me the significance of this river called the Rubicon?"

Sonnet shifted in her desk. "To be honest, sir, I have no idea."

Professor tapped his pointer. "We talked about it last semester in World Civilization."

"I believe it had something to do with … Julius Caesar?"

Professor nodded. "That's a good start. Who can expound on that?"

Marcus's hand shot up. "Prof, it's the river where Caesar and his army crossed on their return to Rome."

"Why was that important?"

"When he and his army crossed the Rubicon, they were in direct opposition to the Roman Senate."

"Good." Prof glanced around the class. "Was it a big river?"

Sonnet's memory had been jarred. "No, sir, it was a small river, that was really a big river."

Prof grinned. "Please explain."

"Once Julius Caesar waded across the Rubicon with his army, there was no turning back. 'Crossing the Rubicon' is still used as a metaphor for making a decision that allows no retreat or change."

Prof nodded. "Good answer, but it isn't a metaphor. It's an idiom." He turned to me. "And Miss Cotton, have you ever crossed the Rubicon?"

I slid down in my desk. "Not that river, but other rivers in my life have been points of no return."

"How so?"

"Last year, my family crossed the Calcasieu into No Man's Land, and I knew there was no going back.

"Why so?"

I ducked my head. "It's complex, and I'd rather not talk about it in public."

Thankfully the lunch bell rang. "I'll see all of you after lunch in Latin," Prof said.

Sonnet walked beside me as we went outside. "You handled that pretty well."

"Whew. He likes putting people on the spot."

"You haven't seen nothing yet. Wait until Latin class."

My stomach was in knots as I walked into Latin with Sonnet. It was Professor Baldwin's prize subject, and I was way out of my league. Even before class started, a boy named Delbert Cole tested me on my knowledge of Latin. He sadly shook his head. "You don't know anything, do you?"

"It's all Greek to me."

The three of us laughed, as Cole said, "Well, at least you've got a sense of humor."

Professor Baldwin tapped his pointer. "Class, come to order."

In a refined dignified script, Professor wrote on the blackboard, "We have no power over external things, and the good that ought to be is found only within ourselves."

Prof stepped back from the board, admiring the statement as well as his crisp handwriting. "A Greek philosopher, Epictetus, wrote this during the time of the Roman Empire. I shakily wrote it on my slate board, twice breaking my piece of chalk."

Then Prof using a yellow piece of chalk and wrote between the lines of the English translation. *Externorum habemus potestatem bonum quod deberet esse obiectum studio, non inveniatur in nobis.*

Sweat beaded on my forehead as I copied it down in Latin. Prof called on students to explain various words in the sentence. Sonnet, when called on, stood. "The first word *Externorum* can be translated as *external*, but a more correct translation would be *foreign*.

"*Bene dictum*, Miss Ireland."

I kept my head down praying he wouldn't call on me, but my prayers weren't answered. "Miss Cotton, what do you think the philosopher is saying?"

I wouldn't even attempt to pronounce the author's name. "I believe he—the writer—is insisting that none of us can control what happens around us, but we can"—I glanced around the classroom— "and must control what happens in us—in our heart and soul."

"*Bene dictum*. Well said, Miss Cotton."

I sweated out the final quarter hour of Latin. Prof said, "All right, I'd like one of you to come write a Latin sentence and we'll dissect it."

"Know-It-All" Delbert Cole raised his hand and strode to the board, where, while copying from a scrap, wrote. *Sic semper tyrannys.*

Professor Baldwin's anger was visible as he stood beside Delbert. He spoke through gritted teeth. "So, Master Cole, please explain your sentence?"

Cole put his finger below each word as he said,

"Sic … Thus.

"Semper … Always.

"Tyrannys … to Traitors."

He smiled wickedly at Prof. "*Sic Semper Tyrannys*—thus, always to traitors."

Prof's face was red. "And please tell the class what prompted you to share that sentence?"

"It's an important part of our history," Delbert Cole said. "When John Wilkes Booth shot Abe Lincoln, Booth shouted 'Sic Semper Tyrannys' as he leapt from the Presidential Box at Ford's Theater."

Prof walked toward him. "And if I recall, that was after he had cowardly shot President Lincoln in the back of the head and then jumped onto the stage and ignobly broke his leg."

Sonnet nudged me. "Prof is a Union man, and Cole loves to aggravate him."

I was trying to figure out what ignobly meant.

"John Wilkes Booth was a Patriot, not a coward," Cole said.

Prof rose to his full height. "No, he was a coward, and he was the traitor."

Cole put his arms on the lectern. "My daddy believes the traitor was the one who was kilt that night."

"The correct word is *killed*."

Sonnet whispered, "The Civil War has never ended for the Cole family, and he cannot resist needling Prof. It always makes for an interesting class."

Prof picked up his pointer, and I wouldn't have been surprised if he'd cracked it over Delbert Cole's head. "This isn't history class, but since young Master Cole is insistent, I'll remind the class that this dastardly act was done after the Civil War had actually ended." He took a deep breath. "And that the coward Booth was justifiably shot and killed in a burning barn. Mr. Cole, do you know what his final words probably were?"

"No, sir."

Prof wrote in large letters across the board, breaking his chalk in the process. "'Finis.' And Mr. Cole,"—he pointed to an American flag hanging on the wall— "may I remind you that we are all Americans in here."

David Cole defiantly stood. "That's not my flag."

Prof took a deep breath, and nodded at me. "Well, Miss Cotton, this is your first day in Latin, but as you can see, it will always be an invigorating class."

I wasn't quite sure what invigorating was, but I knew Latin was never going to be boring—or in my case—easy.

CHAPTER 46

ROOTS

January 29, 1882

As January ended and I settled into a semblance of routine and our house began to feel like a home, then a disturbing event occurred. Tom-Claws, our wagon cat, disappeared.

Ever since we'd left Ten Mile, Claws had been off his feed. Just lying around lethargically with little interest in tormenting caught mice or exploring our new surroundings. Even as we moved into the house, he kept his abode in the corner of the wagon. It was Mom who first noticed him missing. We searched the surrounding countryside for days and even put up a few notices in Sugartown. I even asked Lucky, but he was of no help.

But it was to no avail. Pap shrugged. "Oh, he'll show back up sooner or later. You know how it is about those nine lives. He's probably off tom-catting around."

But the weeks went on with no sign of Tom-Claws, who'd been my cat since I was a girl. It was a devastating loss. At age sixteen, I couldn't carry on about it like I was ten, but I even dreamed of him at night. I spent my days wandering and worrying about him being in trouble and needing my help. But in the coming weeks, we saw neither hide nor hair of Tom-Claws Cotton, our faithful ratter and wagon cat.

Speaking of loss, I still hadn't received a letter from Dan Moore. I'd written dozens to him in care of his brother Mayo in

Alexandria. I wrote him daily, using the letters as a chance to chronicle our new life in Sugartown, the Baldwin School, our house, and with many of the characters that made up the village of Sugartown. Each day as I mailed my letter, I asked the postmistress, Mrs. Singleton, if there was any mail posted for me.

She'd sadly shake her head, "Not today."

A month later I simply quit asking. Mrs. Singleton, sensing my anguish, said, "Honey, you can't stay down because some boy won't write you back. There could be all kinds of reasons. He may not be receiving your letters or his reply letters might be sitting in the post office at Alexandria or Lake Charles."

"I'm sorry, but I've given up. I believe Dan'l Moore has closed the door and moved on."

"Honey, you don't know that." The postmistress came out from behind her counter and hugged me.

The tears burst forth in a torrent. "Well, I had a deep love for him—but it's slowly cooled and has turned to anger. That's been the general tenor of my letters for the past week."

"Honey, writing an angry letter doesn't usually solve a problem."

"I'm just haunted by our final words when we parted in Ten Mile. I asked him if he felt as deep about our relationship as I did."

"What'd he say?"

"Something to the effect of 'Yes, Missouri, it was real. But sometimes even real things don't last.' "

Mrs. Singleton stroked my hair. "Honey, after what y'all'd been through in the Westport Fight, I'd be careful trying to figure out what every word or statement meant."

I wrote Dan three more letters that week. I wished I'd kept a total count of how many I'd sent.

The only number I was sure of was how many letters I'd received back—zero.

The following Monday, I walked into the Post Office and held up a brown envelope.

"This is the last one."

Mrs. Singleton removed her green visor. "What's the letter say?"

"That I've waited long enough and am taking his silence as an answer."

I slid the envelope through the post office slot.

Mrs. Singleton picked up the envelope from her side of the mail cage. "Missouri, once this leaves Sugartown this afternoon, it's too late to take it back. What you've written in ink to this boy will last forever." She tried to hand the letter back across the counter.

"No, ma'am," I ceremoniously dusted off my hands. "It's time to move on."

I walked the streets of Sugartown for most of the morning. I was still hunting. If someone had asked, I'd replied I was hunting a lost cat named Tom-Claws. But there was something much deeper. I was still hunting for a lasting love, a real home, and a feeling of belonging.

Dan Moore and his family were the closest thing I'd had to all of these things.

Although Pap insisted we were staying near Sugartown, I never felt settled. However, that changed in mid-February when he borrowed a middle-buster, hooked up Aunt Em, and began putting in a garden. I suddenly felt much better about our Sugartown roots. I joined him in the plowed field. When a man starts digging in the dirt and putting in a crop, it's usually a sign he plans to be here a while.

Pap was holding a cut potato in each hand. "In the Deep South, folks always plant their Irish potatoes on the Ides of February— February 15."

"I thought you and Ma swore by the *Farmer's Almanac?*"

"We do, but planting taters is different. It must be done on the Ides of February."

He then plowed three more rows on the west side. "We'll plant some field corn and string beans on the waxing of the moon.

We'd seldom been anywhere long enough to plant crops or keep livestock. That week Pap proudly came home with four chickens, swinging them by their tied legs. Ma leaned on her hoe. "Where'd you get money to buy chickens?"

"I still have a little of my horse-race winnings socked away."

"Well, I'd like to find that money sock and get a few things I need," Ma said.

He cut the chickens loose, and they immediately went to scratching in the grass. One of them, a big Rhode Island Red, flapped its wings and cackled.

"They already think they own the place," Pap said as he went into the house.

I was ecstatic. "We're staying, aren't we?"

Ma threw down her hoe. "Don't count your chickens before they hatch."

Then the next miracle happened. Pap got a job. It began when I met a man at the Post Office and as he fumbled through his mail, I said, "I bet you work in a sawmill."

He looked up in mild irritation. "How'd you know?"

"You're missing two fingers, and you smell like pine sap."

He grinned and held up his right hand. "Took my eye off for just a second."

"You've got sawmill fingers."

"Lots of men around here do. At least I've still got three on this hand. Other fellows haven't been as lucky as me."

"Lucky? I guess I'll take your word for it, sir. If you don't mind me saying, my father is an excellent sharpener."

"Crosscuts?"

"Yes, sir. He can hone the big circular saws, too."

"Is he looking for work?"

I hesitated on how to answer. "Well, I'm sure if the price was right."

Three-Fingers said, "My name's Weldon. Tell him to come by my mill, and I'll make him a good offer. We just lost our best sharpener to one of the big mills in Lake Charles.

I told Pap about the sawmill job, and he agreed to take a look. During Pap's circuitous work career, he had worked as a sawyer, or flathead, as they called the lumberjacks in Louisiana. He was a little old to hold up to being on the business end of a crosscut saw all day, but he had another skill always in high demand in the woods. He could sharpen a saw to a honed cutting edge. He'd learned this trade as a boy, and although rusty, he soon earned a reputation around Sugartown as the best man for putting an edge on a crosscut, double-bit ax, and even the big circular blades in the sawmills.

Pap took to his work, going from mill to mill. He was paid various amounts by the different mills, but he received part of his pay in lumber. Each day, on the slip pulled by Mag or Aunt Em, he brought home one-by-sixes and soon built a solid floor for my room. He also had access to leftover sawmill slats, and he and I built a lean-to for Pegasus and Mag and Aunt Em to replace their tattered tent.

The wagon was carefully parked way under a crude shed behind the house.

All of this added up to a miracle. We were putting down roots.

But the defining day of my hope was a Friday when Pap brought home a load of rough lumber. He wouldn't tell Ma or me what he had planned, but the next morning, he began constructing an outhouse. It wasn't fancy, but it was ours and it said a whole lot about permanence and pride.

Ma and I eagerly dug the latrine pit, and by mid-afternoon Pap hooked up the team and dragged the new outhouse over the pit. We were in business.

Each day during the work week, Pap arrived home shouldering several dull crosscut saws. I'd help him brace them as he filed and sanded the teeth. During these times, he was full of stories. "You know, Abe Lincoln was an able sharpener and sawyer. That's how he got his nickname of the rail splitter. They claim he was tremendously strong in his upper body and could outwork any young man. During his boyhood, the ax was still the tool of choice of the woodsman, the crosscuts were just coming into wider use."

Pap flipped over the saw. "Honest Abe once said that if he had six hours to cut a tree, he'd spend the first five sharpening his saw. It don't matter how hard a man works, if his saw is dull he'll work ten times harder."

He pointed the file at me. "A good lesson for life."

I'd never seen Pap more content or kinder.

Speaking of kindness, I was mostly treated well at school, especially by the teachers. On a Tuesday, Miss Collins asked me to stay after school. I was the worrying type, and she sensed it. "You're not in trouble." She handed me an envelope.

I held it as if a rattlesnake might be inside.

"Open it, Girl. It's got your name on it."

I didn't recognize the handwriting on the envelope or enclosed letter.

"Missouri Cotton,

Please go by Lacy's Store at your convenience. A package awaits with your name."

There was no salutation or signature. I twirled the note in my hand, even smelling it as if it might give off some clue. I held it to the light expecting some invisible ink to give off another message. "Who is it from?"

"I don't know. It was stuck in the door when I arrived this morning."

I studied it some more.

"Girl, you don't look a gift horse in the mouth. Go by the store and find out."

"May I be excused?"

She shooed me out of the room, and I made tracks as fast as I could to the store. It'd been raining all week. Even the wooden sidewalks were covered in mud. By the time I reached the store, my legs and shoes were mud-caked. I was so excited that I forgot to remove them at the store entrance.

A man leaned over the counter. He had what I'd call a bemused look on his face. "May I help you?"

"I'm Missouri Cotton. They told me you have a package for me."

He lifted up a box and pulled out a pair of new Wellington boots. They were a waterproof gum boot ideal for tromping through Louisiana mud. "They're for you."

He nodded at my muddy school shoes. "I believe you'll find it a lot easier now to keep your school shoes clean."

He handed me the boots, and I immediately slipped them on. They fit perfectly. "Who got these for me?"

"A secret admirer."

"Who was it?"

"Can't tell." He nodded toward the doorway. "Now, get on

your way. When you return, be sure to take those boots off at the door."

I scooped them up and ran out the door. "Don't worry. I will."

As I hurried home in my new boots, I tried to figure out who had done this. I had several suspects in mind but couldn't be sure. The kindness I received at the Baldwin Academy, was more of a "you're trying to better yourself, so let's see how we can help you pull yourself up."

I still had problems fitting in at the Baldwin Academy. There was a gang of uppity girls who called themselves the Sabine Women. They pronounced it differently from the river as in Say-Bean. Anyway, the Sabine Women claimed they were descendants of a nation of women who were kidnapped by the Trojans for war brides. I found it in one of the library encyclopedias, and it called the incident "the Rape of the Sabine Women." It didn't paint a pretty picture of this legendary story.

The Sabine Women prided themselves on tormenting my every move. I felt like that different-colored chick that the others tried to peck to death. I figured I'd have to whip one or two of the Sabine Women sooner or later, but I chose for the moment to keep my academic and behavioral record clean.

As I walked home that day, I looked down at my new boots and thought, The Sabine Women will still find plenty of reasons to make fun of me, but it won't be due to my muddy school shoes.

The next week an incident happened that involved the Sabine Women and me. Their ringleader was an older girl named Bridget Thompson. She had kin that had been on the Ten Mile side of the Fight, and they'd convinced her I was active in the shooting from inside the store. Bridget and her group spread story after story about me. The worst was that I'd been the one who killed Mr. Whiskey Morrow at the store. Bridget also spread the word that I'd been involved with a colored worker at the Turpentine Camp.

One day, I'd had enough and caught her alone by the washroom. I got her by the arm. "I've had enough from you and your friends. I've tried to ignore your taunts and digs, but I've had my fill."

She smirked. "And what are you gonna do about it?"

I grabbed her by the neck. "You'll stop talking that way about me. I don't want to hear any more of these lies about me. I've had enough."

She coughed and tried to remove my hand. I tightened my grip before letting go. "Is my message clear?"

Bridget Thompson rubbed her neck where my finger marks showed. She had a mixture of fear and hate in her eyes. "I will ... get the last word ... on this. You just wait and see. I'll see you and your trashy family run out of town." But this encounter ended the direct harassment from her and her crew. They gave me plenty of space, evidently convinced I was a little bit crazy.

CHAPTER 47

ST. PATRICK'S DAY

Thursday, March 16, 1882

Ma stood over my bed. "Missouri, get your dress on quick. We've got business in Sugartown.

School had been cancelled by a recent rain that had swollen all of the creeks. I'd looked forward to a lazy day, but Ma was ready to go.

"What kind of business?"

"The kind that I've got to see with my own eyes."

I quickly dressed, and we doubled up on Pegasus. "Now, what's going on?"

"We're going to the Baptist Church. I can't tell you what's there. It might jinx it."

I knew better to waste my breath asking more. As we went through town, I saw Sonnet and waved for her to join us.

Several carriages formed a semi-circle in front of the church. I figured someone had died. But as we climbed off Pegasus, Ma said, "Yesterday, a baby was left in a basket on the church steps. A note was left from the mother, and that's all I know at this point. The pastor's wife took the child, which looked to be about four months old into the parsonage."

The baby was asleep in a basket on the church floor right in front of the communion table. The Pastor's wife lifted the blanket, and Sonnet gasped, "Mrs. Preacher, that baby's half colored."

"He is. The poor child'll have a hard life if he stays in Sugartown."

"Well, I'm sure someone in our church will give the child a home," Sonnet said.

The pastor's wife looked away. "I'm afraid that won't be

possible. It just wouldn't be, uh, proper."

I glanced at Ma, whose arms were crossed and her jaw was set.

"Where do you think the child came from?" Sonnet said.

The Pastor's wife sighed. "A few months ago a young pregnant woman was in and out of town for a few weeks. Word was that she was staying with kin across Sugar Creek. We believe the baby belongs to that young woman." She even left this note. The Pastor's Wife handed the note to Ma, who handed it to me.

To Whomever,

I can't take it anymore, and I sure won't take care of this baby. I hope someone will find it in their heart to raise this child.

Sonnet knelt by the basket. "Well, he's a lovely baby, even if he is a half-breed."

I made a face at Sonnet. "You need to watch how you describe folks. I've been called all of those names my whole life."

"I'm so sorry, Mizz. It's just how we talk around here."

"Well, I don't want to hear those words from you."

She stood. "You won't."

The three of us. Ma, Sonnet, and me, left the church. Sonnet helped Ma into the saddle. "Mrs. Cotton, no one in Sugartown is going to take that baby."

Sonnet reached up to the reins. "You're thinking about taking that baby, aren't you?"

"Someone's got to."

Ma and I rode slowly home. "Pap will never go for it."

"You let me take care of him." She put her hand on my shoulder. "What do you think?"

"I hate to admit it, but I don't want that baby in our home. Things are going so well that I hate to upset the applecart."

Ma sighed. "Missouri Cotton, I know you pretty well. That's not the real reason."

I hung my head. "It'll affect how my classmates look at me and our family. Most of them already view us as white trash. Taking this baby in would add another layer to our reputation."

"Missouri, you ought to be ashamed of yourself."

"I am."

We reached home, and I quickly went to the lean-to to unsaddle Peg. I patted my horse. "I'm ashamed of myself. Been looked down on my whole life, and now I'm doing the same thing to an innocent baby." I left the house and took a long walk along

Whiskey Chitto Creek.

It was dusk-dark when I finally got the courage to return home. Pap and Ma were sitting over our supper of squirrel, gravy, and cornbread.

Ma was in full throttle, holding up her fork. "Henry, you've always wanted a boy something fierce. I've prayed about it for years. We've lost several baby boys, and we're way too old to have a baby on our own. Maybe this is the Lord's way of giving us that boy."

Pap silently chewed on a squirrel leg. I'd seldom seen him this quiet.

That night, it took me a long time to go to sleep, partly due to Ma and Pap talking far into the night. To my surprise, Pap's voice remained calm, and I could sense a softening in his voice.

I drifted off to the knowledge that changes were coming to the Cotton Home. Only time would tell if these changes were good or bad.

The next morning Ma dressed in her best dress and accompanied me to school where she gave me a five-dollar bill. "I want you to bring home a nursing nanny goat tonight."

I held the bill like it was a rattlesnake. "What about its kid?"

"Buy it too." She waved. "I'll see you at home this evening."

I stood on the doorstep as she made a beeline for the Baptist church. I knew there was going to be at least two more kids at the Cotton Farm tonight and one would be bleating while the other one would probably be a squaller.

Today was St. Patrick's Day, and I'd completely forgotten it. Not having a stitch of green on, I was pinched all day. But overall, it was a good day. Word leaked out that we were taking in the new baby, and Delbert Cole went home at lunch and brought back a nanny with a male kid.

"How much do you want for her and the kid?"

"Nuthin'. My folks wanted to help." He handed me the rope and said, "Deborah and her son, Pete, are yours."

When I arrived home from school leading a goat and kid, I had to pinch myself when I saw Ma holding that baby. She smiled. "I've named him Patrick James, since we got him on St. Patrick's Day, but we'll call him James. I had a brother named James, and I just like the way it sounds."

I looked from Ma to Pap. "What possessed you and Pap to take that baby?"

"I've always had a soft spot for underdogs and outcasts." Ma handed the baby to me. "We've always been underdogs. I'm inclined to think that Jesus was for underdogs, too."

Pap shrugged. "Well, I figger we'll take him in until his family claims him."

"Pap, you know that's not going to happen," I said.

Well, I've always called your Ma 'The Patron of Lost Causes.' She'll take in any stray dog or skinny cat and feed any road beggar that knocked on our door.

Ma just smiled and said, "Yep, and I married the biggest lost cause of all."

Even Pap laughed at that but still bitterly complained about having another mouth to feed.

Of course, it became my job to keep Baby James supplied with goal milk, but Deb, as I called her, was a good milker.

By the second day, Pap held Baby James more than Ma or me. Our lives did change, and I mean immediately. The fact that little James lived with us now made the drafty house even more of a problem. Because Ma had lost her share of babies, she worried greatly over any little cough or sneeze the baby made, while Pap was busy covering every knothole and chinking every gap between any logs.

He'd hold the baby every night after supper on the front rocker. Invariably as the four of us watched another day end, Pap would make a statement to the effect, "I sure hope this boy turns out better than me."

Ma would nod in agreement. "I hope he grows up better than all of us." I laid my book in my lap and stared off deeply into the lengthening shadows. I was pretty convinced Baby James would.

Our house was beginning to look and feel like a home, and of course, that's when the trouble started. We were the Cotton family, and whatever alias or summer name we took on, trouble seemed to still find us. This trouble happened as the weather warmed and the snakes began showing up. Early mornings and at dusk were when the snakes moved the most, and we killed several copperheads each morning or evening. With Baby James in our home, the idea of snakes in and around our house sent chills down my spine. After we killed a good-sized four-footer on the porch, we all moved into the wagon to sleep.

However, it was hard to sleep in the wagon due to the battle royale taking place under the house. Lucky, who'd lost a paw to a snakebite, hated snakes with every ounce of his little dog's heart. He spent most of each night barking under the house and normally greeted us each morning with a dead snake in his mouth. He repeatedly popped it with his jaws, slinging it against the wall with a loud plop, as if to assure us it was truly dead.

"That dog's a snaker," Ma said. "He knows how to pop a snake's neck."

Pap lifted the snake on a stick. "It's another copperhead. I wonder how many more are holed up under there?"

Lucky was on a mission from God and was in constant combat under the house. As he'd drag the dead snakes out, I'd haul them off on a shovel. I lost count at eight. Most were small, but Lucky had killed two big ones.

About the fifth morning of the battle, Lucky lay quietly by the door, his muzzle swollen to twice its size. "It looks like Lucky got bit," Ma said.

"Will he be all right?" I asked.

"Should be. Copperheads have short fangs, and dogs are resistant to snake poison. He'll be sick a few days. I'll pick some snake leaves in the swamp and fix up a poultice for him.

The next day I killed a copperhead by the front step with a hoe. Lucky lifted his head but showed no interest in the snake. I wondered if his bite had taken the fight out of our snaker.

During his recovery, I took over snake duty, but I had help. Deb the goat hated snakes as bad as Lucky and instinctively began roaming the yard snake-hunting. It's an amazing thing as to how a goat hoof can dispatch a snake.

My snake duty weapon was a long-handled hoe. One day a good-sized copperhead nipped my boot when I got careless. That's when I got Peacemaker out. I needed some target practice anyway. I'd sit in a straight chair near the collapsed chimney each morning before school and again at dark. Ma supplied me with coffee and Pap threw in some cash for shells. He enjoyed watching me shoot. A .45 caliber has kick to it and the first couple of times I fell out of the chair. Pap laughed. "Looks to me like you got too much gun for a girl your size."

I pointed to the headless copperhead I'd just dispatched. "Take it up with him."

Lucky hardly raised his head at each killing as if he'd retired permanently from snaking. I should have known better. About the third day after the snakebite, Lucky was hopping about on his three legs, rededicated to eradicating every reptile within our place. Once again in the wagon, it was hard to sleep as Lucky carried on nightly warfare with the copperheads. Deb took the day shift while Lucky, barking all night, worked graveyard.

Most mornings, a mangled copperhead lay by the front steps. Ma said Lucky was leaving us a gift. Pap starting calling Lucky "St. Patrick" saying, "He's gonna cast every snake out of this place."

Another thing that endeared Lucky to us was how he hovered over Baby James. If James was on the gallery or in the yard, Lucky kept in step with him. "That snaker's protecting James," Ma said. "Ain't no snake gonna get within striking distance of that baby."

Lucky's battle under the house continued, then slowly petered out. I don't know if Lucky had killed every snake, or the survivors simply surrendered and slithered off to safer pastures in Ireland. We never spotted another snake on our place.

The week after St. Patrick's Day, 1882, featured an encounter that shook me to the core. Sugartown, being on the Confederate

Road, was the main trail for driving livestock westward to the Sabine River at a place called Niblett's Bluff. It wasn't unusual for cowboys to drive hundreds of heads of cattle westward through town.

I tried never to miss it. On this particular day, word spread that a large herd was coming through town within the hour. It hadn't rained in several weeks so the road was dusty. That meant closing every window and door at the businesses and homes. I helped lock down the Baldwin School.

Cowboys, being cowboys, loved running the herd through town at a full trot, and today's drovers were no different. The lowing herd, accompanied by a towering cloud of dust, rushed through Sugartown's main street. The whip-popping, whistling, and yelling cowboys were enjoying their version of busting up town.

Several of the cowboys had bandanas over their faces, but it was easy for me to see that they were from the Ten Mile area.

I wondered if the bandanas were to make them appear as outlaws, or keep the dust out of their nostrils. I surmised it was both. One of the riders stationed his horse not twenty feet from where I stood by the school. He had his bullwhip unfurled and anytime a stray cow tried to veer off, he expertly put her back with the herd.

As the last of the herd passed, he pulled down his bandana. It was Moon Perkins. I had a side profile of him, so he didn't see me. I wanted to call out, let him know I was alive and in Sugartown, ask about his mother and brother Robert and Occupy Church, if he ever saw Unk, and how things were in Ten Mile.

But I did none of that. I stood frozen in time, with my hand over my mouth, watching as he pulled up his bandana, spurred his horse and quickly caught up with the rear of the herd. I quietly said, "Another time. Another place," and walked back into the school.

CHAPTER 48

SURPRISES

March 25, 1882

It was the last Saturday in March and unseasonably cold for this time of year. A cutting north wind penetrated my blouse and jacket as I put dirt on our emerging potato plants. I looked up to see a lanky boy approach the front gate. It was Billy Reed, the sheepherder who'd helped us protect the store at Westport.

I stuck my hoe blade up. "Morning."

"You're the Westport Fight Girl," he said.

"And you're Sheepherder Billy, who went to the 'Who'd a Thought It School.'"

"You have a good memory." He looked around our place. "What are you doing here?"

"Me and my folks moved here after the burnout."

"Yeah, I heard they burned the Westport store. Sorry."

"I guess it was going to happen sooner or later."

"How do you like Sugartown?"

"A lot. I'm in school."

"At the Academy?"

"Yep."

"How'd you swing that, money-wise?"

"It's been a conspiracy of kindness."

Billy shrugged. "So, it has." He held up a pine knot and some matches. "We're setting fire to the woods today. We've been waiting for a strong north wind that'll drive the fire through the pines and today's the day. I wanted to warn you before we start burning."

"Why are you burning?"

"The fire makes for better grass for the sheep. It also gets rid of briars and underbrush and hopefully kills the ticks and chiggers." He pointed toward the road. "The wind'll carry the fire and smoke toward you, but don't worry, we've got plenty of beaters to keep it from crossing the Military Road."

True to his word, it was a fine fire. It scorched the longleafs up to head high and all of the straw and scrub was burned to a crisp. I walked out to the road to enjoy its heat.

Billy came by setting backfires at the road with his pine-knot torch. "This is our Easter cold snap. Happens every year."

"But Easter changes dates."

"Don't matter. We'll have a cold spell right around Easter no matter what."

The Easter cold snap affected us in our house. It was some kind of drafty and cold. Because the chimney was collapsed, Ma still cooked out in the open on the lee side of the house. If we tried to build a fire in the chimney, it quickly smoked the whole house. So, we spent most of the time bone-chilled, even on warmer days. Pap, Ma, and I all kept a fresh cold most of the time. On sunny days, Ma would take her sewing or other housework out on the porch, complaining, "It's a lot warmer outside than in there. We could hang out meat inside ... if we had any."

Pap promised he was going to repair the chimney, but it was just as we'd found it. Several nights I moved into the wagon, where it wasn't quite as drafty.

On one of those mornings I was leaving the wagon, wrapped in a quilt, when I saw a group of men riding up. I ran inside to get decent as Pap walked to the gallery edge warily. "Can I help you fellows?"

"Nope, we came to help you."

"How's that?"

"We're here for the chimney daubing."

Ma welcomed the men to the gallery and made a hot, scalding pot of coffee. I came out to see a wagon loaded with pine straw pulling into our yard. Soon, more riders, most with picks and shovels, arrived. I knew a few of the folks from seeing them around the school and town, but knew none by name, except Billy Reed.

Pap and one of the older men selected an area in the backyard, and the younger men began digging down to the red clay beneath the topsoil.

I'd never been at a chimney daubing and was very interested in the process. Two men built a rectangular frame of 2 x 6's and filled it with straw and red clay. A bucket brigade went to our rain barrel and began pouring water into the mixture. A woman carried an armload of Spanish moss and dropped it into the mix. Billy shucked his boots, rolled up his pants leg, and climbed into the box. I hiked up my skirt to a respectable level and climbed in and was soon joined by another brave girl.

We stompers mixed the clay, straw, and moss into a pulp for the daubing, and our feet were the mixing tools. Within a few minutes we were covered in red clay up to our knees. It was caked on the tools, our feet, and everything within twenty feet of the pit and walls. We were like those Israelites making their Egyptian pyramid bricks, except we had the straw.

The men quickly tore down the old chimney and erected four stout saplings in a rectangular shape. "They're building a frame of sweet gum saplings," Billy said. "They'll drill holes in the saplings to place the stick cross-pieces. Then they'll use our mixture to fill in between the sticks."

Everyone seemed to have a specific responsibility. Two men with shovels carried the clay mixture to the chimney where it was carefully jabbed into the lowest spaces within the framework.

Within hours, a respectable chimney graced our house.

At the same time, another group was chinking the logs of the house. Part of the house's draftiness was the gaps between the logs. Pap had covered some of the larger gaps with sawmill slats, but the clay mixture would make a firmer seal.

I stopped my stomping to watch the chinkers at work. They had brought a small cart loaded down with what appeared to be mostly trash. The workers, mostly women, began filling the gaps from the wagon's contents. They began with small bits of kindling and sticks, which were stuffed into the largest spaces. Then they took oakum, Spanish moss, dried manure, and even old newspaper and made another level of protection.

One of the men said, "This'll seal your house against driving wind and rain, and block any vermin getting in."

Ma stepped up to him. "Whose idea was this?"

"Ma'am, I don't rightly know." The man shrugged. "Word just spread that we were having a chimney daubing for some new neighbors, and here we are."

Ma was still interrogating one of the daubers about how this joint venture came to be. "When's the next one?"

"I'm not sure."

Ma pointed at me. "Mizz here goes to the Academy. You make sure she knows when there's something like this going on. We'll be there to he'p."

"Yes'um, that's how it works."

Finally, the daubers, who'd finished their chimney work, used their trowels to smoothly cover the exterior of the chinks. Pap, who'd always been good with his hands, showed himself adept at making a tight attractive covering to the chinks.

Ma nudged me. "Your Pap's always been good with his hands, whether it's lifting a wallet, doing a Lucky Lady Switch, or working on things like this."

He was quick with the trowel, causing Ma to add, "He's always said the hand's quicker than the eye."

I sighed. "Well, I hope he sticks to this kind of sleight of hand."

Ma pointed at the wall. "Look at that mud sticking to the chinking. It's good to have something to grab onto. It's no different with people. Everyone needs something to latch on to."

"Do you think we're finding that here?"

Ma studied Pap as he joked with several of the men. "I hope so, and I hope it lasts."

The next morning, Pap was saddled up. His bedroll and saddlebags were evidence he was going on a sojourn.

Ma, in her bedclothes, stood on the steps. "Henry, are you sure about this?"

"As sure as I've ever been in my life."

He turned toward me and held up a folded paper. "I'm going to Lake Charles to file for a land patent on this place. I believe I can transfer the Nash homestead deed to our name. If so, we'll own 160 acres."

Ma, ever the realist, said, "If we stay on it for five years."

"I've never owned a foot of land," Pap said. "We've been called white trash, squatters, and clay eaters. If I can clear up this land deed, we'll have a new title. Landowners."

"It won't change how folks look at us here in Sugartown."

"Maybe not, but it'll change about how I look at myself." Pap clucked to his horse. "I hope to be back in a week."

Pap was gone; it was a Sunday with no school, so I took Baby James to town. He always enjoyed being out, and in spite of what anyone might say or think, I was proud to show him off. He especially enjoyed riding on Pegasus. I put him in front of me in the saddle, and off we went.

I was aware that folks whispered. A rumor had spread that James was my baby, and it was kind of like that scarlet letter. It only made me more determined to take him with me. I wasn't ashamed of my new brother, and it would not have mattered if he was green and had horns growing out of his head, he was my brother.

I tied Pegasus at the hitching rack, told Lucky to stay by the horse, and went into the post office. We'd been in Sugartown since January and not received one single piece of mail, but I still checked nearly daily. The postmistress shook her head. "Sorry." Then she stepped out from behind the counter. "Maybe I'll just write you a letter and mail it to you if that'd make you feel better."

I hung my head.

"So, I assume it's a boy you're waiting for a letter from?"

"Well, he's a boy for sure, but he's a boy who hasn't written."

"Sorry." She took a piece of candy out of a drawer. "You mind if I give the little fellow a treat? I don't think he'll choke on it."

I unwrapped it and gave it to James.

"It was mighty brave of your folks taking on that baby."

"It was the right thing to do."

"Yes, it was the right thing, but your folks were about the only ones willing to do it. All of the so-called religious people wouldn't touch him, and then folk like y'all…" She stopped in her tracks.

I waited for her to finish. She didn't need to.

"I'm sorry if that sounded…"

"No offense taken. Thanks for the candy." I walked down the street taking in the sights of a Saturday in Sugartown. Turning to Baby James, I said, "You fit in nice with us. We're just white trash, or maybe brown trash is more like it." He smiled, and it lifted my spirits. "But lots of these people have been as nice and friendly as can be. I guess we'll take the good with the bad."

Baby James pulled on my necklace. I rounded the corner and saw a wagon backed up to Lacy's Store. I froze. Dan Moore stood by the wagon.

Quick as I could, I ducked behind the corner then peeked around. He was leaner than when I'd last seen him, had grown a full beard and had a wilder, older look. I liked that look. However, there was also an unspeakable sadness about him as he worked. I just knew that meant Miss Eliza had died.

If you'd asked me five minutes before now, I'd assured you that I'd sworn off Dan Moore. But as I watched him unloading the wagon, every emotion I'd ever felt came roaring back. There's a saying I put stock in. "You'll think you've forgiven someone who's wounded you or forgotten a lover until they show back up. Then whatever's in your heart comes alive again."

I think love and hate have one similarity. You'll think you're over one. Love or hate. Then you see the object of that emotion— a lover or an enemy—and it all comes back.

For me, Dan Moore held both of those emotions. I was angry at him for not writing and the cavalier way he'd said goodbye on January the first. He'd shown varying degrees of interest in me. It'd been easier if I knew for sure, but I couldn't convince myself that he didn't love me. He just couldn't—or didn't—quite know how to show it. Except for that one night under the stars, and then he acted like it'd never happened.

At the same time, the sadness I sensed made me want to run out and hug him close. Watching Dan, my stomach hurt. Baby James, sensing my anxiety, began to fidget and fuss. I had a decision to make—run home or step out and make myself known. If I went to him, what would his reaction be to Baby James? Under my breath, I said, "I don't give a flying fig what he thinks."

It gave me the moxie I needed to walk straight to the wagon. Dan's back was to me, and I felt a mixture of dread and excitement. Lucky caught Dan's scent and ran up to him and began barking joyfully.

He whirled around and his eyes went from Lucky, then up to me, and finally the baby I was holding, then back to my eyes. "Mizz." He repeated my name several times. "What are you doing here?"

"We live near here."

"I thought you were in Texas?"

"What about you, Dan'l?"

"We've bought Lacy's Store and will be moving here next week. I came down early to take care of some of the particulars."

He nodded at Baby James. "And who is this?"

"He's my new brother, Patrick James Cotton, but we call him Baby James."

Dan reached out and James grasped his finger. "Where'd he come from?"

"He was left as an orphan at the church door, so Ma and Pap took him in."

"He's got beautiful eyes."

"He's a delightful baby," I said.

I studied Dan's eyes. "How have you been?"

"A lot of water under the bridge since Westport."

"Same for us."

Dan smiled at Lucky. "I see you've still got a good dog."

"Man's best friend. Or in my case, woman's." I could hardly speak the words. "What about ... your mother?"

His face dropped, and I waited. "She's weaker. The long wagon ride over here was tough on her."

"But she's ... she's alive?"

"Oh, yeah. She's tougher than an old boot."

Hot tears filled my eyes. "I was so afraid that the fight, then the fire..."

"We were, too. Her heart was broken to leave Ten Mile, but she's soldiered on. She'll sure be happy to see you." Dan's face dropped. "But I do have news of loss—it's Unk. He died in early January not long after we all left.

"Not sweet Unk?"

"Mizz, it was just too much for him. We'd already arrived in

Alexandria and didn't know anything about it until he had been buried two weeks.

"Where did they bury him?"

"It's ironic. They buried him right at the spot where he first hid the money near the town ant colony."

"Does he have a marker?"

"Someone put up a wooden cross, but we couldn't find it or his grave when we came through Ten Mile." Dan smiled wistfully. "Unk was probably the richest man in Ten Mile if we could find his money, yet he was buried like a pauper."

"He was an angel, wasn't he?" I said. "I have a feather he gave me on the first day I met him. I still use it as a bookmark. He told me that wherever a bird feather fell is where an angel had trod. Should be lots of feathers on the ground wherever Unk Dyal walked."

Dan blinked. "Never been a purer heart who walked these Pineywoods than my great uncle, Nathan Dyal."

"How about your father, Mr. Joe?"

"I believe the fight, then Unk's death, was harder on him than Momma. He never mentions Westport, and if the subject comes up, he walks out of the room."

"Where did y'all go after leaving Westport?"

"We crossed the Calcasieu and settled for a while in Hineston, then Alexandria. Daddy scouted around and after rejecting several sites east of the river, decided Sugartown would be the best place to put stakes down and toss his hat over the wall." Dan put his hands in his pockets. "So here we are."

"It looks like we might we sticking around, too. We've got a house south of town."

"A house for the Wagon Girl?"

I studied the way he said it.

"Mizz, I've thought often about how you were the strongest one during the fight."

"I was scared to death."

"We all were, but you were the bravest."

"I'm not sure of that. There was plenty of courage all around that day."

"A heap of stupidity, too."

"Agreed."

"Dan'l, why didn't you write me? At first, I sent weeks of letters to you at Mayo's address?"

"I never got a one. Are you sure you had Mayo's address?"

"I know I used the correct address. I guess they got lost or…"

Dan kicked at the wagon wheel. "Or maybe someone didn't want me to get them."

I was stunned. "Someone?"

He shrugged. "I just don't know."

"Well, I need to know." I stamped my foot. "Well, I need to know about us."

"Us?"

"Yes. Us. Me and you." I searched the ground for a rock to throw at him. "Don't you ever think about our night together before the store burned?"

"Sure, I do."

I wasn't convinced, especially when he deftly changed the subject. "Did you know Gordon Musgrove is still alive?"

I clenched my fists, put Baby James down, picked up a dirt clod, and flung it at him. "You are without a doubt the most unromantic man in the whole world." I looked around for something else to chunk at him. Even Lucky, tail between his legs, scooted out of range.

He held up his hands. "Don't shoot me."

"If I had a gun, I would." I grabbed the baby, burst out in tears, and stormed off, throwing back one last barb. "Dan'l Moore, you don't understand the first thing about women or love."

I left the post office, holding Baby James and huffing down the Sugartown Road toward our place, Lucky trotted beside me at a safe distance. About a quarter mile down the road, I realized I'd left Pegasus and had to angrily retrace my steps into town.

I didn't see any sign of Dan Moore. I'm sure if he saw me stomping back to my horse, he'd hide somewhere safe.

Galloping home, I was still some kind of mad at Dan, but I was mostly mad at Missouri Cotton. It seemed I was always sabotaging relationships. Here was the man I wanted more than anything in the world, and I was driving him away.

Or maybe driving myself away.

CHAPTER 49

REUNIONS

March 28, 1882

Mr. Joe Moore arrived two days later, and I went by the store to greet him.

He put down a box. "Well, if it's not Missouri Cotton."

Suddenly, Queen Esther, the cat, scrambled through my legs. "Well, look who's still around." She'd lost most of her tail and still had a singed look. Other than that, she looked in fine fiddle.

"Still the best ratter we've ever had."

"We lost our wagon cat Tom-Claws. Evidently he liked it better in Ten Mile.

"Now, that's a subject for discussion."

"But I've still got your dog Lucky."

"Lucky adopted you a long time ago. He's yours. How is he?"

"He's still hopping along at full speed. He's become a notorious snaker. Our house had a nest of copperheads underneath. Lucky fought the battle of Whiskey Chitto and came out victorious."

I stepped closer, noticing the sadness in his eyes. "I was so worried about Miss Eliza. I was afraid the fight and fire would be too much."

"It nearly was." He smiled. "She'll be so happy to see you. She and Will should arrive later today."

"Good. I'll drop by after school."

"I'd heard you're a school girl now. That's hard to believe."

"I can hardly believe it's true either."

As soon as classes ended, I rushed to the store. Once again, in spite of my excitement at seeing Miss Eliza, I was nervous.

She was sitting in a straight chair in the store with her legs covered with a shawl.

She was much frailer since I'd last seen her three months ago. Her voice was husky. "Child, I thought I'd never see you again, and here you are."

I nearly fell on her, hugging her with all of my might. In spite of my best efforts, I wept, and I'm not talking about a few tears. I had that case of the sobbing spasms. A torrent that had been bottled up in my soul burst forth, and I couldn't stop it nor say a word. It was as if I had a clod stuck in my throat.

She pulled me onto her lap, and I was afraid I'd break her fragile body.

Mr. Joe brought me a chair, and I flopped into it, still speechless. Miss Eliza stroked my hair. "Are you all right?"

"I just … just never … thought I'd see you again … and here y'all are."

"And that's a good thing, ain't it?" Her dark eyes sparkled. "Is it true y'all have a house near town?"

I nodded. I had the dry heaves and still had that throat-clod. "Yes' um ... and I'm in school here ... at the Academy."

She gestured. "That school is one of the reasons why we chose Sugartown. It's a chance for Will and Dan to get some schooling. I've been afraid they're both going feral." She handed me a hankie. "Is the school as good as they say?"

I blew my nose in a very unfeminine way. "Miss Eliza, I don't have much to compare it to, but it's wonderful. They even have a library."

"What was the name of that book you were searching for?"

"*Les Misérables*. They've got the complete set."

"I've been stewing for months about how it must end. I'm ready to hear it."

"You will, but first I want to hear about Westport and Unk. "What about Westport?"

Mr. Joe, who'd been standing in the doorway, hurried out of the room.

She nodded. "Joe can't even say Westport. All that trouble broke his heart. Losing the store was bad enough, but he still blames himself for Unk's death."

"That wasn't his fault."

"I know, but he took it all real hard," Miss Eliza said.

"I know you miss Unk."

"I miss him like the rain. But the day we left Westport for Alexandria, I knew I'd never see him again. So I was grieving long before I learned of his death."

"How were things in Westport?"

"All of the Outsiders are gone, and we got a cool reception as we passed through. In spite of it being my people, it no longer felt like home."

"Was it hard going by where the store was?"

"Lots of dreams and money in those ashes." She took my hand. "Let's talk of other things."

Just then, Esther the cat ran under my chair and out the door. "I see Esther made the move. She did lose a good bit of her tail in the fire but looks well otherwise."

"I tell her that she's surely got no more than eight of her lives after the fire." She took my hand. "How's your mother?"

"She's doing all right. Getting settled has been so good for her." She didn't ask about Pap, but I felt compelled to share. "Pap's doing better, too. Not drinking quite as bad and has even put in a garden and gotten a job at a sawmill."

"That's good."

"Did you know we have a new baby?"

"Dan said the baby's as dark as you or me."

"He is that." I took her hand. "I was so worried. I thought…"

She winked. "You thought I'd be dead by now. I guess the Lord has something left for me to do."

"There's a lot of folks need you here, especially me." I glanced outside where the sun was setting. "I've got a good walk home, and I'd best be going."

"Where's your horse?"

"I don't ride her to school. They'd make me pay a livery charge." I kissed her on the cheek. "I can't wait to tell Momma that you're here."

"Give us a few days to get moved in, and I want to pay her a visit."

"She could come into town."

"No, I want to see her house and that garden."

I stood to leave, but she grabbed my arm. "I want to hear how your book, Les Mizz, really ends."

I sat on the bed. "I'll tell you the short version. As *Volume Five* begins, all of the main characters are together at the barricades.

Jean Valjean, in spite of his hatred of Marius and his plans to escape with Cosette to England, has shown up at the barricades. Even when he takes off his National Guard uniform, we're unsure if he's there to kill or rescue Marius or simply die in the fighting.

"Don't tell me that he hurts the young man who loves his daughter?" Miss Eliza said.

"Hold your horses. It's a long night as the group awaits the upcoming Army attack. Do you remember the boy Gavroche?"

"I like him in spite of his being a rascal."

"Well, Gavroche crosses barricades, gathering bullets from the cartridge bags of the dead soldiers. He sings, dancing back and forth cat-like. He is finally cut down, wounded. When he sits up and sings the stanza of another mocking song, he is fatally shot down.

"I'm sad to hear that, but he died like he lived—with spunk."

"Miss Eliza, here's the best part. Valjean and the condemned spy Javert recognize each other. This is Valjean's chance on revenge on Javert, and he volunteers to 'blow his brains out.' But when Valjean takes Javert to a deserted alley, he fires his gun in the air, and cuts the spy free, allowing him to leave. Javert begs Valjean to kill him."

"That Javert is one complicated fellow," Miss Eliza said.

"The attack ensues and the soldiers quickly overwhelm the barricade defenders. Marius is seriously wounded, and Jean Valjean, though old, still possesses great strength. He takes Marius on his shoulders and carries him through the underground sewers of Paris to safety. At the grated gate where the sewer enters into the River Seine, he encounters Javert. Valjean asks permission to take Marius home, then he will consent to his own arrest.

The harsh Javert consents. As they part, Javert, driven to desperation, throws himself into the River Seine and drowns."

"That's something."

"Marius' recovery is slow and neither he nor Cosette realize

Valjean saved Marius. The relationship between the young couple and old man is broken, and his decline is sudden and sure.

"At Valjean's deathbed, Marius and Cosette learn that Valjean saved him at the barricades. They are reconciled and Valjean dies a happy man.

"What about Marius and Cosette?"

"As far as we know, they live happily ever after."

"Now, that is a fine story."

Mr. Joe stuck his head in the door. "I hate to break up this talk, but it's getting dark." He nodded to me. "Let me walk with you."

"I believe the end of that book kept Eliza alive until now."

"Do you want to hear about it?"

He put his hands up. "No thanks. Besides, I heard most of it from the porch."

"You were eavesdropping."

"So a man can really change?"

"Sure he can."

We talked small talk until Mr. Joe said, "You know, she's dying."

I looked away, those hot tears returning. "I don't want to hear that."

"It's all right to say it. Eliza's dying. I know it and she knows it. Missouri, my job's helping her get ready to die. That's what folks do in a lifetime marriage. We help each other through the ups and downs. We bring new life into being, weather life's storms, and then we help each other die. It could've been either one of us, but it looks like it's fallen to *me* to help *her*." He smiled. "Unless a tree limb falls on me or lightning strikes me down."

"I'm sorry."

"So am I, but there's nothing I can do. I hate it most of all for the boys." He had that grit in his eye that I'd seen so often.

"You know, no one comforted her better than you did back there at—. Could you ... would you, help her ... us ... again?"

"I'll do whatever I can."

When we neared the lights of our cabin, he turned back. "Good."

CHAPTER 50

A VISIT

April 1882

Saturday was a beautiful spring day as I walked into town. I was to meet Miss Eliza Moore at their store and then bring her out to see my mother.

March had continued warm, and the dogwoods were in bloom under the pines. The contrast in color of the white blooms set against the endless green canopy of the pines was stunning.

When I arrived at the store, Dan was hooking up the wagon. It was the first time we'd seen each other since my blow out.

He stopped, holding a trace chain in his hand. "Well, is it safe for me to go?"

I was embarrassed. "I'll do better. I promise."

"Mizz, I don't know what to do with you."

"I don't know what to do with myself, either. Let's just try to enjoy this day."

"Fair enough. Momma's inside. Why don't you help her get to the wagon?"

"What about Mr. Joe?"

"He has business to take care of."

Miss Eliza was coughing as I entered the store. She tried to put on a good face. "I had a bad night, Child, but I'm ready to go." I helped her down the steps and onto the wagon, where she lay on a pallet Dan had arranged. She wasn't up to the rough ride to our place, but I knew mentioning it was futile.

"Prop me up so I can see the woods."

As we left Sugartown and eased down into the edge of Sugar Creek Swamp, Miss Eliza took a deep breath and waved at the hardwoods. "There's nothing like new leaves of spring." A fresh breeze whipped the limbs. "My man Joe always talks about the forty shades of green in Ireland. I believe early spring in the swamps is our closest thing to it."

The ride in the open air seemed to invigorate her. "It's amazing how the first leaves have a light green color and then darken as summer arrives." She was really chatty. "Now, I love the pines, but they are always the same forest green year-round. There's a stability and comfort in knowing my pines don't change color and drop their leaves.

"But hardwoods are a different story. They reflect the seasons and bring delight in each one. I'm glad we have them both."

I moved closer to her. "My teacher, Professor Baldwin, likes using fancy words. He calls these colors verdant."

"What does it mean?"

"It means awash with lush green vegetation."

"Well, that describes what we're looking at here."

Being outside in the verdant world was evidently good for Miss Eliza. Her color looked better, and her coughing lessened.

The wagon climbed out of the bottomland and we were once again under the canopy of the pines. I pointed out blackened trunks and smaller dead pines. "Last month, a big fire, set by the sheepherders, burned through here. It's a shame the fire killed the young pines."

She raised off her pallet. "Child, help me sit up. Stop this wagon."

I helped her. She pointed at a nearby burnt pine that was about two feet tall and had its straw burnt off, leaving only a small bare stump. "Take a closer look at its top. It ain't dead."

A small white bulb sprouted from the tip surrounded by a few whiskers of green straw. "Mizz, that tree's not dead. It just got burned back. It survived the fire, and it'll be back stronger than ever."

She winked. "Survived the fire. Stronger than ever. That pine's like me and our people. It's been broken and burnt, but the truth is, it's never been stronger." She wrapped her arm around my shoulder and leaned on me.

"Child, my eyesight's pretty dim, but my vision's never been clearer. I can see up ahead and I ain't one bit scared."

We neared our house, passing the stand of field corn and snap beans Pap had planted. She pointed at his hills of potatoes. "Tell your daddy he needs more dirt on those hills if he's gonna have big

Irish potatoes." Miss Eliza took a deep breath. "There's no better smell than fresh-turned dirt."

Surveying our garden, Miss Eliza smiled. "It looks like whoever lives here is putting down roots."

"I sure hope we are."

Ma, wiping her hands on her apron, stepped off the gallery to meet the wagon.

Miss Eliza sat up. "Dan, stop this wagon and help me down."

"Momma, we can pull the wagon up close to the house."

"No. I want off right here."

We helped her down as she flipped off her slippers. She leaned on her cane, walking gingerly between the rows of corn. "I just want to feel cold, fresh dirt on my feet one more time."

Dan leaned against the bed of the wagon. "She's been like that lately. Does whatever she wants when she wants."

"How old is your momma?"

"In her late fifties." He looked away. "Not old enough to die."

I put a hand on his shoulder.

Dan wiped his eyes with his shirtsleeve. "Yep, too young to be dying, but she is."

"It looks to me like today she's living," I said. "Maybe living fuller and better than most anyone I know."

Ma led us up onto the porch, and then brought out a fresh pot of coffee. "I'm sorry we don't have a nice serving set."

Miss Eliza waved her off. "It's best straight out of the pot. It's a perfect morning for fresh, stout coffee."

And it was stout. Ma must've bumped her elbow when she put the grounds in.

After a few minutes of chitchat, Miss Eliza said, "You two young people go off and do whatever it is young folks do."

Dan swallowed hard. "But…"

I wanted to hit him. Why did this man make me so crazy?

His mother shoved him. "Y'all get on."

We walked down the Sugartown Road toward Whiskey Chitto Creek.

"What do you think they're talking about back at the house?" he said.

"Probably us."

"Probably so."

"Missouri, we missed our chance at Westport. It was my fault."

"I'll share the blame."

"Regardless, let's not miss this chance." He pulled me close and kissed me like he did that night under the stars. Once again, my knees went weak and I was determined to make this moment last forever if I didn't fall out.

"We don't know how long we'll both be here. Let's make the most of it," Dan said.

After more than an hour of strolling, kissing, talking, and more kissing, we returned hand-in-hand. Ma and Miss Eliza sat together on a rough wood bench on the porch. Both had an otherworldly smile and snuff dripping down both of their cheeks. Miss Eliza, though visibly tired, was cuddling Baby James. "I believe I've overdid it today." She nodded at my momma. "But it was worth it."

I helped her into the wagon, and we said our goodbyes. As the wagon receded into the distance, I said, "Ma, y'all had a good visit?"

"We sure did. That's a wise woman."

"What did y'all talk about?"

She winked. "If I tell you, I'd have to kill you." She cleared her throat. "It seems you and Dan Moore are getting along."

"It seems so."

"What'd y'all talk about?"

"Ma, you need to mind your own snakes. Besides, if I told you, I'd have to kill you."

CHAPTER 51

SCHOOL'S OUT

May 1, 1882

It was the last weekend before school ended. In the late 19th century, school ended early in May, so students could help their family harvest the early crops and plant the others.

It was late Saturday afternoon when I rode into Sugartown to return several books to Professor Baldwin. Monday would be the final day of school and I was afraid I'd forget during the hustle and bustle of the last day.

I'd seldom been to Professor Baldwin's house which sat behind the school building. I tied Pegasus and, books in hand, knocked on his door.

I heard noise inside but no one came to the door. I continued knocking to no avail and turned to leave.

The door cracked open. Professor Baldwin, wearing a tee shirt and boxers, stuck his face in the gap. "Missouri, what are you doing here?"

"I came to return these books ..."

His face was florid and unshaven as he leaned heavily on the door frame. I knew drunk well, and the good professor was really drunk.

I handed him the books. "I'm sorry if I came at a bad time." A woman's voice echoed from the back of the house. I slowly backed away as he slurred, "Thanks for bringing them by—I'll see on you Monday."

Monday arrived and I walked to school with a troubling emotion of fear and uncertainty. It was the last day of school and everyone was in a chipper mood except me.

I wondered how I would respond when I saw Professor Baldwin. Most of all, I worried over how he'd react to me. Our final Latin class was memorable in that Professor Baldwin was unusually emotional as he went over his favorite subject. Prof, without looking at me, said, "Missouri, I'd like you to give us our Latin quote of the day to parse."

I pulled out a dog-eared notebook and walked slowly to the board and copied laboriously, "*Omnes relinquite spes, o vos intrantes.*"

Professor Baldwin, still avoiding eye contact, stepped back. He then did something he'd never done in the classroom. He pulled out a long cigar, lit it, and the class was soon filled with the aroma of rich tobacco smoke. "Now, who wants to try to decipher it?"

Delbert Cole, of all people, raised his hand. "I believe it is, "Everyone ... relinquish hope ... if you're entering here."

Prof took a deep puff. "Delbert, that's pretty good. Abandon hope all ye that enter here."

He finally looked at me. "Miss Cotton, do you know the name of the author?"

My brain was a fog. "I don't remember."

"He was an Italian philosopher named Dante, and this comes from his most famous work, *The Divine Comedy*." It's a book about the seven circles of Hell."

Everyone in the class stared at me as if I was crazy.

Professor Baldwin walked to my desk, and cigar ashes scattered on my open notebook. "Why did you have this quote in your book?"

"Sir, when you cross the Calcasieu River east of here at Hineston, you enter Louisiana's No Man's Land. A sign in English says, "Abandon hope all ye that enter here."

"Why was it put there?"

"Well, I believe it was to warn that you entered No Man's Land at your own risk ... and you're probably not coming back."

Professor Baldwin arched his eyebrows. "Not coming back?"

I felt a deep sadness as I repeated, "Not coming back."

The school bell rang; the 1882 Spring school term ended. All of the other students hurried from their desks. Prof stood beside my desk and put his finger on the Dante quote in my notebook.

"That's a good word for you to remember."

"Which one?"

"*Spes*. It means hope." He smiled. "Keep your hope."

"I'm sorry for disturbing you at your house on Saturday."

He balanced his cigar on the edge of my desk. "And I'm sorry you saw me in that condition."

"That's okay. I've seen drunk men before." I immediately wanted to kick myself.

"But, Missouri Cotton, you've never seen *me* like that."

"No sir, I haven't."

"And I'm sorry you did. My drinking's gotten worse and I can't seem to control it. I hope a summer away will help."

"So, do I."

He put his finger on the next line I'd written under Dante's quote. "It means 'not coming back.' " He stabbed that sentence with his index finger, then softly said, "Not coming back?" He patted me on the shoulder. "Come on, it's time for the closing assembly in the schoolyard."

At the assembly, Professor Baldwin, back in top form, eagerly talked of next semester. "We're planning for bigger and better things at the Academy. We're building additional boarding for students and are currently interviewing promising new faculty members. The school will be empty all summer, but Miss Collins will be available as needed. My plans are to visit family in New York, confer with colleagues at Columbia, and finish the summer drumming up new students in rural Louisiana and east Texas."

Sonnet winked at me and held up one finger. We had a bet that Prof could not complete a speech without mentioning his alma mater at least three times.

Prof walked back and forth. "While at Columbia, I plan on taking a seminar on new methods in pedagogy and effective teaching methods as we plan for the future and beyond to the coming century."

Sonnet held up two fingers.

"I'll be back in late August and look forward to seeing all of you as the semester begins on September 1. If you need me, write in care of Columbia University." He took a theatrical bow. "Until then, I bid you adieu."

I held up three fingers and mouthed, "You owe me a soda."

A crowd congregated around Professor Baldwin, wishing him the best on his travels and plans for the best school between the rivers.

When the crowd finally thinned out, I walked up to the Professor. "Sir, may I see your pen?"

He hesitantly pulled an expensive pen from his vest pocket.

I uncapped the pen. "Let me see your right hand, please. His hand was shaking as I grasped it. Across his palm, I wrote '24601' and then closed his fist.

I handed him the pen. "It might be … a while before we see each other again. Use that number to remember me by."

Tears filled his eyes as he put his pen back into his pocket. I huskily said, "Remember, a man can change. 24601."

He nodded. "24601."

I hugged him tightly. "Thanks for being part of my resurrection," and then I whispered in his ear, "And all of your secrets, especially last Saturday, are safe with me."

"I already knew you wouldn't tell." He opened his hand. 24601 had already smudged a little.

He then pulled that pen from his vest and placed it in my hand, making a fist around it.

"And this is my parting gift to the Westport Fight Girl. Remember, the pen is truly more powerful than the sword. *Spes.* Keep your hope."

With that, he walked to his waiting carriage, waving one time with his right hand. As he bounded into the carriage, I swore I heard him whisper, "24601."

CHAPTER 52

FORTY-EIGHT LETTERS

May 1

Sonnet was waiting as Prof's carriage disappeared out of sight. She laughed. "Let's go to the Moore Store and get that soda I owe you. School's out and that's worth celebrating."

She studied me. "What's wrong, Missouri?"

"Oh nothing. I've just got a lot on my mind."

"What were you and Professor Baldwin talking about back there?"

"We were just telling each other goodbye ... for the summer."

"Well, it looked pretty personal to me."

"It was." I pulled her toward the store. "Now, you owe me a soda."

As we drank our sodas, I saw Mr. Joe in the store office with what appeared to be a Ten Miler. We didn't see many Redbones in Sugartown. They chose to do their business in Hineston or Alexandria, avoiding this part of No Man's Land.

Seeing me, Mr. Joe motioned me over. "Mizz, you remember my oldest son, Mayo, don't you?"

I hadn't recognized Mayo Moore, with whom we'd stayed with in Alexandria last year. Once again, I was shocked at how different he looked from his Irish father as well as Dan and Will. Mayo was a mirror image of his mother and her people.

He especially had her dark eyes and shy smile, but he wasn't smiling as he stared at me and placed his hand on a twine-tied stack on the counter. I immediately recognized my handwriting on the letters. "These are the letters I'd wrote to Dan'l during our months of separation." My voice was trembling. "Where have they been?" I turned to Mayo. "Did you have them?"

Mayo held up his hands. "Whoa. I had nothing to do with it."

I looked at Mister Joe. "Then who did, and why?"

Mayo looked at the floor. "I'm afraid it was my wife."

"Your wife Ophelia?" I slapped the bundle to the floor, where they came untied. "But why?"

"Ophelia just felt that you ..."—Mayo looked away. — "That you weren't the best match for Dan and decided to do her part in ensuring it never happened."

I scanned the faces of the Moore men. "Neither of you knew about this?"

"I found them stashed away last week," Mayo said. "I came straight here with them. There's forty-eight of them."

I picked up the scattered letters from the floor. "Does Dan'l know?"

"Not yet." Mr. Joe put his hand on my shoulder. "We figure you're the one to give them to him."

I wanted to fling the letters across the room, but at the same time I wanted to guard them against my bosom. "How do I give him a bundle of letters written over a three-month period?" I stalked the room. "Do I give them to him in a big bundle and just walk away?"

"That's the best way I know," Mr. Joe said, "We're celebrating an Irish May Day bonfire tonight. You can give them to him then."

"I might just throw them in your Irish bonfire."

Mr. Joe Moore stepped back. "You can't do that. I'd have to report you for mail fraud and destruction of government property." He winked as he picked up one of the letters. "They're the property of one Dan'l Moore c/o Mayo Moore, 414 Murray Street, Alexandria, Louisiana."

In the hours leading up to the bonfire, I went through about six emotions, most of them anger. Why would Ophelia Moore, Dan's sister-in-law, withhold my letters? She'd acted a little cool toward me, but I never sensed a deep dislike.

I put the letters in my book bag and made my way to the Moore Store as dusk approached. Will was stacking a pile of dried sticks and saplings in the road. He waved. "May Day—May 1—is a major holiday back in Ireland. The May Day bonfire is the culmination of the day."

"What's it about?"

Will shrugged. "You'll have to see for yourself. May Day started as some Irish Pagan holiday. It became a time for folks to gather, prepare for planting, and take the livestock back out to the highlands."

Will turned serious. "Do you have the letters with you?"

I held up my book bag. "You know?"

He nodded. "What are you gonna do?"

"Are you sure he doesn't know?"

"He has no clue."

"I'll give them to him after the bonfire."

"Good idea."

The May Day bonfire, like all Irish events, was celebrated full-force and fortified by good Irish whiskey. Several Irish-blooded families were in attendance as well as a good handful of curious Sugartowners.

Dan held my hand, while he explained each part of the celebration. "We'll let the bonfire burn down, and then the brave ones will jump the fire."

"Jump the fire?"

"Yep. Get a running start and leap over the fire."

"Will you?"

"Sure, no Irish boy worth his salt can pass up the challenge."

"Do girls do it?"

"No. A dress isn't a good outfit." He pointed at his father. "Da's the bonfire master."

Mr. Joe called to Dan. "Son, move those timbers on the roadside around. It needs to be a little lower but longer on the north end."

"It's not just the height that scares me," I said. "That's a long leap."

"That's the whole purpose," Dan said.

I watched Mr. Joe kicking a stray ember back into the fire.

"Does he do the leap?" I asked Dan.

Dan laughed. "He's always been the champion, but several years ago, about the time Momma took sick, he quit. Said he'd gotten too old."

Evidently, the fire had reached the perfect combination of height and length. Mr. Joe stepped off about ten yards and made a line in the sand with his walking stick. "All right, let's see who has it in them."

Without hesitation, Will Moore took a twenty-yard running start and leapt through the flames, nearly clearing them, and came down in the far edge of the cinders, scattering a spray of embers into the night sky. He whooped in a shrill voice, pumping both hands in the air."

Dan laughed. "He's always so scared, he has to do it first, or he won't do it at all."

"What was that yell?"

"It's our family's Irish war cry. Da brought it with him cross the Atlantic."

A line of Sugartown boys, Irish, otherwise, and in all sizes, took the challenge. The Irishman stood at the starting line with a walking stick in his hand. "Watch how Da measures who can go." The Irishman made a boy stand beside the stick, and mussed his hair. "Maybe next year, Lad."

What amazed me was how each boy had no choice but to leap through the flames as they were too high to clear completely. Most came through slightly singed, cussing, praising the Lord, or all three. A good swig from a jug awaited each one.

Dan pointed at three older men with buckets of water. "They're the Bucket Masters, in case someone's clothes catch fire."

"No way."

A few of the older boys and men cleared it completely. Others came down with one or more feet in the fire.

One fellow landed butt-first in the edge of the fire and his tattered jeans caught fire. He did a fine jig as he was doused with water, steam pouring from his pants.

The Sugartown crowd whooped and hollered, slapping him on the back like he was named Shadrach or Meshach.

Dan, let go of my hand. "I guess it's my turn." He calmly took off his shirt, boots, and socks, handing them to me. "Meet me at the far end."

None of the other leapers had been bare-footed, and all of them had taken liberal running starts. But not Dan Moore. Instead, he toed the line made by his father's stick. I heard the Irishman whisper, "Are you sure?"

Dan's answer was a burst toward the fire. The flames illuminated his face and every muscle signified determination. His legs were still pin wheeling as he passed through the tiptop of the fire. He seemed suspended in space and I immediately thought of Pegasus the Flying Horse.

Every eye was focused on the far end of the fire. It is no exaggeration that Dan's heel struck the last far ember. His momentum was such that he tumbled headfirst in the street, turning several awkward cartwheels.

The crowd went wild.

I walked over and handed him his boots and shirt. He didn't exult or raise his hands in triumph. He quietly shook the dirt off his body, sat in the street, and dressed.

Behind us, I heard someone say, "Those Irishmen are crazy."

Joe Moore, the Irishman, stood over his son. "Even the Irish aren't that crazy. That was Redbone crazy."

Dan looked up. "Or maybe a combination of the two."

His dad only shook his head. "That's a dangerous mixture."

The fire was dwindling and the Irishman, after raking the embers into a tighter circle, let a few of the younger boys go.

Then he walked from his ceremonial post to a spot about thirty yards shy of the fire. Most of the crowd wasn't even watching. Dan saw it first. "Da's gonna go."

Mr. Joe grinned, and rushed toward the fire. His war cry was otherworldly and he stumbled as he made his yell and leap and we held our breath. There was no way he was going to make it. And he didn't. He cleared about three-quarters of the fire, coming down in the fire, which erupted in embers and smoke.

He did an awkward somersault out of the fire and landed on his hands and knees, before being doused by the Bucket Masters, twice each for good measure.

Steam roiled off him and Dan ran to where his father sat in the sand. "Da, are you all right?"

He held up his hands. "Singed my palms a little, but other than that, I'm great."

The crowd helped him to his feet, pounding on his back. I

watched from the fire's edge and wondered if this was the moment the Irish storeowner Joe Moore went from being an outsider to a Sugartown legend.

Now, it wasn't the smartest thing I'd ever done, but I had to do it. I stepped out of the shadow. I had no pretense that I could clear the length of the fire, but I figured I had a chance to clear the width.

I hiked my skirt up and knotted it the best I could, and then stepped off my approach. I didn't care if anyone saw me. I was doing it for myself.

But Will Moore saw me and hollered, "Missouri Cotton!" Every head in the crowd turned my way. I knew if I didn't go now, someone would step in my way and stop me.

I ran with every muscle in my body and soul. Someone later told me I screamed out, 'Feet, don't fail me now,' but I have no recollection. I simply felt flames coming up to envelop me.

The next thing I knew I was in Dan's arms on the safe side of the fire. "Girl, you are some kind of crazy."

I unknotted my dress, letting it fall to appear decent, but knew a woman leaping a bonfire probably forever removed the word "decent" from any future description.

Mr. Joe stood, arms crossed, in front of me. "Moxie. You've got grit. He shook his head. "I'm not sure I've ever seen this much of it in a woman."

"You showed a good bit of moxie in your own long leap," I said.

"It was pretty crazy, wasn't it?"

It took a while for all of the excitement to calm down. One by one, and in clumps, everyone left Sugartown's first May Day Bonfire.

Dan and I sat on the store steps, watching the fires burn down to ashes.

"I've got something for you." I pulled the stack of letters out of my bag. "These belong to you."

He walked over near the fire where he could see. He squinted, then looked up. "These are your letters to me. Where were they?"

"At the address listed." I said.

"Mayo had them?"

I shook my head. "No, his wife had them."

"Ophelia? She hid them from me?" He cussed under his breath. "But why?"

"You'll need to ask Mayo. The main thing is that those letters belong to you."

He held them awkwardly. "I don't quite know what to say ... or do."

"Read them ... when you're ready."

"I'm not ready, right now." He took my hand. "I want to talk. Just you and me."

We stretched out on the gallery.

"Mizz, I'm just not sure I'm the man you think I am."

"You're the man I want and that's all that matters."

"Well, we've got a lot to sort through. I guess these letters will help us get started." Dan Moore lit a lantern and one by one, from the first postmark to the last, read each letter aloud. He made few comments until he reached the final two weeks of letters. "You were getting pretty mad by then."

"I thought you'd abandoned me."

"I hadn't, and I won't."

Just then the first glint of daylight lit the horizon and a cardinal began singing in a nearby pine oak.

Tonight wasn't quite as romantic as our night in Ten Mile under the Milky Way, but it was another night with Dan Moore I knew I'd never forget.

Two days later, I entered the post office and Mrs. Singleton waved a letter. "Well Missouri Cotton, you've finally got mail."

It had no return address and I didn't recognize the handwriting, but I knew who it was from. I went straight to a bench on the post office gallery and tore it open.

"Dear Missouri,

"I spent all morning re-reading your letters. In spite of no sleep last night, I couldn't stop until I'd completed all of them. Reading nearly fifty letters takes some time. I'm a slow reader and even slower writer. Please excuse the shortness

of this letter and my poor handwriting compared to the wonderful words of your letters. I was touched beyond words as I read. I'm not always good at expressing how I feel. It's something I'm working on. Please know that I love you and am committed to seeing where this goes in the coming days and weeks lead our love. You are the bravest and most courageous woman I've ever met. I love you for that and a hundred other reasons.

Lovingly,
Dan'l Moore"

It probably wasn't the most romantic letter ever written, but I knew it came from Dan Moore's heart. I was uneasy with his "committed to seeing where this goes," but decided to just enjoy the beautiful stretch my life was currently taking.

CHAPTER 53

INDEPENDENCE DAY

July 4, 1882

With school out, I spent every day working at the store or being with Miss Eliza. Things were busy at the store. Mr. Joe, though new to town, loved to talk, laugh, and make new friends. Many of these new friends soon became regular customers at the store.

As he loved to say, "I'm an Irishman? How can I know what I'm thinking if I don't say it out loud?"

Mr. Joe was also excited about this being the height of watermelon season in Sugartown, and the entire front gallery of the store was stacked with fresh melons. There is no sweeter watermelon in the world than those grown in the Sugartown area, and the porch at the Moore store was piled high with melons of all sizes. Independence Day meant celebration, and no celebration was complete without an ample supply of Sugartown melons cooled down in the creek or well.

Beginning on July 1st, the store melon pile decreased by the day. Will and Dan were busy getting resupplied from local growers as farmers and even a few businessmen from Lake Charles arrived with wagons.

By the morning of July 4th, I counted eighty-four on the porch and felt sure we'd sell them all.

This Irishman did two things on Independence Day 1882 that I'll always associate with that day. Early that morning, using a rickety ladder, he posted a fine hand-painted sign from the eave reading, *Moore General Store/Sugartown, Louisiana, United States of America*. He nailed it to the store with eight big nails.

"You planning on staying a while?"

He balanced the ladder on his shoulder. "I don't want any gust of wind blowing down my sign."

The second Independence Day act by Joe Moore was the erection of a sweet gum sapling and his tying his American flag on it. Sugartown was an odd place; people seemingly had no quarrel with the U.S. flag, they just chose to ignore it. Most days, Mrs. Singleton at the post office simply forgot to raise her small flag.

The big flag at the store drew lots of attention. First of all, it was the flag that had survived the Westport Fight, and its singed corners and tattered corners were a real conversation starter.

Secondly, the erection of the flag immediately created controversy. About noon, a rabble-rouser named Cole, whose son Delbert loved needling Prof. Baldwin about being a carpetbagger, showed up with the intention of removing the flag at the Moore Store. The elder Mr. Cole brought a small crew with him. However, another group of patriots got wind of the siege and met the attackers at the flagpole.

I followed Mr. Joe as he came out of the store, arms folded, and studied the mixed crowd. In a strong but calm voice, he said, "I bought this store and the land beneath it. My deed says it's part of Imperial Calcasieu Parish, and it also states that this is Louisiana and therefore the United States." He pointed at his new store sign. "This is my country, my flag, and I have the right to fly it."

"Fellow, you're not even a real American," Cole said. "You're Irish."

"I'm as American as any of you, and besides that flag has great value to me. It survived the burnout at my store in Westport. I kinda feel special about it."

A guy in a tattered Rebel cap stepped to the flagpole. "Lots of my friends died fighting against that flag."

Mr. Joe planted his feet at the base of the flagpole. "So did plenty of mine. I served faithfully at Vicksburg. Nearly starved. Saw the surrender myself on July 4th."

A lean rawboned man, who had a resemblance to a young Abe Lincoln, stepped to the flagpole. "Look, I was born under that flag. Like most of you, I fought against it during the Rebellion, but the minute the War ended, that flag .... He choked up. "... That flag there became my flag again, and it will be until my dying day, and I'll fight any man who tries to molest it."   I saw several men nervously fingering their guns. A few women, sensing trouble, shooed their children away.

It was at this tense moment when Will Moore walked to the

flag, munching on a slice of watermelon. He pointed. "That flag ain't the right American flag anyway."

He immediately had the attention of the crowd. I glanced at Mr. Joe who was doing a poor job of hiding both his irritation and puzzlement.

Will hopped up on the gallery. "That's the 1877 flag. It's only got thirty-seven stars. Colorado got added as a state and the official U.S. flag now has *thirty-eight* stars." He glanced up at the tattered flag and then took a look around the crowd. "I can't believe y'all are fixing to have a fight over a flag that ain't even a *real* American flag." Will took another bite of melon, turned and walked into the store.

A voice behind me said, "Who in the 'ell was that?"

"I think it was the storeowner's boy," a man said.

Will's presentation had seemingly taken all of the spunk out of both groups. Mr. Joe used this moment well. "I'm asking you fellows to respect my store, my land, and my flag, whether it's the right one or not."

"Are you asking or telling us?" Cole said.

"I'm asking you as a friend, neighbor, and fellow American." The Irishman extended his hand.

Mr. Cole stood for a few seconds studying the Irishman's hand before shaking it. "Well, since you've asked us, we'll leave you and your flag alone." But he raised his voice. "But let me be clear, it ain't my flag." He motioned to his remaining friends. "Let's go, men." They marched off as if they were returning to their battle stations, awaiting a Union cavalry attack.

The defenders of the flag, satisfied of their victory, retired to the store's bar for a good day of drinking.

I elbowed Mr. Joe. "I thought we were back at Westport for a minute."

That afternoon, reports reached the store about several incidents near the Post Office that had alarmed the populace. It began when a patron leaving with their mail spied a woman's purse left on the road edge. When he opened the purse, a garter snake slithered out, accompanied by youthful laughter from behind the building and the purse being snatched away on a long piece of fishing line.

A few minutes later, another Good Samaritan, this time a woman, picked up the purse and took it in the Post Office before opening it. When the wood rat jumped out, the three women in the building and the rat nearly tore it trying to get out first.

The next citizen never had the chance to open the purse. Just as they reached for it, it was jerked away by the fishing line.

Several men went to investigate and only found the ragged purse, still tied to the fishing line. Some folks thought it was hilarious, while others bemoaned the future of the youth of Sugartown.

The story reached the store and Mr. Joe immediately looked around. "Where is Will Moore?"

I immediately whispered. "Gavroche."

Dan, stacking boxes, said, "I'm glad to have a good alibi. I only hope my brother does too."

Will Moore walked in the store just as store hours ended. He had his shotgun and laid four squirrels on the counter.

"Where have you been?" Mr. Joe asked.

"Hunting over in the backwoods bay with the hounds."

"Squirrels aren't good eating this time of year." His father said. "It's too hot."

Will shrugged. "Couldn't resist a 4th of July hunt."

Dan, after sniffing the squirrels, whispered to me. "Those squirrels aren't fresh. They were killed yesterday."

"You don't think?" I said.

Dan nodded at his brother's smirk. "I know."

Mr. Joe was interrogating Will in the corner, but I couldn't help but noticing how he seemed to be stifling a smile.

Dan walked by me. "You've got to admit, it was pretty original."

All I could say was "Gavroche."

As the store closed, one single melon remained on the gallery. Joe Moore hefted it and asked me. "Think you can carry it home?"

"Is the Pope a Catholic?"

He laughed. "Last time I checked, he was." He balanced the melon on my shoulder.

"Can I ask you one thing?" I said. "What would've you have done if those fellows had tried to take down your flag?"

He rubbed his beard. "Well, since they didn't, we'll never know, will we?" He doffed his cap and in his strongest Irish accent said, "And Happy Independence Day, Missouri Cotton."

I saluted back. "And the same to you, Sir."

CHAPTER 54

THE PAST RETURNS

July 11, 1882

About a week after Independence Day, Mr. Joe and Will made a supply trip to Alexandria. Joe Moore had some legal business and took Will along for company and to keep him out of trouble.

They were gone nearly a week, and afterwards, Will rushed to me. "I've got to talk to you in private."

"About what?"

"Meet me at Sugar Creek Crossing today at ten. We'll tell everyone we're squirrel hunting."

I dutifully met him near the Old Campground Cemetery. He had his 20-gauge shotgun and hunting vest on, and we slipped along the creek as if we were hunting.

"Well, what is it?"

He lowered his voice. "It's about Buzzard."

"What about him?"

"Well, when I got to Alexandria, I couldn't stand not knowing whether he was dead or not, so I went to the business where he worked in Alexandria. I saw Mr. Perry, the proprietor, and asked for Buzzard. Mr. Perry eyed me cautiously. 'What do you want to know about him?'

"'He owes me some money,' I said.

"'Buzzard's gone.' Mister Perry scoffed. 'He owes me a lot more than he probably owes you.'

"'When will he return?' I asked.

"'Never,' Mister Perry said.

"I stuttered, 'You mean ... he's dead?'

"'No, Buzzard's in Memphis. He got in a bad accident here, and after recuperating, he moved to live with a sister in Memphis. Last I heard he's painting houses.' "

Will Moore shouldered his shotgun. "Mizz, I was so relieved that he was alive that I said, 'Don't worry about the money he owed me. It's just paper, anyway.' Then I ran faster than a martin flies to its jug. It was like a two-ton weight had been lifted off me. I wasn't a murderer after all."

"Does anyone else know?" I asked.

"Just you and me. Not even Dan."

"Especially not Dan'l Moore," I said.

Will browsed the treetops. "Since we met in the woods to squirrel hunt, we'd better bag several squirrels so as to give us an alibi."

He quickly located a nest of cat squirrels in an old beech. "Mizz, go around the tree and shake that muscadine vine." When I shook the vine, five squirrels raced in five directions. Will dropped one that fell right at my feet.

His second shot wounded a cat squirrel. It hung on bravely by one paw until falling into a briar patch. Reloading his shotgun, Will plowed into the thicket to finish off the squirrel.

It was part of the Moore family code that you never wasted a shell and never left a wounded animal on the ground or on the water. As Will hurried into the thicket in pursuit of his squirrel, a saw-briar vine the size of your finger raked him across the face. The briar had sliced him across the forehead, cut his cheek below his eye, and then across his lip and chin. His face was a mask of blood.

"Will, come out of there. Forget that squirrel."

He'd moved deeper into the thicket. "I'll be out as soon as I get my squirrel."

I tried to follow him in but was soon entangled in thick briars and vines. I felt a panic building as if I was in the clasp of something alive and sinister. It was as if I was in Buzzard's clutches again with no way to get free.

The shotgun blasted. "Got him," Will said.

I fought myself back out of the thicket and met him under the beech tree. His long cut extended from his forehead to his chin, and blood was everywhere.

He proudly held up the squirrels. "Two shots. Two squirrels."

"Actually, you shot three times. The third shot was the coup de grace.

"Well then, I stand corrected. He wiped the blood off his face with his sleeve. Blood had soaked into the collar of his shirt. "Missouri, you're cut too."

Both of my arms were scratched elbow to wrist with blood oozing down my fingers.

Will backed away. "You're not going to try any of that black magic bleeding stuff on me, are you?"

"Nah, it's only for saving lives." I took a sock off and used it to wipe my arms clean of blood. "I believe you're going to make it."

Will got his knife out and cut a section of the saw-briar vine that had sliced him. "I figure I'll be explaining this some, might as well have some evidence."

"If you saw yourself in the mirror, you'd realize you'll be telling this story a lot. I believe you're bleeding as much as Buzzard did."

Will wiped his cheek with a bandana. "Man, am I glad to know he's alive."

I wasn't feeling very gracious. "He deserved everything he got."

"But I'm sure glad he ain't dead and I ain't no murderer."

Will and I both created quite a stir when he entered the store. I rolled my blood-soaked sleeves down and slipped to a side room.

"Son, what happened to you?" Mister Joe said.

"Got in a fight with a wildcat."

"Well, I can see it won. What really happened?"

"I got in a fight with a saw-briar vine trying to root out a cat squirrel."

"It looks like the vine won."

"Maybe, but I got the squirrel."

Mr. Joe pulled out an assortment of bottles of ointments, iodine, a stack of bandages, and a blue bottle of Phillip's Milk of Magnesia.

"Da, I don't think I need that."

After being patched up, Will looked like the bandaged fifer and drummer I've seen in a Revolutionary War painting in an old copy of a magazine in Mobile.

Every medicine had been used to cleanse Will's cuts and

prevent infection. Only the bottle of milk of magnesia sat unused on the counter.

Customers who came in had all kinds of questions for Will. He finally slipped out back to clean our squirrels.

As Mr. Joe returned to sorting nails, it was evident he was disturbed.

"What's wrong?"

"John Watson's dead."

It took me a second to put it together. "John Watson, our sharpshooter at Westport?"

"He was murdered across the river."

Mister Joe pulled out a folded *Louisiana Democrat* article from his wallet. "A peddler brought it to me this morning."

I read the article aloud.

"Westport Gunman Killed in Ambush

"Local timber man and pioneer, John Watson, was killed near the village of Calcasieu in an apparent revenge killing last Tuesday. Mister Watson, age 46, along with two other men, was helping a woman named Mrs. Tompkins move to Hineston. About sundown, they'd set up camp near New Hope Church, at milepost 32 on the Sugartown Road. According to witnesses, Watson got up during the night to put knots on the fire and was shot from in the dark with a shotgun. He was struck by buckshot in about ten places. One entered his skull, another right in the heart. He slumped down (and) mumbled, 'Hand me my gun.' That was it. He was dead. A Grand Jury will be assembled to investigate the killing, but so far there are no suspects.

Mr. Joe leaned on the counter. "Since the Westport Fight, John Watson was a marked man. He got the blame for killing both Old Tom Perkins and Simon Morrow. He'd wisely avoided No Man's Land's side of the Calcasieu, but evidently traveled too close to the river. Speculation in Hineston is that this was a setup involving the woman and one of the men."

"But he didn't shoot either Perkins or Morrow." I handed the note back.

"That's not what folks believed."

I placed my elbows on the counter. "That day, as the fight ended, Watson told me that he believed in fate, and a bullet couldn't touch him unless it had his name on it."

Mr. Joe shook his head. "So evidently, that bullet—or those ten buckshot—did."

When Will walked back in, I re-read the article aloud. He shook his head. "We thought Watson was ten-foot tall and bulletproof. I guess the second part weren't so."

Mr. Joe tapped his pipe against the counter edge. "He was the true hero of The Westport Fight. He saved the day—and our hides—that day at the store. He stemmed the final charge with his sniping. I'll never forget how he never flinched as shots peppered his spot at the window."

"When they started that full-throated Rebel Yell charge, I just knew we were goners," Will said. "While the rest of us hid under counters and in empty barrels, John Watson stood his ground and stopped the attack in its tracks."

"We owe our lives to him," I said. "And now he's dead."

Mr. Joe tamped his pipe full of tobacco. "He lived by the sword … and died by the sword."

My head was spinning. Buzzard, who probably intended on killing me after molesting me, was alive, while John Watson, who had saved our lives, was dead.

It was late August and everyone had their crops laid back or harvested, which left folks with more leisure time. Country folks love any kind of meeting, especially what is called a protracted meeting. That's a fancy name for a church revival, and folks in Sugartown in 1882 loved meetings like this. It was a chance to be together and free, often with good food and good music. Even those not really religious would attend at least part of a revival meeting.

The Baptist Church in Sugartown was about four years old, and trying to get traction in the community, so they decided to hold a revival. These meetings were protracted because they could go on for weeks if the preaching was good, people were getting saved, and the offering was adequate.

They were held at night, and with school out and most crops at a standstill, people didn't mind being out later. That was good because many of these meetings could go late into the night.

The men of the Baptist and Methodist churches in Sugartown constructed a brush arbor on Sugar Creek at the Old Campground Site. An evangelist from North Louisiana named Boltz had been invited to preach the series of meetings.

Ma and I attended the first night. We met the Moore boys, and I was assigned to sit between Will and Dan. Will's reputation for the baby-swapping revival caper had preceded his arrival in Sugartown, so I served as both his bodyguard and watcher. It was the first time I'd seen him since the saw-briar fight. Even in the torchlight, his cuts looked bad. "It's lucky that one of those thorns didn't get your eye."

"I got the squirrel. That's what matters."

"Get quiet, Frankenstein." Dan nudged his brother. "The service is starting." Dan, from the moment he saw Will's face, gave him the nickname. The book, *Frankenstein*, by a lady named Mary Shelley, was the most popular book checked out by boys in the Baldwin Academy Library. It was the perfect nickname for Will, and he seemed to take it in relatively good humor.

There were about forty folks, mostly women and children, present on the first night of the revival. The smoke fires built outside the arbor discouraged the mosquitoes but created a fog under the brush arbor.

The best part of the meeting was how Dan held my hand tightly the whole sermon. Because of that, I didn't mind how long the message was. Reverend Boltz preached a fiery sermon that brought plenty of amens and a host of folks coming forward for an altar call. As the meeting dismissed, Reverend Boltz said, "Lord willing, tomorrow night we'll have a special guest. He's one of the survivors of the recent Westport Fight and has a strong testimony you'll want to hear."

Dan, Will, and I all came wide-awake. "Who could it be?" I said. We named the men who were in the store with us and none seemed a good candidate for a revival speaker.

"Maybe it's one of the Redbones?" Will said.

Dan laughed. "I don't think they'd feel any more welcome here than we'd be at Occupy."

I prodded the two brothers. "Go ask the preacher who it is."

We argued back and forth about approaching Pastor Boltz. Finally, all three of us went, with Will as our spokesman. "Reverend, who is the Westport Fight man?"

The Reverend surveyed the three of us, then grinned. "I guess you'll have to come tomorrow night to see for yourself."

We continued our argument outside the arbor. "It's got to be Frank the Surveyor," Will said. "He was pretty shaken up during the entire fight."

Dan punched his brother in the shoulder. "He was too drunk to remember a thing. It's not him, and I don't think it's Sam Nolan. He lives here now, and I've not seen the slightest conversion in him."

Dan shook his head. "It might be one of the LaCazes. I heard they moved to Slabtown."

"Mizz, what do you think?" Will said.

"I believe it's Musgrove."

"Musk?" Both brothers burst out laughing.

At the store the next day, we quizzed Mr. Joe about the mystery man. He had no clue, but said, "I plan to be there to see for myself."

We took our same bench that night, joined by the Irishman. The crowd was much larger and, during the singing, I checked the crowd for anyone with any connection to the Fight. The four of us, sitting on one of the back benches, were the only ones that fit that description.

Will leaned over to his father. "Da, I bet it's you. The preacher's gonna call you up there."

A look of fear swept over the Irishman's face. "I'll get up and run."

Will nudged his brother. "What if he calls on you?"

"I'll wet my britches. What about you?"

Will, never at a loss for words, said, "I'll march up front and tell the whole story from start to finish. They'll have to relight the pine knots by the time I get through." He turned to me. "Mizz, it might me you."

"No way. The Reverend said it was a 'he' and that's not me."

Reverend Boltz's sermon was just as long as the night before. Not a word was mentioned about the speaker from the Westport Fight. The Reverend finally closed his *Bible* and wiped his brow.

"Before we have an altar call, I've brought a special guest. Most of you have heard about the Westport Fight back at Christmas."

Half of the congregation turned toward our bench. It was a well-known fact we'd been there.

The Reverend evidently was unaware of this. "This man was nearly killed in the fight, but survived and has repented and given his life to Christ. He's been preaching east of the river, and I asked him to come share tonight." He motioned toward the edge of the arbor. "Come on out, Brother Musgrove."

Dan, Will, and I all gasped when Musk walked out. The Irishman, whispered under his breath, "Well, I'll be damned."

Then Will busted out laughing, and Dan punched him. "Shut up."

Gordon Musgrove was dressed in a black suit, much different than the leather he usually wore. He walked with a slight limp and was about thirty pounds lighter. The most amazing thing was his hair. It'd turned completely white, except for one small dark spot on the crest of his head.

Will noticed it too. "Look, he's white-headed except for that one black spot where they split his head open trying to club him to death. That by itself should've killed him."

Gordon Musgrove began in the strong rough voice that we knew well. "Most of you don't know me from Adam's housecat, but folks on both sides of the river can attest that I was as bad of a man as ever walked the face of the earth. I didn't care nothin' about religion or the things of God. I viewed myself as one tough hombre and said and did what was on my mind."

Every eye and ear was on Musgrove. Even a crying baby in the corner had quieted.

"My big mouth is what started the Westport Fight."

Will whispered, "Amen."

Musgrove began a blow-by-blow account of the fight on the porch, and then moved on to how he was left outside when the shooting started. Now, I won't retell the story because you've heard it before, but Musgrove told it from his perspective and it was basically accurate in both his details and timeline.

He took off his black coat. "Being caught outside, I knew I was a dead man, so I hid behind a water trough. For the first time in a long time, I prayed. Promising the Lord that if I got out of this mess alive, I'd change my ways.

"Just then, one of the attackers found me and aimed his pistol and shot me three times. After that, I was in and out of consciousness. Later, someone beat me on the head with a pine club and that's the last thing I remember."

He pulled out a bandana and wiped his eyes. "When I awoke, I was inside the Westport Store on the floor. I was the most surprised man to ever draw a breath. I should've been dead."

Dan leaned to his Father. "He don't know we're here."

Mr. Joe lifted his hand. "Shh."

Musgrove was obviously nervous and sweating. "Two teenage boys braved the shooting and dragged me inside the store where a Doctor, James Hamilton, saved my life. I was bleeding to death from the gunshots, but the good doctor patched me up and staunched the bleeding."

I was sitting like a stone statue.

"He's not even gonna mention you," Dan said.

"That doesn't matter."

"I lingered between life and death for weeks. It was a month before I could stand on my own."

His voice lowered and he stepped from behind the pulpit. "Now lots of folks make promises to God when they're in trouble, then forget them when things get better. But I'm a man of my word. God saved my life at Westport and I promised Him if He did, I'd give my life to Him. He kept his promise, and I've tried to keep mine. As soon as I was able, they baptized me in Spring Creek near Amiable Church. Folks came by the hundreds to see me baptized. That's how bad of a man I was. Some of them came, saying, 'I won't believe it unless I see it.' "

Musgrove turned to Reverend Boltz. "The preacher that baptized me said we should've charged admission and used the money to pay off the church building." The crowd laughed appreciatively.

"That day at the Westport Store, I was as close to death as you can be. When I woke up, I didn't see or hear no bright lights or harps, but I knew something had happened. Being born again can be instantaneous or a process. For me, it was both."

"Some folks ask me how I can forgive the men who shot and beat me. I can't really explain it. I'm just so happy to be alive that I ain't got time nor energy to hate anyone. If you'd known me before, you'd know what a change that is."

I nodded my head, recalling my first visit to the store with Musk blocking my way and the suggestive insults he'd tossed my way in the presence of the other men.

"Yep, if ever a man's needed being born again, I'm one, and the change God made in me can't be argued with."

I glanced at Mr. Joe. He was leaning forward against the bench in front of him.

Musgrove made a fist. "Since then, I've felt the call of God on my life to preach the Gospel of Jesus. Right now, I'm just going wherever I'm asked to share my testimony."

An older man on the front bench said, "Can't have a testimony without a test."

Musgrove nodded. "That's true. And my testimony is that if God can change me, he can change anybody."

Young Deacon Will chimed in, "Amen."

Dan squeezed my hand harder.

You could tell by Musgrove's voice that he was nearly through. "I was kind of like the Apostle Paul. He wasn't looking for God on the Damascus Road, but God found him. That's kind of how it was for me at the Westport Fight. God found me. I ain't changed because of being baptized or being called to preach, I been changed by God. I was born again and you can be tonight too."

There followed a fine altar call. Musgrove sat down on the front bench, and none of the four of us could take our eyes off him.

When the service ended, the crowd gathered around Gordon Musgrove, asking questions and just touching him. Mr. Joe slipped toward the dark. I grabbed his arm. "You don't want to speak to him?"

"Not now. I'll catch up with him later."

Dan, Will, and I stood in line. Musgrove looked at the brothers, a light of recognition in his dark eyes. "You're the two younger Moore boys?"

"Yes, sir," Dan said. "I'm Dan and this is Will."

Musgrove looked at Will. "Son, you must've got in a fight with a buzz saw."

"Yeah, and you shoulda seen the buzz saw."

Gordon Musgrove motioned to the remaining crowd. "Y'all come over here. These are the two boys who dragged me inside the store. They were the real heroes of the Westport Fight." The congregants looked at Will and Dan as if they were Hercules and

Ulysses.

Dan pulled me forward. "Mr. Musgrove, you remember Missouri, don't you?"

He bent down to see my face. "I don't believe I do."

"She helped drag you inside, and she doctored on you along with Doctor Hamilton," Will said.

A look of confusion clouded Musgrove's face. "I don't remember any girl being there."

Dan looked from him to me. "Surely, you remember ..."

"I wish I could say I recall, but I don't. I guess that clubbing messed up my head."

"It gave you that dark spot, didn't it," Will said.

Musgrove smiled. "And turned the rest of my hair white."

We said our goodbyes and went out into the darkness. Dan said, "Little brother, you run on ahead. I need a few words with Mizz."

Dan turned to me. "Do you think he really didn't remember you putting that spell on him?"

I shrugged. "It seems he didn't. Besides, it wasn't a spell." I'd always wondered what Dan Moore saw and heard when I staunched the bleeding in Musgrove's leg. Evidently, he'd seen more than I thought.

"Well, whatever you did saved his life. I saw it with my own two eyes."

I sighed. "I'm still not sure if Ma's gift was passed on to me that day, or if it was just the mighty hand of God."

"Or maybe both," Dan said.

"You see, the thing about gifts is that you don't go around bragging about them. You seek to silently stay behind the screen, using these gifts for good with little notice. That day on the floor of the Westport Store, for the first time in my life, I welcomed the fact that I might have some gifts."

I walked faster, and Dan Moore caught up with me. "And Musk didn't remember how you claimed his soul for God."

I froze. "You heard that?"

"Heard it and saw it."

"Have you told a soul?"

"No one." He squeezed my hand. "Your secret's safe with me. But I do know you saved his life and his soul."

"I didn't save him. God stopped the bleeding. I just did what

I'd been taught. And no one can save a soul but God. And from the look of the new Gordon Musgrove, that's what happened."

I grabbed Dan's hand. "And you promise to never tell about my part."

Dan pulled me close, kissed me, and whispered, "All of your secrets are safe with me."

The revival went on for two weeks, and several things happened on the last night of the meeting worth mentioning. Miss Eliza, who spent most of her time bedridden, went to the service. Everyone tried to talk her out of it, but she said, "I'm going if I have to crawl."

Mr. Joe had taken a liking to the Evangelist, Reverend Boltz, who came by the store each day. He agreed to attend with Miss Eliza.

The crowd had thinned down the second week, but the closing night was packed. The service itself wasn't that memorable, but when the altar call was given, Will Moore was the first one down the aisle. He spent several minutes talking with the evangelist and then they got down on their knees and prayed. A whole line of young people and several women followed Will. We sang the five verses of "Just As I Am" over and over until I knew the words backward and forward.

As the Evangelist closed out the altar call, and we awaited the closing prayer from the Methodist preacher, Joe Moore stood and nervously cleared his throat. "Now, most of you know I'm new here, and if you'd heard me speak, you know I'm Irish." The crowd murmured. "Where I come from, we're all Catholic, so this Protestant stuff is a little strange, but I've been impressed with Reverend Boltz. And I want to make sure he leaves Sugartown knowing we appreciate him." Mr. Joe held up a five-dollar bill. "I want us to take a collection for this man of God, and I'll start it off with a five."

A buzz went through the crowd. Five dollars was a princely sum in this part of the Pineywoods. A Frenchman named Landry, another Catholic, stood. "Well, if an Irishman can give five dollars, so can a Frenchman."

Mister Joe turned toward him in mock indignation. "Well, if a Frenchman can give five, an Irishman can surely give ten more."

Someone in the back said, "Amen."

Mr. Landry stood to his full height, which wasn't much. "If an Irishman can give ten, so can this Frenchman." He held up a ten-dollar bill.

The Irishman turned to the Evangelist. "Sir, if you'll come by my establishment tomorrow, I'll have your money ready." He turned to the crowd. "Now if two Catholics can give thirty dollars, you Baptists and Methodists ought to be able to match it." He placed his upturned hat on the front bench. "If anyone else wants to give, put it in my hat."

Reverend Boltz looked as if he was going to faint. Thirty dollars was probably more money than he made in several months of preaching. He was speechless, something evangelists seldom are.

The Methodist preacher prayed a long, flowery, heartfelt prayer, and after he said, "Amen," the faithful filed by the hat. I watched closely, mainly hearing the clink of coins, but there was some quiet money too. I even saw a folded silent twenty go in the hat.

The next morning at the store, I cornered Mr. Joe. "I believe that was a setup between you and the Frenchman Landry. Y'all had it planned."

He sat on a keg. "There's no way that tightwad Cajun would ever give fifteen dollars to anything. I got to his pride."

"So you planned it?"

He shrugged. "It did go well, didn't it?"

"I'd say so. How much did you end up with?"

"Nearly a hundred dollars."

"Wow."

Mr. Joe leaned on the counter. "Missouri, recently Reverend Boltz was scheduled to preach in the Green Oak community, not far from the Coushatta Indian village. The creeks were out of banks for three days running. Finally, the Reverend took his clothes off, wrapped them in a bag, then balanced the bag on his head, and swam his horse across the river. He was that determined to get there to preach." He smiled. "That hundred dollars is a good investment in a good man."

I found Will, who was stocking the shelves with a new order of laundry soap that had just arrived.

"What happened to you last night?"

"I got saved."

"What's that?"

"The preacher invited anyone who wanted to be saved to come forward. I took him up on his offer."

"Did he save you?"

"Heck no, preachers can't save nobody. I asked Jesus to."

"Do you think he did?"

"Mizz, I think he did. In fact, I know he did."

"How can you know?"

Will grinned. "I just know that I know that I know that I know."

I'd had a restless night before. I wasn't quite sure about all of this religion and Will's decision. During the revival, I'd been in church more and heard more preaching and biblical reading than in all my earlier life combined.

After work, I made my usual visit to Miss Eliza. She was propped up in bed, sleeping. I slipped in, and quietly put a straight chair by her bed. It was one of my favorite things to do. Being in her presence gave me a sense of peace and purpose. Sometimes I'd do my homework or read a book, but most of the time I just sat there watching her. In my heart of hearts, I knew my opportunities to do this were slipping by.

There was a downside to these silent vigils. Sometimes she'd draw a deep labored breath, then lay silent for what seemed like half a minute, before struggling for more air. Tuberculosis was a cruel way to die, and no one deserved this type of life or death.

Presently, she stirred and saw me. "How long you been sitting there, Child?"

I shut my Latin book, which I hadn't looked at in fifteen minutes. "Not long. Just came by to check on you."

"You must've been quiet." She held my hand. "You'd make a good squirrel hunter."

"Maybe I'll be Will's squirrel-hunting partner."

"Keep him out of the briars." She tried to sit up. "Child, would you hand me my Garrett's sweet snuff? I need a good shot."

"Miss Eliza, you promised your family you'd quit using snuff. You nearly choked to death last week on it."

"But I didn't promise you. Hand me my can." I reluctantly threw it on the bed and she quickly filled her lower lip with the light brown powder. In a few minutes, she'd worked it up and had a string of amber spittle on her chin. "Excuse my messiness. The sicker I get, the more mess I make with my snuff, but it's one of the few things left that I really enjoy."

I waved her off. "Enjoy yourself. I'll keep your chin wiped, and if you choke to death, I'll take the rap." I leaned forward. "I guess you heard about Will last night?"

"Yes. I left midways through the service. Just couldn't sit any longer. Will came in and woke me up to tell all about it."

"What do you think happened to him?"

"Prop this pillow up, Child." Once she was comfortable, she said, "Will responded to the Lord speaking to him. We call it a lot of things. getting saved, being born again, being converted."

"What do you call it?"

"I just call it making peace with God."

"Is it like turning over a new leaf?"

"Not really. It's more than that. You can turn over a leaf and still have the same mean sap inside you." She pointed to her heart. "It's an inside thing."

"Has it happened to you?"

"Yep, when I was a girl, a little younger than Will. There weren't no lightning flashing or Damascus Road experience, I just made a decision to follow Jesus. Made my peace the same night I made my decision to follow Jesus. It's kind of a package deal, I guess." She shifted in the bed where she could look straight at me. "But you make peace on God's terms, not yours."

She pointed to her spit can. "Hand me my can. In my child-like mind, I just realized I couldn't get to God on my own. My sin was in the way, but I realized he'd already made a way. That's where Jesus comes in. He made the way. I've always loved it where he said, 'I'm the way, the truth, and the life.' That 'bout sums it up."

"I'm not sure I'm ready for that kind of commitment."

I waited for her assurance or comment.

"Child, there's only two kinds of truth. What's in your head and in your heart. What we're talking about now are the things of the heart. What we're talking about here don't take place in your head. It's a matter of the heart.

I moved closer to her. "I know something happened inside my heart inside the store during the Fight. I can't explain it, but I did feel God's presence."

"How was that?"

"I was working on Gordon Musgrove, who was bleeding out. "I tried everything. Direct pressure, even was ready to use a tourniquet." I lowered my voice. "I even used one of Ma's incantations from Ezekiel, but it was right after that when I prayed directly to Jesus; no I begged ... Jesus to help, and the bleeding stopped immediately."

"Missouri, I can't look in a person's heart, but doing something—even saving the life of Musk—don't make you born again. It's when you accept what Jesus has already done for you. Child, the way I see it, it doesn't matter if the Scripture from Ezekiel or prayer to Jesus did it, it was God that healed him."

"I believe it was Jesus. I felt his presence." I crossed my arms. "I've felt his presence ever since then."

"And that's a good thing."

"Seeing and hearing Gordon Musgrove the other night really affected me. He's not the same man."

"That's what I heard. I guess he really was born again. The *Bible* says somewhere that if any man is in Christ, he's a new creature."

"I was around Musgrove before this all, and he wasn't even a good creature, much less a good man."

"No one is beyond the reach of God."

I hesitated. "What about my pap?"

"He ain't no more beyond God's reach than Musgrove."

"But he'd have to go a long ways to get there."

"Who? Your Pap or Jesus? I didn't say your pap didn't have a long ways to go, but he may be closer than you think, or Jesus may be sneaking up on him." She laughed and spittle went all over the sheet.

"I guess we'll see."

"That we will."

"Miss Eliza, are you strong enough to walk out to see something parked outside?"

I helped her to her feet and we made our way to where our wagon was parked.

"I ain't seen that fine pair and your wagon in a spell. What's their names again?"

"The mule is Aunt Em and the ox is Mag."

"They still look in fine fettle."

I led her to the wagon bed and uncovered the granite slab.

She craned her neck. "What is that?"

"It's a marker for Unk's grave."

She rubbed her hand over the smooth granite. "That cost a pretty penny."

"It was what I wanted to do."

"What does it say?"

"Nathan Dyal,

"Known as Unk

"And loved by all."

"I didn't put a date because he was so elusive about when he was born."

"Child, he wasn't much with numbers."

"But he was the best."

"Yes, he was," she said. "What does the rest of that writing say."

I read it to her.

"He sleeps. Although his fate was very strange, he lived. He died when he had no longer his angel. The thing came to pass simply, of itself, as the night comes when day is gone."

"It's from the gravestone of Jean Valjean at the end of *Les Miserables*. It's what Cosette and Marius put on his tombstone."

"What does it mean?"

"That Unk Dyal, although strange, truly lived. In fact, he may have lived the best and fullest life I've ever known."

"I wouldn't argue with that," Mrs. Eliza said. "But what about the part 'he died when he had no longer his angel?'"

I'd wondered how I'd speak to this. I did it the only way I knew to be frankly. "You were his angel, Miss Eliza."

She ran her fingers along the engraving of the slab.

I touched her elbow. "You're not the reason he died, but losing you and your family was the beginning of the end."

She looked up peacefully. "But, my leaving Ten Mile *is* the reason he died. I fully expected it. I wasn't a bit surprised when we received word. I hate I wasn't there with him at the end, but he was ready and it was time. Now, what does the end of your wording on the tombstone say?"

"The thing came to pass simply, of itself, as the night comes when day is gone."

"I like that. That's how his passing was." She nodded. "He left at the time he chose and he left as he lived, simply. Where will you place this marker? We're not even sure where he's buried."

"Miss Eliza, where I place it won't be important. It'll be a permanent reminder that he lived. A reminder, long after you and I are gone, that Unk Dyal lived."

"And didn't he live!" She smiled and leaned forward. "Why don't you put it out there close to the town ant colony where he originally buried the treasure? We think he was buried near there.

"I was thinking of putting it where they think his treasure was last buried."

"That's even better. He won't be forgotten, will he?"

"Not as long as I'm alive.

"He was my angel," she said.

"And you were his."

"Won't be long before I join him."

I wanted to argue but held my tongue. "It'll be a fine reunion, won't it?"

Miss Eliza Moore stared off into the distance, making me wonder what she saw. After several minutes, she said, "It'll be the finest reunion ever."

CHAPTER 55

OMENS

Late August 1882

I tried not to take stock in all of those signs and omens that folks like my parents based their lives of fear and hope on. Ma had moved past her fixation on crows, and it wasn't a day too soon.

But I should've recognized the day when the fox showed up as an omen.

Summer was supposedly ending, but it was still hot as blue blazes in the Louisiana sun. There's nothing more miserable than Louisiana in the dog days of July and August. Even the nights remained hot and made it hard to rest. As August ended, I looked forward to school starting and the first cool spell. Our first day of classes would be Labor Day.

Baby James was playing with some blocks of wood from the sawmill on the front porch. Because the house faced east, late evening was when the front gallery was a refuge from the sun. Even though school didn't start for a week, I was struggling through a Latin primer, trying to get a running start before classes began.

As always, Lucky was sitting near the baby on eternal patrol. Suddenly, the dog's hackles rose and it ran to the gallery edge, barking fiercely. A dog was coming down the lane. As it neared, I realized it wasn't a dog, but a red fox. It was wobbling and I immediately knew it was rabid. It was foaming at the mouth and had no fear of approaching our house. I made a split-second decision and raced in the house for Pap's shotgun, but couldn't find it.

I ran in my bedroom to retrieve my pistol from its hiding place, up where the baby could never get near it. I always kept five of the chambers loaded with only the barrel empty. As I raced to the porch, I clicked the trigger once. It was ready.

I'd made a terrible mistake in going for the gun. Instead, I should've gotten the baby safely in the house, I'd left him on the porch.

The fox was sickly looking but stood on the top step engaged in a snarling contest with Lucky, who'd placed himself squarely between the fox and baby. I tried to grab Baby James, but he was screaming and had scooted to the corner of the porch.

Lucky and the fox were within a foot of each other. Although the baby was my one and only priority, I didn't want my faithful dog bitten by a rabid fox. Against my better judgment, I kicked Lucky out of the way to avoid the fox's snapping teeth. That left me as its primary threat and as it lunged at me, I fired three times.

Fortunately, a Colt .45 has a good kick on both ends. The bullets knocked the fox in a flip off the porch. Lucky, sensing victory, lunged at the fox, and I grabbed his collar as he went by. I figured a dog biting a rabid fox could get rabies. I dragged Lucky, who was straining and barking, back onto the porch, shoving him inside the house. Then I grabbed Baby James and put him indoors, then propped the screen door shut with a straight chair.

I sat on the steps, not six feet from the dead fox, and trembled. I couldn't hold the pistol, so I set it down beside me.

Within five minutes, I heard a horse approaching at a trot. As the rider neared, I recognized Mister Burnett, our closest neighbor down the creek. He pulled up reins. "I heard the three shots. What's the matter?"

"I pointed at the fox."

"Rabid?"

I nodded.

"I'm glad you gave the three-shot warning."

I was puzzled.

"I heard three shots in close succession," Mr. Burnett said. "That's the signal for help in this neck of the woods. You didn't know that?"

"No sir. I was just stopping that fox before it got to the baby or my dog."

Lucky was scratching at the door and James' wailing hadn't subsided.

"You got an old feed sack or something I can haul the fox off in? I'll take it and bury it in the woods." He climbed off his horse while I grabbed a sack off the line. He used his boot to push the fox in the sack, which I held open.

"Now, get some kerosene. We need to burn the spot where the fox lay. If your dog licks up any of that blood or slobber, it could get the rabies. I'd recommend you tie your dog for the next couple of days. Are you sure the fox didn't nip him?"

"I don't think so."

"Let's have a look." We went in the house and I took the baby in my arms. James had the dry heaves and was trembling as much as I was.

Mr. Burnett took a long time examining Lucky. "I don't see any skin broken. How close were they?"

"Right at each other."

He lowered his voice. "Now, I don't want to say this, but the right thing would be to put your dog down right now. If it gets the rabies, it could bite the baby or anyone."

I stepped to the gallery edge. "Over my dead body."

The old man shrugged. "If your dog gets the rabies and bites you, it will be over your dead body."

"That fox didn't bite Lucky, so he ain't gonna get rabies."

"I still think ..."

I didn't realize I was holding my pistol. "Mr. Burnett, that's the last we'll hear of it. Lucky saved the baby's life and probably mine, too. He deserves to live."

He nodded at the pistol. "You're a real pistol yourself." He tipped his hat. "I'll best be going." He tied a plow rope to the sack so he could drag the fox behind his horse, which made the horse finicky, and it danced in circles trying to get away from the fox. Our neighbor mounted up. "Now, tell your daddy that if I were him, I'd still ..."

I waved him off. "Goodbye, and thank you for your help."

They took off at a gallop, the horse trying to get away from the fox in the sack, but only pulling it along.

When Pap and Ma came home late that evening, they made me

repeat the fox story at least four times, asking more questions with each telling. The entire time, Pap was examining Lucky for any sign of cut or tear.

As we later sat around supper, Pap dropped a bombshell. "I'm leaving in the morning for Alexandria and then Baton Rouge. I'm going to get Louisiana Lottery tickets. There's money to be made here on selling those tickets."

Ma, who didn't read much, said, "What's the Louisiana Lottery?"

"After the War, the state legislature needed money to recover. They passed the only legal lottery in America." Pap tapped the table. "It's been a huge income for the state with ticket orders coming from all over the nation. In Louisiana's larger cities like New Orleans or Shreveport, ticket sales are brisk, and on the days of a drawing, entire cities stop to hear the numbers announced.

I'd read about it in the *Louisiana Democrat* and the paper made it sound like the greatest thing that had ever happened to our state. I knew better. Louisiana has always held the record for scandal and the lottery had scandal written all over it.

Not so with Pap. He continued walking in a circle. "This lottery will be good for everyone. To ensure honesty, the drawings are held on a stage in New Orleans under the watchful eyes of two of our Confederate generals, Jubal Early and P.G.T. Beauregard. The numbers were actually drawn out of the hopper by two boys from the Louisiana School for the Blind.

Ma scoffed. "Old Generals and young blind boys. Only in Louisiana. I wouldn't trust it if Peter and Paul were overseeing it and Moses was spinning the number cage.

I knew my pap well enough that there was some sliminess to this plan. Henry Cotton and the Louisiana Lottery were not a trustworthy combination in my opinion. "Pap, how will you make money on this?"

"Folks here on the frontier don't have access to purchasing Lottery tickets. I'll buy a passel of them, mark the price up a little, and sell to the locals. It'll be providing a service to the community with me serving as the middleman."

"But you know the chances of anyone winning in Sugartown are nigh impossible," I said.

"But folks will buy. Lotteries give folks hope."

"I'd call it false hope." I stood. "What I don't understand is that you're doing so well here. You've got steady work, making friends, your drinking's in check. So, why go off chasing something like this?"

"I was made for better things than filing saws. This could take us to places we've never been."

It sounded like an omen. A harbinger that bore no good.

The next morning, Pap left, saying he expected to be gone about two weeks. Ma and I, through practical experience, had no idea when he'd return.

It was late August and nearly time for school. Things seemed to be flowing along well for me in Sugartown, when another omen occurred. Bridget Thompson, leader of the Sabine Women who tormented me at school, was hired on at the store. I wasn't sure I could work with her, but Dan told me to just do my job and keep my mouth shut. It seems her uncle in Ten Mile had been a good friend of Mr. Joe, and hiring Bridget might rebuild some burnt bridges between Ten Mile and Sugartown.

Mr. Joe, aware of Bridget and my history, made sure she clerked on days I was with Miss Eliza, so we seldom crossed paths in the store. When I did come in, she'd quickly move to another area.

I'd told Dan about my throat-grabbing scene with Bridget in front of the washroom earlier that spring. He was amused at my moxie to take on the bullies, but darkened at Bridget's threat to get even. "Mizz, you do have some moxie, but you'd better watch your back. She's capable of causing you trouble."

School was scheduled to take in on the first Monday of September. I'd seen some of my school friends all summer since they lived near Sugartown. Others I'd not seen since May, and they trickled in on the days leading up to classes. There were several new students, and chief among them was Will Moore. His saw-briar scabs were healing, but "Frankenstein" stuck with him like blackstrap molasses on a Sunday shirt.

Dan was waiting until next semester to begin. He was needed at the store, and money was too tight for two tuitions in the Moore home.

However, as students and teachers and supplies showed up, one thing was missing. Professor Baldwin.

As classes began on Monday, Professor Baldwin was nowhere to be seen. This wasn't completely out of the ordinary. Early in the semester, he often traveled on weekends to nearby cities, digging around for more students.

Miss Collins called a school assembly and announced in a shaky voice that "Professor Baldwin is rounding up some new students in Orange, Texas, and he should be here, with them in tow, by the end of the week." She coughed. "Students, classes will start in fifteen minutes. Professor Baldwin's classes will be covered by Mr. Sanders from the neighboring 'Who'd A Thought it School.' By then, we hope Professor Baldwin will be back.

I watched her closely, knowing she was lying, but wondering what she knew. I felt sorry for her, surmising that she probably knew no more than the rest of us.

At lunch, Sonnet Ireland cornered me. "Missouri, you know something about Professor Baldwin that the rest of us don't."

I bit off a large slice of cornbread. It's hard to talk with a mouth of cornbread. Instead, I just shrugged at Sonnet.

She wouldn't give up. "You know something. It goes back to the last day of school and your 'personal' conversation with him."

She said this in a saucy tone that irritated me, so I said, "Well, if I told you, I'd have to kill you."

"What's that supposed to mean?"

"Ah, it's just a common idiom they use in the Ten Mile Country. Sonnet, honestly, I don't know one thing more about where he is than you do."

A rooster crowed from the school henhouse. "He's flown the coop for sure," Sonnet said. "He's not coming back."

On Wednesday morning, the school bell rang without the Professor, and it dismissed that day with still no sight of him. By Friday, the rumor mill was rolling hard and the fear that the Professor might have skipped out grew. Worry really set in on Friday when he was still absent.

I had enough to worry about with Pap being gone and my class schedule. It included Latin II, American History, grammar, geometry, algebra, and a new course on public speaking.

I dove into the rigors of this new schedule. My math was weak and the twin classes of Algebra and Geometry filled me with dread. Then there was public speaking. I had a well-earned reputation for speaking my mind, but the idea of getting up in front of others and giving a speech gave me the willies. However, it was a requirement to get a teaching certificate, and that was my goal at the Academy. I still wasn't clear on the requirements that female teachers remain single. Someone tried to explain about this thing called the marriage bar. Dan Moore was moving so slowly in our romance that I didn't feel too worried.

On the day school started, Pap had been gone sixteen days. We'd received no post of where he was. I laughed at the thought of Pap and Professor Baldwin sitting together at some watering hole at Natchez-under-the-hill. They would definitely make strange bedfellows.

Ma simply shrugged. "This ain't our first rodeo. He'll show up sooner or later. He's kind of like that cat with nine lives."

"Yes'um, but even Tom-Claws ran out before he got to nine." I tried to focus on school and not let my father's crazy antics distract me. I kept recalling his parting words, "This could take us places we could never go."

I wondered if I'd be going on to the next place Pap planned to take us. I was feeling some independence, but there were two major problems about that freedom I felt. Ma and Baby James. Ma was a fragile soul, becoming more so by the year. I wasn't sure what she'd do without me.

And the thought of not being with Baby James chilled me. I'd fallen in love with him and looked forward to every moment around him. I stayed busy with Dan, school, my work at the store, and taking care of Miss Eliza, but made sure every day ended with me home before dark. With Pap gone, I felt as if I was filling in a gap that Baby James needed.

CHAPTER 56

THE TIDE TURNS

September 1882

It seemed the story of my life. Just when things would be going great, the bottom would fall out. It had happened in so many river towns of the South. It had happened in Westport. And now it was happening in Sugartown, the place I'd liked best in all of my travels.

Classes continued at the Academy, but nobody knew about the long-term future of the school. Miss Collins had shared a letter with us, purportedly from Professor Baldwin, that he had been deathly sick and in the hospital at Waco, Texas. The letter mentioned nothing of his return.

The remaining faculty were bound and determined that we would shuffle on. The student body pressed on and everyone did their best to keep things moving and maintain morale.

But each day we lifelessly marched into the Academy. We all knew it was the beginning of the end.

About two weeks after school started, Pap returned. As usual, he was mum about his trip, but plopped down a thick wad of bills and a sheaf of Louisiana Lottery certificates and tickets.

"Henry, where did that cash come from?" Ma said.

"Ask me no questions, and I'll tell you no lies."

"What do you plan to do with the Lottery tickets?"

"Sell them."

I picked one up and held it to the lantern light. "Are they genuine?"

"As far as I know."

I shot him a glance. He was the master of hiding behind the how-could-I-know alibi.

Ma picked them up. "Where do you plan to sell them?"

"I've talked to Mizz's boss about selling them out of his store."

I shuddered. "Pap, please don't do that. Those folks have been so good to me and I—"

"Joe Moore has been good to you, and that's exactly why I want to share the profits with him."

I grabbed his arm. "Pap, please don't."

He jerked away. "I'm your father, and I'll decide what's best for this family." He bagged up the cash and tickets. As he left the room, he said, "No one's to touch this bag or say a word about it."

I went to bed troubled, knowing that storm clouds were brewing.

I was secure in my job with the Moore store and sitting with Miss Eliza. I was bringing in enough cash to buy my own clothes, take care of my school supplies, and kick in cash to help the family, but I knew in my heart that this lottery scheme would collapse in a house of cards, and my job at the store would be one of those cards.

Pap spent most of the next day at the store. I studied the interactions between him and Joe Moore. I wanted to pull Mr. Joe aside and say, "Don't do business with him. It won't end well." But how do you say that to your boss about your own father?

The locals were excited about finally being able to be part of the infamous Louisiana Lottery. Before, they had to travel to Alexandria or Lake Charles to buy a ticket. Now, they could take their chances in Sugartown. Pap set up a table in the corner of the store and was busy all morning trading cash for tickets. I walked by him and he winked. "I'm raking it in like Grant took Richmond."

I bit my tongue and walked on.

Mister Joe, his arms crossed, stood off to the side. I detected uneasiness in him. "Are you all right?"

"It's just a little more than I expected."

"I bet."

He smiled. "That's a bad pun."

"It is," I laughed. "Well, I hope it works out well for everyone and some Sugartown dirt farmer wins and builds a tall building, stockyard, or railroad here."

He was still smiling, but I looked up and saw Bridget Thompson, and she wasn't smiling. I was soon to learn why.

The cash at the store was kept in a strong box in the office. During the day, each clerk had a bag in his or her apron. Throughout the day, we'd check in our money, place it in the top of the safe, and record our sales as well as cash.

That evening at closing time, Mr. Joe and Dan checked the day's receipts against the cash. I could tell something was amiss. They counted and recounted the cash and coins, then flipped through the receipts.

I walked over. "What's wrong?"

"We've done a preliminary count and this bag should contain $237.33, but we're missing $125 of that. We're also missing the small red bag that we place the big bills in. That's where the $125 was."

I swallowed hard. We seldom had a two-hundred-dollar day, and to be missing over half of that was devastating.

All of us—Dan, Will, Mr. Joe, Bridget Thompson, and me—searched the store high and low for the money. It had to have been misplaced.

Then Mr. Joe locked the doors, went into his office, and closed the door. One by one, he called us in. Will, then Dan, and then me.

"Mizz, I'm not accusing anyone of taking this money, but I've got to question everyone. I'll ask you the same things I asked my own boys. Did you record all of your receipts and check in your cash sales?"

"Yes, sir, just like everyday."

"Did you see the red bag on the top shelf?"

"Yes, sir. I checked my cash in three times, and it was there each time. I placed two twenties in it."

He turned in his chair. "Did you see anyone around the safe that doesn't work for us?"

"No sir."

"What about your father?"

Hot tears welled in my eyes. It was a moment before I could speak. "Mister Joe, I never saw Pap even close to the office here."

"I'm sorry to even ask that, but he was here all day and there's money missing."

I couldn't think of what to say, so I mumbled, "I understand." But it was a lie. I was cut to the quick. I'd built up a pretty good bank account of trust with the Moore family and felt it crumbling below me.

"I'm sorry Mizz. You can leave." It was a long walk to the office door.

"Mizz, send Bridget in."

I nodded at her. "It's your turn."

She smirked at me as she shuffled by.

I sat beside Dan. He put his arm around me. "I know he asked about your daddy. I'm so sorry."

"It's just what it is."

I should've noticed how long Bridget was in the office. It was much longer than any of us other three.

When she came out, she had that same smirk, but Mr. Joe's face was red. Despite that, his voice was soft. "Mizz, go get your book sack."

My legs melted beneath me. I sensed where this was going before I even handed him the bag.

He called all of us into the office. The Irishman opened my book sack and pulled out the red bag. He shook it and one twenty-dollar bill fell out. A look of sorrow crossed his face. "Where is the rest of the money?"

"I never had the money, and I didn't take that red bag."

Mr. Joe nodded toward Bridget.

"Missouri Cotton," Bridget said, "I saw you take the bag from the office, remove most of the cash, and stuff the bag in your sack."

"Mr. Joe, she's a liar, and this is all payback."

"I saw you do it," Bridget said. "You thought no one was looking."

I glanced toward Dan and Will. While Will studied the floor, Dan's eyes were fixed on me.

"Dan'l, I didn't take that money. I've always been as honest as the day is long."

"Missouri, you know I believe you."

Bridget laughed. "That's not true about being honest. Everyone in Ten Mile knows how you got your start at the Westport Store. You were stealing. My uncle told us all about it." She turned to Mister Joe. "Once a thief, always a thief. You were born to thieves and that's all you'll ever be."

Joe Moore held up his hand. "That's enough for tonight. I want everyone here early in the morning. We'll try to get to the bottom of this."

I arrived home to Pap's manic excitement. He'd made a large amount of money on the tickets that day. "Found a bird's nest on the ground. I only have twelve tickets left and will sell them in the morning. Then we'll ..." He saw my face. "What's wrong with you?"

"I'm in trouble at the store."

Ma, holding Baby James, came into the room. "What happened?"

"Over a hundred dollars was missing from today's receipts. Bridget Thompson said she saw me take it."

Ma bounced the baby on her hip. "Who is Bridget Thompson?"

"She's a girl from school who hates me and has been working at the store for the past month. The missing bag and some of the money were in my book sack. Bridget said she saw me do it. It's a frame up."

Pap stood. "I'll go in the morning and straighten this out."

I looked away. "Please let me take care of this myself. I know you'd like to help, but…"

"You just think I'd just make it worse?"

"Pap, I didn't say that." I turned for my room. "I just want to go to bed."

I went to bed, but didn't sleep. I replayed the day's events over and over. Dan had warned me that Bridget was dangerous and would try to get even. He was right. She was both dangerous and crafty. It was my word against hers and at the moment, with the missing bag being in my possession, it didn't look good.

I was up early, wanting to be the first at the store. The store was still locked when I arrived, so I sat on the front porch. I heard keys rattling and the door opened. Mr. Joe leaned on the frame. "Come on in the office."

He didn't look like he'd slept either. "Mizz, I spent all night mulling this back and forth in my mind. Since your first day officially on the job, I've never had reason to doubt your honesty. We've had you in our home, you've traveled with us, I've given you more and more trust on handling the money." He sighed. "But…"

"Go ahead, sir."

"I have no choice but to let you go. There's an eyewitness who said she saw you take it. Bridget described it in pretty good detail."

"I'm sure she did."

"And the bag, and some of the cash, was in your sack."

"She put it in there."

"I'm sorry, Mizz." He looked away. "I've got to let you go."

"If you got to the bottom of this and I was innocent, would you reconsider?"

"Nothing would make me happier." He stood. "But for now, you're fired. You can go ahead and slip out before the others arrive."

It was the longest walk of my life back to our house. Lucky limped along beside me. I believe even my dog sensed my house of cards had collapsed.

Reaching home, I sat in the rocker and held Baby James. There was nothing else to do. I racked my brain for a way to prove my innocence and expose Bridget Thompson, but my mind was a cobweb of confusion and pain.

Ma rubbed my shoulders. "How was it?"

"He let me go."

"I'm sorry."

"So am I. Where's Pap?"

"He's sleeping it off. He got a little wound up after the big day and then your troubles. He spent most of the night on the front gallery, getting as drunk as Cooter Brown."

I'd always wondered. "Who in the heck is Cooter Brown?"

Ma smiled wryly. "I guess he's the measuring stick that all drunks are gauged against."

I listened to Pap's snoring. "I guess his lottery ticket customers will have to wait."

About two hours later, he stumbled out of the bedroom. I motioned at the dozing baby. "Shh. He's sound asleep."

"When I go sell the last of my tickets, I'm going to have a talk with that Irishman."

I held my finger to my lips. "It's too late. He fired me."

"I'll straighten him out. Prove to him you're innocent."

"Pap, for the love of God, let it be."

After three cups of coffee, he seemed eager to get back to business and headed out the door.

I sat waiting for Dan to come. Surely, in spite of this, he would at least come check on me. I'd laid Baby James down and got out *Les Miserables*. It felt like the exact book to read on a day like this. I flipped to the passage where Marius, after being rescued from death at the barricades, returns to the café where he and his young friends had so naively planned their revolution.

They were all dead except Marius. He was alone.

That's exactly how I felt.

I drifted off to sleep with *Les Miserables* in my lap.

I was awakened by loud knocking on the screen door. "Missouri, it's me. Sonnet. You need to come quick. Your father's in trouble at the store."

"What is it?"

"I'm not sure, but it involves the Law."

Ma was in the pea patch out back. I leaned out the back door. "I'm running into town. James is asleep."

Sonnet and I doubled up on Pegasus and galloped into town. Sonnet filled me in. "All I know is that your father was out on the gallery selling those Lottery tickets when a lawman from Rapides Parish arrived accusing your father of running a scam as well as a long list of cons and robberies."

"What'd he look like?"

"Real tall fellow. Dressed in black topped off with a long black coat."

"I call him Javert. He's not the Law, just a sorry bounty hunter." I spurred Pegasus with my boot heels.

Sonnet clung tightly. "There were two other rough-looking characters with him. They were all armed to the teeth."

"They're bounty hunters."

"After your father?"

"Afraid so."

We reached town to see a crowded gallery at Moore Store. I pushed my way through to where Pap stood in front of his lottery tickets table. Javert and his partners stood on either side of him. Javert had cuffed Pap by one arm to a table leg. The bounty hunter held up a lottery ticket to the crowd. "These tickets are frauds. Counterfeit." He pointed at Pap. "Just like this fellow here. You'll never win a dime with these tickets, and this scoundrel has your money. These tickets are fake."

Pap raised his free hand. "Folks, this is all a terrible mistake. I bought these tickets last week in good faith in Alexandria."

The crowd didn't seem convinced and crowded closer around Pap.

"This man, whom you know as Henry Cotton," Javert said, "goes by a long list of aliases. The crimes he's committed in Rapides Parish are longer than your arm. He's wanted in Alexandria, Hineston, and Natchitoches for running scams and cons. He's a grifter and I plan to return him, and his family, to Rapides to face charges."

Sonnet elbowed me. "He's after you too."

I suddenly regretted not bringing my pistol. I wasn't sure I'd shot Javert or anyone, but would've liked having the option.

I looked at the doorway, where Dan Moore stood watching me without expression.

Someone in the crowd blurted out, "Henry Cotton has been a model citizen here. He's the best saw filer we've ever seen."

Suddenly, the Irishman stepped through the crowd and approached Javert in front of the table. "Sir, where is your badge?"

"I have none, but I have warrants allowing me to cross this parish line and arrest this man as well as his wife and daughter, and take them back across the river to justice."

A voice in the crowd echoed. "He ain't nothin' but a bounty hunter."

This was answered by, "But Cotton's taken our money and I want mine back."

Mister Joe reached out to Javert. "Let me see your papers." He put on his spectacles and carefully read the three pages. "Your papers require you to work with one of our Parish law officers to take this man into custody."

"That is correct. I would like to see one of your local deputies."

"We only have one, and he's not here. He's in our Parish seat at

Lake Charles, a two-day ride by horse. We expect him back late tonight."

"I'll gladly wait."

Mr. Joe flipped another page. "This warrant is written to be carried out in Vernon Parish."

"That's correct."

The crowd murmured as the Irishman said, "This ain't Vernon. You're in Imperial Calcasieu Parish. That's why our deputy's in Lake Charles." He held the papers aloft. "These sheets aren't worth the paper they're written on."

Javert was off balance and the crowd pushed their way toward him. "Folks, listen to me. I'm your only chance to get your lottery ticket money back. You've been scammed."

Meanwhile, Mr. Joe lifted the table leg and freed Pap from his temporary confinement. He jerked Pap by the arm and pulled him onto the gallery where they had an animated conversation. Pap's face went from relief to disgust, and then resignation. Mr. Joe led Pap back to his table and waved his hands. "Due to this misunderstanding, Mr. Cotton has agreed to refund all tickets, and as a show of good faith, he will attach a 25-percent bonus for your trouble."

I thought Pap was going to faint. Instead of making a killing on this, he was losing a quarter on each dollar. He gritted his teeth but managed a pained smile as folks with tickets lined up for their payoff. In spite of the situation, it was humorous watching a man with one handcuff doling out money for tickets.

Javert, surrounded by his henchmen, stood firm. He rose to his full height. "When your deputy returns, I will serve these papers and return these scoundrels to face justice in Alexandria."

There'd been thunder to the northwest for the last hour, and at this opportune moment, a lightning bolt split the sky and a cloudburst opened up. Everyone ran for cover on porches and in doorways. Pap paid off the last of the folks in line and I pulled him away. "Let's get." The crowd and rain blocked us off from Javert as we stepped around the side of the store. As I passed Sonnet Ireland, I kissed her on the cheek. "Thanks for coming to my rescue."

The only good thing about the rain was that it gave us cover for our escape. By the time we reached the house, everything we had was soaked. "Pap, you'll have to dry out all of that money you made.”

“After your boss's fine announcement, there's not much to dry out.”

“I bet that big wad you hid is still dry.” I grabbed him by the shoulders. “What do we do now?”

“Clear out. Head for Texas.”

“Why don't you go? Ma, James, and I can stay. I really don't think the fellow wants to arrest all of us. It's your head he wants on a pole. You go and we'll catch up with you later.”

“You heard that fellow. He said he planned to arrest all of us. That includes you. Whatever we do, we'll do it as a family. Start getting your stuff ready to leave.”

“But I can't leave Sugartown until I clear my name for robbery that's been pinned on me.”

“Your reputation ain't my problem right now. Keeping us out of jail is.”

BOOK FOUR –
LEAVING: THE RIVER

Tell me who you are, and I'll tell you where you're from.
  – Wallace Stenger

CHAPTER 57

ON THE ROAD AGAIN

September 1882

We ran into the house like two soaked rats. Ma grabbed some towels so we could dry off. "What's going on here?"

"We're leaving." Pap looked in the side cabinets for one of his bottles.

Ma looked around the house that had truly become our home. "We can't leave this."

"We are and we're leaving tonight. That bounty hunter is here and says he's gonna arrest all of us."

He found a half-filled whiskey bottle. I knew it wouldn't be half-full for long.

I thought I was going to be sick. "But Pap, I've finally found a place— "

"There's other places."

"But my schooling."

"There's other schools. A girl don't need that anyway."

"And Tom-Claws. If we leave here, we'll never find him again."

"All of this trouble and you're worried about a cat?"

I begged "Leave me behind, and I could…"

He grabbed me by the sleeve. "You're going and that's the end of it."

Ma stepped forward. "But, Henry, the girl's finally…"

He slapped her. "Enough. Get ready. We're leaving after dark."

Ma rubbed her face. "Where to?"

"Texas."

Then he played his ace in the hole. "If we stay here, they're gonna arrest all three of us." He pointed to Baby James. "And what happens to him?"

Neither Ma nor I had a good answer to that. Giving up James wasn't an option. We began throwing things together, quickly deciding what to take or leave.

Pap walked over to me as he took a swig of the bottle. "Missouri, write a note telling that we've returned to Alexandria. That'll put them off our trail." There was no use arguing. I dutifully wrote the letter and tacked it to a gallery post.

It continued raining hard after supper, and the weather and darkness aided in our leaving undetected. We slipped unseen through Sugartown. A few lights twinkled in the distance. As we passed the school, I turned my head away. Whether I liked it or not—for now at least—my star was hitched to this wagon and Pap and Ma.

I'd written a second note and wrapped a rock in it. As we passed the post office, I quietly leaned off Pegasus and tossed my missive toward the porch. It hit a window, and I cringed at the sound of breaking glass.

Ma stiffened. "What was that?"

A dog barked and Pap clicked at the team, picking up speed.

My only hope was for the right person to find the note and pass it on to Dan Moore.

We sloshed along all night as the rain came harder and we moved slower. There was a full moon and breaks in the clouds kept us on the road. We stopped for the night at Whiskey Chitto Creek. As soon as it was daylight, Pap forded the creek, which was muddy and rising due to the overnight rain. We forded a succession of smaller branches until we reached another good-sized stream, Bundick Creek, that afternoon.

A local man took us to the best crossing, remarking that there'd been more rain upstream and the creek was on the rise. "You'll be the last to ford this creek for a few days." The water came up to the wagon bed and it began floating free. Ma, praying loudly, held on tight to Baby James, praying aloud.

Peg lost her footing and began swimming. I guided her over to the wagon and reached for Baby James. "Let me have him because neither you nor Pap can swim."

I took the squalling baby, holding him close to my body. I knew that no matter what, no current or obstacle could pry him loose. I might drown, but he wouldn't.

We finally all made it across, exhausted. Ma said it so simply,

"We are defeated."

As we made camp on the west side of the creek, Pap watched the muddy creek rising. "No one will be able to trail us for the next few days. We'll make Texas for sure."

CHAPTER 58

AT THE RUBICON

September 30, 1882

Our travel from Sugartown to the Texas border was a blur of tangled emotions, and I barely remember any of it. Pap was impatient to be moving faster. The sooner we crossed into Texas, the better. The road we were on led to a Sabine crossing called Hickman's Ferry.

We encountered a lone horseman heading west. "What's between here and the river?" Pap said.

"Lots of pines, then some prairie, and then the Sabine River Swamp."

Four days after leaving Sugartown, we neared the Sabine River and the Texas border. The tall pines gave way to an equally majestic cypress swamp. We wound our way through several miles of bottomland, crisscrossed with sloughs of coffee-colored water, switch cane, and saw palmetto. The Sabine, known by the Spanish as the Rio Sabinas or The River of Cypress, was lined by its towering namesake trees with their swollen trunks and root-like knees protruding up to a man's height.

Spanish moss hung in curtains on the cypress trees, and the thick mist made the root-like cypress knees look like mountain peaks.

Ma saw the cypress knees differently. "They look like the tops of tombstones."

In spite of the late hour, Pap insisted we cross into Texas. The ferryman was a young man who tried to talk Pap out of making a crossing this late in the evening. "Sir, the river's high but dropping. Tomorrow will be much safer."

"We're going now."

The ferryman shrugged and began preparing the ferry.

A low fog settled over the river as sunset approached, and the shade of the cypress canopy over the murky water made for an eerie scene. Ma, who was in one of her dark moods, shivered. "I don't like being under this cypress shadow any more than I did the yellow longleaf when we entered No Man's Land. I'm ready to see a long stretch of open country again."

We'd traversed the width of No Man's Land from the Calcasieu at Hineston to this lonely outpost on the Sabine River. This gloomy place matched my despair. I'd given up hope of a white knight riding up to rescue me. Nobody was coming, not even Dan Moore.

"Pap," I said, "how far are we from Sugartown?"

"Not far enough." He looked over his shoulder and nearly fell off the wagon due to a day of heavy drinking. He'd reached his surly mood and I moved away to give him room. He threw a bottle and it shattered against a cypress.

I thought about the rock and note I'd thrown, breaking the Sugartown Post Office window with it. I wondered if it'd gotten to Dan Moore. I wondered if it even mattered now.

I stood forlornly at the river, looking back. Ma, noticing my stare, said, "Child, ain't no use staring back. You might turn to a block of salt."

I already felt like one. A block of something dead. There was a rock where my soul should be. If I fell in this river, I'd sink like a stone, and that might be the best thing for me.

Suddenly, from under a towering cypress, a blue jay feather wafted down to the sandbar. I picked it up, twirling it in my fingers. I glanced up into the canopy but neither saw or heard a bird.

"Unk," I said. *Everywhere a feather falls, an angel has walked.* I didn't know where this journey was heading, but felt a peace in my heart. I wasn't alone. I put the feather in my saddlebag and led Peg to the ferry.

The young man running the ferry shook my shoulder. "Hey, where y'all going?" He had a crooked smile and a dog lick. "You look like you're a thousand miles away."

"I am."

"Well, where are y'all headed?"

"West, as always."

"What's your name?"

"Mizz."

"Like Miss?"

"Nope—like Missouri."

"Missouri. Now that's a name. My name's Wade."

"Wade?" In spite of my despair, I laughed. "That's a right fine name for a boy running a ferry."

"I ain't no boy."

"As I said, that's a right fine name for a man running a ferry."

"That's better. When will y'all be back?"

"We won't." I pointed at Pap and the wagon. "Pap doesn't plow the same ground twice. We've crossed lots of rivers but seldom the same one twice."

Wade picked up a mooring rope. "Wish I could go with you. Ain't never been more than five miles in any direction from here."

I looked him in the eye. "I wish I could stay."

"Then let's change places."

I laughed. "Have you ever heard of the two boys in *The Prince and the Pauper?*"

"What?"

"Mark Twain's new book, *The Prince and the Pauper.*"

"Who?"

"Twain. Mark Twain."

"He must not live around here." He shrugged. "But you and I could trade places."

"Ain't possible. You're obviously a boy—I mean man—and I ain't."

"Speaking of that, you don't have a man?"

"I thought I did."

"Thought?"

"I put my trust in a man, but he cooled off when trouble came. So here I am, on the move again. I thought he might come after me." I looked back at the swamp. "But I was just wrong. Plain wrong." I shrugged. "By the way, what's the name of this place?"

"This is Hickman's Ferry, but I call it Hades."

"Why?"

He pointed toward the next bend. "There's where my brother drownt two year ago." Wade loosened another rope from a cypress stump. "This here river is wicked. No matter how well you think you know it, it'll take you if you ain't careful."

"Why do you stay?"

"Not much choice. My mom's been a basket case since Pete drownt. She swears she'll die if I leave. There's three other children younger than me." He tightened the tether stretching across the river. "So here I am, tied to this place like this here rope."

I pointed at Ma. "I'm caught in the same guilt trip myself. Do you have a father?"

"Been gone for years." He nodded at Pap. "Is he your father?"

I wasn't sure how to answer. "He's really my grandfather, but until a year ago I thought he was my father. He's not much of either."

I stepped into the edge of the Sabine as the cold water rushed by. A leaf floated by, spinning on the foam until the current sucked it under.

Wade saw it, too. "Like I said, it's a mean ole river. It takes whatever it wants." He led Peg onto the ferry behind the wagon. She balked at the ramp, so Wade took his jacket off and covered her eyes, calmly whispering to her as he coaxed her aboard. I stepped aboard the ferry as Wade untied the mooring rope, and grabbed a hold of the thick crossing rope bridging the river. The Sabine was high and muddy, and I feared Wade might lose his grip, so I helped by pulling along the rope. Pap joined us as we drifted into the current.

"Rubicon," I whispered.

Pap jerked on the rope. "What's that?"

"The Rubicon. A European River I learned about in the Academy."

"This ain't Europe, and this river's the Sabine."

"Nope. For me, it's the Rubicon. There's no going back."

He shrugged as he got a new grip.

We reached the far bank and began unloading. We were finally in Texas. Pegasus was trembling, so I walked her off the ferry and to the river for a drink.

Ma gestured across the river. "Who's that hollering over there?"

"Mizz! Missouri!"

I could barely make out shapes through the fog on the river, but

I knew the voice. It was Dan Moore. He walked to the river's edge, where I could make out his silhouette. He cupped his hands. "Mizz, the answer is yes. Wait for me."

I climbed onto my horse for a better vantage point and carefully led her into knee-deep water. Pap waded out to the horse, his shotgun cradled in the crook of his arm, and jerked the reins with his free hand. "Time to go." He nodded across the river. "You ain't his kind. You'd never fit in over there."

Ma, still holding James, waded into the water and approached me from the other side of Pegasus. Waiting for Pap to walk out of earshot, she said, "Missouri, if you leave, we'll never see each other again but … this may be your one and only chance for a better life."

"What about Baby James?" I said.

"He'll be fine. It's time for you to think for once about what's best for Missouri Cotton."

This was my Rubicon decision. Either way, there was no turning back.

Pap returned, and grabbed my leg roughly. "If you go, you won't never see your mother, me, or Baby James again."

I hung my head as Pap led Pegasus and me out of the river and back to the wagon, where he angrily cinched Peg to the wagon.

I looked back. Dan Moore stood stock still, arms crossed, watching the scene unfold.

From the ferry, halfway across the river, Wade hollered, "Do you want me to come back?" I knew if I waited for that ferry, someone was going to be killed, so I waved him away.

Pap walked knee deep into the river and pointed his shotgun toward Dan Moore. "Son, you'd best get outta here." Pap often kept his gun loaded with squirrel shot but always carried buckshot in his shirt pocket. I wasn't sure which shot he was loaded with, but believed buckshot could kill a man across the river's width.

I alit from Peg and ran, wading in and placing myself in front of Pap. He didn't flinch. "Get out of my way."

"You'll have to shoot me first."

"Before I let you cross that river, I will." He nodded toward the wagon. "Now get back on your horse."

"What are you loaded with?"

"Double-aught buckshot."

I stood between two worlds and two men. If I responded to

Dan, it might cost him his life, and I wasn't willing to do that. Slowly, I turned my back on Dan and the river, walked back to the wagon and climbed onto Pegasus.

Pap took Baby James from Ma and tried to hand him up to me. "This is your brother. Hold him." James, sensing our tension, began screaming and reaching for Ma, who took him and climbed on the wagon. I turned away, keeping my hands on the reins.

Pap climbed onto the wagon, laid the shotgun under his feet, and clicked to the team as they struggled forward in the wet sand.

I reached for my knife.

One word echoed in my mind. Moxie.

Leaning forward, I pulled Peg's rein taut and sliced it. As the wagon lurched forward, the rein came loose, and I jerked on it with all of my might, turning Pegasus toward the river.

I slapped her on the side of her neck, and she lunged for the water. With only one rein, I didn't have much control, but Peg never hesitated as she plunged off the bluff bank into the river's swift current.

A shotgun blast rang out, followed by Ma's scream. I flinched but felt no pain. Across the river, Dan Moore hadn't moved. Who—or what—had Pap shot at? I refused to look back.

I tried to make for the ferry, but Peg and I were pulled downstream by the Sabine's strong current. Wade knelt along the ferry's stern and threw a coiled rope, but it fell far short of us.

I was hanging onto Peg for life when my dress snagged on a submerged limb, and only my death grip on the saddle horn kept me on her. The limb also tore loose my saddlebags and I caught them with my free hand. Everything material that mattered in my life was in those bags.

The Sabine truly was a wicked river, but for some reason, I felt an encompassing peace. No matter whether I lived or died, I'd made my decision.

Strangely, in the middle of the river, time seemed to stand still. They say your life passes before your eyes at such a time as this, but it was another life I saw—Cosette and her bleak life at the beginning of *Les Miserables*. How, in spite of everything, her story had a happy ending.

Some folks would say that was true just in fairy tales and fiction, but I was ready to find out for myself. I knew one thing. I'd never cross this river again.

Several onlookers had gathered downstream as Pegasus fought the current. I'd lost my saddle horn grip and was hanging onto her mane with both hands.

Someone said, "She's crazy."

Pegasus found river bottom and splashed toward the bank.

A man pointed to the river. "That dog ain't gonna make it."

Lucky was mid-stream, fighting the current. A three-legged dog dog-paddling in a flooded river is an unfair fight. Several times his head went under, but eventually he'd bob up, struggling for the bank.

"Come on boy, you can make it," I shouted.

Peg was standing in water up to her belly, and Lucky finally reached us, and I pulled him up on the horse's back. Lucky licked my face. "I knew you'd come, too."

Once on shore, both horse and dog shook water off their backs. One of the observers said, "That dog ain't got but three legs. He's lucky he made it."

I laughed. "He was named right." Lucky sat on his haunches, his perpetual smile never leaving him, his eyes locked on mine.

So much was happening so fast that I nearly missed Dan Moore running toward me. He tripped over a cypress knee and fell face-first in the sand, sprang to his feet, and continued running until he reached me. He pulled me close and turned me away from the river. "Don't look back. They're gone."

"Who was Pap shooting at?"

"I'm not sure."

"I can't go back."

"To them or Sugartown."

"To them."

"You don't have to." He kissed me with a mouthful of Sabine sand. "Mizz, are you sure about this?"

"As sure as I've ever been about anything." I grabbed his arm. "But I do have a question. why didn't you come sooner?"

"Momma died three days ago."

"Oh, Dan'l, I'm so sorry."

He held me closer. "The last thing she told me was that if I didn't get on my horse right then and come get you, I wasn't as smart or brave as she thought I was. She died within an hour and I saddled up and have been riding hard since. My horse road-foundered about twenty miles back and I walked and ran the rest of the way.”

"You missed your own momma's funeral.”

"She wanted it this way.” He kissed me again.

"It won't be easy going back.”

"Nothing good ever is.”

"I'll never get the cloud of the missing money off me.”

"Your protector Will Moore took care of that,” Dan said. "He caught Bridget Thompson red-handed with her stash of the money and receipts.”

"Wow.”

"Will Moore is a rascal, but he's a smart rascal. He said to tell you that he's always got your back.” Dan shrugged. "He said you'd understand what he meant.”

Dan helped me onto Pegasus and led her up the Louisiana bank of the Sabine.

"How far is it back to Sugartown?” I asked.

"As the crow flies, about thirty miles. But it shouldn't take long,”—he patted Pegasus on the flank— "since we're riding a flying horse.”

Just then a flock of east-bound squawking crows flew over in the darkness. Dan Moore winked. "They don't mean a thing.”

And as usual, Dan Moore was right.

"Perched Crow” by my father, Clayton Iles. circa 1980

Coming Next in November 2018

No Man's Land: 1918
A Novel by Curt Iles

November 11, 1918. The Great War is over. American soldiers Watson Moore and Billy Reed are eager to leave France and return to their previous lives in Pineywoods Louisiana. Unlike many of their friends, they've survived the brutal modern war with its barbed wire, machine guns, poison gas, and deadly no man's land between the trenches.

Nurse Jessica Maye has left the European field hospitals before the war's end to return to Lake Charles, Louisiana. She's thrust into two events that shake her homeland: the Great Storm of August 1918 and a Flu Pandemic that is doing what bullets couldn't do.

All three veterans return to a land that has changed forever. The clearcutting of the vast longleaf forests is in full swing. Barbed wire is now strung where livestock grazed freely for centuries. Men and women who'd never traveled a day's journey from home have now seen the world.

Together, the three of them, Watson, Billy, and Jessica, carry a shared secret from the war that will affect each of them for the rest of their lives. The three friends discover that sometimes even after the war is over, the battles go on, and often the toughest battles are fought inside the soul of a man or woman.

1918: No Man's Land is the novel that ties the novels *As the Crow Flies* and *A Spent Bullet* together.

Expected publication is November 2018. Stay in touch at www.creekbank.net for details and dates.

AUTHOR'S NOTES

"The historian tells what happened.
The novelist tells how it felt."
– E.L. Doctorow

I stand in front of a class of Alexandria fourth-grade students. They've just finished a month reading *The Wayfaring Stranger,* the first novel in the Westport Series. I hold in my hand note cards featuring their questions about the novel.

I read the first card. "Were Joe and Eliza real?"

"Yes," I say. "They were my great grandfather's grandparents, and they owned the Westport Store."

Second card: "Was there really a place called Westport?"

I nod. "It's nothing but a country crossroads now, but it did exist."

Third card: "Was Unk real?"

I always dread this question, especially from my young readers. I shake my head. "No. Unk Dyal wasn't real. I made him up."

The entire class groans, and it's as if I've just burst their life bubble and *kilt* Unk Dyal.

But I quickly address their dismay. "Unk Dyal *is real.* His name is Greg Johnson and he lives near Westport at Union Hill, Louisiana. I patterned Unk Dyal's unique personality after Greg Johnson."

I explain to the class that Greg has been a special friend for nearly twenty years. He is just as kind, wise, spiritual, and innocently simple as his namesake, Unk. I've learned more from the wisdom of Greg Johnson as any professor or preacher in my life.

Yes, Unk Dyal is real. He just goes by another name, resides in a different era, but lives within miles of the events and places of my Westport Series. I wish each of the students could meet Greg Johnson. I guess they have as they've learned to love Unk.

As a boy, I grew up in the shadow of the stories of The Westport Fight. My great grandfather, Frank Iles, was the grandson of Joe and Eliza Moore. He was born about the same year (1881) as the Fight, and his mother, Addie, wrote the oldest version of the fight. It's now found in the McNeese State University Archives. Grandma Addie's manuscript is one of the accounts of the fight. I was brought up on the Moore version of the Christmas Eve Fight of 1881.

The other Westport Fight account is best known and was written (and quoted below) by Webster Talma Crawford and is responsible for keeping the story alive. It is beautifully written and I am so grateful for his account. It seems to have been written in the early twentieth century.

Remarkably, both surviving accounts are nearly identical.

I've always been bothered that there is no written Redbone version of the Westport Fight. Even today, this tribe is hesitant to talk about *The Fight,* and their versions have been handed down orally.

History is *normally* written by the winners, but the Westport Fight is an exception. The two written accounts were from the standpoint of the losers: those who were driven out.

What makes this memorable is how, for one of the few times in American history, the natives won. Instead of being forced out, they—the Redbones—dug in and ousted the Outsiders.

I've always liked stories where the underdogs prevail, and the Westport Fight is one of those.

The object of the feud was who would control the land, pines, and resources of the Ten Mile area. Crawford's narrative ends with a paragraph worth quoting:

> *The Redbones won, and as we view the valley and the land about, we are glad somehow that they did, for it is lovely there. The streams flow sweetly, sheep graze on the rolling hills, and there is a peace over everything, which makes Cherry Winchie Valley more like it was a hundred years ago than those who have not seen it will believe.*

Even today, the Ten Mile area in the corner of Rapides Parish has its own unique independent character. One of my older friends recently drove through the Ten Mile Country for the first time in a half century. "The only thing that's changed," he said, "is that there are now pulpwood trucks parked in the yards instead of stump trucks."

As I travel weekly through the heart of Redbone country on Louisiana 113 between Glenmora and Pitkin, a cursory glance at road names and mailboxes proves the Ten Milers are still there. There's a marker to the Westport Fight at the intersection of Louisiana Highways 113 and 462 and it was erected by the victors, the descendants of the Ten Milers.

Once again, Crawford's account speaks of the men and women who were involved in the Westport Fight:

Every man in the Westport Fight was a hero. The Neutral Ground, as history shows, bred a race of heroic figures, but having passed across the stage of American life at a time when the attention of the nation was centered on bigger events, those heroes of Western Louisiana remain pretty well unknown. Every man engaged in the Westport Fight was a hero. Only heroes lived in Western Louisiana in the early 1880's.

I've had a lifelong love for the Ten Mile people. The old saying is that they are the world's best friends and worst enemies, and I can truly attest to the first part of that adage. I'm thankful to be the recipient of their friendship and hospitality.

They have a deep love of the land and fresh spirituality that always amazes and humbles me. To visit a Ten Mile church, whether Freedom, Shady Grove, or one of the Occupy's, is an experience to be savored. These folks worship with a passion and depth that always moves me.

At the same time, my years as a high school basketball coach reinforced the legend of their fierce competitiveness. If you've ever fought your way in, through, and out of the gyms at Pitkin, Fairview, Elizabeth, or Plainview High Schools, you know they still don't take kindly to Outsiders in their territory, or on their basketball courts.

I'm sure I'll take my lumps for this fictional account of the Westport Fight. Writing about the past and telling stories of people's ancestors can elicit strong feelings. In spite of that, it was still a story I was *compelled* to write.

I was motivated by one thought. *If I didn't tell about the Westport Fight, it would be lost to history.* I hope my deep love of the land, people, and culture of the Redbones shines through. This will be my last Redbone-centered book. I'm ready to explore other parts of our area.

Additionally, I wrote *As the Crow Flies* to celebrate the small town that Sugartown once was. As I drive past the deserted crossroads where Louisiana highways 113 and 112 intersect, I find it hard to believe that it was once a thriving community with stores, churches, and yes, the Baldwin Male and Female Academy. As I crawl through the grown-up scrub trees and briars to visit the former palatial home of Sugartown's last doctor, Henry Ray Officer, I'm reminded of why I call this former community, "Sad Sugartown."

All of my Iles and Moore kin come from Sugartown, and to "bring it back to life" is a privilege.

I've written thirteen books, and *As the Crow Flies* has been, by far, the most difficult. It took six years to finish. It was written around our selling of everything we had in Dry Creek and leaving the Pineywoods for three years in Red Dirt Africa.

Amazingly, returning to Louisiana in 2015 was even more difficult than leaving. DeDe and I realized how much America had changed, and so had we. We chose to not return to the Pineywoods, but the flatland cotton country of central Louisiana. There were seven reasons for this decision—seven grandchildren who live in the Alexandria area.

2017 has been a year of ups and downs. I was dropped by my agent (it happens) and received enough publisher rejections to fill Ten Mile Creek. Throw in a stint in the psych ward hospital (now, that's a story to tell) along with many births, deaths, joys, and sorrows.

Like Missouri at the Sabine, I've spent a good part of the last year swimming in the river, sometimes with the current, most often against it. But *As the Crow Flies* is done and I've told the story—

hopefully in a fair way to the real folks who were there.

At least, they won't be forgotten.

I'm still not sure what kind of book this is. It has tested who I am as a writer. I've not had writer's block, but I sure as heck have had writer's doubt. I recently read a fine quote by the famed composer, Richard Strauss, "I may not be a first-rate composer, but I am a first-class, second-rate composer." That probably describes me as a writer.

I am comfortable with the fact that I'll probably spend the remainder of my life as a regional Louisiana writer. But as they say, "Write about what you know and love," and I both *know* and *love* my part of Louisiana—the Pineywoods. For the rest of my life, I'll write stories about our people and history. Don't worry that I'll run out of stories or ideas, I have a mental list of dozens of books and stories stretching across our history.

As the Crow Flies is no longer my book. I've done my part (with the help of so many others). It now belongs to you. Read it. Enjoy it. Pass it on to friends and family. Tell your world about it. Word of mouth is the best friend a book ever has.

It's a good book that tells a good story about a forgotten area where memorable stories and (mostly) good people abound. It's the place I always return to in my writing—the Pineywoods of western Louisiana.

Curt Iles
Alexandria, Louisiana/Dry Creek, Louisiana
September 2017

If enjoyed *As the Crow Flies*, you'll want the first two books in the Westport Series.

The Wayfaring Stranger
Joe Moore's journey to America and the beginnings of he and Eliza's lives together in in the Ten Mile country.

A Good Place
Set during the Civil War, and narrated by Mayo Moore, oldest son of Joe and Eliza.

Get the complete Creekbank Collection:

As the Crow Flies

Deep Roots

A Good Place

The Wayfaring Stranger

The Mockingbird's Song

Hearts across the Water

Wind in the Pines

The Old House

Stories from the Creekbank

Trampled Grass

A Spent Bullet

Uncle Sam. A Horse's Tale

Christmas Jelly

Much more at www.creekbank.net

For further reading about the unique Ten Mile/Cherry Winchie/Westport area, as well as what is fact and fiction in our Westport Trilogy, visit http.//bit.ly/TheWestportStory.

Acknowledgements

Gina Arnold
Lynnne Boggs
Debra Bird Tyler
Allen Green
Diann and Dean Mills
Dean Burns
Hallee Bridgeman
Chip MacGregor
Jan and Linda Schekman
Paul Conant
James & Shannon Newsom
Dry Creek Camp Staff
Tall Timbers Camp Staff
James and Shannon Newsom
Clara Springs Camp Staff
Peyton Christian
Tamp and Grind Coffee
In Memory of Jeff Phillips
Steve McCloud/Tipitina's
Chuck Reed
Hannah Ciccarelli
Bill Iles
Mary Iles
Jared Ramsey
Clint and Amanda Iles
Terry and Sara Iles
Clay and Robin Iles
Noah, Jack, Jude, Syd & Luke Iles
James L. Rubart
Mary DeMuth
Connie Vallery Book
Ugly Mug Marketing
Wayne Mullins
Louis Blankenbaker
Richard Churchman
Christina Griffin

Aquilla Young
Ricky Airhart
Billie Richmond
Sharon Joyce
Greg and Angie Harrison
Eddie Boniol
C.W. Johnson, Jr.
Kendal Gott
Robert McLendon
Victor Hugo
Thomas Umstattd, Jr.
Doug Cooley
Marybeth Anderson
Robert and Selena Friday
David Miller
Tim Reeves
Carlos Nichols
Lisa Fussell
Barbara Baumgarten
Holly Wilson
Lindsey Torbett
Connie Vallery Book
Coleen Ritter
Lisa Adams
Billy Davis
Sharon Cook
Lance King
Mike Gallien
Lloydell Iles Mullican
JoAnn Iles Edwards
Webster Talma Crawford
Don Marler
Jane McManus

A personal word from Curt:
Join us on the Journey

Since you're reading *As the Crow Flies*, I consider you part of the Creekbank Tribe. As an Independent Author, I depend on readers and friends like you to spread the word. I'm personally asking you to do one (or all) of the following:

1. Tell your friends and family about the book. Word of mouth is an author's best friend.
2. If you've read any of our books, write an Amazon review.
3. Better yet, purchase *personally* autographed copies as gifts for birthdays, stocking stuffers, anniversaries, and special occasions.
4. If you have an *independent* (not the chains) bookstore in your area, support it, and ask them to purchase copies/set up signings.
5. Bug your local newspaper to do a feature story on our book.
6. Ask your local public library to place *As the Crow Flies* (and our other books) on their shelves. Simply show them your copy and the ISBN number on the front flyleaf.
7. Share *As the Crow Flies* with local book clubs. If contacted, I will send a free copy to the club leader. Book clubs, whether through personal appearances, Skype/Facetime, or on the phone, love chatting with authors they've read.
8. Tell your local school(s) about *As the Crow Flies*. My books are enjoyed by all ages (Last year, a fourth-grade class read *The Wayfaring Stranger*. It was a joy to visit with them and share the background and history of my first novel.)
   I'd recommend *As the Crow Flies* for middle school through high school. I believe students will enjoy getting to know Missouri Cotton and her story. Just as with clubs, I'm available, whether in person or through the Internet, for book discussions. Some elementary schools have bought individual student copies of our children's book, *Uncle Sam: A Horse's Tale*.

Thank you in advance for helping spread the word about *As the Crow Flies* and Creekbank Stories.

Curt Iles
curt@creekbank.net
Facebook: curtiles/creekbank
www.creekbank.net
PO Box 6060 Alexandria, La 71307
To learn about special discounts for bulk purchases, book club sales, school visits, and speaking, contact us at www.creekbank.net.

47185181R00208

Made in the USA
Lexington, KY
05 August 2019